NIGHTINGALES AT WAR

NIGHTINGALES AT WAR

by

Donna Douglas

Magna Large Print Books
Long Preston, North Yorkshire,
BD23 4ND, England.

British Library Cataloguing in Publication Data.

Douglas, Donna
  Nightingales at war.

  A catalogue record of this book is
  available from the British Library

  ISBN 978-0-7505-4226-5

First published in Great Britain by Arrow Books in 2015

Copyright © Donna Douglas 2015

Cover illustration © Colin Thomas

Published in Large Print 2016 by arrangement with
Arrow Books, an imprint of The Random House Group Ltd.

Magna Large Print is an imprint of Library Magna Books Ltd.

Printed and bound in Great Britain by
T.J. (International) Ltd., Cornwall, PL28 8RW

Acknowledgements

As I say every time, you would not be holding this book in your hands if it wasn't for the help and support of a lot of people. First, I'd like to thank my agent Caroline Sheldon, and editor Joanna Taylor for bravely stepping into the world of the Nightingales and guiding the project along. I'd also like to thank the whole Random House team, especially Selina Walker and the ever-innovative Andrew Sauerwine and his great sales team.

I'd also like to thank the Archives department of the Royal College of Nursing for their tireless help in tracking down facts, the Imperial War Museum, the Wellcome Library and the Bethnal Green Local History Archives. Not to mention all the brilliant nurses who have shared their stories (most of which are too shocking to include!) and the lovely readers who have taken the Nightingales to their hearts.

Last, but not least, I would like to thank my husband Ken, who has put up with more hysteria than any man should ever have to suffer, and my daughter Harriet, who read each chapter as I wrote it, cheered and booed and cried in all the right places, and whose comments and enthusiasm kept me going. I love you both very much.

To the newlyweds, Harriet and Lewis

Chapter One

On the Friday in May 1940 that Winston Churchill became Prime Minister and the Germans launched a Blitzkrieg of bombs over Holland, Dora Riley went back to the Nightingale Hospital to ask for a job.

It was six years since she had stood before Matron as a student nurse at the Nightingale. But standing in that book-lined office, with its heavy dark furniture and leather-covered chairs, listening to the slow, ponderous ticking of the mantel clock, her heart still raced like a nervous probationer's as she faced the woman on the other side of the desk.

The world might have changed a great deal over those six years but Kathleen Fox was as serene as ever, sitting tall and graceful in her black uniform, her face framed by an elaborate starched white headdress. Her calm grey gaze fixed on Dora, weighing her up, just as it had on that very first day they'd met.

'So, Mrs Riley,' she said. Her soft, well-spoken voice still bore a trace of her Lancashire roots. 'You wish to come back to us, do you?'

Dora laced her fingers behind her back and stood up a little straighter, as she had been trained to do when speaking to her seniors. Old habits died hard. 'Yes, Matron.'

'How long is it since you were a staff nurse here?'

'Two years, Matron. I passed my State Finals in nineteen thirty-seven, and I left to get married the following spring.'

She kept her eyes fixed on the top of Miss Fox's headdress as the Nightingale's Matron considered the notes in front of her. 'And why do you want to come back, may I ask?'

'I want to do my bit, Matron. For the war.'

'Indeed.' Miss Fox paused. 'Your husband is serving, I take it?'

'That's right, Matron.' Dora pressed her lips together, not trusting herself to say any more. She had too much pride to show her true feelings. She was a tough East End girl, brought up in the back streets of Bethnal Green, barely a stone's throw from the hospital itself. Where she came from, it didn't do to go around weeping and wailing about your troubles. You just buckled down and got on with it, as her mother and grandmother had always taught her.

But inside she was raw from thinking and worrying about Nick. He had been sent off to France in March, and Dora missed him with every fibre of her being.

That was the real reason she had decided to come back to the Nightingale. She had to do something. Not just to help the war effort, but because she knew she would go mad if she stayed at home, fretting and fearing the worst.

'May I ask why you have applied to us directly, and not to the Civil Nursing Reserve?' Matron interrupted her thoughts. 'Surely that is the proper channel for former nurses wishing to offer their services?'

Dora looked at her squarely. She had a feeling Miss Fox already knew the answer to that one.

'I did, but they won't have me,' she said bluntly. 'They don't want mothers.'

'Ah, yes.' Matron's mouth curved. 'You have twin babies, don't you?'

Dora wasn't surprised she knew about Walter and Winnie. Even with everything else going on around her, Miss Fox still managed to keep up with all her 'girls', past and present. 'Yes, Matron,' Dora confirmed.

'How old are they?'

'Just a year, Matron.'

'They're still so young. I must say, I'm surprised you want to leave them and come back to nursing.'

Dora said nothing. She could already tell from Miss Fox's expression that she was going to be turned down again, and braced herself for another rejection.

'I do admire you for putting yourself forward,' Miss Fox said finally. 'But the Civil Nursing Reserve rules are there for a reason. As you know yourself, nursing is a vocation. The hours are long, the work is very hard, and war or no war, we expect our nurses to dedicate themselves to this hospital. It's no job for a wife and mother.'

'I'll manage,' Dora insisted. 'I've moved back home so my mum can look after the twins while I'm working. We've got it all worked out.'

'I see. And supposing you're in the middle of your shift, nursing several patients on the Dangerously Ill List, and you receive word that one of your babies is poorly. What will you do then? You can't drop everything and go home, and you'll hardly be able to do your job properly if you're worrying about your little ones either.'

'I won't have to worry, if my mum's there,' Dora said stubbornly. 'She brought up six kids of her own, she'll know what to do.'

Miss Fox gave her an almost pitying look. 'I think you may find you feel differently about that when the time comes,' she said kindly. 'A mother's instinct is to look after her own children, not someone else's.'

'Yes, well, I ain't got much choice, thanks to Hitler!' Dora hadn't meant to snap, but she was sick and tired of having doors closed in her face when all she was trying to do was help. They'd been exactly the same at the Labour Exchange, looking down their noses at her when she'd gone to volunteer. 'Believe you me, I'd like nothing better than to be at home with my husband and kids, but old Adolf and his mob have put a stop to that,' she went on, ignoring Miss Fox's startled expression. 'Now I can either sit at home, twiddling my thumbs and going off my head, or I can be here, making myself useful. And the way I see it, Matron, you could do with some help. From what I hear, you're having to rely on nursing auxiliaries with five minutes' training. I know it ain't ideal, but wouldn't it be better to have someone like me working here? I want to be useful, and I know I can do a good job. I'll work as hard as I can, I promise. At any rate, surely I've got to be more use than a volunteer who doesn't know a bedpan from a bandage?'

Dora caught Miss Fox's frozen stare, and

14

realised that yet again she'd gone too far. Why did she always have to let her temper run away with her? Matron would never have her back now, not if this war went on for a hundred years. She would have to join the Women's Voluntary Service, making tea and mending socks for soldiers.

'I see you are still as outspoken as ever,' Miss Fox remarked, her brows lifting.

'Sorry, Matron.' Dora lowered her gaze to the rug. It wasn't Miss Fox's fault. She was just following the rules, the same as everyone else. But the whole world seemed to be rules, rules, rules these days. Posters plastered on walls, leaflets from the government through the letter box, all telling her what she could buy, what she should eat, where she could go and who she could speak to. Do this, do that, do as you're told. It was bad enough that they'd taken her husband away from her, without them trying to run her life too. She was sick of the whole lot of them.

She came back to the present when she realised Matron was addressing her.

'I hope you realise, Nurse Riley, that if you do return to this hospital you will never be able to speak to me like that again,' she said.

Dora stared at her blankly. She had barely heard what Matron had said, she was too busy trying to take in the fact that she had just been addressed as Nurse. It was a long time since anyone had called her that, and she hadn't realised how much she missed it. Pride flowed through her, straightening her spine and making her stand even taller.

But still she could hardly trust herself to believe it. 'Do you mean – I can come back?' she asked.

'As you said yourself, we don't have a great deal of choice,' Miss Fox admitted frankly. 'And while I'd argue with you that most of our nursing auxiliaries do know a bedpan from a bandag—' Dora withered under her stern expression '—I can't deny it would be useful to have more staff nurses on the wards.'

'Thank you, Matron.'

'But as I've said, you must not expect any special treatment,' Miss Fox went on. 'You will be treated as any other staff nurse here, although of course you will not be expected to live in. But you will be expected to follow orders and to put your duties first, is that understood?'

Her voice was still soft, but with that underlying note of steel that Dora remembered well.

'Yes, Matron. Thank you, Matron. I won't let you down, I promise.'

'See that you don't, Nurse Riley.'

Dora stared at the older woman's serenely implacable face and thought she detected the slightest twinkle in her grey eyes.

Dora Riley was right about one thing, Kathleen Fox reflected. Everything was changing. She barely recognised the hospital any more. The windows of the elegant Georgian building were scarred with crosses of brown anti-blast tape, and banks of sandbags were stacked deep against its walls, all but obscuring the ground floor.

Most of the wards had been emptied the previous September when war was declared. The convalescent patients were sent home, and those who were too ill were evacuated, along with most

16

of the staff, down to the Nightingale's sector hospital in Kent.

Eight months on, and with no sign of the bombs and gas attacks they'd all feared, several of the London wards had reopened. But they had lost a great many skilled nurses to the Queen Alexandra's Imperial Military Nursing Service. Kathleen didn't begrudge them going off to serve their country, but it made it very difficult for her to run the hospital. They were having to rely on former nurses like Dora Riley, and an army of girls from the Voluntary Aid Detachment, or VADs as they were known.

Volunteers who didn't know a bedpan from a bandage. Kathleen smiled at the description. Dora had a point. They were willing and cheerful enough, but a few Red Cross classes barely prepared them for the rigours of life on a busy hospital ward.

There was a knock on the door and Veronica Hanley the Assistant Matron strode in without waiting for a reply. Kathleen's heart sank at the sight of her tall, masculine figure. Now there was someone she wouldn't have minded sending abroad. She was sure Miss Hanley could have terrified the wits out of the Nazis, far more effectively than the British Expeditionary Force.

She fixed a smile on her face. 'Hello, Miss Hanley. What can I do for you?'

Miss Hanley slapped a piece of paper down on the desk in front of her. 'The new linen order,' she pronounced, in her deep booming voice. 'There are to be no new sheets or pillowcases. The factory that makes them has been given over to war work.'

17

'I see.' Kathleen picked up her pen to sign the form. 'I daresay we will soon be asking our patients to bring their bedding in with them.'

Miss Hanley shuddered. 'Perish the thought, Matron! Are you aware that many of our patients come from homes infested with vermin?'

'I was joking, Miss Hanley.'

'Oh.'

Kathleen smiled at the puzzled look on the Assistant Matron's square-jawed face. Miss Hanley had many excellent qualities, but a sense of humour wasn't one of them.

It was just one of the many differences that separated them. Veronica Hanley was of the old school, Nightingale-trained and a stickler for tradition. She had never been able to hide her distaste for Kathleen Fox, with her inferior training, brisk northern ways and new ideas.

When the war started, Kathleen had offered Miss Hanley the chance to go to Kent as Acting Matron of the sector hospital. She had thought her assistant would jump at the chance, but Veronica Hanley had surprised her by refusing.

'I would prefer to stay in London, if you don't mind, Matron?' she'd said. 'It doesn't seem right to desert my post during the Nightingale's hour of need.'

Kathleen had reluctantly conceded to her request, even though she suspected it had more to do with Miss Hanley's wanting to keep an eye on her.

As she signed the order, she could sense the Assistant Matron looming over her, poised to speak.

18

'Was there something else, Miss Hanley?' she asked patiently.

'The decorators telephoned. They won't be able to start work on Holmes and Peel wards for at least another two weeks.'

'That's a nuisance.' Since the hospital still wasn't full to capacity, the Trustees had taken the decision to have two of the empty wards on the top floor painted. 'Perhaps they could decorate them both at the same time, to make things quicker?'

'Is that wise, Matron?' Miss Hanley frowned. 'Surely it would be better to decorate them one at a time, so we always have a spare ward available in case of emergencies–'

'We will have them decorated together,' Kathleen cut across her, irritated. Why did her assistant have to argue with her over everything? 'I very much doubt we'll be needing them in a hurry,' she added more calmly. 'We barely have enough nurses available to staff the wards we do have open.'

'Speaking of nurses...' Miss Hanley cleared her throat, and Kathleen knew what was coming next. 'That girl I saw coming out of your office earlier – am I right in thinking she trained here? Let me think. Nurse...' She made a great pretence of searching for the name. 'Nurse Doyle, wasn't it?'

Kathleen bent her head so her Assistant Matron wouldn't see the smile on her face. Poor Miss Hanley would make a very poor fifth columnist, she thought. She lacked the subtlety for subterfuge. Her broad, plain face gave her away every time.

19

'That's right. Except she's Mrs Riley now.'

'So she is. And what brought her here, I wonder?'

As if you didn't know! Kathleen thought. Miss Hanley would have been listening at the door for the past half-hour.

Playing along, Kathleen said, 'She wants her job back.'

'Then she should apply to the Civil Nursing Reserve,' Miss Hanley said promptly.

'They won't have her because she has children.'

'Ah.'

'Nevertheless, I have taken her on as a staff nurse.'

'Really, Matron?' Miss Hanley couldn't have looked more scandalised if Kathleen had told her Mussolini himself was going to be working at the hospital as a porter. 'But the hospital rules clearly state that married women with young children–'

'I fear we may have to disregard our rules a great deal more than that before all this is over. War changes everything, Miss Hanley. And at least Nurse Doyle – I mean, Riley – trained here, which is more than some of our nurses have these days.'

'Hmm.' Veronica Hanley's mouth firmed. From what Kathleen could recall, Miss Hanley had never really approved of Dora anyway. In her opinion nursing, especially at the Nightingale, was strictly for well-brought-up young ladies from respectable families, and not working-class girls like Dora.

As if she knew what Kathleen was thinking, Miss Hanley sighed and said, 'I suppose we must trust your judgement, Matron. You are in charge, after all.' God help us, her forbidding expression implied.

Kathleen turned her gaze back to the linen order, the various items crossed through with red pencil. Life was difficult enough, without having to fight her own daily battle with Miss Hanley, she thought.

Chapter Two

Dora ran all the way back to Griffin Street.

No one living in the street ever used their front door. Only rent collectors and tallymen turned up on the front step. Dora hurried down the narrow back alleyway, hemmed in by high, rough brick walls that led up to the railway embankment on one side and the tiny backyards of the terraced houses on the other.

She lifted the rusting latch and let herself in through the wooden back gate that led into the yard of number twenty-eight. Like its neighbours, it was small and square, with spindly weeds nosing their way through the cracks in the paving slabs.

Her younger brother Alfie was squatting beside a battered cardboard box in the middle of the yard, dangling a lettuce leaf over it.

'What you got there, Alfie?' Dora approached and peered into the box. A twitching nose and a pair of black eyes stared back up at her. 'Blimey,

21

a rabbit. Where did that come from?'

'I caught him on Hackney Marshes. His name's Octavius and he's my pet, but Nanna says he's going in the pot.'

He pulled a face. All the family called him Little Alfie, but at eight years old he was a sturdy boy who nearly came up to Dora's shoulder.

She crouched beside him and put her hand out to stroke the rabbit's soft brown fur. 'You don't want to take any notice of Nanna. You know she's all talk.' She nodded towards the leaf in his hand. 'All the same, you'd best not go feeding it too much, or she might change her mind.'

She left her brother, ducked past the drooping washing line and let herself in the back door.

Her mum Rose was in the scullery, making tea.

'Hello, love.' She smiled at Dora over her shoulder. 'You must have heard the kettle boiling.' She turned, wiping her hands on her pinny. 'How did you get on at the hospital?'

'Matron says I can start next week.'

Her mother beamed. 'There, what did I tell you? I said they'd give you your job back, didn't I?'

But Dora wasn't listening. Her attention was fixed on the thin curtain that separated the scullery from the back kitchen. The gurgling sound of her children's laughter lifted her heart, and it was all she could do not to run to them. 'How were the kids?'

'As good as gold.' Rose Doyle gave her a knowing look. 'You go in and see them, and I'll bring you a cup of tea. You look as if you could do with one.'

'Ta, Mum.' Dora gave her a quick, grateful smile and pushed through the curtain.

The little kitchen had always been the heart of the house, the place where the whole family gathered to talk, laugh, cry and fight. Nanna Winnie was in her usual place in her rocking chair by the hearth, mending socks. It gave Dora a pang to see how close she held the darning to her face these days, squinting over her spectacles. Her eyesight was failing, although she would never admit it.

'All right, Nanna?' Dora greeted her cheerily, but her gaze was already fixed on little Walter and Winnie, propped side by side on the rug at Nanna's feet. Nick's brother Danny was with them, patiently building up towers of wooden bricks for them to knock down with their chubby, flailing hands.

Walter caught sight of her first, and promptly burst into tears. Winnie joined in, and soon they were both wailing.

'Typical! They haven't cried all day until you walked in,' Nanna grumbled.

'They're just excited, that's all. Hello, darlings.' Dora scooped them both up, one in each arm, and kissed their fat little cheeks. They looked so like their father it was heartbreaking, with their dark curls and intense blue eyes.

Dora buried her face in Winnie's neck, breathing in her achingly familiar baby smell. 'Are you sure they've been all right?' she asked.

'I told you, they've been little angels,' her mother said, coming in with the tea tray. 'I've hardly had to look after them, as a matter of fact.

Danny's been doing it all, ain't that right, Dan?' Rose looked affectionately at the young man kneeling on the rug, tidying up the bricks. Danny gave her a shy, lopsided smile in return.

'He's devoted to them, all right,' Nanna agreed.

'I should think so,' Dora said. 'They're your niece and nephew, ain't they, Danny?'

He nodded earnestly. 'They're my f-family,' he said. 'N-Nick said I had to look after them while h-he was gone.'

'Quite right, too.' Dora smiled indulgently at him. Danny Riley was a curious-looking young man, with his mop of pale hair and vacant eyes. He was in his early twenties, but he had the mind of a child. His mother told everyone he'd had a terrible accident, but Nick had confessed to Dora that it was a beating by their brutal father that had left his brother so broken and damaged. Nick had also told her that when he'd found out, he'd given the bully a taste of his own medicine. He hadn't gone into details, but knowing her husband Dora could well imagine. Whatever Nick had done, he'd frightened Reg Riley so badly that he'd left town, never to be seen again.

Nick had been protecting his brother ever since. Apart from herself and their babies, Dora knew Danny was the only person in the world Nick Riley truly loved.

Dora loved Danny too, so she was happy to have him come to live with them after they were married. With a good home, and surrounded by love, Danny had started to thrive. He fitted right into their happy family, and since the twins came along he'd been utterly devoted to them. He would play patiently with them for hours, singing to them, making silly faces or letting them yank handfuls of his hair. He would help Dora settle them and then he would sit for hours watching over them while they slept, marvelling at their tiny fingers and toes.

He would have taken them from her now so she could drink her cup of tea in peace, but Dora couldn't bear to let go of them. She sat at the table with one twin on each knee, chatting to her mum and her grandmother.

She told them all about her interview with Matron, and how she'd asked all kinds of questions about why Dora wanted to leave her children and go back to work.

'Well, she's got a point, ain't she?' Nanna said. 'It ain't right for a mother to go out to work. She should be with her kids.'

Dora was crestfallen, but once again her mother stepped in.

'Listen to yourself, Ma! You were working down the laundry when you were nine months gone with our Brenda and me, so don't you try to tell anyone different. And I was just the same.' She turned to Dora. 'Take no notice of her, Dor. She's just in one of her cantankerous moods. You should hear her talking about you to the neighbours. Anyone would think you were Florence Nightingale herself the way she goes on about you.'

'I do not!' Nanna Winnie denied, two bright spots of colour staining her jowly cheeks. 'And as for you,' she turned her attention to Little Alfie, who had the misfortune to walk through the back door at that moment, 'you get out there and take those filthy boots off before you come into my nice clean kitchen. I ain't having you tramping mud all the way through. And I hope you ain't been feeding that sodding rabbit again? I'm telling you, the sooner that gets made into a pie, the better!'

Rose caught Dora's eye across the table and winked at her. Dora grinned back. Typical Nanna Winnie. God forbid anyone should think she'd gone soft in her old age.

Rose put down her cup and stood up. 'Anyway, I'd best get on, or I'll never get any food on the table.'

'Can I help?' Dora offered.

Before her mother could reply, Danny scrambled to his feet, a tangle of lanky arms and legs.

'I'll h-help,' he said. 'I l-like cooking.'

'Well, then, I won't say no.' Rose smiled at him. 'Come on, Danny. You can help me cut up the greens.'

'If the bloody rabbit ain't had 'em all!' Nanna muttered.

When they'd gone, Dora turned her attention to the official blue military envelope propped up on the mantelpiece. She'd spotted it the moment she came in, and her heart had bounced in her chest, hoping it might be from Nick. But peering closer, she realised the neat, round handwriting was nothing like her husband's untidy scrawl.

'Is that from our Josie?' she asked.

'It is.' Nanna plucked the letter from behind the clock and handed it to her. 'And this came with

26

it, too.' She passed over a black-and-white photograph. 'Don't she look lovely in her uniform?'

Dora felt a choking lump rise in her throat at the sight of her little sister Josie, looking so smart in her WAAF uniform. 'She looks so grown up,' she murmured.

'That's what I said to your mum. Hard to believe she's turned twenty, ain't it?'

Dora stared at her sister's smiling face. She was the only one of the family to inherit their mother's slender dark beauty and not their father's red hair and sturdy limbs. She was the quietest of the rowdy Doyle clan, as well as the cleverest. She and Dora were very close, and now Josie was up in Lancashire learning how to repair aircraft, Dora missed her almost as much as she missed her Nick.

There was another letter from her sister-in-law Lily. After Dora's brother Peter was called up, Lily and their little daughter Mabel had been evacuated down to Kent. Dora was supposed to go with them, but she couldn't face being away from the rest of her family.

Her other younger sister Bea came home from work in time for tea, and soon they were all gathered round the table, talking and arguing as usual.

'The girls at work reckon we'll be invaded now,' Bea announced, helping herself to potatoes.

Dora caught Danny's look of dismay across the table. 'It won't come to that,' she said.

'How do you know?' Bea pouted. 'It makes sense, don't it? Now they're in Holland, we'll be next.'

'Not now Churchill's in charge,' Nanna predicted confidently. 'That old beast will stand up to Hitler, don't you worry.'

'It's our soldiers I feel sorry for,' Bea went on, through a mouthful of food. 'How do you think our Pete's going to get on, stuck out there? And your Nick,' she added, looking at Dora.

'He'll be all right, don't you worry about that.' Dora glared at her sister across the table and willed her to be quiet. Seventeen-year-old Bea had always been the troublemaker of the family, keen to stir it up whenever she could.

'Yes, but—'

'Can we talk about something else?' Dora cut across her sister's objection. 'What was Mickey Malone doing hanging around our back alley first thing this morning?'

A dull flush rose in Bea's face. 'I dunno, do I?'

'Really? He looked as if he was waiting for you.'

Rose put down her knife and fork. 'Mickey Malone? Round here? I hope you ain't having anything to do with him, young lady!' she warned.

'That family's nothing but trouble,' Nanna chimed in.

'I dunno what you're talking about,' Bea mumbled, shooting Dora a filthy look across the table. Dora hadn't meant to get her sister into trouble, but at least it had stopped Bea from talking about Nick and the war. Dora was finding it hard enough to keep her spirits up without her sister making it worse.

After tea, Dora went upstairs to put the twins to bed. Danny insisted on helping her.

'Don't you want to listen to the wireless?' she

28

asked him. '*Sandy's Half-Hour* should be on soon. You know how much you like listening to the music.'

Nick had bought the wireless for them just before he left, and it was Danny's pride and joy. He would sit for hours, twiddling the knobs, his ear pressed to the polished wooden set, grinning with delight at each crackle and whine. He listened to everything. He would cackle with delight at *It's That Man Again*, hum along to the band music, and listen earnestly to the news broadcasts and the advice from *The Kitchen Front*, even though he didn't understand them. It made Dora smile to see him so happy.

'I'd r-rather help you.' He slanted a shy smile at her. 'B-besides, you always say I can g-get them off to sleep b-better than you.'

Dora smiled. 'That you can, Danny,' she agreed. 'Come on, then, let's get this pair washed and changed.'

She was amazed at how deft Danny was at changing the babies' nappies. The young man who was so clumsy he couldn't tie his own shoelaces, was gentle and careful when it came to folding and pinning the towelling squares into place. He was an expert compared to the ham-fisted attempts of the student nurses Dora used to see on the children's ward.

Once they'd got the twins washed and powdered and in their nightclothes, Dora tucked them up in the middle of the double bed with bolsters on either side to stop them rolling. Walter went to sleep straight away, but Winnie twisted and grizzled, holding out her chubby hands.

'She w-wants Aggy,' Danny said, pulling the battered rag doll out of his pocket and handing it to Dora. 'She won't sleep w-without her.'

'Thanks, Dan. I might have known you wouldn't forget.' Dora took the doll from him and tucked it in beside her daughter. Sure enough, Winnie gave a satisfied sigh and her eyelids fluttered closed.

If only all our problems could be sorted out so easily, Dora thought.

She left Danny singing to them while she went to sort through the pile of washing her mum had left in a corner of the room. 'You Are My Sunshine', as usual. Danny had heard Jimmie Davis singing it on the wireless and hadn't stopped humming it since.

It was strange, she thought. Danny usually stammered words when he spoke, but for some reason he could sing without a single stumble.

Dora joined in, humming to herself as she picked up his shirt to fold it. But the sight of it in her hands stopped her in her tracks. Why did even the simplest job have to remind her that Nick wasn't here? His absence permeated every part of her life, from the moment she woke up without him in bed, to the moment she went to sleep thinking about him.

'Nick will come home, w-won't he, Dora?'

She looked up, shocked to hear her own thoughts put into words. Danny had stopped singing and was watching her carefully. She hoped he hadn't seen her falter, or the tears she'd quickly dashed away.

'Of course he will, Dan.' She forced lightness into her voice.

'B-but Bea said–'

'Take no notice of Bea,' Dora dismissed instantly. 'She talks a lot of nonsense.'

Danny was silent for a moment. 'Nick w-won't get killed, will he, Dora?' he asked finally.

Dora turned away from him, hoping to God Danny wouldn't see the doubt that flickered across her face. Whatever she felt, she had to be strong for her family. 'Of course he won't.'

Danny paused for a moment, and she could see his worried expression as he struggled to take it in. 'All the s-same, I w-wish he'd stop fighting and c-come home,' he said at last.

Dora smiled sadly as she folded the shirt.

'So do I, love,' she sighed. 'So do I.'

Chapter Three

'No, I'm not having it. No daughter of mine is going to wipe strangers' backsides!'

Alec Caldwell brought the flat of his hand down on the table, making the cups rattle. He was a big, burly policeman, and his voice filled the tiny back kitchen where the family sat having their tea.

Jennifer regarded him, unperturbed. She was used to her father's bark, and she knew it was nowhere near as bad as his bite. 'But it won't be like that. I'm going to be a proper nurse. They'll teach us how to give injections and all sorts.'

'My Aunt Fanny they will! You think they're

31

going to trust you to stick needles in people, my girl? Mark my words, you'll be nothing but a skivvy emptying bedpans and cleaning up God knows what.'

Jennifer wrinkled her nose in disgust. That wasn't what the nice woman at the Red Cross had said. She'd made it sound as if Jennifer would be saving lives, or at least cooling a few fevered brows. She hadn't mentioned anything about bedpans.

'She thinks she's Florence Nightingale!' Jennifer's younger brother Wilf cackled, through a mouthful of bread and dripping.

'Shut up, you!' she turned on him. At fourteen, he annoyed her constantly. 'I've got to do my bit, Dad,' she explained to her father. 'It's either that or go into the forces. And you wouldn't want that, would you?' she reasoned.

She saw his face go pale, and knew her words had struck home. The thought of his daughter being in danger was almost too much for Alec Caldwell to bear, she could tell. Not that she would join up in a million years. But it was worth mentioning the possibility now and then, just to see her father panic. Bless him, she had been twisting him round her little finger since the day she uttered her first word.

Her mother stepped in. 'She's right, Alec. She's got to do something, now she's turned eighteen. And there are a lot worse things than nursing. Mrs Armitage's eldest girl has just joined the WTS. I was talking to her when we were queuing at the butcher's yesterday. She's beside herself with worry.'

'You see?' Jennifer pushed the forms across the

32

table towards her father. 'Just sign them for me, Dad. Please?'

Her heart lifted when he picked the papers up, only to plunge when he put them down again. 'All the same, I still don't like the idea. That's not what I brought my daughter up to do.'

'She ain't Princess Elizabeth!' Will muttered into his cup.

'Cissy's doing it.' Jennifer refilled her father's cup, trying to be every inch his dutiful little girl. It wouldn't do to let frustration get the better of her now. 'We thought we'd sign up together.'

'Oh, well, if she's doing it, you're going to have to do it too, ain't you?' Her father smiled reluctantly. 'I reckon if she jumped in the Thames, you'd have to follow.'

'The terrible twins!' her mother said with a smile.

Jennifer was offended. 'It was my idea, actually. I'm the one who wanted to do it.' She and Cissy might be best friends, but everyone knew she was the leader. It had been that way ever since they were kids.

'And what does Cissy's father think about it?' Alec Caldwell asked. 'Not a lot, if I know him!' He and Bob Baxter had been friends and neighbours for years.

'As a matter of fact, he's all for it,' Jennifer lied. In fact, she knew Cissy was two doors down, having the same conversation with her own father at that very moment, and probably telling him exactly the same story. That was what they'd planned earlier as they arranged gloves in the glass display cabinets at the draper's shop where

33

they worked.

'Is he now?' Alec Caldwell scratched his chin thoughtfully. Jennifer could see he was wavering, but she also knew that she wasn't safe yet. One wrong word could still ruin everything. Her father adored her and would never deny her anything, but he couldn't bear for the wind to blow on her either. He would have wrapped her up in cotton wool for ever if he could.

She looked at her mother, silently appealing to her. If anyone could sway her husband's opinion, it was Elsie Caldwell.

Sure enough, Alec turned to his wife and said, 'What do you reckon, Mother?'

Elsie picked up the form and glanced through it. 'Well, it would be better than her going into the forces,' she said. Then, before Jennifer could let out her sigh of relief, she went on, 'It would mean she could stay at home, too, if she got a job at one of the local hospitals.'

Jennifer's dreams disappeared like a bubble popping before her eyes. 'I'm not staying at home!' she blurted out. 'I want to work at a military hospital!'

That was what had been in her mind when she came up with the idea. She had visions of herself drifting from bed to bed, an angel of mercy bringing light and hope into handsome soldiers' lives.

'She wants to find herself a boyfriend!' Wilf chimed in, ruining her daydream.

'I thought I told you to shut up?' Jennifer reached across the table and grabbed his earlobe, twisting it hard until he yelped in pain.

'Stop it, you two,' her mother said mildly,

offering her husband the plate of bread across the table. 'Another slice, Dad?'

'Thank you, don't mind if I do.' Her father took some bread and spread dripping on it. 'And you can pack that in, Wilf,' he added, pointing his knife at his son. 'Our Jen doesn't have boyfriends. She knows she's far too young for all that.'

Jennifer picked at a loose thread on the chenille tablecloth and avoided her father's eye. As far as Alec Caldwell was concerned, she was still his little girl and that was the way he liked it. And Jennifer wasn't about to put him straight either. She didn't want him putting his big boot down and spoiling her fun.

'I don't think I'll have much choice anyway.' She shrugged, doing her best to sound nonchalant. 'I daresay they'll send me wherever I'm needed.'

'I'm sure that's not right, love,' her mother put in. 'According to these here forms, you ain't allowed to serve in a military hospital until you turn twenty. And you can't be sent overseas until you're twenty-one.'

'Let me see that!' Jennifer snatched the papers from her mother's hand and scanned them. The nice lady at the Red Cross hadn't mentioned *that* either.

'Is that right? Oh, well, if that's the case...' Her father took the forms from her with a broad smile. 'Fetch us a pen, Wilf, and I'll get these signed.'

Jennifer scowled at her mother, who smiled benignly back at her. Trust her to know everything! Elsie Caldwell might not always show it, but she could be very canny when she wanted to be. She also knew everyone from Tower Bridge to the Isle of Dogs, so there was no getting anything past her.

Jennifer lapsed into furious silence, but no one seemed to notice as they went on chatting around the tea table. Her mother was telling them about a row that had broken out in the queue outside the greengrocer's. Jennifer clattered her cup around in its saucer a few times to draw attention to her frustration, but all her mother said was, 'Be careful, dear. If that gets broken we ain't going to replace it in a hurry.'

Jennifer blew out an angry sigh. Until you're twenty-one... It felt as if she'd grown up listening to those words. They drove her mad. She was still almost three years away from that magical day, and it felt like a lifetime.

'How did you get on?' Jennifer asked Cissy when they met up later. As usual on a Friday night, they were going dancing at the Palais. It was a wet, dismal night, and they huddled under an umbrella together so they wouldn't ruin their carefully set curls.

Cissy grinned. 'My dad was all for it.'

Jennifer stared at her. 'You're having me on? What did he say?'

'He reckoned he quite liked the idea of me being a nurse. "A nice, respectable profession for a young lady," so he said.'

Jennifer stepped into a puddle and cursed under her breath. She wished she hadn't decided to wear her new calfskin sandals. They would be ruined in all this rain.

'I wish he'd talk to my dad,' she grumbled.

Cissy's face paled. 'He didn't say no, did he?'

'He might as well have done,' Jennifer sighed. 'Did you know we're not allowed to be mobile until we're twenty?'

'No! But I thought we were going to work in a military hospital?'

'So did I, but we can't.' Jennifer stopped to brush splashes of mud from her stockings. 'I must say, the idea of being a nurse doesn't appeal to me so much now. I want to look after soldiers, not horrible old men with boils and piles and God knows what else!'

'Me too.'

Jennifer saw the faraway look come into her friend's blue eyes and her heart sank. Of course Cissy was thinking about Paul Maynard again. They had been courting for nearly a year, but she never missed a chance to mention his name.

And she was even worse since he'd joined the Royal Navy. Hardly an hour went by when Cissy wasn't going on about how much she missed Paul, and how worried she was that he was away at sea. The way she went on, anyone would think he was fighting the war single-handed!

Privately, Jennifer thought she was daft to fall in love at such an awkward time. Life was hard enough without pining away and upsetting yourself over a man.

'Maybe I should join the Wrens instead?' Cissy mused, as they queued in the rain outside the Palais for their tickets.

'What?' Jennifer turned to her, aghast. 'Why

would you do that?'

'I just want to be closer to Paul.'

'But what about me?' The words were out before Jennifer could stop them.

Cissy looked at her blankly. 'What about you?'

'I thought we were going to stick together?'

That's what they'd always done, ever since their mums had parked their prams beside each other in the street. They had sat next to each other all the way through school, then got jobs together at Wells the draper's on Old Ford Road. They spent practically every waking moment together, laughing and larking about. Everyone called them the terrible twins, even though they didn't look at all alike. Jennifer had always been jealous of Cissy's bouncy blonde curls, until she'd seen Vivien Leigh in *Gone with the Wind* and decided that being dark and sultry was far better.

'You'll understand when you fall in love,' Cissy told her.

There was something about the way she said it that irritated Jennifer. Hadn't they always agreed that neither of them would start courting properly until the other had found a boyfriend? But then Paul came along and swept Cissy right off her feet. And now she was acting as if she was a grown up, and Jennifer was a silly young girl.

But Jennifer's bad mood lifted as soon as they walked into the dance hall and she heard the band playing. As usual on a Friday night, the place was packed. Groups of soldiers stood at the bar, laughing and drinking and eyeing up the girls. Other people sat at tables around the edge of the room, but most couples were on the dance floor, twirling and whirling in each other's arms.

Jennifer and Cissy had barely taken off their coats before two soldiers claimed them and led them on to the floor for a foxtrot. From then on, they didn't stop. They went from one dance to the next, pausing only to change partners. The music was too loud for conversation, but Jennifer didn't mind. She wasn't particularly interested in whoever she was dancing with, as long as he didn't tread on her toes too often. For her, it was all about having fun and forgetting about the boring old war for a while.

She was glad to see Cissy was having a good time, too. The music and atmosphere of the dance hall seemed to have chased all thoughts of Paul out of her mind, and she was more like the happy-go-lucky girl Jennifer used to know, whirling around the dance floor, laughing.

Jennifer was pleased for her friend. She also secretly hoped Cissy might finally realise what she was missing out on, moping after her boyfriend. They were only eighteen, far too young to get serious about anyone. Why tie yourself down when there were so many handsome men in the world to flirt with?

And flirt she did. One young man in particular, a soldier, was especially keen to claim all her attention for himself. Jennifer didn't mind. He wasn't her type, but his smart khaki uniform made him seem quite dashing. He bought her drinks, and after a while she danced every dance in his arms, until her new shoes rubbed blisters on her heels and she had to stop.

'Let's go outside for some fresh air,' the young

man said. He'd told her his name, but Jennifer hadn't caught it above the sound of the band playing. It didn't matter anyway, since she wouldn't be seeing him after tonight.

Jennifer eyed him shrewdly. She knew exactly what he was after, and it wasn't fresh air.

'It's raining,' she pointed out, mock innocent.

'I'm sure we could find a nice doorway to shelter in.' There was no mistaking his suggestive smirk. 'Come on, I'll walk you home.'

They were in a darkened corner of the dance hall, tucked behind a pillar away from the crowds. The young man had somehow manoeuvred her so her back was against the wall. Over his shoulder, Jennifer could see Cissy spinning around the dance floor, her laughing face illuminated by the coloured lights overhead.

'No, thanks, I'm with my friend,' she said.

'She can find her own way home, surely?'

'I promised my dad we'd stick together.'

'Your dad ain't here, is he?'

Lucky for you, Jennifer thought. Uniform or not, Alec Caldwell would have torn this skinny young man limb from limb for even looking at his daughter.

The soldier frowned. 'Come on, love. Why do you think I've been buying you drinks all night?'

Jennifer met his eye boldly. 'Because I was thirsty?' she said.

His smile was cold. 'You're a smart one, ain't you?'

'Too smart for you, mate.'

'We'll see about that.' He pressed his body closer to hers, and she could smell beer and cigarettes on his breath. 'You've had your fun, now I want mine.'

He made a grab for her breast through her blouse, squeezing roughly. As he moved in, Jennifer lifted her knee just as her dad had taught her, ready to let him have it as hard as she could between his legs.

But before she could make another move, the soldier suddenly staggered backwards away from her.

'You heard the lady, son. She ain't interested,' a gruff voice said.

Jennifer stared in shock at the man who loomed out of the shadows. He was tall and heavily built, with slicked-back dark hair.

The soldier shook himself free and squared up to the newcomer. 'You want to mind your own business, mate, or I'll stick one on you.'

'Try it.' The man's voice was menacing in its softness.

A thrill ran through Jennifer as the two men stood toe to toe. She loved men fighting over her. But then, to her disappointment, the soldier shrugged and muttered, 'Nah, she ain't worth it. You can have her, if you're that bothered.'

As he walked off, Jennifer turned to the stranger. 'What did you do that for?' she demanded. 'I could have dealt with him. I know what I'm doing.'

A slow smile spread across the man's face. The dim light of the dance hall illuminated a faint silver scar running down the length of his cheek. 'I'll bet you do,' he said softly.

Before Jennifer could reply, Cissy hurried over.

'What was that about? Was there a fight? I might have known if there was trouble you'd be right in the middle of it, Jen Caldwell.'

'It's all right,' the man said. 'I saved your friend's honour.'

Cissy turned to him. 'And who are you, when you're at home?'

He smiled at Jennifer. 'Just call me a knight in shining armour,' he said.

'Very mysterious, I'm sure.' Cissy turned to Jennifer. 'Come on, let's go home. I promised my mum I'd be in by ten and you know how long it takes to walk in this rotten blackout.'

'I could give you a lift, if you like?' the man offered. 'My car's just round the corner.'

A car! Jennifer didn't know anyone with a proper motor. Most of the boys around Bethnal Green couldn't afford more than a second-hand pushbike.

But before she could accept, Cissy jumped in with, 'No, thank you. We'll make our own way home.'

'Suit yourself. Some other time, maybe?' He winked at Jennifer. 'Mind how you go, won't you?'

They spilled out of the brightly lit dance hall into the pitch darkness of the blackout. It was still raining, and they clung to each other under their umbrella as they stumbled along the street.

'My hair's going to be ruined. We should have let that bloke give us a lift,' Jennifer grumbled, turning up the collar of her raincoat.

'You must be joking! I ain't getting into a stranger's car. Especially not someone like him,'

42

Cissy replied primly.

'What was wrong with him?'

'I dunno. But there was definitely something not quite right about him.'

'Well, he seemed like a perfect gentleman to me. He came to my rescue, after all.'

'Hmm.'

'What's that supposed to mean?'

'If you ask me, it's a case of out of the frying pan and into the fire.'

'Do you think so?' Jennifer smiled in the darkness, glad that Cissy couldn't see her face. The last thing she wanted was another lecture from her friend.

But Cissy knew her too well. 'I mean it, Jen. There's something not quite right about him. Something – I don't know – dangerous.'

I know, Jennifer thought. God only knew, she could do with a bit of danger and excitement in her life.

Chapter Four

It felt strange to be in uniform again. Dora barely recognised herself as she stared at her reflection in the cloakroom mirror. Was it really only two years since she'd last put it on? It felt like a lifetime ago. But she had got so used to being a wife and mother, she suddenly felt like a young girl again in her heavy blue dress, white apron and black wool stockings.

43

She immediately felt a pang, wondering if she'd done the right thing. It had seemed like such a good idea to go back to nursing, but now she was actually here Dora couldn't imagine how she would cope. What if she'd forgotten everything she'd learned? She had a sudden, horrible picture of herself going blank and getting in everyone's way.

And then there were her babies. Her heart ached when she remembered how the twins had sobbed and reached out their chubby arms imploringly to her when she'd left them that morning. She had been so close to taking off her coat again, but her mother had insisted she should not.

'Go,' she'd said, pushing Dora gently but firmly towards the door. 'They'll stop before you get to the end of the alley, I promise.'

They might have stopped crying, but Dora hadn't. Tears had run down her cheeks all the way to the hospital gates. Poor little mites, she hadn't been away from them for a whole day before.

But at the same time she knew she couldn't give up her plan to return to nursing. She was so frantic with worry about Nick, if she didn't do something to occupy her mind, she felt she would go completely mad.

She gave herself a mental shake. You chose this, my girl, she told herself sternly. You were the one who made such a fuss about wanting to nurse again, and you've got to see it through. If you walk away now you know full well you'll never come back.

At least she'd been assigned to the Casualty department, where Helen Dawson was in charge.

44

The two girls had shared a room at the students' home while they were training, and they had been friends ever since. At least Helen wouldn't be as hard on Dora as some of the other sisters might be, which was some comfort.

But her fingers still fumbled over the studs on her starched collar and cuffs. And to think a couple of years ago she'd been able to put them on with one hand while hurrying down the stairs of the nurses' home, late for breakfast! Now she was as clumsy as a nervous probationer.

And as for her cap ... no matter how hard she tried, she couldn't fold the square of starched linen into something resembling a headpiece. As she tried and tried, she could feel the crisp white fabric wilting in her clammy hands.

She was still cursing quietly over it when the door opened and a dark-haired student nurse stuck her head round.

'I just wanted to remind you, Sister will be on duty at eight and we're supposed to be ready – oh, I see you're having a bit of trouble.' She came forward, her hands outstretched. 'Would you like me to help?'

'Thanks,' Dora replied, handing it over.

'There's a knack to it,' the girl said. 'You have to take this corner over to this edge, you see? And make sure this crease is at the front, like so ... there.' She folded it deftly.

'Thanks – I'm sorry, I don't know your name?'

'Kowalski. Devora Kowalski. All my friends call me Dev.'

'I'm Nurse Riley. My friends call me Dora.'

'Pleased to meet you. Pass me your pins and I'll

fix it in place for you.'

'Thanks.' Dora handed over the pins she'd remembered to bring with her. 'Sister Sutton used to despair of me because my hair was always escaping. She used to say if she saw another ginger curl poking out she'd shave my head!'

Nurse Kowalski's brows lifted. 'You're a Nightingale girl?'

Dora nodded. 'I took my State Finals nearly three years ago.'

'The same time I started training.'

'So you're in your final year?'

'I would be, if it weren't for this wretched war. Our training has been "officially suspended until further notice".' She quoted the words with a grimace.

'Bad luck.' Dora remembered how she couldn't wait to take her Finals and be able to wear the hospital badge and finally call herself a real nurse. 'This war's a nuisance all round, ain't it?' she said.

'It is,' Dev agreed with a sigh. 'But at least they've let us come back to London now, which is something. It was so dull when the students' home moved down to the country.'

'Is Sister Sutton still in charge?'

'Yes – worse luck!' Dev's nose wrinkled. 'We all thought she might retire when the war started, but she's still here. And she's got even worse since we arrived back in London. Now she can nag us about remembering our gas masks as well as everything else. And as for that awful little dog of hers...'

'You mean Sparky?' Dora laughed. 'For gawd's

46

sake, don't let Sister Sutton hear you calling him that!'

'Well, he is awful,' Dev said with feeling. 'Nasty, bad-tempered creature. I swear he lies in wait for us at the bottom of the stairs so he can nip our ankles. He made a hole in my stocking the other morning. And then Sister Sutton had the cheek to tell me off about it!' She finished pinning Dora's cap and stood back to admire her handiwork. 'There,' she, said. 'I think that's straight enough. Now hurry up, or Sister Dawson will report us. She's an angel, but she still likes things done her way!'

They hurried back to the main Casualty Hall just as Helen Dawson was coming on duty. It gave Dora a jolt to see her friend in the uniform of a ward sister. The severity of the grey dress suited her, emphasising Helen's tall, willowy figure, while the starched linen bonnet tied in a bow under her chin framed the perfect oval of her face. When Dora had first met her back in their student days she had thought Helen the most beautiful creature she had ever seen, and she still thought it now.

Dora immediately stood to attention beside Dev Kowalski, her hands folded behind her back. She and Helen might be friends off duty, but while in uniform Sister Dawson was still Dora's superior.

'Welcome to Casualty, Nurse Riley.' Her greeting was formal, but Dora caught the hint of warmth in her brown eyes.

'Thank you, Sister.'

'I must say, we'll be glad to have an extra pair

47

of hands, won't we, Kowalski? And I know you've worked in Casualty before, so your experience will be useful.'

'I hope so, Sister,' Dora replied.

'You might notice a few changes since you were last here,' Helen said. 'The department has been extended over the past year or so, and we now have two further emergency treatment rooms and a gas cleansing station. Although fortunately we haven't had to put it to use so far,' she added. 'We also have some extra consulting rooms, and a recovery ward at the end of the corridor.'

Dora frowned. 'Aren't patients transferred up to the main ward, Sister?'

Helen shook her head. 'Not unless it's completely necessary. We don't have the staff to look after them, you see. Which is why we're so pleased to have you.'

'Hear, hear!'

Dora turned to see Dr McKay the Senior Medical Officer approaching them. He had been in charge of the Casualty department ever since Dora started training at the hospital. He was in his mid-thirties, dark-haired, with a sharply intelligent face and horn-rimmed spectacles that completely disguised his terrible sense of mischief. Dora knew from experience that there was never a dull moment with David McKay. He was also a brilliant and dedicated doctor.

'Good morning, Nurse,' he greeted her with a grin. 'First day back, is it?'

'That's right, Doctor.'

'It'll be good to have you.' His dark eyes twinkled behind his spectacles. 'Although I daresay you'll

48

notice there have been quite a few changes around here.'

'Sister Dawson was just telling me about them, sir.'

'Oh, yes, indeed. Quite a lot has changed around here. Although some things are a little harder to spot than others. Isn't that right, Sister?'

He glanced at Helen. She didn't meet his eye, but Dora could see the delicate pink colour rising in her friend's pale cheeks.

'Anyway, um, as I was saying, I'm sure you'll find your way around soon enough.' Helen lost her composure for a moment, her blush deepening as she stumbled over her words, much to David McKay's amusement. Dora saw the grin lighting up his face as he sauntered away. Poor Helen, she thought. Her friend was desperately trying to keep their romance a secret for the sake of hospital rules, but he looked as if he wanted to shout it out to the whole world.

Helen pulled herself together and gave Dora her instructions for the morning. She was to assist in the General Surgical Outpatients clinic.

'Dr Jameson will be taking the clinic. I'm sure you remember him?'

'Yes, Sister.' Although if it was the same Simon Jameson she recalled, he had been a humble medical student when Dora had last seen him.

Helen finished giving the nurses their orders and dismissed them. As they watched her walking off, Dev whispered, 'Poor Sister Dawson, she was trying so hard to stay professional. Dr Mac really shouldn't tease her like that.'

Dora looked at her. 'What do you mean?'

49

'Can't you tell? They're madly in love.'

Dora hoped her face didn't give her away. 'What makes you say that?'

'Oh, everyone knows,' Dev said airily. 'I think it's such a silly rule that they aren't allowed to be together, just because they both work here.' She sighed. 'Poor Sister Dawson, I think she deserves some happiness. You do know what happened to her, don't you? Her husband died of scarlet fever, just a few days after they were married. But of course you'll probably remember that, won't you?' Dora made a non-committal reply, and Dev went on, 'She married him in hospital, didn't she, knowing he was going to die? Don't you think that's romantic?'

Dora gritted her teeth to stop herself from snapping at the girl. There was nothing romantic about the way Helen's heart had shattered into a thousand pieces after Charlie's death. Nor was there anything romantic about watching her struggling through every day, until finally it all became too much for her.

Dora had been convinced her friend would never recover, but then David McKay had come along and with his doctor's skills, put Helen's heart back together.

But Dora knew her friend well enough to realise that she would be mortified to think everyone was gossiping about her.

'Can you show me the way to Outpatients?' she asked, changing the subject. 'And then you can tell me all about Dr Jameson...'

It was indeed the Simon Jameson she remembered. He arrived a minute before his first patient, handsome, ruddy-cheeked and fair-haired, his white coat stretched over his broad rugby player's shoulders.

'Bless my soul, if it isn't Nurse Doyle!'

Dora smiled. 'It's Nurse Riley now, Doctor.'

'So it is. I heard you'd got married. Such a loss to the rest of us.' He pulled a face that was more comical than tragic.

Dora laughed. 'Go on with you! As I recall you always preferred blondes.'

He grinned back at her, looking even younger than his twenty-four years. 'Trust you to remember that!'

His good humour helped Dora to feel more confident. But she was still trembling with nerves when the first patient, a post-gastrostomy, was brought in to have his stitches removed. It was all she could do to stop her hands from shaking as she carefully cleaned the gastrostomy tube and handed it back to Dr Jameson.

But once she'd got used to it, it didn't seem so daunting. Dora soon fell back into the swing of things, losing herself in the business of cleaning and sterilising instruments, checking and cleaning wounds, changing dressings and administering massages. Many of the patients were post-operative cases whose wounds had become infected. Dora swabbed them out and dusted them with antiseptic powder, holding her breath behind her mask so she didn't have to breathe in the awful smell.

'It's the war,' Dr Jameson said. 'The idea is to send post-op patients home as soon as possible these days, instead of allowing them to recover on the ward. The trouble is, most of them don't look after themselves or bother to keep their wounds clean, and then they end up just as bad as they were before.' He shook his head regretfully. 'But who are we to question, eh, Nurse? Now, who do we have next on the list? We'd best get a move on, I'm due up on the ward in half an hour.'

'Sorry, Doctor.' Dora fumbled through her notes, immediately flustered. 'I'll try to be quicker.'

'It's no trouble, Nurse. It takes a while to get back into the swing of things, doesn't it? Besides, it's not as if there are any dire emergencies waiting for my attention upstairs.'

He was just as kind the first time she had to give an intramuscular injection. Her hands started shaking again, but fortunately the patient was face down on the bed and didn't seem to notice.

Dr Jameson gave her a knowing smile. 'Dear me, Nurse, I wasn't sure if that needle was going to end up in the patient's buttock or the mattress!' he commented afterwards.

The rest of the day was just as busy, and by the time Dora's shift finished at five, she was so tired she could barely move.

She was in the cloakroom, trying to massage the life back into her aching feet, when Helen came in. In contrast to Dora's own bedraggled appearance, Helen looked as fresh and uncreased as she had first thing that morning.

'Hard day?' She smiled at Dora.

'I'd forgotten what it's like being on your feet all

day,' Dora groaned. 'I'm going to have blisters the size of footballs by the end of the week.'

'Methylated spirit should help.' Helen smiled sympathetically. 'I'm sorry I haven't had a chance to speak to you much today, but we've been busy as usual.'

'That's all right, Sister.' Dora grinned back at her. 'I don't expect you to hold my hand!'

Helen grimaced. 'You don't have to call me that when it's just the two of us!'

'I might forget in front of the other nurses if I don't.' Dora remembered something then, and added, 'By the way, I wanted to warn you Kowalski seems to know all about you and David.'

Helen looked stricken. 'Does she? How? I thought we'd been so careful.' She shook her head. 'It must have been David. He can't resist teasing me. I've told him about it, but he can't seem to stop himself.'

'He can't help it if he's besotted with you, can he?'

Helen smiled reluctantly. 'All the same, he shouldn't flirt in front of the nurses. It's only a matter of time before Matron finds out about it.' Her smile faded a fraction. 'Although I don't suppose it matters, as he'll probably be gone before too long.'

Dora looked at her sharply. 'I thought he'd deferred his call-up?'

'Only because he thought he'd be needed here. But now he's talking about signing up for the Medical Corps.' Helen bit her lip. 'I honestly don't know how I'd cope if he weren't here. It's bad enough my brother being in the RAF, without worrying about David, too.'

'I know what you mean,' Dora said quietly.

She bent her head on the pretext of putting her shoes back on, but she could feel her friend watching her.

'Oh, Dora, I'm sorry,' Helen said. 'Listen to me going on about my silly fears, when you're going through just the same thing. How is Nick? Have you heard from him?'

'Not for a while.' Dora kept her head down, still tying her shoelaces.

'Poor you, you must be so worried.'

Dora took a moment to compose herself, only looking up when she could trust herself to smile. 'Oh, you know Nick. He can look after himself,' she replied breezily. 'Now, I meant to ask you, can you help me practise my injections? I made a right mess of my first one earlier.'

She looked into Helen's warm brown eyes, willing her to get the message. Fortunately, her friend was wise enough to understand what Dora was trying to say to her.

'Yes,' she said. 'Of course I can help you.'

Chapter Five

Jennifer had no idea making a bed could be so difficult, but the Red Cross instructor seemed to be making a right meal of it.

'Where possible, bed making should be done by two persons,' the woman intoned at the front

54

of the class. 'You must make sure you have everything to hand, and always ensure the patient is not exposed to any draught...'

Her gaze swept the room. She was in her fifties, her iron-grey hair tucked up into her navy blue cap. The uniform did nothing for her, Jennifer thought. She decided there and then that if nursing meant putting her feet into those ugly brogues, then she would have none of it.

'Blimey, I've never heard so much fuss over making a bed, have you?' she whispered to Cissy, who stood at her side.

Cissy nudged her. 'Shh, you'll get us kicked out before we've even started!'

'Place a chair a yard from the foot of the bed-stead,' the instructor continued. 'Remove the pillows and untuck the bedclothes...'

Jennifer tried to listen attentively as the woman went on to explain how to make a bed with an immobile patient lying in it, but it was all too much like school for her liking, and she found her attention wandering.

She looked round the church hall. It was full of young girls like her and Cissy, plus a middle-aged woman in a tweed suit who looked like a spinster librarian.

'Take off the bedclothes one at a time, folding the upper corners to the lower corners, lift and place them on the chair...'

Jennifer's gaze snagged on a young girl standing at the back of the class, her back pressed against the wall. She was an odd little thing. It was hard to tell if she was pretty or not as her face was mostly hidden behind a drab curtain of mousy hair. Her slight frame was swamped by a shapeless skirt and blouse.

She caught Jennifer staring and looked away quickly, ducking her head.

'Now it's your turn.' Jennifer came back to the present just in time to hear the instructor's final words. 'Get into pairs, please, and we'll take turns making a bed without disturbing the patient.'

Jennifer grabbed Cissy's arm straight away. 'I hope you were listening to what she said, because I wasn't,' she whispered.

'I tried,' Cissy hissed back. 'But it can't be that difficult, can it?'

As it turned out, it was harder than it looked.

The dummy was surprisingly heavy, with contrary limbs that seemed to flop about exactly where Jennifer didn't want them. How had the instructor made it look so easy? she wondered, as she struggled to loosen the bedding while the dummy leaned drunkenly against her shoulder.

And it didn't help that the teacher stood over them, barking instructions. 'No, no, roll the soiled sheet towards the patient's shoulders ... tuck the ends of the clean sheet in before you try to lift the patient ... support her, for heaven's sake!' The back of Jennifer's neck began to prickle with sweat as the instructor kept up a running commentary of criticism.

Finally, it was over. Jennifer and Cissy eyed each other despairingly across the bed as the teacher inspected their work with a disapproving frown. 'Well, you didn't let the patient fall out of bed, which is something,' she sighed. 'But no self-respecting ward sister will tolerate those wrinkled sheets. The patient would have bedsores in no time.' She looked around the room. 'Would anyone else like to try? How about you?' She picked out the mousy-haired girl standing at the back. 'And you.' She pointed at a middle-aged woman. 'Come on, don't be shy. You've all got to have a go some time.'

The girl stepped forward to the centre of the circle, her gaze fixed on the ground. Close to, she looked even more odd. Behind her curtain of hair was a little face with a pointed chin and wide-spaced grey eyes the colour of dirty dishwater. She wasn't wearing a scrap of make-up, not even a dab of powder, Jennifer noted with astonishment.

She and the middle-aged spinster seemed nervous at first as they faced each other across the bed. But once they started, they quickly got into their stride. They worked in perfect unison, removing pillows, untucking bedclothes, folding the upper corners to the lower corners then lifting them carefully, the girl putting her half down on the chair before the older woman did hers.

The instructor watched them approvingly. 'Very good,' she said. 'You see how they're working together? It makes the job so much easier.'

The girl deftly rolled the soiled sheet down and had the clean sheet smoothed in its place before her partner had even managed to lift the dummy's shoulders.

But it was her appearance, not her bed-making skills, that took Jennifer's attention. She looked as if she had been making do and mending far longer than anyone else. The frayed collar of her blouse had been repaired several times with row upon row of careful little stitches. The flowery pattern had faded with washing to little more than smudges on the thin fabric. Jennifer wouldn't have been seen dead in it.

'Look at her,' she whispered to Cissy. 'Have you ever seen anyone dress like that? I know there's a war on, but you'd think she'd make some effort, wouldn't you?'

'At least she can make a bed,' Cissy said.

'She looks like she's just fallen out of one, with that hair.'

Cissy snorted with laughter. The instructor whipped round to face them

'Pay attention, please. You might learn something,' she snapped, her grey brows drawing together over her hooked nose.

The girl and her partner continued, but the girl's movements seemed slower, more faltering. Jennifer wondered if she'd heard her comment.

Finally, they finished and stepped back for the instructor to inspect their work. She paced around their bed, bending down to inspect the neatly tucked corners, and smoothing her hand over the sheet. Then she asked them their names.

'Eve Ainsley, Miss,' the girl whispered, flinching as if she had been struck.

'This is excellent work, Miss Ainsley.' The instructor smiled at her. 'I couldn't have done better myself, and I've been in the Red Cross for thirty years!' She turned and addressed the rest of the room. 'Everyone, please look at what Miss Ainsley and her partner have done. This is the kind of standard we expect from our volunteers.'

Eve kept her gaze fixed on the floor, but Jennifer could see her blushing deeply. She couldn't imagine why. If she'd been praised she would have made sure she enjoyed every second of it.

Not that there was much chance of that. She couldn't seem to do a thing right as for the next two hours they made and remade beds, stripping them off, folding mattresses, dusting bedsprings and wiping down bedsteads. By the end of it, Jennifer's arms ached so much she could barely lift them and she was feeling thoroughly disgruntled.

'I'm really not sure I want to be a VAD after all, if it's that difficult,' she grumbled as they left the class just after eight o'clock. The evening air was cool, and darkness hadn't yet fallen, so at least they could still see where they were going.

'It wasn't that bad,' Cissy said.

'My dad was right. It isn't real nursing. We're just glorified skivvies. I don't want to spend all my time making beds and sweeping floors.'

'All the same, we've got to do our bit,' Cissy replied.

Jennifer stared at her friend. 'Why are you taking it so seriously all of a sudden?' she asked. 'It was supposed to be a laugh!'

'We need to take it seriously,' Cissy said. 'We could be looking after real casualties one day. Sooner than we think, if the news is anything to go by...'

'Not again!' Jennifer sighed, irritated.

The news that the Germans had launched an attack on France had galvanised everyone. Suddenly there were ARP wardens on every corner, Jennifer's father had joined the new Local Defence Volunteers, and her mother was terrified. She was certain they were going to wake up any day and find German soldiers at the end of their beds. She had started to carry her gas mask again, and forced Jennifer to dig hers out from where it had been gathering dust on top of the wardrobe.

'If the Germans are going to invade then I wish they'd get it over with, because I'm sick and tired of all this doom and gloom!'

'You can't say that!' Cissy looked shocked.

'Can't I? At least then this wretched war would stop. We wouldn't have to stumble around in the dark any more, and we might get some decent food to eat. And we wouldn't have to mess about making beds either!'

'You wouldn't say that if the man you loved was out at sea, fighting for his country,' Cissy said.

The pious look on her face made Jennifer snap, 'Oh, here we go again!'

'What's that supposed to mean?'

'Nothing,' Jennifer muttered.

'I can't help being worried, can I? Paul's out there somewhere, and I don't know where he is or whether he's safe.' Cissy's voice trembled. 'I know you think I go on about it, but I can't help it.'

Jennifer sent her a sideways glance. She had never seen her friend so upset. Cissy was usually so much fun.

'I know,' she sighed. 'Sorry for snapping, Cis. I didn't mean to upset you. You know I'd be just the same if I were in your shoes. Worse, if anything. And you can go on about it as much as you like,' she said. 'I'm your mate, and from now on I promise I'll listen to you all you want.'

'And I'll try to stop moaning so much,' Cissy said, her mouth twisting.

'It's a deal.' Jennifer grinned. 'In that case, why don't we go to the flicks tomorrow and cheer ourselves up?'

'Are you sure we shouldn't stay at home and practise our bed-making?' Cissy suggested wryly.

'You're joking, ain't you? I've got better things to do with my time, thanks very much! Anyway, what do you fancy seeing at the pictures?' Jennifer changed the subject. 'I wouldn't mind seeing that new Deanna Durbin film. You know I've always liked Deanna...'

Chapter Six

'Where do you think you've been?'

Eve closed the front door and braced herself, seconds before her Aunt Freda's silhouette appeared in the lighted kitchen doorway at the end of the passageway.

She forced brightness into her voice as she shrugged off her coat. 'My nursing class, Aunt. I told you it started this week.'

Her aunt advanced down the narrow, darkened passageway towards her The fading light through the coloured fanlight cast jewelled stripes of green and red across her pinched face.

'You're later than you said you'd be,' she accused.

'I had to wait a long time for the bus, Aunt.' Eve hung up her coat and hat on the hallstand. As she turned round, her aunt was standing close to her, so close Eve could see the deep lines etched around her narrowed eyes.

'I'll know if you're lying to me, my girl. I can always tell a liar.' She stared down her long, pointed nose.

'I'm not, Aunt, I promise.'

'Deceit is in your bones, child. You are your mother's daughter, when all is said and done. Evil begets evil.'

Eve hung her head. 'Yes, Aunt.'

She tensed, waiting. But to her relief, Aunt Freda turned and headed back down the passageway to the kitchen. 'Your tea's in the oven,' she snapped over her shoulder.

'Thank you, Aunt.'

Eve's heart sank at the sight of the congealed dollop of greasy stew and grey mashed potatoes on her plate. But she knew better than to leave it, especially with Aunt Freda watching her. Waste not, want not, her aunt always said. At least there wasn't much of it, Eve consoled herself as she wrapped a tea towel around her hand and carried the hot plate to the kitchen table. For once she was grateful for her aunt's stinginess.

She picked up her knife and fork, but her aunt's bony hand flashed out and locked around her wrist, gripping like a vice. Eve jumped, her fork falling from her hand.

'Aren't you forgetting something?' Aunt Freda said. 'Or are you so above yourself you don't need to thank the Lord any more?'

Eve looked into her aunt's cold grey eyes and realised her mistake. 'Sorry,' she mumbled. Her aunt released her grip and Eve locked her own hands together, bowing her head as she waited for her aunt to start her prayer.

'Heavenly Father, we humbly thank thee,' Aunt Freda intoned solemnly. 'Bless us, O Lord, and these your gifts, which we are about to receive from your bounty...'

Eve risked opening one eye and watched her aunt's thin lips moving. She could have sworn her prayers went on longer each time.

'And grant forgiveness to thy servant Eve, that she may become worthy of thy grace, though she may be steeped in sin...'

Eve shut out her aunt's words, and thought instead about the First Aid class, and how the instructor had praised her work. Eve glowed with quiet pride, remembering her words. She so rarely received a word of praise, she nursed it like a precious jewel, keeping it tucked away and taking it out to enjoy every now and again.

Finally Aunt Freda ran out of steam, and ended her prayer with a heavy and meaningful 'Amen'. Eve waited for a moment, then picked up her knife and fork again. But her aunt still wasn't ready to leave her in peace. She sat at the table, her arms folded, and reeled off a list of jobs that needed to be done.

'We've had a lot of mending come in today,' she said. 'When you've finished your tea you'd best get down to the workshop and make a start.'

Eve looked up in dismay. Usually she wouldn't have dreamed of contradicting her aunt, but she was weary and the thought of going down to the dark cellar filled her with horror. 'Can't they wait until tomorrow morning, Aunt?' she pleaded.

Aunt Freda's eyes hardened. 'Are you giving the orders around here now?' she snapped.

'No, but I'm quite tired—'

'Well, I can't help that, can I? I've told the customers they can pick them up in the morning, and I'm as good as my word. If we don't give them a good service they'll end up going elsewhere, and then where will we be?' She glared at Eve. 'And there's no need to look at me like that It's not my fault if you choose to go gallivanting off to First Aid classes when you're needed here, is it?'

Eve thought about explaining again that it wasn't her choice, she had been ordered to do war work. But what was the point? Aunt Freda never listened.

'No, Aunt,' she agreed heavily. She tuned out her aunt's critical voice and stared up at the heavy wooden cross over the mantelpiece, the only adornment in the bare, cheerless room.

'You've got to earn your keep,' Aunt Freda continued. 'We're not made of money, and since I've been good enough to take you in, the least you can do is try to make yourself useful!'

'Yes, Aunt.'

After tea, Eve washed up her plate. She started when she accidentally caught sight of herself in the speckled scrap of mirror over the sink. She looked such a scare, no wonder that girl Jennifer had given her such a scathing look.

No one in their right mind could ever have called her pretty, or even attractive. Her skin was so pale and washed out, it was almost the colour of the greying dishcloth she held in her hands. Her thick eyebrows sat low and straight over a pair of sad, tired eyes. She was only nineteen, but she looked like a careworn woman of thirty.

She wondered what she would look like if she wore make-up like Jennifer, and Cissy. But then they were pretty to start with. She doubted if anything could ever improve her unremarkable looks.

'You'll crack that mirror if you stare at yourself much longer.' Eve caught sight of her aunt's reflection over her shoulder and ducked her head guiltily.

'Sorry, Aunt.'

'Your mother was very fond of looking in the mirror, too. Always admiring herself, she was. And look what happened to her.'

Eve let her gaze drop to the worn wooden draining board. She knew very little about her mother, apart from what her aunt had told her. All she knew was that Lizzie Marshall had fallen pregnant outside wedlock, that she'd given birth to Eve in secret and then died of childbed fever – 'or shame, more like', as her aunt always said. Aunt Freda and Uncle Roland had then taken Eve in and brought her up as their own child, since they had none of their own.

Aunt Freda never missed a chance to remind Eve where she'd come from, or that her mother was a sinful whore who'd brought scandal down on her respectable family.

'She was no sister of mine,' she always said. But Eve secretly preferred to think of her mother as a young woman who had been led astray and made a mistake, and not the reckless wanton her aunt always painted her as.

But whatever the truth, Eve knew she owed her aunt everything. If it hadn't been for Aunt Freda taking her in, she would have ended up in the workhouse. Instead her aunt had given her a home and respectability.

Eve sometimes wondered if she might have led an easier life in the orphanage, but she would never have dared say such a thing.

After she'd finished washing up, she went down to the workshop. A rush of icy air came up to greet her as she opened the heavy door and stepped into the gaping dark mouth of the cellar. There was no light switch at the top, so she had to inch her way down the narrow wooden staircase all the way to the bottom in pitch blackness, her left hand pressed against the rough brickwork to steady herself. The wood creaked under her feet at every step, deafening in the silence. Eve forced her feet forward, knowing that if she stopped for a moment her nerve would fail her.

Once, her aunt had recounted the grim story of how her great-grandfather's apprentice had killed himself down here. Spurned by his sweetheart, he had hung himself from the low beams.

'My grandfather found him swinging the next morning,' Aunt Freda told Eve. The story haunted her, and when she was very young and her aunt used to lock her in the cellar as punishment, Eve would cower in the corner, terrified that his unhappy corpse would find her in the darkness. Even now she still feared the dark, and working late in the workshop she would jump at every creak and groan. The smell of damp was like the stench of death to her.

After what seemed like a lifetime, her feet found the last step and she fumbled for the light switch and clicked it on. The weak light from the single bulb cast eerie shadows over the deep recesses of the cellar, illuminating the grey damp patches blooming on the whitewashed brickwork.

Eve hurried across to her worktable and lit the lamps, comforted by the extra glow they offered. But her heart sank when she saw all the clothes piled up beside the table, ready for mending. Most of it looked like hand sewing, which was particularly tiring to do by the weak lamplight. There was enough to keep her busy until after midnight.

Wearily, Eve sat down at the sewing machine and got out her needles, thread and scissors, ready to begin. She had learned the tailoring trade from her aunt's husband, Uncle Roland. It was really Aunt Freda's shop, passed down from her father, but she had married his apprentice and together they had run the business until Uncle Roland died six years earlier.

Poor Uncle Roland. Why such a kind, gentle man had ever married someone like Aunt Freda, Eve didn't know. Perhaps the rumours were true and he had been after her money and her shop? But if that was the case, his plans had gone badly wrong. Uncle Roland had been under Aunt Freda's thumb as much as Eve was. Her aunt had bullied him mercilessly, treating him more as a glorified employee than as her husband.

But he'd taken it all meekly, just as Eve did. They both knew that it was no use fighting Freda. She had God and a vicious tongue on her side.

At any rate, Uncle Roland had passed his skills on to Eve, teaching her how to cut patterns, how to tailor a garment to the body, how to mend, stitch, pleat, dart and transform an old, worn-out piece of clothing into something new and special. She was a natural, so he said.

'It must run in the family,' he'd told her once, as they sat side by side at the bench. The cellar didn't seem such a frightening place when Uncle Roland was there.

'Was my mother a good seamstress too?' Eve had asked him once. But Uncle Roland had shook his head, his eyes darting towards the door, as if he feared Aunt Freda might appear.

'Best not talk about her in front of your aunt,' he'd whispered. 'You know it upsets her.'

After he'd died, Aunt Freda had taken Eve out of school and set her to work in his place. Eve hoped that she had done her uncle proud with her skills. Not that anyone would know it to look at her. While Aunt Freda was happy for her to sew for other people, she only allowed Eve to wear the most shapeless and dowdy of garments herself.

'You're not a beauty and you never will be,' she'd told her firmly. 'Besides, I don't want you dressing like those hussies you see walking down the Mile End Road, showing everything the Good Lord gave them.'

Like Cissy and Jennifer. Aunt Freda would have a fit if she saw them, with their rouged cheeks, glistening pink lips and high heels. They were exactly the kind of girl her aunt despised.

But Eve was entranced by them. Everything about them fascinated her – their carefully curled hair, their clothes, their confidence. Jennifer and Cissy were as glamorous as a pair of movie stars. Or at least, what Eve could imagine movie stars looking like, if she'd ever seen one. But her aunt considered the cinema to be a den of sin, and Eve had never been allowed to go.

Had her mother been that pretty and carefree? Eve wondered. She had always longed to ask her aunt, but knew she would never dare. Aunt Freda had destroyed every photograph of Lizzie Marshall after she'd died.

'I tossed them all on a bonfire in the back garden,' she'd declared. 'I don't want any memories of that woman in my house. Not after what she did.'

Eve could understand it, but she dearly wished she could have seen her mother's face or had a keepsake of her, even if it was only a faded snapshot.

As it was, the only memory she had was given to her by Uncle Roland. He had described Lizzie once as they worked at the big cutting table.

'Always laughing, she was. When she smiled, it lit up her face,' he'd whispered, all the while shooting nervous glances over his shoulder to make sure Aunt Freda wasn't listening. 'She had your grey eyes too, but her hair was very dark.'

'I suppose I must get my light brown hair from my father,' Eve mused.

'I daresay.' But before he'd had a chance to add any more, the cellar door had opened and they'd heard Aunt Freda's tread coming down the stairs.

From that day on, Uncle Roland had refused to be drawn into talking any more about her mother. But it was enough for Eve to build up a mental picture of her.

And in her mind, the smiling, dark-haired young woman looked exactly like Jennifer Caldwell.

Chapter Seven

Kathleen Fox and Veronica Hanley stood motionless side by side in the office, their gaze fixed on the wireless as they listened in silence to the broadcast from Westminster Abbey. The Archbishop of Canterbury's voice was grave as he intoned the prayers 'for our soldiers in peril'. It was strange to think that the very same prayer was being said in churches all around the country.

The broadcast came to a close and Kathleen raised her gaze to look at Miss Hanley. The Assistant Matron's square-jawed face was rigid.

'Those poor men,' she murmured.

'Indeed, Miss Hanley.' For once they were in agreement.

Up until that morning, they had received little news of what was happening to their troops in France. But then they had woken to find that the Germans had driven the British Expeditionary Force back to the coast of northern France. Thousands of soldiers were now cornered on the beach at Dunkirk, fighting for their lives as they desperately awaited evacuation.

'In peril' must be putting it mildly, Kathleen thought. She couldn't imagine what the government was doing about it, but the situation must be hopeless indeed if the King himself was on his knees, praying for their salvation.

'We should prepare ourselves to receive casualties,' she said.

'But surely they will go to military hospitals, Matron?'

Kathleen looked at her assistant's bemused face. Miss Hanley clearly hadn't grasped the scale of the problem at all. 'I daresay the military hospitals will take all they can,' she agreed. 'But we are talking about thousands of injured men, Miss Hanley. Far beyond the capacity of the military establishments.'

'Surely not, Matron?' Miss Hanley said briskly. 'The British forces will prevail. They must!'

Kathleen wondered if Veronica Hanley had been listening to the radio broadcast at all. She looked so utterly sure of herself as she stood there, bristling with self-righteousness. Had Miss Hanley been on that beach at Dunkirk, Kathleen felt sure she would never have taken shelter or feared for her life. She would have been leading a last, desperate charge against the Germans.

'Nevertheless, I think we should prepare ourselves,' Kathleen said quietly.

Before Miss Hanley could reply, there was a knock on the door and James Cooper strode in. Previously a consultant at the hospital, he had taken over as the Nightingale's Senior Surgical Officer when the war started.

'Have you heard the news?' he asked.

Kathleen nodded. 'We were just discussing it.'

'I've just spoken to the Area Medical Officer on the telephone, and he's asked that we ready ourselves to receive casualties within the next twenty-four hours.'

Kathleen sent Miss Hanley a sideways glance. 'How many casualties should we expect?'

'Around forty. Possibly more. We can take them, can't we?' Mr Cooper asked.

Kathleen took a deep breath. 'Of course,' she said. 'We have Holmes and Peel wards standing empty for just such an emergency. All we'll need to do is reallocate nurses–'

Miss Hanley cleared her throat loudly. 'Excuse me, Matron, but have you forgotten Holmes and Peel are both currently being decorated?' she reminded her.

Kathleen's heart sank. Why hadn't she remembered that? Mr Brewer and his men had moved in on Friday, clattering up the stairs with ladders and paintbrushes.

'Surely they're not both out of commission at the same time?' James Cooper looked irritated.

'I'm afraid so, Doctor,' Miss Hanley said.

'But whose idea was that?'

Kathleen caught her assistant's smug look. 'It

72

was my decision,' she admitted.

'Matron thought it would save time,' Miss Hanley added.

James Cooper sighed. 'That's a nuisance, I must say. But we'll just have to do the best with what we have, I suppose. What do you suggest?'

Kathleen rallied. 'Well, if we put some extra beds in Everett, we could clear Blake...'

'Surely it would be better the other way around, Matron?' Miss Hanley interrupted again. 'Blake has a much larger balcony than Everett. That could accommodate at least half a dozen beds, if it had to?'

'Good idea.' Mr Cooper nodded. 'And what about Parry? There aren't many children there at the moment, from what I recall.'

'That's true, Mr Cooper,' Miss Hanley said. 'We could send most of them home and make use of the beds there. And that would mean we didn't need extra staff...'

Kathleen listened to them, feeling all the while like a silly schoolgirl who wasn't allowed to join in with the adults' conversation. If only she had thought for a moment about the foolishness of putting two wards out of action at the same time, instead of allowing her annoyance with Miss Hanley to cloud her judgement. But she'd been so determined to prove a point to her Assistant Matron, she had blundered ahead without thinking. Now she was being allowed to play no part in sorting out the mess she had created.

But it was more than just her pride that was hurt. Her error had caused a crisis at the hospital, and possibly put the lives of injured soldiers

73

in danger.

She had to redeem herself somehow.

'Can't we finish decorating at least one of those wards by tomorrow?' She hadn't realised she'd said the words out loud until she caught the astonished looks on Miss Hanley's and Mr Cooper's faces.

Miss Hanley gave her a patronising look. 'I hardly think so, Matron,' she said. 'May I remind you, the decorators only started work on Friday? They've barely begun.'

'Then it wouldn't be too difficult for them to stop, would it? I'm sure we can put up with an unpainted ward for a little longer.'

'It really isn't that simple, Matron,' Miss Hanley said. 'The paintwork has already been stripped, and there is undercoat on the walls. If you had been up there to see it, you would realise–'

'Then we'll get the decorators to come back and finish it today!' Kathleen snapped.

'On a Sunday, Matron? I hardly think that's possible.'

'We won't know until we try, will we?' Kathleen could feel herself growing flustered. Miss Hanley was right, of course. She wished she had never come up with such a desperate suggestion. Now she had made herself look even more foolish in front of Mr Cooper. She could feel him staring at her. He probably thought she'd lost her senses.

'Excuse me,' he said patiently. 'This is all very interesting, but what shall I tell the Area Medical Officer?'

Kathleen turned to him. 'You can tell him to send his casualties,' she said.

James Cooper's brows rose. 'All of them?'

'All of them,' Kathleen said firmly, ignoring Miss Hanley. 'We will have a ward ready for them by tomorrow morning.'

Even if I have to stay up all night and paint it myself, she thought.

'Well, that was a waste of time.'

Aunt Freda pulled on her gloves, her face pinched with disapproval. Eve's heart sank. When her aunt disliked the church service, it could put her in a bad mood for the rest of the day.

'All those prayers for the soldiers in peril,' Aunt Freda continued. 'One comes to church to be enlightened and instructed, not to pray for souls who aren't worth saving anyway.'

Eve shot a wary glance towards a group of women who stood at the back of the church, weeping and comforting each other. She hoped they hadn't heard her aunt's comment. 'A lot of the people here have sons and husbands fighting in France,' she said.

'Yes, and most of them had never set foot inside a church until this war broke out,' Aunt Freda scoffed. 'I've seen those women out in the street. I've seen the way they act, laughing and using profane language and taking the Lord's name in vain. But as soon as it suits them, they're in here on their knees, praying to Him to help them. Much good it will do them,' she said with a grim smile. 'God will judge them, you see if He doesn't. He will punish the sinners.'

She raised her voice and Eve cringed, seeing the women look their way. She wished her aunt would shut up, but nothing would stop Freda Ainsley when she was in one of her moods. She glared back at the women, as if daring them to approach her.

'Really, Mrs Ainsley, that's hardly Christian.'

Reverend Stanton stood behind them, a young man at his side. Eve had never seen him before, but she could tell at once the two men were related. They were both tall and sandy-haired, with lively green eyes and wide, friendly smiles.

Aunt Freda turned on him. 'Reverend,' she said, tight-lipped, 'I was just saying, I felt this morning's service left a lot to be desired.'

Eve saw a look of astonishment appear on the younger man's face. But Reverend Stanton's smile only broadened.

'As usual, I welcome your comments,' he said smoothly. 'I'm sure they will be most – incisive.' Then, before Aunt Freda could enlighten him further, he added, 'Have you met my son Oliver? He's just returned from France.'

Aunt Freda's brows rose. 'You were fighting?'

The young man shook his head. 'I was at art school in Paris.'

'Unfortunately his studies have been curtailed by recent events, so he'll be staying with us for a while.' Reverend Stanton smiled at Eve. 'You two are a similar age. Perhaps you could befriend him, since he doesn't know anyone in the area?'

Eve glanced at Oliver Stanton. He looked as horrified by the idea as she was.

Thankfully, her aunt stepped in. 'That won't be possible,' she said tautly. 'Eve has far too much work to do helping me in the shop. Besides, I

76

don't hold with girls consorting with young men,' she added. 'It isn't decent.'

'I'm sure I wasn't suggesting anything improper, Mrs Ainsley,' Reverend Stanton said, as Eve blushed.

'All the same, I don't hold with it,' Aunt Freda insisted. 'Especially not for my niece. She has sin in her blood,' she confided.

Eve stared at the worn stone flags beneath her feet. She didn't dare look at Oliver Stanton, she could only imagine what he was thinking.

'Anyway, it's time we were going,' Aunt Freda said. She gripped Eve's shoulder, propelling her towards the church door. 'Good day to you, Reverend. And you, Mr Stanton.'

'It was nice to meet you,' Oliver called after them as they hurried away.

Reverend Stanton's wife and daughter were waiting at the door. Muriel Stanton was a few years older than Eve, tall and fair-haired like her father, with the same green eyes and bright smile.

'Ah, Mrs Ainsley,' Mrs Stanton greeted Aunt Freda. 'I'm so glad I ran into you both. I've been meaning to thank you for the wonderful work you did, altering Muriel's dress for her.'

'I thought it was ruined when I ripped the skirt so badly,' Muriel put in. 'But honestly, when Mother showed me how you'd mended it, I couldn't believe it. I could hardly see it had been damaged at all.'

Aunt Freda allowed herself a small smile. 'You're quite welcome, I'm sure.'

Mrs Stanton turned to Eve. 'You really are a gifted seamstress, Eve. I wonder if you would accept a small token of our appreciation...'

She reached into her handbag for her purse, but Aunt Freda put out her hand to stop her.

'Don't,' she said. 'Eve doesn't need it, thank you.'

'But I just wanted to–'

'She was just doing her job, that's all. No more and no less.'

'But–'

'Come along, Eve.' Once again, she felt her aunt's grip on her shoulder. Her fingers seemed to be digging even harder into her flesh this time.

As they walked away, Aunt Freda muttered, 'And you needn't get above yourself either. She was only being kind.'

'Yes, Aunt.'

'You're nothing special. You just remember that,' Aunt Freda warned her.

'I – I know that, Aunt.'

As they left the church, Eve risked a glance back over her shoulder. Muriel Stanton was still standing at the church doors, chatting to another parishioner. Her mother stood at her side. The look of smiling pride on Mrs Stanton's face as she gazed at her daughter gave Eve a painful pang of envy.

How she wished her aunt could love her like that. She longed for nothing more than to make Aunt Freda proud. And yet no matter how hard she tried, nothing she did was ever good enough.

How unlovable must she be, Eve wondered, if her own flesh and blood could despise her so much?

Chapter Eight

It was almost midnight on Sunday evening when James Cooper emerged from the basement operating theatre, exhausted and in low spirits. It always affected him badly when he lost a patient. After nearly twenty years as a surgeon, he knew he should have been used to it, but each time he felt the same sadness and frustration when he had to admit defeat.

There was no shame in giving up in this case. The emergency appendix operation had been long and difficult, and no one but he had truly expected the patient to live. The appendix had perforated, and the entire peritoneal cavity was a toxic mess. But still James had battled on long after he sensed Dr Jameson and the nurses losing heart.

Everyone thought it was his professional pride that refused to allow him to give up. But it was more than that. James dreaded facing his patients' families. He hated to see the hope die on their faces when he had to explain that, in spite of his best efforts, he had failed to save their loved one's life. They had put all their trust in him, and he'd let them down.

It was particularly hard in this case, as the patient was a young father. James had sat rigid behind his desk, watching the man's widow weeping and not knowing what to say or do to comfort her. All he could do was repeat the facts over and over again.

'It was too late ... the appendix had already perforated ... too much damage...'

He didn't think she'd taken in anything he'd said, and he didn't blame her. All the poor woman knew was that she'd lost the man she loved, and her children had lost their father. And there was nothing he could say to take away the pain.

He wondered if Simone would cry for him the way that woman had wept for her husband. He doubted it. It would probably be a blessed release for both of them.

He thought about going home, but couldn't face it. Once upon a time Simone might have been waiting up for him, but after more than twenty years of marriage, he knew her bedroom door would be firmly closed. Unless she was in one of her argumentative moods, in which case he would face endless hours of questions and accusations about where he'd been and who he'd been with. Then there would be tears and bitter recriminations, and he would end up apologising just to make it all stop.

No, it wasn't worth going home. As he wearily climbed the stairs, James wondered how his life had gone so badly wrong that he preferred a hard couch in his office to his own marital bed.

James Cooper had been just twenty years old and a young officer when he'd first met Simone in Amiens. She was a young girl then, helping her father run the village inn where many of the men went to escape during their rare periods of rest.

After the horrors James had witnessed on the battlefield, she had proved a welcome escape, a breath of sweet, fresh air to chase away the stench of death and despair. Young and romantic as he was, James had fancied himself in love. He had married Simone as soon as the war was over, and brought her home with him to England.

But it wasn't long before he realised that the urgent passion fuelled by the intensity of war couldn't be sustained in the quiet of peacetime. They were like strangers, unable to find any common ground between them. And it didn't help that Simone was desperately unhappy in her new home. Like a beautiful, exotic hothouse flower, she simply couldn't survive in the chilly, grey climate of England. She hated the people, the weather, the language. But most of all she hated James for bringing her there. He did his best to make their marriage work, but Simone's indifference, combined with her violent, jealous moods, eventually proved too much for him. Now they were like barely civil strangers, existing side by side in an atmosphere of mutual resentment.

He had reached the landing that led to his office when he heard a curious sound from above him. At first he thought it might be exhaustion playing tricks on him. But as he paused on the stairs to listen, he realised it wasn't his imagination. Drifting down the stairs were the sounds of laughter – and music.

Curious, he followed them to the top floor, where the empty wards were situated. From along the passageway came the strong smell of fresh paint. As James approached, he could hear the hubbub of voices. It sounded as if someone was having a party in Holmes ward.

He opened the double doors, and an extraordinary sight met his eyes. The cavernous ward, stripped of beds, furniture and curtains at the tall windows, was filled with people. James recognised nurses, medical students, porters, even a couple of ward maids, all merrily wielding paint brushes side by side. The decorators were there, too, in their brown overalls, looking askance at the efforts of those around them. Over in the corner, a gramophone was playing.

And in the middle of it all was Kathleen Fox. James picked her out straight away, halfway up a ladder, painting a window frame. He barely recognised her in paint-spattered overalls, her chestnut hair wrapped up in a colourful scarf.

He stood in the doorway, watching her for a moment as she chatted happily to the young medical student beside her. But then she spotted him and came down the ladder to greet him.

'Mr Cooper!' She had a smudge of white paint across her nose. 'This is a surprise. What are you doing here?'

'I've just come out of Theatre.' He gazed around him. 'You seem to have mobilised quite an army!' he commented.

'Oh, I can't take the credit for it,' she dismissed. 'I simply explained the situation and everyone volunteered to help the decorators get finished in time for tomorrow. Although between you and me, I'm not sure they're entirely appreciative of our efforts!' she confided with a smile.

'I'm sure that's not true.'

'I wouldn't be too certain. Poor Mr Brewer the foreman is doing his best to keep control of everyone, but I feel the situation is getting away from him!'

She grinned. James didn't think he had ever seen her looking so full of life. Out of her severe black uniform, she looked far younger than her forty-odd years, laughter sparkling in her grey eyes.

'It's looking splendid anyway,' he said.

'Do you think so?' Kathleen looked around her. 'We won't be able to get all the furniture back in place and the curtains up until the paint's dry tomorrow morning, but hopefully it should all be ready by the time the casualties start to arrive.'

'You've done very well.'

She blushed. 'I felt I should correct my mistake,' she admitted quietly.

'Not to mention prove Miss Hanley wrong?'

Kathleen sent him a quick look, then a slow smile spread across her face. 'I'm afraid you may be right,' she admitted shamefaced. 'Is that very terrible of me?'

'Not terrible at all, if it means the ward is ready for when the men arrive. But you do realise if you manage to pull this off, Miss Hanley will probably claim it was all her idea?'

'You may be right about that, too.' Kathleen looked rueful. James had to fight the urge to reach out and rub the smudge of paint from her nose. 'But we still have quite a lot to do, so I'm afraid Miss Hanley may yet have the last laugh.'

'Could you use an extra pair of hands?'

She frowned. 'Surely you'll want to go home, if

you've been in Theatre all this time?'

He thought about Simone, waiting for him, spoiling for another fight. Or his house, dark and unwelcoming. 'I'd like to do my bit.' He shrugged off his jacket and rolled up his shirtsleeves. 'So where do you want me to start?'

'Well, you'll need to change first ... if you go and see Mr Hopkins, he'll kit you out in something suitable. Then...' Kathleen looked around the ward, 'if you have a head for heights, you could make a start on the ceiling?'

As they worked on into the early hours, James was surprised to find he was enjoying himself. The medical students and nurses seemed to have an endless supply of energy, even breaking off from their painting to perform a spirited rendition of 'The Lambeth Walk'.

James caught Kathleen Fox's eye across the ward. She was still perched on her ladder, watching the couples and clapping along to the gramophone music. She had exactly the right idea, he thought. She understood that everyone would work a lot harder if they were allowed to have fun at the same time.

He was just glad Miss Hanley wasn't there to see it. She would have had a fit, he decided.

'Have you ever seen anything like it?' Mr Brewer, the decorators' foreman, said from below his ladder. 'In all my born days, I don't think I've ever worked on a job quite like this one. Don't think I've ever worked on a Sunday either, come to think of it.'

'It's very kind of you to give up your day off to help us,' James said.

84

'Didn't have much choice.' Herbert Brewer nodded towards Kathleen. 'Turned up on my doorstep she did, just after my missus and I had finished our dinner. She explained about the lads coming back from France, and how she needed the ward to be ready for them, and of course I couldn't refuse. Neither could any of my lads. We've all got sons and brothers in France, we'd want them to be looked after. Wouldn't like to think they didn't have a decent place to come home to.' He grinned up at James, showing wide-spaced gaps between his yellowing teeth. 'Wouldn't like to try saying no to Miss Fox neither. She's got a way about her, your Matron,' he said.

James looked at Kathleen again, still perched on her ladder, clapping in time to the music. 'Yes,' he agreed. 'She certainly has.'

Chapter Nine

Helen was already waiting in the Casualty Hall for Dora when she reported for duty first thing on Monday morning. Matron was with her.

'Oh, there you are, Riley,' Miss Fox greeted her. 'I just wanted to let you know you'll be moving today.'

'Moving, Matron?'

'We're opening up Holmes ward for the Dunkirk casualties, and I want you to help out for the next few weeks. I know you've settled here in Casualty,

85

but we have urgent need of you elsewhere, I'm afraid.'

'Yes, Matron.' Dora's reply was automatic but her heart was beating rapidly against her chest, as if it could fight its way out of her ribcage.

'Get changed and report to Holmes as soon as possible, would you? I know Sister Holmes would be very grateful for some help. The casualties are expected within the next hour, and there is a great deal to do before then.'

'Yes, Matron.' Dora watched her walk away, glad she had managed to resist the urge to argue. It wouldn't have done any good, since Matron's decision was always final.

'I'm sorry,' Helen said, when Miss Fox had gone. 'I wanted to keep you, but Matron insisted.'

'Why me?' Dora asked, trying to sound calm. 'Why couldn't she send Kowalski instead?'

'From what Matron told me, they need an experienced nurse up there. They only have Sister Holmes and one of the new VADs to look after the whole ward.'

Yes, but why me? Dora repeated silently. It was her worst nightmare come true. She had started work at the Nightingale hoping it might help take her mind off what was happening to Nick across the Channel. And now she had been put on a ward looking after servicemen just like him. They would be badly wounded, too, in just the way she feared Nick might be one day. How she would ever cope she had no idea.

'You heard what she said. It'll only be for a couple of weeks.' Helen's voice broke into her thoughts. 'If you really can't manage then I'm

sure Matron will send you back, under the circumstances—'

Dora stared at her friend's sympathetic expression, appalled she had given herself away. She'd
had no idea her fears were written so clearly
across her face for all to see. The last thing Dora
wanted to do was let on how afraid she really
was.

She quickly readjusted her features. 'Oh, I'll be
all right,' she said as breezily as she could. 'I just
thought I might be of more use here, that's all.'

'Are you sure? I thought you might be worried
about Nick.'

'Why should I be? I told you, Nick can take care
of himself.' She gritted her teeth into what she
hoped was a convincing smile. Helen sent her a
sideways look but said nothing. Once again, Dora
was grateful to her friend for her wisdom. She
wasn't sure she could have kept up the pretence if
Helen had questioned her further.

Up on Holmes ward, she found a state of orderly
chaos. The porters were still wheeling empty beds
and lockers on to the ward and setting them up in
two tidy rows either side of the vast room. Two
VADs were making the beds as quickly as they
arrived, while another was cleaning the floor, and
yet another sat at the table in the middle of the
ward, stitching hooks into blackout curtains. The
tall windows had been thrown open, but the whole
ward still smelled strongly of fresh paint.

In the centre of it all stood Miss Pallister, Sister
of Holmes ward. She was another familiar face
from Dora's training days. Sister Holmes was in
her late thirties and movie-star glamorous, with

her rounded figure, pillowy lips and wavy blonde hair. She was also living proof that appearances could be very deceiving indeed. Those soft curves hid a spiky temper and a heart of pure granite.

She barely bothered to greet Dora, ordering her instead to start making up hot water bottles.

'I sent the new VAD to do it half an hour ago, but the muddle-headed girl doesn't have the first idea what she's supposed to be doing,' she sighed, rolling her eyes heavenwards. 'And you,' she called across the ward to the girl who was making the bed. 'What did I tell you about making sure all the wheels point the same way?'

Dora found the new ward VAD in the sluice, filling hot water bottles. Sister Holmes was right, she did seem to be making rather a meal of it, carefully expelling the air from each bottle by pressing it against the flat bib of her apron, then fastening the stopper and checking it over and over again for leaks. At the rate she was going, the bottles would be cold long before she got them into the beds.

She greeted Dora with wide-eyed enthusiasm. 'Oh, hello, you must be Nurse Riley?' she lisped. With her blonde plaits and buck teeth, she looked and sounded as if she'd just skipped off the lacrosse pitch of a posh girls' boarding school. 'I'm Daisy Bushell.'

'Pleased to meet you.' Dora nodded towards the hot water bottle in the girl's hands. 'How are you getting on with those?'

'Nearly done, I think. It's all terribly exciting, isn't it?' Daisy whispered. 'I can't wait for the patients to arrive.'

I can, Dora thought grimly.

'My fiancé is in the RAF,' Daisy continued. 'I applied for a military hospital, so I was awfully disappointed when I was sent here instead. But now it looks as if we're going to be nursing real war casualties after all.'

Dora stared at her blankly. 'Real war casualties?'

'You know – wounded soldiers and so on. Isn't it thrilling?'

'Thrilling isn't a word I'd use,' Dora muttered. 'Besides, sick and injured people are all the same, whether they're in uniform or not.'

'Well, you say that. But there is a difference, isn't there?' Daisy smiled knowingly. 'I mean, you really feel as if you're doing your bit when you're nursing soldiers, don't you?'

She was young, Dora told herself. Young and naïve, and she didn't know what she was saying. But with Dora trying to hold on to what was left of her nerves, the last thing she needed was a chatterbox like Daisy Bushell trampling all over them with her nonsense.

'If you really want to do your bit, you'll get those bottles into the beds before they turn stone cold,' she snapped.

They had finished airing all the beds as the telephone rang on Sister's desk, warning of the first casualties' arrival. Dora busied herself, straightening her cap and adjusting her apron to steady her nerves, while all the time Daisy chattered on behind her. It was all Dora could do not to turn round and shake the girl until her teeth rattled.

89

And then they arrived, a filthy, bleeding mass of exhausted humanity.

As the porters wheeled them in, Dora, Sister Holmes and the doctors got to work immediately, peeling off dirty dressings and examining wounds. Sister Holmes had already instructed Dora that she was to assess the men herself, treating those she could and sending the worst cases down to Theatre, or referring them to one of the doctors.

With Daisy Bushell still behind her, craning over her shoulder to get a good look, Dora approached her first case, a young man whose leg had been blown off. As Dora peeled the filthy dressing from the bloody stump of his leg, she could already see the wound seemed to be moving. Sure enough, she lifted the dressing to reveal a seething mass of maggots.

'Oh, my gosh!' she heard Daisy whisper from behind her hand. 'How revolting...'

'It's not as bad as it looks,' Dora said. 'The maggots will eat away at the dead tissue, so it's less likely to get infected.' But it was too late. Dora heard the thump behind her as Daisy Bushell slid gracefully to the ground.

At least it shut her up for a minute.

From that moment on, they didn't stop all day. They worked steadily, cleaning, stitching and dressing wounds, setting up infusions, and giving morphine injections. As she was plunging the needle into another patient's arm, it suddenly occurred to Dora that her hands were no longer shaking. The nerves that had plagued her on her first day in Casualty had been chased away by the adrenaline surging around her body.

The men were in a shocking state when they arrived – dirty, exhausted and starving. Some had been lying on stretchers on the beaches for twenty-four hours. They had been sent straight from the Casualty Clearing Station on the south coast, and wore scrawled labels from the army medics, stating their injuries. In most cases no label was needed. The filthy makeshift dressings wrapped around shattered limbs or bloodied stumps were all anyone needed to see.

The whole time she was working, Dora's heart was in her mouth, terrified that the next body she encountered would be Nick's.

She tried to push it out of her mind, determined to stay focused. The men didn't need her sympathy. They needed her help, and she gave it unstintingly, until her eyes ached and her hands were sore and her legs could barely hold her up any longer.

Unfortunately, Daisy didn't have the same strong stomach or capacity for hard work. Every time she caught a glimpse of blood she would keel over. Dora got so tired of stopping whatever she was doing to haul the girl off the floor, that in the end she dumped her in the sluice with a bottle of sal volatile.

'I don't know why you want to work in a hospital if you can't stand the sight of blood!' she snapped.

'I didn't know, did I?' Daisy wailed. 'I had no idea how awful it would be. I couldn't imagine–'

'What did you expect? They've been in a war, they ain't going to come back with grazed knees, are they?' Dora stared at her. 'And to think you wanted to work in a military hospital! You couldn't nurse a cold!'

'I'm sorry!' Daisy burst into noisy tears. 'It's just every time I see one of those poor men, I think of my fiancé Richard. What if he's been injured? What if he's dead?'

'You can't think like that,' Dora said.

'I can't help it!'

Dora watched her sobbing, huddled on the floor of the sluice. In spite of her annoyance, she couldn't help but feel sorry for the girl.

'Wait there,' she said. She hurried off to fetch a tot of brandy from the locked cupboard in the kitchen, and handed it to the VAD. 'Here,' she said. 'Now pull yourself together, and don't let Sister catch you crying or you really will be in trouble.'

'Thank you.' Daisy sniffed back her tears and lifted the glass shakily to her lips, grimacing at the taste. 'Sorry for being so wet, Nurse Riley. I only wish I could be as strong as you, I really do.'

Dora didn't reply. Deep down, she wished she could be as wet as Daisy Bushell. Perhaps letting go and having a good cry might stop the terrible ache in her chest.

Chapter Ten

When Eve arrived for the final First Aid lecture, the first thing she noticed was Jennifer, sitting on her own in the back row. There was no sign of Cissy.

Eve scuttled past her to her usual place in the far corner of the room as the instructor began her lecture on bathing.

'If a patient is too ill to bathe themselves, then you will have to do it for them,' she said. 'Washing a patient is the most important of your duties. Do it skilfully and you will make the patient feel better and gain their confidence. Do it clumsily and you will badly affect their comfort and health.'

Eve glanced across at Jennifer. She was inspecting her nails, hardly listening as usual. She was dressed up to the nines in a cornflower blue dress, her dark hair carefully curled.

'I would like you to experience for yourselves what it feels like to be washed, as it may give you a better understanding of what you're doing,' the instructor continued. 'So this evening you will be practising giving each other a blanket bath, rather than the dummy. We will assume for the purpose of the exercise that it is a medical patient without any obvious injury. Get into your pairs, please.'

Eve looked around for her usual partner, then remembered that Miss Witchell had told her she had to visit her elderly mother in Basingstoke, and wouldn't be coming to the class. Her gaze travelled the room, looking for another partner – and found Jennifer. For a moment their eyes locked, and Eve saw her own dismay reflected in Jennifer's face.

'You two,' the instructor said. 'Pair up quickly, please.'

Eve felt Jennifer's dark mood as they set the trolley together. She clattered the nail scissors, hairbrush and comb, and splashed water into the hand basin so carelessly Eve had to rescue the flannel, sponge and soap before she soaked them.

It's not my fault, Eve wanted to shout. I'm not enjoying this any more than you are. But she bit her tongue as they set up the screens and pulled the upper bedclothes off the bed.

'I'll go first,' Jennifer announced abruptly, slipping off her dainty sandals and hopping on to the bed before Eve could argue.

Not that she would. She was relieved not to have to submit to Jennifer's rough ministrations. She could only imagine how she would wield the flannel, the mood she seemed to be in.

'Where's your friend this evening?' Eve asked, as she carefully rolled the mackintosh sheet and blanket underneath her.

'She's not feeling well,' Jennifer replied, tight-lipped.

'What's wrong with her?'

'She's making herself ill, that's what!' Jennifer looked cross. 'She reckons she's too upset to come out. She's spent all week shut away indoors, listening to the news on the wireless.'

Eve was thoughtful as she covered Jennifer with

94

a warmed blanket and went through the pretence of removing her clothes in preparation for washing her.

'Is her boyfriend in France, then?' she asked.

'He's in the Royal Navy.'

'Oh, dear, no wonder she's so worried.' Even Aunt Freda had been glued to the wireless for the past few days, waiting for news. 'Those sailors are so brave, aren't they, going in under fire like that? And with so many ships being sunk—'

'Don't,' Jennifer cut her off coldly. 'I hear enough about it from Cissy. I'd rather not talk about it any more, if it's all the same to you?'

'Sorry.' Eve fell silent, concentrating on her task. She was surprised by the way Jennifer had spoken about Cissy and her boyfriend, though. She and Cissy were such good friends, surely Jennifer should have been more sympathetic.

Perhaps that was just the way friends were with each other, she thought, as she finished the job and covered Jennifer with a dry blanket. She had never had a close friend of her own, so she didn't know.

Then it was Jennifer's turn to perform the blanket bath. She made no effort to hide her disdain for the task as she roughly set about Eve's face and limbs with the sponge.

'Just think, soon we'll be doing this for a real patient,' Eve tried again to make conversation.

Jennifer gave a bored sigh. 'I can't wait.'

Before Eve could reply, the instructor came over.

'How are you getting on?' she asked.

'All right,' Jennifer replied.

'I think that's for your patient to judge, don't you?' The woman turned to Eve. 'What do you say about it, Miss Ainsley? If you were a patient, would you feel reassured by Miss Caudwell's treatment?'

Eve caught Jennifer's warning look over the instructor's shoulder. 'Yes, Miss,' she mumbled, her blush rising.

'I'm glad to hear it.' The instructor sent her a sceptical look, but didn't question her further. She turned back to Jennifer and said, 'It's a pity you can't look the part as well, Miss Caldwell. How many times do I have to remind you, the rules governing a VAD's appearance are the same as for any other trained nurse? There is to be no make-up or jewellery, hair must be covered at all times, and nails are to be unvarnished and cut short.'

'Yes, Miss.' Jennifer waited until she had gone, then rolled her eyes. 'How typical! The first time she could actually say something nice, and all she can do is look for faults. I really don't think that woman likes me.' She held up her hands, displaying her pink-painted nails. 'Well, I don't care what she says. I'm not cutting these off for anyone.'

The class dragged on and finally finished just after nine. Eve panicked as they stepped into the darkness of the blacked-out street. She watched Jennifer arranging her hat on her dark curls, wondering if she should say anything. Finally, fear drove her to blurt out, 'Do you mind if I walk home with you?'

'Why? Don't tell me you're frightened of the dark?' Jennifer mocked. Then she caught sight of

Eve's expression and her mouth twisted. 'You are, aren't you? For goodness' sake, what a baby!'

So would you be, if you'd been locked in a cellar as often as I have, Eve thought, but didn't reply.

'Why don't you get the bus, if you're that scared?' Jennifer said.

'The bus doesn't always run at this time, not since they changed the timetable. I waited ages for it last week, and it didn't come.' Eve hadn't got home until after ten o'clock, and her aunt had gone mad. She didn't want to risk that again.

Jennifer sighed. 'All right, I suppose you could walk with me,' she agreed. 'But only as far as Cable Street, mind. I'm not going out of my way.'

But they hadn't got as far as the corner before a sleek black car drew up beside them and a man's voice said, 'Going my way?'

Eve was so startled she almost broke into a run. But Jennifer gave a funny little smile of recognition and sauntered over to the car.

'Depends where you're going, doesn't it?' she purred.

'Wherever you like, sweetheart.'

'I suppose you could give me a lift home.' Jennifer shrugged. She opened the car door, then turned to Eve. 'Are you coming, or what?'

Eve stood rooted to the spot, dry-mouthed with panic. 'I – I can't,' she said.

Jennifer's mouth twisted. 'What d'you mean, you can't? Don't tell me you're frightened of cars as well as the dark?'

Eve stared at her. She simply couldn't imagine what her aunt would do if she saw her getting out of a stranger's car. And even if Aunt Freda didn't see her, one of her church cronies was bound to be spying. Word would get back to her aunt, and then Eve's life wouldn't be worth living.

'Suit yourself,' Jennifer said carelessly, climbing into the passenger seat. 'Don't let those monsters get you in the dark, will you?'

The man flashed a wolfish grin at her in the darkness of the car. He looked every bit as dangerous as he had that night when he'd rescued her at the dance hall.

'Alone at last,' he murmured. 'Are you sure you don't want to get out too, while you've got the chance?'

Jennifer's heart raced in her chest. 'No, thanks,' she said. 'I'll take my chances.'

His smile broadened. 'I like a girl who ain't afraid to take chances.'

Jennifer did her best to act cool. 'Haven't seen you around for a while,' she commented.

'Been looking for me, have you?'

'No!' she replied, a bit too quickly. No need to let him know she'd been back to the Palais every Friday.

He looked over his shoulder, pulling into the road. 'Where to?' he asked.

'Flint Terrace,' Jennifer replied. Then, remembering her father would be at home, she added, 'But you can drop me in Cable Street. I don't want to go all the way.'

'I bet you say that to all the boys!' the man said.

Jennifer laughed, but her palms were clammy. Perhaps Eve had the right idea, after all? It suddenly occurred to Jennifer that she might have been a bit rash, climbing into a car with a virtual stranger in the dead of night. She barely knew him, apart from that one incident when he'd rescued her from the soldier. She could only imagine what Cissy would say about it.

'So where have you been this evening?' he asked. 'Out with your boyfriend?'

'If you must know, I've been to nursing class.'

'You're going to be a nurse?'

'No, I'm going to be a bricklayer, what do you think?'

His mouth slanted. 'I bet you'll make a good nurse. I wouldn't mind waking up to find a pretty girl like you at my bedside!'

'Cheeky!' Jennifer smiled, forgetting her nerves. She loved flirting, and he was a good partner. Not every man understood the rules, but he did. 'If you're going to talk to me like that, you ought to tell me your name.'

'It's Johnny. Johnny Fayers.'

'Pleased to meet you, I'm sure. I'm–'

'Jen,' he said. 'I heard your mate speak to you the first night we met.'

Jennifer did her best to look aloof, but inside she was squirming with pleasure. He'd remembered her, that was a good sign. 'Jennifer Caldwell, actually.'

'Oh, I beg your pardon, Miss Caldwell.'

She looked across at his profile, craggy in the moonlight. His slicked-back dark hair emphasised his flattened nose and the silvery scar, running down his cheek. He was a few years older than her, she guessed. His presence seemed to fill the car, the smell of his cologne, the powerful, masculine scent of him. Cissy was right, he was definitely dangerous.

'How did you get that scar?' She said the first thing that came into her head.

'You're not backward in coming forward, are you?' He smiled. 'If you must know, I was in a fight.'

'Did you win?'

'I always win, darlin'.'

Jennifer studied him from under her lashes, noticing his height and his muscular build under his suit jacket. 'You look like you can take care of yourself,' she remarked.

'I reckon I can, at that.'

Johnny glanced across at her, and she caught the challenging glint in his eye. 'So don't your boyfriend mind you getting lifts off strange men?' he asked.

'I haven't got a boyfriend.'

His brows lifted. 'No? I'm surprised. Pretty girl like you, I thought you'd be courting.'

'For your information, I have plenty of offers. Just no one serious.'

'Prefer to play the field, eh? You sound like a girl after my own heart.'

'Something like that.' Jennifer craned her neck to peer into the darkness. 'You can drop me off here.'

'You sure you don't want me to take you to your door? It's not safe, you know, in the blackout. You get all kinds of ne'er-do-wells hanging about.'

'I know. I'm looking at one,' Jennifer said.

He put his hand to his heart and pretended to be wounded. 'You're a very cruel young lady, do you know that?'

'So I've been told.'

He pulled the car up and she started to get out. 'Well, thanks for the lift,' she said.

'It was my pleasure.'

She paused, waiting for him to ask her out. They all did, sooner or later.

'Well?' he prompted. 'Was there something else you wanted?'

'No,' Jen replied, disappointment making her voice sharp. 'No, not at all.'

'Well, then, I'll bid you goodnight.'

As she got out of the car, Jennifer caught a glimpse of Johnny's knowing smile and slammed the door angrily in his face.

She stood on the pavement in the darkness and watched him drive off, the blackness swallowing up the car at the end of the road. Was he teasing, or was he really not interested in her? It was hard to tell.

Jennifer frowned. She had always fancied herself as being very good at the flirting game. But she had the distinct feeling she'd met her match.

Chapter Eleven

Eve watched the car disappearing off into the darkness, and wondered if she'd done the right thing. Not that she'd had much choice, she told herself. Even if she'd tried to stop Jennifer going, she doubted if she would have taken any notice.

Eve was worried for her, but at the same time she couldn't help admiring her. Jennifer Caldwell was utterly fearless, striding out boldly in her heels, her head held high under the cheeky angle of her hat. How Eve wished she could be more like her, so sure of herself and filled with confidence, instead of being scared of her own shadow.

She looked around, waiting for her eyes to adjust to the all-enveloping darkness of the blacked-out street. She started walking, concentrating on putting one foot in front of the other in the darkness. Every so often someone would brush past her, knocking her sideways, followed by a muttered apology and receding footsteps before she had even managed to recover her balance.

She headed towards the river, following the acrid, tarry smell that hung on the warm night air. Somewhere ahead of her lay the shining ribbon of the Thames. But as she walked further, she began to realise that all was not as it should be. Instead of narrow terraces of houses, great warehouses seemed to loom up on every side of her. As she looked up, she thought she could make out the tall, skeletal shape of a crane.

Eve stopped, trying to get her bearings, panic filling her chest. Somewhere she must have taken a wrong turn, come down a side road. Instead of seeing the familiar shops of Cable Street, she had ended up close to the docks.

And then she heard the footsteps, coming out of the darkness behind her.

Eve held her breath and listened. It was her imagination, she told herself. Fear was playing tricks on her. But the footsteps were definitely getting closer. Sinister footsteps – not quick and purposeful, but slow, heavy, dragging...

Panicking, Eve ran blindly out into the middle of the road, and straight into the path of a bicycle.

She heard a screech of brakes, and the next thing she knew she was sitting in the middle of the road, a tall shape bending over her.

'Are you all right?' a male voice asked.

'I'm fine, thank you. Just a bit shaken, that's all.' Eve scrambled to her feet, brushing herself down.

'I'm terribly sorry. I didn't see you until it was too late. Did I hit you? I thought I was going slowly.'

'Really, I'm quite all right. It was my fault for dashing out into the road.'

She paused, listening. The heavy, dragging footsteps had vanished. Just her imagination after all, she decided. And now the moon had emerged from behind a cloud, she could finally make out where she was, too.

'It's Eve, isn't it?'

She looked up into the face of the stranger. In the dim, silvery moonlight, she could vaguely make out his tall, slim outline looming over her.

'I'm Oliver – Reverend Stanton's son? We met on Sunday at church.'

'Oh, yes. Of course.' She recognised him now she could just about make out his features in the gloom.

'Perhaps I could walk you home, since we're both heading the same way?' Oliver offered.

'Really, there's no need.'

'But it's the least I can do, after giving you a scare like that–'

'I said no!' Eve cut him off, nerves making her abrupt. 'Really, I'm fine,' she said, more calmly.

'Well, if you're sure?' She could hear from the faltering of his voice that she had offended him. But she couldn't help it. She couldn't imagine what her aunt would do if she turned up with a young man in tow. Even if it was Reverend Stanton's son.

'Quite sure, thank you. Now, if you'll excuse me, I must be getting back. My aunt will be worried if I'm late.'

'Of course. It was nice meeting you again,' he called after her. But his voice was already lost in the distance as Eve hurried away.

Aunt Freda was waiting for her, sitting tall and gaunt in the high-backed armchair beside the unlit kitchen fireplace. She was half asleep, her Bible resting in her lap. But her eyes snapped open as soon as Eve walked in.

'You're late,' she remarked.

'I had to walk all the way back from my class,

104

and I got lost in the dark.'

'Got lost? I've never heard such nonsense. Surely you should know your way by now? Unless you've been up to no good,' she said.

Eve thought guiltily about running into Oliver Stanton. She wondered if she should tell her aunt about it, but there was really nothing to tell.

Thankfully, for once her aunt changed the subject. 'Now you're back you can make yourself useful and put the kettle on,' she said. 'I have a slight headache.' She pressed her fingers to her temples.

'I'm sorry to hear that, Aunt. Shall I fetch you an aspirin?'

'If I'd wanted an aspirin, I would have asked for one, wouldn't I?' Aunt Freda shot back. 'Just make a cup of tea, and be quick about it.'

Eve picked up the kettle and filled it at the sink.

'How much longer are these wretched classes going to go on?' Aunt Freda asked. 'You know I don't approve of you being out until all hours.'

'Tonight was the last one.' Eve lit the gas and put the kettle on the bob to heat. 'I start work at the hospital next week.'

She sensed it was the wrong thing to say. Aunt Freda was already vexed about her abandoning the shop to work as a VAD three days a week.

'Yes, well, we shall have to see about that,' she muttered. But before she could say any more, there was a loud knock on the front door that startled them both. Aunt Freda sat bolt upright in her chair. 'Who on earth is calling at this time of night?' she said.

'I'll go, shall I?' Eve started towards the door,

but her aunt put out a hand to stop her.

'Certainly not. It's my house, and I shall answer my own front door.'

She rose stiffly to her feet and headed up the passageway. Eve warmed the pot and spooned in the tea and wondered if her aunt was going to make much fuss about her going to work at the hospital. Taking the First Aid classes had made her realise how much she wanted to put her skills into practice. But she didn't want to show what it meant to her, because then her aunt would forbid it completely.

At least she had the law on her side, thought Eve. She had to do some kind of war work, whether her aunt liked it or not. She just had to approach it very carefully...

She turned round and almost dropped the teapot when she saw her aunt standing silently in the doorway.

Eve put her hand to her hammering heart. 'Oh, Aunt, you gave me quite a start–'

Then she saw the leather strap hanging loosely from her aunt's hand, and a ripple of dread ran through her. She straightened up, trying not to tremble. 'Aunt Freda?' she whispered.

'You had a visitor,' Aunt Freda said. She held out her other hand, and Eve saw her own purse. 'Reverend Stanton's son. He says you dropped this earlier on?' Her brows arched questioningly over cold, hard eyes.

'I can explain...' Eve started to say. But the leather strap whistled through the air, catching the back of her hand with a sharp crack. Eve flinched back, snatching her hand away.

'Don't you dare speak to me!' Aunt Freda's voice rasped. 'I don't want to hear your lies.' She advanced towards Eve, her eyes pinpricks of venom. 'You've been sneaking around behind my back, haven't you?'

'N-no, Aunt. I–'

'And I suppose you've been lying to me about those classes of yours, too, haven't you? Telling me you're off learning to be a nurse, when all the time you've been getting up to all sorts!'

Eve backed away, her eyes fixed on the twitching leather strap. 'I haven't, Aunt, honestly. I was walking home, and he ran into me on his bicycle. I – I must have dropped my purse then.'

'Liar!' The leather strap cracked through the air again, narrowly missing her. Aunt Freda advanced towards her, face taut with fury. Eve's legs buckled and she groped behind her, fingers closing around the worn wood of the draining board.

'I swear to you, Aunt, it's the truth.'

'Swear, would you? So you're a blasphemer as well as a whore.' Aunt Freda's face twisted. 'I should have known, no matter what I did you'd turn out just like your mother.'

'But Aunt–'

'You need to be punished.' Aunt Freda's voice was suddenly low and calm, belying the madness in her eyes. 'I will not have a lying whore in this house, do you understand me? You need to have the evil beaten out of you, for your own good.'

'Aunt, please,' Eve begged, her voice hoarse with fear.

'It's for your own good, child. "He that doeth

wrong shall receive for the wrong which he hath done." Colossians, chapter three, verse twenty-five. How do you ever expect to learn, if no one teaches you a lesson?'

'Please, Aunt–' She was whimpering now, unable to stop herself even though she knew her pleas would only goad her aunt further. 'Please, don't–'

The leather cracked, and she felt the hot snap of pain across her cheek, sending her reeling backwards. All she could do was cower, her arms over her head, and wait for it all to be over.

Chapter Twelve

The nightmare jolted Dora into wakefulness and she jack-knifed upright, gasping for breath, her heart hammering. It took a moment for her to remember where she was, lost in the sea of her double bed, the sheets tangled around her legs, her nightgown damp with sweat. But slowly, as her eyes got used to the darkness, she started to make out the familiar shapes of the wardrobe and chest of drawers, and the soft breathing of her babies on either side of her.

She put her hand to her chest and tried to breathe deeply as the sound of Nick's screams slowly faded from her mind. But they didn't disappear completely. When she closed her eyes, she could still see his face, caked with dirt and blood and glistening with sweat, distorted with pain and terror.

It wasn't the first time she'd had the nightmare. She'd had the same dream every night since the news came from Dunkirk. For the past week she'd woken to the same awful vision.

But this was too vivid to be a dream. It was as if he were there, so real and solid she could have reached out and touched the rough serge of his uniform, stiff with dirt and blood. Even now, she could still hear the deafening sound of machine-gun fire, the explosions, the sound of panicked screaming, and–

Waves. Underneath the deafening bombardment, the muted roar of the sea, and the smell of salt...

Beside her, baby Walter stirred and started to whimper. He was a far lighter sleeper than his sister, who went on breathing softly, her plump little arm curled over Aggy the rag doll. Usually Dora would have waited for Walter to go back to sleep by himself. But this time, glad of the distraction, she got out of bed, disentangling herself from the sheets, and picked him up.

'There, there, sweetheart,' she crooned softly, burying her face in the warmth of his shoulder, calmed by his comforting baby smell. Holding her son close, she could feel her frantic heartbeat slowing down at last.

Walter soon nodded off, his head heavy on her shoulder. Dora tucked him back into bed beside his sister, but she couldn't face getting back in herself. Weary as she was, she was afraid to sleep in case the nightmare came back and she saw Nick's face again in her dreams. She pulled on her dressing gown and went downstairs to the kitchen.

She tiptoed past Danny, curled up on his mattress under the window. Not that he stirred – Danny always slept so soundly, his innocent mind untroubled by fears and nightmares. She envied him that.

Dora crept into the scullery and put the kettle on. While she waited for it to boil, she went over to the window, lifted a corner of the heavy blackout curtain and looked out. It was a balmy June night, and the air was still. There were no street lamps, but the full moon cast a silvery light over the backyard, illuminating the coal bunker, the outhouse and the makeshift rabbit hutch that Little Alfie had put up for Octavius after he gnawed his way out of his cardboard box.

The day after he'd built it, Nanna Winnie had made a show of going out into the backyard with her knife, much to Little Alfie's dismay.

'You can't eat Octavius!' he'd cried, distraught. 'He's my pet.'

'He's another bleeding mouth to feed!' Nanna shot back. 'I'm sick of him eating all my best greens. He's going in a pie.'

As Dora and her mother tried to console Alfie, Nanna had returned five minutes later empty-handed. 'There ain't more than a morsel of meat on him yet,' she'd declared. 'I'll wait till he's filled out a bit.'

Rose had winked at Dora. 'I knew she wouldn't do it,' she whispered. 'I caught her out there feeding him carrot tops the other day.'

Was that really only two weeks ago? Everything

110

had seemed so normal then. If Dora had known what was to come, she would have cherished their laughter, held on to it with everything she had. Now she longed for those days, when they were full of hope...

'I'll have a cuppa, if you're making one?'

Dora looked over her shoulder. Her mother stood in the doorway to the scullery, her dressing gown drawn around her.

'Sorry, did I wake you?' Dora said. 'I tried to be quiet.'

Rose shook her head. 'I don't sleep much these days, to be honest.' She smiled sympathetically. 'I don't suppose you do either?'

Dora turned away, taking an extra cup from the cupboard. 'The kids were restless,' she said. 'I think Walter might be teething again–'

'It's all right, Dor. I'm your mum, you don't have to pretend with me.'

No, she thought, but I have to pretend to myself. If she stopped pretending, she wasn't sure if she would have the strength to go on.

It was only in her dreams that the mask came down and reality clawed at her. Dora thought again about her nightmare, about the incessant rattle of gunfire, the rush of waves. If she breathed in, she could still almost smell the salty tang in the air.

That was why she couldn't sleep. She was too afraid.

'It's all right to be worried,' Rose went on. 'It'd be a strange thing if you weren't. But you'll get some news soon.'

When? Dora wanted to cry out. It had been

over a week since the evacuation began. They had already had a letter from her brother Peter to say he was safe, and at the hospital not a day went by without one of the nurses hearing good news from a loved one. Dora celebrated with them, but at the same time her heart broke that she still hadn't had news of Nick.

With nothing else to go on, she could only imagine the worst. And working on the ward, being surrounded by men with devastating injuries, men whose lives and bodies had been shattered by war, only made her imagination run riot.

'Chin up, love. You heard what Pete said in his letter. It's been that chaotic bringing all the men back, even the War Office can't keep track of who's where.'

'I know, Mum.' Dora tried to smile.

'You know what they say. No news is good news.'

Dora looked into her mother's tired brown eyes. Rose didn't believe that any more than Dora did. But she was desperate to give her daughter hope, and Dora was desperate enough to take it.

What else could she do? She was trying her best to keep smiling, but with each day that passed it was growing harder and harder to believe that the news would be good.

The following morning Dora arrived on the ward to find more casualties had arrived during the night, including a wounded airman in one of the private rooms.

'He has suffered extensive burns over his face and body.' Sister Holmes recited the gruesome details in a flat voice. 'He is being kept sedated with morphia for the pain. He will need his dressings changed every two hours, and a daily saline bath.'

But her face told a different story. The private rooms were for patients on the Dangerously Ill List, who needed extra nursing care. They were also, although no one would admit it, the patients with little chance of recovery.

Dora glanced sideways at Daisy Bushell. The colour had already drained from her face.

'Sister won't expect me to help with his dressings, will she, Nurse?' she whispered anxiously, after Sister Holmes had dismissed them. 'I honestly don't think I could manage it.'

There isn't much you can manage, is there? Dora bit back the retort that sprang to her lips. Daisy should have been used to the men's injuries by now, but she still turned faint at the sight of blood. But Dora couldn't be too angry with her. The girl gamely turned up every day and did her best. And even though her skills were limited to scrubbing floors, making beds and emptying bedpans, Dora knew they couldn't do without her.

There was talk of a new VAD arriving the following morning. Dora only hoped she had a stronger stomach than Miss Bushell.

Yet more casualties arrived during the day, including a gas gangrene case. Dr Jameson arrived for his rounds as the patient was being wheeled into a private room.

'Poor devil,' he said grimly to Dora. 'He's in a wretched state. Mr Cooper amputated his arm and has given him antitoxin, but it probably won't be enough to save him.' He shook his head.

'Frankly, I'm astonished the poor chap made it back across the Channel. He must have been determined to get home.'

Dora suddenly thought of Nick. Was he out there too, struggling to get back to her?

Sister Holmes summoned her over. 'You'll have to deal with the new patient since I'm busy with Dr Jameson's round. He'll need an intravenous infusion of saline. I've already set it up for you.'

'Yes, Sister.'

As she walked into the room, the putrid sweetness of the gas gangrene hit Dora like a sickening wall. She held her breath, forcing herself not to gag as she attached the infusion and arranged the warmed blankets and hot water bottles around the man.

She consulted his notes. His name was Sam Gerrard, and he was twenty-five years old. The same age as Nick. Bile rose in her throat again, but this time it had nothing to do with the man's injuries.

She was replacing his notes when his eyes suddenly fluttered open.

'Where am I?' he whispered, his voice as dry as sand.

Dora came to the side of the bed, where he could see her. 'You're in hospital, ducks. In London.'

'I made it home, then?'

'Yes, you're home. Safe and sound.'

'I dunno about that.' His mouth curved in the sketch of a smile. 'I'm in a bad way, ain't I?'

Sam was an East End lad, she could tell it from his accent. He sounded so much like Nick it

114

almost broke Dora's heart. She forced her brightest smile as she lifted his wrist to check his pulse. It skittered beneath her fingers like a trapped bird. 'You've got home, and that's something,' she said. 'Now, can I get you something to drink?'

'A pint would be nice.'

'I don't know if I can manage that! How about some water?'

Private Gerrard had drifted off to sleep by the time she'd poured his water for him. But he woke up again as she was setting up a heat cradle over his bed.

'What's that?' he asked.

'Something to keep you warm.'

'I'd rather have my missus.'

Dora smiled. 'You're married?'

'With two kids. Twins.'

Her throat dried. 'How old are they?'

'Just turned a year.'

Dora stared down at him. It could have been Nick lying there in that bed.

'I – I'll get you that drink I promised you, shall I?' She forced herself to stay calm as she carefully lifted his head and held the cup to his lips for him to drink.

'Are you sure that machine's on?' Sam said, as she laid him down again. 'I'm bloody freezing.'

'Give it a minute,' Dora tried to smile, but anxiety uncurled inside her. 'Are you in any pain?'

He shook his head. 'Not as much. Hardly any, I'd say. Whatever you gave me must be doing the trick.'

'That's good news.' Dora turned away so he

115

wouldn't see her face. It was a good sign, she told herself, even though all her training and experience told her the opposite. The pain stopped when the toxins took hold.

She switched off the heat cradle. 'There, we'll leave it for half an hour then put it on again.'

'Miss?' She'd reached the door when Sam called her back.

'Yes?'

'I will be all right, won't I? Only I promised my wife I'd come home for her and the kids.'

Dora hesitated for a moment, not sure if she could trust herself to speak. Dr Jameson's words came back to her. *He must have been determined to get home.*

'You'd better keep your promise then, hadn't you?' she whispered.

Dora was still thinking about Sam Gerrard as she made her way home later. It was another warm June evening, and Victoria Park was closing. As Dora passed, it made her smile to see the park-keeper with his bunch of keys jingling on his belt, ushering people out of the yawning gap that had once been the park gates.

She thought of another young woman, just like herself, cuddling her baby twins in the small hours of the morning, wondering and worrying and waiting for news.

Her husband would come home to her, Dora decided. Sam was a fighter, just like her Nick. He had made his wife a promise, and he meant to keep it. That promise alone would keep him alive, just as it would keep her Nick alive.

But then she turned the corner and saw her

116

mother standing at the end of the alleyway, and her heart stopped in her chest.

Her mother never came to meet her. Not unless she had news...

Dora saw the envelope in her mother's hand and suddenly she wanted to run, to turn and flee and not have to face whatever lay ahead of her. But her legs seemed to melt away from underneath her, and the next thing she knew she was sitting on the kerb as her mother walked slowly towards her, holding out the telegram she had been dreading.

Chapter Thirteen

'The whole ward will need to be swept and damp-dusted every day, including the floors, the window sills and the lockers. Be sure to dust the bedsprings and clean the wheels of each bed, too. Sister will check it's done properly. You'll find brushes and everything else you need in this cupboard here...'

Jennifer stifled a yawn with the back of her hand and wondered if Nurse Riley would ever stop talking. She'd been going on and on for the past ten minutes, listing all Jennifer's duties. They seemed never-ending.

'And this is the linen room,' Nurse Riley went on. 'This is where we keep all the clean sheets and pillowcases. The beds will need to be changed every day, and remade several times a day. It's very important to make sure the patient is comfortable. You have been taught how to make a bed, I suppose?'

She regarded Jennifer with a frown, and the girl stared back at her. The staff nurse was a few years older than Jennifer herself, sturdily built, with muddy green eyes, gingery eyelashes and a freckled face. She looked fierce enough that Jennifer knew she wouldn't want to cross her.

'Yes, Nurse.'

'Good. I hope you can do it quickly, too. Sister expects a bed to be made from start to finish in under two minutes. Any dirty linen needs to be rinsed in the sluice, and then packed up and left in those bins out there for the porters to take to the laundry.'

Jennifer stifled another yawn. She really shouldn't have gone up west with Cissy the night before she started her new job at the hospital. But Cissy had just heard that Paul was safely back in England, and she was in the mood to have some fun.

Boy, they'd really kicked up their heels! There were no British boys in London any more, but the city was teeming with all kinds of exciting foreign soldiers from all over the world. Jennifer had danced all night with Canadians, Polish, Frenchmen, all lonely and looking for some lively company. But in the end it was a young Norwegian who had caught her attention, a handsome blond giant in a blue serge suit. She hadn't been able to understand a word he'd said, but that didn't seem to matter when she was in his arms.

She and Cissy had finally crept home just as

118

dawn was breaking, their shoes in their hands, having cadged a lift on the back of a milk float from Aldgate. Thank God their dads had both been working nights, or there would have been hell to pay.

'Am I keeping you up, Caldwell?'

Jennifer came back to the present to find Nurse Riley staring at her.

'Sorry, Nurse,' she mumbled.

Nurse Riley tutted. 'Really, I hope you're livelier than this when Sister's around. She won't take any of your nonsense. Now here's the kitchen, where you'll boil up the urn for the drinks round, and here are the bathrooms – they'll need to be scrubbed thoroughly every day, although most of the patients will need to be bathed in bed, due to their injuries.'

Was there an inch of the ward that didn't need to be scrubbed or mopped or polished or dusted? Jennifer wondered as she followed Nurse Riley out of the bathroom. As she left she caught sight of herself in one of the mirrors and paused to adjust her cap to a more rakish angle on her dark curls.

The uniform rather suited her, she thought. She'd always looked good in blue, and the crisp white apron emblazoned with a red cross gave her an air of importance.

'Caldwell!' Nurse Riley snapped at her again, breaking her out of her daydream. 'Follow me, and I'll take you down to the sluice.'

Nurse Riley led the way down the ward, her shoes squeaking on the polished floors. Jennifer looked around at the patients. What a terrible, sad sight they were, some with limbs missing, others with their faces and bodies swathed in bandages. Some of the beds had screens around them, shielding them from view. Jennifer wondered what shocking sights lay behind them.

'Don't stare,' Nurse Riley snapped. 'These are wounded men coming to terms with their injuries and the last thing they need is you gawping at them. You must try not to be silly or insensitive when you're on the ward.'

Who are you calling silly? Jennifer felt like asking. But she didn't want to get on the wrong side of Dora Riley. She seemed short-tempered enough already.

None of this would have been so bad if Cissy had been with her. It was so unfair that they'd been separated. Jennifer had been pleased when she found out she was going to be looking after soldiers on the Male Acute ward, until she found out Cissy was being packed off to Casualty. What had seemed like an adventure was turning out to be very dull indeed without Cissy to share it.

'This is where we keep the trolleys and the screens that go round each bed when the patient is being washed or examined.' Nurse Riley pointed them out as she swept past. 'And these are the private rooms.'

Jennifer peered in through the first door, which was half open. The curtains were pulled, shutting out the June sunshine. But in the shadowy darkness, she could make out a figure in the bed, lost amid what seemed to be a complicated arrangement of bandages and straps.

'Who's that?' she asked.

'He's one of Mr Cooper's patients.' Nurse

Riley's voice was clipped with impatience. 'You don't need to go in there. Now this way is the sluice, where you'll be spending most of your time...' She swung open the door to a small room. The stench caught the back of Jennifer's throat, making her eyes water. She reeled back, holding her apron to her face.

'That awful smell...'

'Bedpans,' Nurse Riley said. 'You'll get used to them. Have you ever cleaned one before?'

Jennifer shook her head. Her gaze was fixed on the towering pile of porcelain pans ranged on the floor beside the large sink. They were covered, but the smell still made her stomach churn and her throat tighten.

'Bushell will show you what you have to do.' Nurse Riley nodded towards the skinny blonde girl standing at the sink. 'Be quick about it, mind. No chattering, please. I will be keeping my eye on you,' she warned.

'She's a laugh a minute, isn't she?' Jennifer said, when the door had closed behind Nurse Riley.

'She's actually very nice, usually.' Daisy Bushell shrugged. 'Although I must admit, she has been rather snappish this morning... But still, she's much kinder than Sister. *She's* the one you really have to watch out for. Now, about these bedpans...' She reached for the topmost one. 'Here's what you need to do. You have to empty the contents down here–' She pointed to the large hole in the centre of the sink '–unless you've been told to keep them for inspection. Oh, and make sure you pick out any bits of tow before you empty it away.'

'Tow?' Jennifer said faintly.

'It's a kind of wool stuff that the nurses use to wipe the patients when they've finished using the pan,' Daisy said. 'They shouldn't throw it in the bedpan, it really needs to go in a separate receiver dish, but sometimes they forget so you have to check and fish it out with forceps before you empty it.'

'Fish it out ... with forceps...' Jennifer echoed queasily.

'Once you've emptied the bedpan, you tip it upside down over this spray,' Daisy went on briskly. 'Remember to put it over before you switch on the spray, otherwise you'll make an awful mess. Clean the pan out thoroughly, then use this mop to scrub each one with plenty of disinfectant. Keep the mop in the disinfectant when you're not using it. Then rinse out the pan again, dry the outside and then put it up here.' She pointed to a rack on the wall. 'Do you think you can manage that?'

'I suppose I'll have to, won't I?' Jennifer replied gloomily. She looked around. 'Where are the gloves?' she asked.

'What gloves?'

Jennifer stared at her in horror. 'You don't mean I'm supposed to clean these – things – out with my bare hands?'

'That's the idea,' Daisy shrugged. 'Don't worry, you'll get used to it soon enough. And mind you scrub inside the handles, too. Sister always checks the handles.'

'And what about those?' Jennifer pointed to a row of bottles, covered by calico cloths.

'You clean them in the same way, by emptying them out and then rinsing them. But be sure to check first with Sister or Nurse Riley that they don't need to take a specimen.' She looked anxiously at the clock on the wall. 'We'd better get a move on,' she said. 'The consultant is due to do his rounds at half past ten and we need to have all these done, the ward cleaned, the patients washed and the beds all made by then.'

Jennifer gazed at her hands despairingly. The thought of picking up one of those revolting bed-pans was more than she could stand.

Gingerly she picked up the first pan and held it at arm's length. Holding her breath, she whipped the lid off another pan, gave it a quick half glance and tipped it over the sinkhole, her face turned away. The slopping of the contents down the hole made her retch.

Daisy watched her with amusement. 'I don't actually mind the bedpans,' she lisped. 'It's the patients I can't cope with. All those horrible, gaping wounds, and the missing limbs – ugh!' She shuddered.

'They didn't seem too bad to me.' Jennifer shrugged.

'You haven't seen them up close,' Daisy warned her. She picked up one of the bedpans from the draining board, dried around the outside, then hung it up on the rack.

'What about those patients in the private rooms?'

Daisy stared at her in horror. 'Oh, you must never, ever go in there,' she warned, her voice hushed. 'Sister would have a fit, apart from anything else. Only the trained nurses are ever allowed in those rooms, even to clean.'

'Is that right?' Jennifer was intrigued.

'I mean it, Caldwell. You mustn't ever go in there.'

'All right, keep your hair on. I wasn't going to break the rules. I just wondered who was in there, that's all.'

'Well, so far as I know they were both brought in yesterday. One is a soldier. He's suffering from gas gangrene and he's had his arm amputated. And the other is an airman whose plane crash-landed.' Daisy pulled a face. 'It's a very sad story, from what I've been told. Apparently he had the chance to escape, but he went back to try and pull his wireless operator free. That's when he got burned by the exploding fuel tank.'

'How awful.' Jennifer thought about the figure in the shadowy room, swathed in straps and bandages. 'Will he live, do you think?'

Daisy sent her a strange look. 'I don't know, do I? Goodness, don't you ask a lot of questions?'

'I can't help being curious, can I?'

Sister Holmes appeared as Jennifer was finishing off the last bedpan.

'Are you still in here? What on earth has taken you so long, girl?' she demanded. 'I hope you two haven't been gossiping instead of getting on with your work?' She looked at Daisy, who blushed guiltily.

'Just finished, Sister,' Jennifer said

'Let me see.' Sister Holmes picked a pan off the rack and turned it around in her hands, peering down the hollow handle. 'Still filthy,' she declared, handing it back to Jennifer. 'You'll have to do them all again.'

'They seem clean enough to me, Sister–' Jennifer started to protest, but Sister Holmes snapped her a look that shocked her into silence.

'I don't care how they seem to you,' she said. 'I am telling you they are not cleaned to my satisfaction. I want you to clean them again. And make sure you do it properly this time. Good heavens, at this rate by the time you finish them the patients will be wanting to use them again!'

She turned and left, slamming the door behind her.

The rest of the morning didn't go much better for Jennifer. Once she'd finally finished the bedpans, Sister made her rinse the soiled bedlinen before it went off to the laundry, and scrub and dry the mackintosh sheets. Then it had been time for more bedpans and bottles, and cleaning the bathrooms from top to bottom. By the end of the morning three of her nails were broken and her skin itched from being constantly doused in disinfectant.

And then Sister made her help with serving the patients their meals before she was finally dismissed to the dining room for her own.

Cissy was already there, sitting at a long table with the other VADs.

'I didn't think you were coming,' she said.

'Neither did I. That wretched woman kept me working right up till the last minute.' Jennifer collapsed into a chair and stretched out her aching legs. 'That's better. I haven't sat down all morning.'

'I was lucky,' Cissy said. 'Sister Casualty is an angel, she sent us off on time.'

'You are lucky.' Jennifer grimaced. 'I don't suppose you've been scrubbing bedpans with your bare hands all morning either?'

Cissy pulled a face. 'You haven't?'

Jennifer held out her hands. 'Look. And I've got the broken nails to prove it.'

'All we have to do is tidy up the consulting rooms between patients, and make sure no one vomits while they're waiting to be seen,' Cissy said.

'I wish I was on Casualty with you, in that case.'

'Me too.' Cissy leaned forward. 'You'll never guess who I've been paired up with?'

Jennifer followed her friend's gaze to the end of the table, where Eve Ainsley sat alone, picking at her food.

'No! Poor you. I don't think I envy you at all, in that case. How's she been getting on?'

'Oh, she's already in Sister's good books. She's a real teacher's pet, just like she was in the classes.'

Jennifer looked down the end of the table. 'What's that mark on her face?' she asked.

Cissy shrugged. 'Reckons she walked into a wall in the blackout,' she said, helping herself to another slice of bread.

Jennifer frowned to see the fading bruise on the girl's cheek and felt a pang of guilt. She wondered if she'd had her accident after Jennifer had abandoned her to go off with Johnny. Oh, well, it was Eve's own fault, Jennifer told herself. She should have accepted a lift when she had the chance.

Thinking about that night reminded her of Johnny Fayers. Not that he was ever far from her thoughts. She was annoyed with herself for thinking of him so much when he clearly didn't care about her.

It had been a week now, and she still hadn't seen him. Jennifer kept trying to tell herself that he didn't know where to find her, but she had a feeling that someone like Johnny would be able to find out if he'd been interested. Unfortunately, he hadn't bothered.

And that was exactly why he fascinated her so much. Unlike most of the men she met, he actually presented a challenge to her. Jennifer's mum had always said she only wanted what she couldn't have, and she was right.

Cissy sighed. 'And to think, last night I was dancing with a handsome Frenchman!' she said.

'If he could see you now!' Jennifer laughed. 'What about your Norwegian – what was his name?'

'Nils.' Jennifer smiled at the memory. His name was about the only thing he'd said that she understood.

Cissy giggled. 'That's right. I knew it was something odd. Are you seeing him again?'

Jennifer shook her head. 'He wasn't my type.'

'Really? You seemed quite keen when you let him kiss you?'

'It was only a kiss!' Jennifer shrugged. 'Anyway, can you imagine my dad's face if Nils turned up on our doorstep? He'd have a fit!'

But not as big a fit as he would have if Johnny Fayers rolled up in his car, she thought. Not that there was much chance of that happening.

Back on the ward after lunch, there were more bedpans and yet more cleaning.

As Jennifer passed the private rooms on her way to the sluice, she couldn't resist peeking through the first open door at the injured airman. She could barely make out his shape in the dimly lit room. Surely it wouldn't hurt to take a closer look, she thought. As long as she didn't touch anything...

The room was dark and very warm. The man's laboured breathing was the only sound.

Jennifer crept closer to look at him. His face and the upper half of his body were swaddled in bandages. A complex arrangement of straps suspended him above the mattress. The room reeked of disinfectant, masking another, more acrid smell. Jennifer sniffed for a moment, then realised with a shock that it was the odour of burned flesh.

'What do you think you're doing?'

Jennifer swung round. Sister Holmes stood in the doorway, her shape outlined against the bright light from the corridor.

'Who told you to come in here?'

'No one, Sister.'

'Then what are you doing?'

Jennifer glanced at the figure on the bed. 'I – I just wanted to look at him,' she said.

'You mean you wanted to gawp?' Sister Holmes snapped. 'I've a good mind to take off those dressings and let you have a look at him. That would soon stop you being nosy, I can tell you!' She glared at Jennifer. 'May I remind you, Caldwell, that this is a hospital, not a sideshow? These men have been badly wounded while serving their country. They deserve your respect, not your morbid curiosity.'

'I didn't mean anything by it,' Jennifer murmured lamely. She stared at the floor, unable to meet Sister Holmes's basilisk stare. Daisy Bushell was right, Sister was far more terrifying than Nurse Riley.

'Since it is your first day I will overlook it,' Sister Holmes said finally. 'But be assured, if I find you breaking the rules again, I will report you straight to Matron. I will not have—'

She was interrupted by a cry from the next room. She immediately hurried away and Jennifer followed her.

Next door Nurse Riley was standing over the bed, so pale and still she looked as if she had been carved from wax.

'Nurse Riley?' Sister Holmes spoke sharply to her, but she didn't move. 'Nurse Riley, whatever is the matter? For goodness' sake, speak to me, girl!'

Nurse Riley looked up slowly, and Jennifer saw her cheeks were wet with tears. 'Private Gerrard's dead,' she whispered.

Jennifer looked towards the young man in the bed. She had never seen anyone dead before. She would have liked a closer look, but a second later the door slammed in her face.

That was when Nurse Riley started screaming.

Chapter Fourteen

Kathleen sat beside Dora Riley's bed in the sick bay, gazing down at her. Dr McKay had given her a sedative to calm her, but a pair of defiant green eyes still stared back at Kathleen, fighting sleep.

'I should be on the ward, Matron,' she insisted. 'Sister Holmes needs me.'

'You're not going anywhere until you've rested.'

'But I'm not tired. I just had a bit of a – funny turn, that's all. I'm all right now, honestly.'

'That's not what Dr McKay thinks. He says you're suffering from nervous exhaustion.'

Dora Riley pressed her lips together, and Kathleen could see her fighting back a sharp retort. She certainly seemed more like her normal tight-lipped self, in contrast to the hysterical, tearful girl who had been carried up to the sick bay earlier.

But Kathleen wasn't sure that was a good thing. According to Dr McKay, it was the pressure of holding in her emotions that had caused her to collapse.

'Why don't you tell me what's troubling you, my dear?' Kathleen urged.

Dora turned her face away to stare at the wall. 'It's nothing,' she mumbled. 'There's nothing wrong, Matron, I promise you.'

'But we can't help you if you don't tell us.'

'I don't need help!' A dull flush rose in the girl's freckled cheeks. She appeared to be more embarrassed about her outburst than anything else.

Kathleen regarded her steadily. She had never met anyone as stubborn as Dora Riley. Her dogged determination might have helped her to overcome a great deal in her life, but it also meant she could be her own worst enemy at times.

'There's no shame in accepting help,' she said quietly. 'Everyone needs a helping hand from time to time.'

'I can manage, Matron.'

Kathleen looked at the girl's bitten-down nails. They told a very different story.

She tried again. 'You seemed very badly affected by Private Gerrard's death,' she commented.

Dora winced at the sound of his name. 'It came as a shock, that's all, Matron,' she muttered.

'Surely not. With your experience, you must have known he was unlikely to recover from his injuries?'

Dora kept her gaze fixed on the wall. 'I thought he was going to fight it,' she said quietly. 'For his wife and kids.'

So that's it, Kathleen thought. At last she was getting closer to the truth. 'And I suppose it made you think about your own husband?'

Dora flashed her a look of dismay and Kathleen realised she was right.

'Tell me,' she prompted gently, 'has he been injured?'

Dora turned her face to the wall. 'He's in a military hospital. In Oxford.' The words seemed to be dragged out of her.

'I see.'

'He was shot in the chest,' Dora went on in a

flat voice. 'I've telephoned the hospital to find out how he is, but all they'll tell me is he's comfortable...' Her voice trailed off, lost in misery.

Kathleen was silent for a moment, taking it in. No wonder she'd reacted so badly to that soldier's death. The poor girl must see her husband's face in every wounded soldier she tended.

Comfortable. It was a term they often used when patients' families telephoned the ward. It was supposed to be reassuring, but Kathleen only realised now what an empty phrase it was. Especially to a nurse, who would know what it really meant.

'We must arrange for you to have some time off, so you can go and visit him,' she said. 'Oxford isn't that far.'

'I can't.' Dora shook her head. 'Families aren't allowed to visit patients in military hospitals.'

Kathleen thought about it. 'Surely under the circumstances, they would allow a short visit?'

'What circumstances, Matron? I'm no worse off than a lot of other wives and girlfriends, am I?' Dora's voice was flat. 'I'm luckier than a lot of them, too. Some men never even made it off the beach. At least my Nick has a chance—'

'And if he's as brave and determined as his wife, then I'm sure he'll grab it with both hands,' Kathleen said.

'I hope you're right, Matron.'

Kathleen stood up. 'At any rate, you should take some time off, to recover your strength.'

'If it's all the same to you, Matron, I'd rather go back to work. I'd feel better if I was keeping busy.'

'Very well. But I will have you transferred to another ward.'

Dora looked appalled. 'But Sister Holmes will be short-staffed!'

I'm sure Sister Holmes would prefer that to having nurses collapse in a tearful heap on her, Kathleen thought. The ward sister had looked most shaken when Kathleen had gone up to the ward to see her.

'Sister Holmes can manage. You must put yourself first,' she advised.

Dora gave her a long look. 'With all due respect, Matron, I've got a family to think about. I ain't got time to think about myself.'

'I don't understand.' Kathleen couldn't hide her frustration. 'Surely there must be someone you could speak to about this? I wouldn't ask if it weren't important.'

'I know, and I wish I could help,' James Cooper's voice was sympathetic at the other end of the telephone line. 'But as a military matter, it's quite out of my control. I'm sorry,' he said. 'You know I would do something about it if I could. But rules are rules, especially where the army is concerned.'

'I know,' Kathleen sighed. She looked up as Miss Hanley entered the room with the staff rotas in her hand. 'It just seems so sad, that's all. All she'd need is to see him for a few hours, just to reassure herself...'

'I understand you're trying to help, but if you want my advice I'd let it go,' James Cooper said.

That's the trouble, Kathleen thought. I can't let it go. She had spent all afternoon trying to find a

133

way to help Dora Riley. She had even pondered the idea of asking that Nick be transferred to the Nightingale Hospital. But she realised that was impractical. Their resources were stretched enough, without her putting more pressure on everyone.

'But if you'd seen the state the poor girl was in—'

'So are a lot of other girls.' James Cooper echoed Dora's words. 'You can't help everyone, Miss Fox.'

'I suppose not.'

As Kathleen put the phone down, Miss Hanley was still waiting by the door. Kathleen already knew she'd been listening to every word. 'I take it Mr Cooper couldn't help, Matron?'

Kathleen shook her head. 'Unfortunately not.'

Miss Hanley sighed. 'I did try to tell you.'

Something about the smug way she said it made Kathleen's hackles rise. 'And you were quite right, Miss Hanley – as usual!' she snapped.

Her assistant looked offended. 'I'm sure I take no pleasure in it, Matron.'

Don't you? Kathleen thought. She wished she'd never shared her worries about Dora Riley with the Assistant Matron. Miss Hanley had spent all afternoon making her feelings about the matter very plain.

She made them plain again now. 'It's probably for the best,' she said. 'As Matron of this hospital, I'm sure you have better things to do with your time and energy than to involve yourself in nurses' private matters.'

'But don't you see? This isn't just a private

matter,' Kathleen said. 'A young nurse is on the point of collapse because she's so worried about her husband. If we could help ease some of her anxiety, she might be able to continue with her duties.'

'Yes, but–' Miss Hanley started to argue, but Kathleen held up her hand to silence her. She had heard more than she could stand from her assistant on the matter. 'There is more to a hospital than wards and beds, Miss Hanley. What makes the Nightingale work is the people within it. And I don't just mean names on a duty list either.' She waved the rota that Miss Hanley had placed on her desk. 'If we don't care for the staff, then we won't have a hospital at all.'

A mottled flush spread up Miss Hanley's neck. 'I didn't realise you felt so strongly about it, Matron,' she muttered.

'I feel strongly about everyone in this hospital, Miss Hanley. That's my job.'

Even you, she thought, as the Assistant Matron huffed off, slamming the door behind her. Kathleen rested her elbows on the desk and buried her face in her hands as the weariness of the day caught up with her. Sometimes she felt life would be a lot simpler if she took Miss Hanley's view and ran the hospital like a military operation. Perhaps her assistant was right and she shouldn't allow herself to get too involved?

But then she thought about poor Dora Riley, and all the other hard-working nurses and sisters who dedicated so much of their lives to the Nightingale. How could she stop herself from caring about them?

She was pleased to see Dora Riley had followed her orders at least. There was no sign of the young staff nurse when Kathleen did her rounds the following morning. With her usual unerring efficiency, Miss Hanley had arranged for a student, Nurse Padgett, to step in from the Female Acute ward.

'I'm sure it's for the best, under the circumstances,' Sister Holmes said as they began their inspection. 'Riley's been under a great deal of strain, unbeknownst to us all.'

'Indeed.'

'Still, at least the poor girl will be able to set her mind at rest now.'

Kathleen stared at her, mystified. 'What do you mean, Sister?'

'When she visits her husband.' Now it was Sister Holmes's turn to look mystified. 'Surely you know, Matron? Miss Hanley has arranged for her to go up to Oxford on Saturday morning.'

'No,' Kathleen replied. 'No, I didn't know.'

'It seems she has a connection in the War Office. One of the top brass, no less. Very convenient for us, don't you think?'

'Very,' Kathleen agreed, tight-lipped.

Miss Hanley was rearranging the duty lists yet again when Kathleen returned to her office later. Various papers were set out in front of her, and she was drawing lines between them with a pencil and ruler. It looked like a complex geometrical puzzle.

'What's all this I hear about Nurse Riley?' asked Kathleen.

Miss Hanley didn't look up from her drawing.

'After our conversation yesterday, I decided to make a telephone call to my cousin,' she said. 'He's in the War Office. I thought he might be able to help, and he did.'

She picked up her eraser and scrubbed at the paper, rubbing out the line she had just drawn. Kathleen stared at the top of the Assistant Matron's head. She had always known Veronica Hanley came from a distinguished military family. 'Why didn't you think to mention it yesterday?' she asked.

Miss Hanley looked up, meeting her eye for the first time. 'Because I didn't think the situation warranted it yesterday. But then I considered what you'd said, and I decided to trust your judgement.'

They faced each other across the desk. Kathleen didn't know whether to be pleased or to reach over and strangle her. Miss Hanley had had the solution within her grasp all the time, but had kept it to herself. And probably would have continued keeping it to herself if she hadn't had a belated change of heart.

'Thank you,' Kathleen said shortly. It was all she could trust herself to say.

Chapter Fifteen

The furthest Dora had ever been out of London was Kent, in the summers she'd spent hop-picking as a child, so travelling to Oxford felt like the other end of the world to her. The train moved slowly, inching past fields and countryside, pulling into sidings every five minutes to allow another troop train to pass. The other passengers crammed into the packed carriage threw open windows and complained about the delay and the sweltering heat, but Dora scarcely noticed as she stared unseeingly out of the window. Part of her wanted to get there quickly, but another part wanted the journey to go on for ever, so that she didn't have to face what lay ahead of her.

At Oxford station, the porter laughed when she asked about the next bus to Fairdown Hall.

'You've just missed it, love. Next one doesn't go for another three hours. And don't go looking for a taxi, neither, 'cos there ain't one to be had.'

'I'll have to walk, then.'

'But it's nigh on five miles!'

'That don't matter. Can you point out the way?'

The porter regarded her with sympathy. 'Your young man at the military hospital?'

Dora gritted her teeth against the pain that shot through her. 'My husband,' she muttered.

'My boy was at Dunkirk. Bad business, that was.' He shook his head in sorrow. 'He made it back all right, but plenty of his mates didn't. Bad business.' He looked at Dora, then consulted his watch and said, 'Look here, the next train ain't due for another two hours. Why don't I give you a lift up to the Hall? You'll have to walk back, mind, but at least I can get you there.'

Dora blinked at him, shocked by his unexpected kindness. 'If you're sure it's no trouble?'

'No trouble at all, love.' He smiled at her. 'I expect you'll be keen to see your husband, eh?'

Dora hesitated. 'Yes,' she said. 'Yes, I am.'

As they made their way through the narrow country lanes, Dora was glad of the porter's kindness. She might never have found her way otherwise. It wasn't at all like the streets of London, full of familiar buildings and landmarks to guide her way. Here it was nothing but endless trees and hedgerows, with not even a signpost to mark the way.

'They took 'em all down a few weeks back,' the porter explained. 'Meant to confuse the Germans if they invade, but it's just a bloody nuisance for the rest of us. Pardon my French.' He smiled. 'You'll have to remember the way for when you come back. Although I daresay someone will be coming to the station, if you ask 'em.' He sent her a sideways look. 'What happened to your husband, then?'

'He was shot in the chest.'

Dora stared out of the window, watching the scenery roll past, thinking about Nick. She was grateful that Miss Hanley had managed to organise her visit, but at the same time she'd had several sleepless nights wondering what she might find when she finally saw him.

'He'll be all right.' The porter's voice broke into her thoughts. 'He's in good hands. Those nurses, they really look after 'em up at the Hall.'

Dora caught his look and realised her fears must have shown on her face. She forced herself to smile back, grateful again for his kindness.

'I know,' she said.

Fairdown Hall had once been a girls' boarding school. But the dormitories had been turned into wards, and the outside tennis courts given over to rows of military vehicles. Dora made her way up the drive, grateful yet again for the porter's offer of a lift. It was another glorious June day, with the sun blazing out of a cloudless blue sky, and just walking up the drive was enough to send rivulets of perspiration running down the back of her neck. How she would have felt after walking five miles she didn't know.

The house itself was beautiful, with mullioned windows and ivy creeping over its mellow stone walls the colour of honey. On the spreading lawns in front of the house, wounded servicemen in wheelchairs sat under the dappled shade of trees, enjoying the sunshine.

The front doors were open and Dora stepped into the cool shade of the grand entrance hall, with marble floors, wood-panelled walls and a wide, sweeping staircase before her. It might have been a palace, but for the nurses and VADs going back and forth.

An elderly porter emerged from a doorway to greet her. He bore such a remarkable resemblance to the Nightingale's own Head Porter Mr Hopkins, short and stocky with a bristling moustache and an air of self-importance, that Dora almost laughed in spite of her nerves.

'Can I help you, Miss?' he asked.

'I've come to see one of your patients – Private Nick Riley?' She clenched her hands together to stop herself shaking as she said his name. 'I'm Mrs Riley. His wife.'

The man opened up a large ledger in front of him. 'Do you have an appointment?'

'I'm not sure... I think someone from the War Office telephoned to say I was coming.'

The man looked impressed. 'The War Office, eh? Let's see...' He consulted the list in his ledger. 'Well, there's no sign of a Mrs Riley here. Do you have an appointment card?'

'Do I need one?'

He looked up at her, his eyes sharp over his bristling moustache. 'This is a military hospital, Madam. Everyone needs an appointment.'

'But I was told I could come. It was all arranged by–'

'The War Office. So you say.' The porter sent her a sceptical look. 'But no one comes in here without an appointment card. Not even Mr Churchill himself.'

Looking at his truculent face, Dora could almost believe it. 'But I've come all the way from London!' Her nerves, already at breaking point, began to stretch a little thinner.

'I don't care if you've come from Timbuctoo. Rules are rules.'

Dora glared at him. He looked as if he was enjoying every minute of his job. She thought again about Mr Hopkins, and the satisfaction he always seemed to get from reporting nurses to Matron.

'All right, then,' she said. 'I'll wait.'

He stared at her. 'What do you mean, wait?'

'I'll wait here until you let me see my husband.' She dumped her bag at her feet.

'But – you can't do that!'

'Why not? I won't be in the way. And I've slept in worst places than this, I assure you.'

She pulled up a chair and sat down, crossing

141

her arms firmly to let the porter know she wasn't going anywhere.

'I'll have you removed,' he threatened.

'Try it.'

Their eyes met and held. The man blustered with impotent rage, but Dora ignored him. Finally, he gave in. 'I'll let Sister West know you're here,' he said, waving over one of the other porters. 'But I'm warning you, if she doesn't give her permission then that's it.'

Luckily, Sister West turned out to be more helpful than the porter. She came down the sweeping staircase to greet Dora herself. She was in her forties, a tall, graceful woman who reminded Dora very much of Miss Fox, with her pleasant smile and serene manner.

'Mrs Riley,' she greeted her. 'I'm so sorry you've been kept waiting. We had a telephone call from the War Office to tell us you were coming, although the message obviously didn't get through to everyone.' She glanced meaningfully at the man behind the desk.

'How's Nick?' Dora was so anxious she forgot her manners, blurting out the question that had been burning in her mind all the way from London.

Sister West smiled. 'He'll be all the better for seeing you, I imagine. Come up to the ward, and we'll talk on the way.'

They climbed the staircase. Grand-looking portraits in gilded frames frowned down on Dora as she passed.

As they approached the ward, Sister West explained that Nick had suffered a gunshot wound

142

to his upper chest that had missed his heart by a few inches. 'To be honest with you, Mrs Riley, it was a miracle he survived,' she said. 'And it was an even bigger miracle that the medics did a final sweep of the beach and found him, otherwise he might have been left for dead...'

Dora's knees buckled and she gripped the polished banister rail to stop herself from stumbling.

'I'm sorry, my dear, I didn't mean to alarm you.' Sister West's face was full of concern. 'I can assure you, your husband is making an excellent recovery. His will to live is very strong indeed. I wish all my patients were like him.'

Dora thought about poor Private Gerrard. His will to live had been strong, too. But sometimes willpower wasn't enough.

His widow would have received his belongings by now. They were all she had left to remember him by. Whatever happened, at least Dora had been given the chance to see Nick again. She was grateful for that, at least.

Sister West pushed open the door to the ward. 'Right, here we are,' she said. 'Your husband's bed is out on the balcony, down there on the right.'

It was all so familiar to her: the smell of disinfectant, the rows of beds and the busy, purposeful air of the nurses and VADs moving between them. It felt very strange for Dora not to be with them, tending to the patients.

She saw Nick before he saw her. His bed was out on the covered balcony, facing away from the rest of the ward. He had his back to her as he stared out across the grounds. She fought the desperate urge to throw herself into his arms.

143

'If you've come to tell me I need to occupy my time, you can bugger off,' he threw carelessly over his shoulder as she approached. 'I'm all right as I am, thanks very much.'

'I hope you're not being a difficult patient, Nick Riley?'

He turned round quickly, wincing with pain. 'Dora?'

She barely recognised him, his dark curls shorn into a severe army haircut. He'd lost weight, and his face seemed all harsh planes and sunken hollows. There was a line of scars and yellowing bruises across his jutting cheekbones and flattened boxer's nose.

'What are you doing here?' He blinked at her.

'Oh, you know. I was just passing and thought I'd drop in.' She grinned with delight at the stunned look on his face. It wasn't often anyone caught Nick Riley unawares.

He recovered his composure, giving her that slanted half smile that she had missed so much. 'I'm glad you did.' He looked her up and down, devouring her with his inky blue eyes. 'I'm surprised you managed to get past the front desk, though. They never let anyone in.'

'I've got friends in high places, ain't I? Besides, I told the porter I wasn't going anywhere till I'd seen you.'

His mouth twisted. 'That's my girl. You never give up without a fight, do you?'

'Nor do you, from what I hear.'

His smile faded. 'I suppose not,' he said quietly.

Dora sat down beside his bed. 'So how are you?' she asked, diverting her gaze from the

144

dressings that swathed his broad chest.

'Oh, I'll live.'

She recognised his dismissive reply. It was the same thing she heard every day from the soldiers on the ward. Some were desperate to talk about their experiences, to share their stories with anyone who might listen. Others played it down, kept it locked away inside, unable to give voice to what had happened to them.

Dora wished she could ask Nick what she needed to know. But he was like her, he kept his feelings to himself. He might tell her one day, but only when he was good and ready.

'Never mind about me anyway,' he dismissed. 'How are you? How are the kids?'

'They're fine. Getting bigger every day. They'll be toddling soon, I expect.'

'Their first steps, eh? Shame I won't be there to see it.'

Dora saw his expression falter, and hastened to cheer him up. 'I've brought you something...' She rummaged in her bag. 'We went to the photographer's and had it taken a few weeks ago, on the twins' birthday. I was going to send it to you, but...'

Her voice trailed off. Two weeks after the family photograph was taken, the evacuation of Dunkirk had begun. 'Anyway, it's a good likeness of the kids, don't you think?' she went on.

Nick stared at the photograph and Dora could see his face working as he struggled not to cry. 'They've got so big. I bet they'll hardly recognise me when they next see me.'

Dora caught the trace of sadness flitting across

his face. 'Of course they will,' she said firmly. 'You're their dad.' She cleared her throat. 'Look at Danny's face. It's a real picture, ain't it? I don't think he could make out what was happening at all.'

'I'm not surprised. No one's ever taken his picture before.' Nick smiled fondly at the image of his beloved brother. 'Can I keep it?'

'Of course. I brought it for you.'

'Put it there, on the locker, where I can see it.'

Dora propped the photo against the water jug. 'There, that should be all right.' All the time she was aware she was trying to keep herself busy, doing silly little things to ignore the fact that her husband was gasping so painfully for every breath. Trying to convince herself that everything was normal and that Nick wasn't in a hospital bed recovering from a gunshot that had nearly claimed his life.

Recovering. She clung to the word desperately. Nick was alive, and he was recovering. He was luckier than many, and so was she.

They chatted about inconsequential things. Dora told him how well they'd settled back in Griffin Street, funny little stories about the twins and the rest of the family. She even told him about Octavius the rabbit.

'Nanna keeps talking about cooking him, but she picks him up and cuddles him when she thinks no one's looking,' she said. 'When I came home the other night he was in the house sitting at her feet like a pet dog. She reckoned she didn't want to leave him out in the rain.'

Nick laughed. 'Your nanna always was contrary!'

146

After a while, Dora stopped thinking about his injuries. It was as if they were together in London again, and he'd just come home from work and she was telling him some funny tale.

'I wish I could see them all again,' Nick said suddenly.

She reached for his hand and squeezed it. 'You will,' she promised. She hesitated. She didn't want to ruin their time together by thinking about the future, but she couldn't help it. 'Have they said anything about what's going to happen?'

His expression darkened. 'Not really. But I've been told once I recover they'll send me back.'

She forced herself to stay composed. 'Do you mind going back?'

Nick's smile was grim. 'I'll have to go where they send me, won't I? Anyway, it's got to be better than being stuck in this place, doing bloody jigsaws!' he added.

Dora's face must have given her away, because his fingers tightened around hers. 'Don't worry about me, love,' he said. 'I'll be all right. I survived Dunkirk, I reckon I can survive anything. It's you I worry about.'

'Me?'

He nodded. 'You've got so much on your plate. I just wish I could be there to protect you and Danny, and the kids.'

Dora managed a smile, even though she was aching inside. 'Don't you worry about us,' she said. 'We'll be all right. I'll look after them all until you get home.'

They talked for another half an hour, holding hands and chatting about everything and nothing. Dora wished she could put her feelings into words, but it wasn't her way. It wasn't Nick's way either, but she could read his love for her in the way his gaze never left her face.

All too soon, she had to leave to catch the last train back to London.

'I don't suppose I'll be able to visit you again,' she said glumly, as she gathered up her belongings.

'I don't expect you will,' Nick said. 'Besides, I don't want you rushing down here every five minutes, not when you've got the kids to look after. I should get some embarkation leave before I'm sent back, so I'll see you then.' He held on to her hand. 'You will be all right, won't you?'

'I told you, don't you worry about me. I can take care of myself.'

They were both making light of it, but she could see in his eyes that he was as afraid as she was.

She leaned forward and he kissed her. The touch of his lips on hers opened floodgates of emotion and desire.

'You'd best go,' Nick said hoarsely.

Dora's smile wobbled. She felt a tear rolling down her cheek, but Nick brushed it away with his thumb.

She smiled. 'You just make sure you come back safe,' she said.

He smiled back. 'You just make sure I have a home to come back to,' he replied.

She walked away. She took a few steps, then turned. He was staring at the photograph, sadness darkening his eyes, as if he wanted to commit their faces to memory for ever.

Chapter Sixteen

'You don't mind, do you?'

Eve caught the appealing look Cissy gave her from under her lashes, and her heart sank.

'Sister asked me to assist in Outpatients this morning–' she began, but Cissy cut her off.

'Oh, she won't mind, as long as one of us is there,' she dismissed airily. 'Go on, you know you're so much better at this sort of thing than I am.'

'This sort of thing' was an elderly tramp who sat between them on the wooden bench, stinking of stale sweat and cheap booze. He looked up from one to the other with sad, yellowing eyes, then coughed wheezily and spat into a dirty handkerchief.

Cissy winced. 'Please?' she begged. 'He's so dirty. I'm afraid he might have TB or something. I don't want to catch it.'

'Shh! He'll hear you.'

'Nonsense, he's as deaf as a post. Aren't you, you old goat?'

'Baxter!'

'So will you swap with me? Go on, as a favour,' Cissy wheedled.

Eve sighed. There was no point arguing. Once Cissy had made up her mind not to do something, that was it.

And she was very fussy about what she did and

didn't do, as Eve had found out in the three weeks they'd been working together. Cissy didn't like going near any patient who was dirty, or smelly, or whose head needed delousing. She wouldn't clean up vomit because it made her retch, and she would only scrub the toilets if Eve had checked first that there was nothing unpleasant for her to encounter.

As usual, Cissy took her silence for assent.

'You will? Thanks, you're a brick. I won't forget this,' she called over her shoulder as she hurried off to Outpatients. 'We can have lunch together, how about that?'

If you remember, Eve thought. Cissy was full of promises she never kept. She turned to the old man with a resigned sigh. 'Come on, mister,' she said, encouraging him to his feet. 'Let's take you to see the nurse. She'll sort you out.'

It was a struggle to get the old man into the consulting room. He could barely shuffle and leaned heavily against her, his arm around her shoulders. Eve nearly buckled under his weight and the stench of his filthy clothing.

Nurse Kowalski raised a quizzical eyebrow as they staggered in. 'I thought you were in Outpatients today?' she said.

'I was, but I swapped with Baxter.'

'Did you indeed?' Dev Kowalski sent her a shrewd look. 'And I suppose that was her ladyship's idea? You shouldn't let her bully you, you know, Ainsley. You ought to stand up for yourself.'

'I didn't mind,' Eve murmured.

'Yes, well, you should. I've heard the way she speaks to you, ordering you about as if you're her

150

servant. It's not up to her what she does and what she doesn't.' Kowalski shook her head. 'Honestly, the way she goes on anyone would think she ran this place, not Sister. Anyway, what have we here?' She turned to the old man.

'He says he's got a rash on his feet.'

The old man's cough rolled up from his chest like an approaching train, ending in another noisy session with his grubby handkerchief. Nurse Kowalski frowned. 'He's got a nasty chest infection too, by the sound of it. Let's get his shoes and socks off and we'll take a look, shall we? You'd best give him a hand, I don't think he can manage by himself.'

Eve crouched down to unlace his old boots. They had been patched and crudely mended several times, and the soles were hanging off.

Meanwhile, Nurse Kowalski was still holding forth on the subject of Cissy Baxter.

'You know why she wants to help in Outpatients today, don't you? So she can throw herself at Mr Cooper.' Dev Kowalski shook her head in disgust. 'As if a respectable married man like him would ever be interested in a silly little thing like her!'

'But Cissy has a boyfriend,' Eve said.

Kowalski laughed. 'That wouldn't stop someone like her. I'm telling you, you'd do well to keep your distance from that one, Ainsley. She's a cruel little cat.'

Eve was silent as she struggled to unpick the knotted laces. Whatever Kowalski said, as far as Eve was concerned, Cissy Baxter was everything she wanted to be. All right, so she could be a bit selfish sometimes, but that was only because she

151

had the confidence to know what she wanted. If Eve was only a fraction as pretty and self-assured as Cissy was, she was sure her life would be completely different.

She pulled off the old man's boot, exposing a worn, filthy sock. The ammonia tang of ancient sweat nearly knocked her backwards.

Holding her breath, she pulled off the sock, exposing weeping, crusty patches that spread up over his ankle and crept beyond the ragged hem of his trouser legs.

Nurse Kowalski looked over her shoulder. 'Ringworm,' she declared. 'We'll put some iodine on it and see if that helps.' She turned to Eve. 'Perhaps you'd like to have a go at applying it?'

'Me?' Eve looked around, to see if one of the junior students had come into the room behind her. 'Why?'

Dev Kowalski smiled. 'You always seem interested in what we're doing. And if you learn how to do these things, you might be able to help us out a bit more when we're busy.'

Eve couldn't imagine a time when anyone would trust her enough to let her loose on a real patient, but she nodded eagerly.

'I'd like that,' she said. 'If you're sure you don't mind showing me?'

The rest of the morning went by in a blur of cuts, coughs, boils, burns and infections of various types. Dev Kowalski was very kind, showing Eve how to clean wounds and apply fomentations, and letting her practise her dressings. But it all took longer than usual, and by the time Eve finally emerged from the consulting room for lunch,

Cissy had already gone.

Eve was disappointed, but not surprised. She washed her hands, took off her apron and hurried off to find her.

Cissy was deep in conversation with Jennifer when Eve arrived in the dining room. They were sitting at one end of the table, their heads together, having a lively chat. Eve went to the hatch to collect her plate of stew and dumplings, then found a seat beside them.

Jennifer looked up at Eve as she put her plate down. 'Do you mind?' she said coldly. 'This is a private conversation.'

'It's all right,' Cissy said. 'I told her she could join us.' But she sounded half-hearted about it.

It was a very awkward mealtime. Eve sat beside them, her head down, feeling left out as they whispered together. From what she could make out, Jennifer was telling Cissy all about someone called Johnny who had sent her a note asking her out. From what she could also gather, Cissy didn't seem too keen.

'Are you sure, Jen?' she kept saying. 'There's something not quite right about him, if you ask me.'

Eve looked up and caught Jennifer's eye. Jennifer glared back at her and turned her shoulder to Eve, deliberately blocking her out. A moment later, she got up to leave and Cissy followed, with an apologetic shrug at Eve.

So much for having lunch together, she thought.

She was heading back across the courtyard after her break when she heard footsteps behind her.

153

'Excuse me,' a voice said. 'Could you direct me to the Porters' Lodge? I seem to have lost my bearings.'

Eve turned around and found herself yet again looking up into the lively green eyes of Oliver Stanton.

'It's you!' He grinned and whipped off his hat in greeting. 'We seem to bump into each other everywhere, don't we? It must be fate.'

'I suppose so.' Eve tried to smile back at him, but all she could think about was the last time they'd met, and the terrible thrashing Aunt Freda had given her.

'I didn't know you worked here?' he said. 'I thought you helped your aunt in her shop.'

'I'm here three days a week. War work,' she explained.

He nodded. 'Same here. That's why I have to report to the Porters' Lodge. I'm starting my first shift at two o'clock.'

'Oh.' Eve frowned. 'You're not joining up, then?'

'No, I'm not.' Oliver was silent for a moment, then went on, 'I haven't seen you at church recently?'

'No, I've been busy. There's a lot to do in the workshop now I'm not there every day.'

For all her strict observance of the Sabbath, business came first for Aunt Freda. Eve also suspected she was trying to keep her away from Oliver. Her aunt still didn't believe their meeting in the blackout had been an accident.

They stood in awkward silence for a moment, then Oliver said, 'Anyway, if you could point me in the direction of the Porters' Lodge...?'

'Of course. Sorry.' Eve pulled herself together. 'You need to go back past the main building the way you came, down the drive, and it's the little brick building just inside the main gates.'

'I must have walked right past it. I didn't realise the Nightingale was such a big place,' he said.

'It is a bit of a rabbit warren,' Eve agreed. 'But you get used to it.'

'I hope so.' He glanced up at the clock tower. 'Anyway, I'd better get a move on. I don't want to be late on my first day, do I?' Oliver turned on his heel and hurried across the courtyard. 'Thanks for your help,' he called back to her. 'I expect we'll bump into each other again before long!'

Not if I see you first, Eve thought, hurrying away. The last thing she wanted was to give her aunt another reason to be suspicious.

Chapter Seventeen

'Going out again?' her mother asked, as Jennifer applied her lipstick in front of the mirror.

'It's Friday night, ain't it? I always go out on a Friday night.'

'And where are you going tonight?'

'The Palais, with Cissy. Same as always.' Jennifer didn't meet her mother's eye in the mirror.

'Well, that's odd. When I met Marge Baxter in the queue for the butcher's earlier she told me she was going out to bingo with her Cissy to-night.'

Jennifer caught her mother's shrewd gaze reflected in the mirror and knew the game was up.

'So who is he?' Elsie Caldwell asked. 'I'm guessing there's a boy involved in all this? And I want the truth this time, my girl. None of your stories!'

Jennifer paused. 'His name's Johnny,' she said slowly.

Her mother folded her arms. 'And what's he like, this Johnny? Is he a local boy?'

Hardly a boy, Jennifer thought. 'I don't know.'

'You don't know? Where did you meet him?'

'At the Palais. You'd like him, he's a real gentleman,' she put in quickly.

Elsie Caudwell's frown deepened. 'I'm not so sure about that. And I can't imagine your father will like the idea, either.'

'Oh, Mum! You don't have to tell him, do you? This is the first time I've been out with Johnny, it might not even come to anything!'

'All the same, I expect your father will want to meet him. You know how protective he is of you.'

'Don't I just?' Jennifer muttered as she turned back to finish her lipstick. It was a good thing her father was on duty at the police station tonight. Being hauled up in front of Sergeant Alec Caldwell would put any man off!

'What time's he supposed to be picking you up?' her mother asked.

Jennifer glanced at the grandfather clock. It was ten past seven, but she didn't want to admit to her mother that Johnny was late. She just hoped he didn't stand her up, or she'd never hear the last of it.

But before she could reply, her brother Wilf

called out, 'There's a car outside. It's stopping outside our house!'

'That'll be him.'

Her mother looked stricken. 'You didn't tell me he had a car!'

'You didn't ask.' Jennifer shrugged. She dropped her lipstick into her bag and closed the clasp. 'Don't you dare go running out there!' She made a grab for her brother as he slipped past her towards the front door.

'Get in here, Wilf!' Elsie seized him by his collar and pulled him back. 'Your sister doesn't need you embarrassing her.'

Jennifer gave him a smug look. In truth, she was more worried about him reporting anything back to her mother.

Elsie smoothed the lapels of her daughter's coat. 'Enjoy yourself, love,' she said. 'But take care, won't you? Be sure to keep yourself respectable,' she added in a low voice.

'Mum!'

'I mean it, Jen. I know what men are like. Especially men with cars,' she said. 'Your dad will be off duty at eleven, so I want you home by then. No sneaking in in the early hours like you do when you're out with Cissy. And you'd best tell your – friend to park that thing around the corner,' she added as an afterthought. 'I don't want your dad seeing it before we've had time to get him used to the idea of you having a boyfriend.'

'Thanks, Mum.' Jennifer gave her mother a quick peck on the cheek, and dashed out of the door.

Johnny was leaning against the car, smoking. As

he looked up, Jennifer made sure she slowed her hurried steps to a nonchalant saunter.

'Hello, gorgeous,' he greeted her. Jennifer felt a thrill run through her as his gaze travelled lazily up and down her body from head to toe, but she refused to show it.

Johnny had kept her waiting for two months before he finally sent a note to the hospital asking her out. Not even asking, come to think of it. More like telling her he would be in Flint Terrace on Friday at seven o'clock, and she should be ready.

No one had ever treated her like that, and she'd had a good mind to throw the note straight in the bin. That would teach him a lesson. And she might have done, if she hadn't been so desperate to see him again.

But that didn't mean she had to give him an easy time.

'You're late,' she snapped.

'I had a bit of business to attend to. But I'm worth waiting for, ain't I?'

She lifted her chin. She'd waited long enough. 'I'll be the judge of that. Where are we going?'

'It's a surprise.' He opened the passenger door for her, and she climbed in.

'I've got to be home by eleven.'

'You're joking?' He grimaced. 'Blimey, it's hardly worth going out. Most places don't get going till well after midnight.'

'I know, but my dad will go mad if I'm not back.'

'Can't have that, can we?'

She glanced across at Johnny's smiling face as

he started up the car. Was he making fun of her? she wondered. She suddenly felt stupidly young and gauche.

She felt even more gauche when it turned out he was taking her to the Café de Paris, just off Piccadilly Circus.

'I wish you'd told me, I would have dressed up!' Jennifer grumbled, as they made their way down the darkened staircase towards the basement ballroom.

'You look fine to me.'

'Do I?' She didn't feel fine. She was wearing her best dress, red with a black flower print, and her high heels, and her dark hair was caught up with a clip on top of her head. But she looked like a child next to all the elegant ladies in their cocktail dresses and diamonds.

'You're young and you're beautiful. That's something no amount of couture frocks and posh jewellery can match.'

'Do you really think so?' Jennifer said, pleased.

'Trust me. You could be wearing an old sack and you'd still be the loveliest girl in this place.' He held out his arm to her. 'Let's go and have some fun, shall we?'

Jennifer had never been anywhere like it. It gave her a thrill when the maître d' recognised Johnny and greeted him like an old friend. He showed them to the best table in the room, overlooking the dance floor. A band was playing, and some couples had already taken to the floor. The whole place reeked of expensive perfume and money.

Jennifer tried not to stare but she couldn't help it. Johnny, by contrast, seemed perfectly at home

159

as he summoned the waiter and ordered champagne.

'That's all right with you, isn't it?' he asked.

'Of course.' Jennifer affected a nonchalant shrug. She'd never tasted champagne before, she wasn't even allowed to drink. But after Johnny's comments about her being young she didn't want to admit it.

She watched as the waiter popped the cork from the bottle and poured the champagne into fancy flat glasses. The bubbles rose like tiny strings of beads to pop delicately at the surface. It looked as if it would be sweet, like lemonade.

She took her first mouthful, and nearly choked at the dry taste fizzing in her mouth. She swallowed it quickly but it went down the wrong way. Tears streamed down her face as she coughed and spluttered.

Johnny laughed. 'Serves you right. You ain't supposed to guzzle it like dandelion and burdock, girl. Sip it slowly or you'll be under the table in no time.'

'I know that!' Jennifer snapped back, to hide her embarrassment. 'It just went down the wrong way, that's all.' She wiped her eyes with the back of her hand and hoped her mascara hadn't run down her face.

After her initial embarrassment, Jennifer started to relax and enjoy herself. Johnny seemed to know everyone. Every minute or two, someone glided up to the table to talk to him. Once, he excused himself and followed a man to the door. Jennifer watched them standing in the doorway, their heads together in hushed conversation. How rude to walk away and leave her, she thought. If the champagne hadn't worked its way through her limbs, making her feel light-headed, she would have been quite cross about it.

Johnny returned after five minutes. 'Sorry about that,' he said.

'Who was he?'

'Just an acquaintance with a business proposition.'

'What kind of business are you in?'

He smiled and poured her another glass of champagne. 'You ask a lot of questions, don't you? If you must know, I'm in the supply and demand business.'

'What's that supposed to mean?'

'It means people want things, and I get them.'

'What kind of things?'

He leaned forward and took the glass out of her hand. 'Let's dance,' he said, leading her on to the floor.

Johnny was a good dancer, not at all clumsy like the young men Jennifer usually danced with. She felt safe in his arms as he glided her around the floor with style and self-assurance. She noticed several of the other women sending him interested looks, and she smirked back at them, feeling like the cat who had got the cream.

They sat down again, and Johnny signalled for more champagne, and the menu. Jennifer wasn't sure she would be able to eat, until she read what was on offer. Foie gras, lamb chops, steak – food she hadn't ever seen in her life, even before rationing started.

'Can I really have anything I like?' she asked,

wide-eyed, forgetting to be sophisticated.

'Anything you like.'

'But where do they manage to find all this food? Don't they have rationing here?'

'Perhaps they know the right people.'

Jennifer stared at him, mystified. She felt sure he was being clever, but the champagne had addled her brain and her thinking was fuzzier than it might have been.

She ordered oysters, and Johnny ordered Steak Diane cooked rare, whatever that meant.

'Do you like oysters?' he asked.

'I've never tried them,' Jennifer admitted. 'But I've always wanted to. Film stars eat them, you know.'

'Is that right?'

She still wasn't sure if he was making fun of her. But she was having such a nice time, she really didn't care.

She gazed at Johnny across the table, the candlelight flickering on his rugged features. No one could call him handsome, but there was definitely something compelling about him.

Emboldened by another glass of champagne, she decided to ask more questions.

'Why aren't you fighting, Johnny?'

'I'm an invalid.'

She squinted at him across the table. 'You look all right to me.'

His mouth curved. 'Thank you very much. But if you must know, I have an ulcer.'

'I'm surprised you can manage champagne and steak, in that case.'

He winked at her. 'I won't tell if you don't.'

She frowned at him. Once again, she had the feeling he was teasing her. 'How old are you?' she asked.

'Twenty-eight.'

Ten years older than she was. Her dad would have a fit.

He seemed to guess her thoughts. 'Too old for you?' he asked, his eyes meeting hers over the rim of his glass.

She pulled herself together, rearranging her face into what she hoped was a suitably casual expression. 'As a matter of fact, I've always preferred older men,' she said.

'Is that right?'

She nodded. 'They're so much more sophis–sophisticated,' she struggled over the word. Why wouldn't it come out properly? 'They know how to treat a lady.' She hiccuped delicately.

'You sound as if you speak from experience?' he said, his dark brows lifting.

'You'd be surprised,' she said, hoping she sounded suitably mysterious.

Their dinner arrived, brought to their table under great big silver domes which the waiters removed with a flourish. As it turned out, oysters weren't nearly as delicious as she'd imagined. She couldn't think why film stars made so much fuss about them. She'd rather have pie and mash any day, although she didn't dare admit that to Johnny as she swallowed them down.

They talked as they ate. Johnny made her laugh with his outrageous stories. He was as big a gossip as she was, Jennifer was pleased to discover. It made a change to find someone who knew how to make interesting conversation. Most of the boys she usually went out with were only interested in making saucy remarks and finding out what they could get away with before she batted them off.

Afterwards she wanted to dance again, but he said they had to go home.

'You've got to be tucked up in bed by eleven, remember?' Johnny reminded her.

As they drove home, Jennifer slumped in the passenger seat, feeling decidedly odd. There was a tight pain in her temples, as if she was wearing a hat two sizes too small. She could barely focus on her own hands, knotted in her lap. She'd also lost her hairclip along the way, but she couldn't remember where. And it was her favourite, too.

Johnny parked the car around the corner, as she'd asked him to. 'All right?' he said. 'Are you sure you can find your way home? You don't want me to drop you at your door?'

She shook her head, and her eyeballs swivelled painfully in their sockets. 'My dad would go mad.'

'I don't think he's going to be very impressed in any case, seeing you in that state.'

'I don't feel very well,' Jennifer confessed. 'I think it must have been those oysters.'

'It must have been,' Johnny agreed. But there it was again, that mocking smile. He'd been making fun of her all evening, she realised.

Usually she would have come back at him with some sharp retort, or even got in first and given him the brush-off. But something, whether it was the oysters or the champagne, or just the realisation that she liked him more than any man she'd ever met, took away all her pride.

'You're not going to take me out again, are you?' she said sadly.

'Whatever gave you that idea?'

'I don't know.' She lifted her shoulders in a gloomy shrug. 'But I know you think I'm not old or sophisticated enough for you.'

'Is that right?'

He was smiling again. Before she knew what she was doing, Jennifer lunged forward and kissed him full on the lips. She sensed his hesitation for a moment before he kissed her back. His tongue slipped between her lips, hungry and exploring.

When he pulled away, his eyes were glittering. 'What was that for?'

'To prove I'm not a little girl.'

He grew serious. 'You don't want to make promises you can't keep,' he said in a low voice.

'Who says I can't keep them?'

Johnny smiled, but this time there was nothing mocking about his smile. It was that wolfish grin that had made her heart stop the first time she'd seen it.

'In that case,' he said, 'I reckon we'll definitely be seeing each other again.'

Chapter Eighteen

'And did I tell you about the band? Snakehips Johnson, the bandleader's called. He's famous, so Johnny said. Been on the BBC and everything. Honestly, Cis, I've never heard music like it. And the way he moved–'

'So you've said,' Cissy sighed.

It was Monday morning, and they were walking to the hospital together, up Old Ford Road. It wasn't yet seven o'clock, but the sun was already high in the sky, promising another bright, hot July day.

'And the champagne ... did I tell you about that? I had three glasses, and they went straight to my head! You would have laughed if you'd been there,' Jennifer giggled. 'And the oysters! They were so expensive, but Johnny insisted on ordering them, just because I said I wanted to try them...'

She didn't add that they'd tasted horrible, or that she had been up most of the night being ill.

She didn't mention she'd made a fool of herself by lunging at Johnny for a messy kiss either. There were some things even her best friend didn't need to know.

Besides, she wanted Cissy to be impressed. Although she wasn't showing much sign of it at the moment. She was listening to Jennifer's stories with an indifferent expression, as if going up west and drinking champagne was something that happened to them every day.

'Talk about how the other half lives!' she tried again. 'There were so many rich and famous people there. And Johnny seemed to know them all. They kept stopping at our table to talk to him, and of course he introduced me... I felt like royalty, I really did!'

'I know, you told me.'

Jennifer glanced sideways at Cissy's face, and wondered if perhaps she'd gone on about it too much. After all, this was the third time she'd told her friend about it since Saturday morning. But then, she'd listened to Cissy going on about her Paul for the past year, and that was a lot less interesting than the tale Jennifer had to tell.

Perhaps Cissy was jealous. After all, she had never been to the Café de Paris, or drunk champagne. And Paul Maynard could barely afford the bus fare up west, let alone a swanky car!

'What's the matter with you?' she asked. 'I thought you'd be pleased for me?'

Cissy was silent for a moment. Then she said, 'So how has he come by all this money?'

'I told you, Johnny's a businessman. Supply and demand.'

'What does that mean?'

'It's complicated. You wouldn't understand,' Jennifer replied airily. She wasn't about to admit that Johnny hadn't told her.

'I don't reckon your dad would understand, either.'

Jennifer sighed. 'You sound like my mum!'

'I'm just saying, I don't think your dad would

approve of you courting an older man.'

'He's not that much older,' Jennifer defended. 'Besides, the King of England could come courting me and my dad wouldn't approve! Honestly, Cis, I thought you'd be pleased for me. You're always on at me to find myself a boyfriend.'

'That depends on the boyfriend, doesn't it?' Cissy muttered.

'What's that supposed to mean?'

'Couldn't you find yourself a nice young man, Jen?'

Like yours, you mean? Jennifer thought sourly. 'Johnny *is* nice.'

'If you say so.'

'You don't know him.'

'Neither do you.'

They walked the rest of Old Ford Road in silence, Jennifer seething with resentment. Why did Cissy have to act as if she was better than her, just because her boyfriend was in the Royal Navy?

Jennifer had been so looking forward to telling her friend all about her big night – it had always been part of the fun for her, sharing all the details. But then Cissy had taken the wind right out of her sails on Saturday afternoon by rushing round with a letter she'd had from Paul. Jennifer's mum and dad and brother had been there, and Elsie Caldwell had poured Cissy a cup of tea and sat her down at the table and soon the whole family was listening agog as she read how Paul's convoy had narrowly escaped being sunk by a German U-boat in the Atlantic.

They'd all lapped it up, sitting around the table, listening to her eagerly.

'Your young man's a hero,' Alec Caldwell declared. 'He deserves a medal, I reckon.'

Jennifer had listened and tried to smile and looked interested, but inside she was cross because she knew she would never be able to boast about Johnny to them. Cissy was right, her father would never be impressed by him, no matter how wealthy and successful he was.

It wasn't fair, she thought. She was sure Johnny would have willingly gone off and done his bit if he'd had the chance. It wasn't his fault he was an invalid.

The two girls didn't speak again until they said a curt goodbye to each other at the hospital gates and went off to their respective wards.

'I'll see you at lunchtime,' Cissy called out, but Jennifer was too cross to reply. She was still smarting after her friend's comments. Cissy might not approve of Johnny, but at least she could be pleased for Jennifer. She was supposed to be her best mate, after all, and best mates stuck together.

Walking on to the ward, she was greeted by a chorus of catcalls from the soldiers. A few weeks of rest, good food and nursing care had been enough to restore their spirits. Even though their injuries were still severe, they had started to behave like young men again, teasing and flirting with the nurses.

'Look out, lads, it's Vivien Leigh!'

'How's my favourite nurse this morning?'

'Looking lovely this morning, Nurse!'

Jennifer pretended to take no notice, but she couldn't help smiling to herself as she headed

169

down the ward.

But the smile was knocked off her face a moment later when Nurse Riley stepped out of the kitchen and confronted her.

'You're late,' she snapped. 'Get changed immediately and go and help the night staff clear away the breakfast. Then you can make a start on cleaning the ward. The floor will need polishing this morning.'

'Good morning to you, too,' Jennifer muttered, when Nurse Riley was safely out of earshot.

'Best to stay out of her way,' Daisy Bushell advised, coming up behind Jennifer. 'Miss Hanley's inspecting the ward first thing, and it's put everyone in an awful mood.'

'I wish she'd leave it to Matron,' Jennifer said. Miss Fox's daily visits to the ward were quite jolly in comparison to the Assistant Matron's weekly swoops.

Next to rinsing out the bedpans and scrubbing the blood off mackintosh sheets, polishing the floor had become one of Jennifer's least favourite jobs.

She and Daisy started by pushing all the beds from one side of the ward into the centre. Then came the strenuous use of the buffer, a block of wood on the end of a six-foot pole, with a piece of felt attached. Jennifer's job was to spatter polish over the floor, then swing the buffer from side to side, reversing down the ward. It was terribly cumbersome, and when her arms began to ache, the pole slipped and the buffer collided with the soldiers' beds, rattling the frames and making them groan and swear in pain.

170

'Oi! Watch what you're doing with that bloody thing!'

'Christ Almighty, don't you think I'm in enough pain without you making it worse?'

'I can't help it,' Jennifer shot back. 'You should try, it's more difficult than it looks.'

'You there! What do you think you're doing?'

Just her luck, at that moment Miss Hanley rounded the corner with Sister Holmes and Nurse Riley in tow. In the month she had been there, Jennifer was sure Miss Hanley hadn't taken the trouble to learn her name. She was always 'you there' or 'wretched girl'.

'What do you think you're doing, disturbing the patients?'

As if the Assistant Matron's bellowing like a wounded bull wasn't disturbing them, Jennifer thought crossly. But she'd learned it was never a good idea to answer Miss Hanley back, no matter how much Jennifer might feel she was in the right. So she stood and waited as the Assistant Matron bore down on her from the other end of the ward, marching like a drill sergeant, arms swinging, feet stomping.

Jennifer noticed the patch of polish on the floor a second before Miss Hanley's sturdy brogue landed in it. She tried to cry out but shock rendered her speechless as the Assistant Matron's foot slithered away from under her. She caught a disturbing glimpse of directoire knickers as Miss Hanley's legs went up in the air and she landed heavily in a heap at Jennifer's feet.

In the fuss that followed, with nurses rushing to haul her upright, Jennifer could only stare down

171

at her shoes and fight the urge to laugh. She knew she would suffer for it, but somehow she still couldn't stop herself. Her eyes watered from the effort of keeping her face straight. It didn't help that the soldiers were all roaring at the sight of the Assistant Matron sprawled on her well-upholstered backside.

When Jennifer finally risked a glance upwards, Miss Hanley was on her feet again, the picture of wounded, red-faced pride.

Nurse Riley appeared at Jennifer's shoulder. 'Make yourself scarce,' she hissed.

'But I haven't finished—'

'Go. Now.'

She didn't need telling twice. Jennifer fled from the ward, down the passageway to the only place she knew no one would look for her – Mr Chandler's room.

Philip Stuart Chandler was the name of the airman. Jennifer had read it on his notes. She also knew that he was twenty-three years old, a flight sergeant from Hampshire, stationed on the south coast. His next-of-kin were his parents, Eileen and Donald Chandler. She also knew that he had lost three fingers from his left hand and most of the flesh from his face and upper body when his aircraft caught fire.

Jennifer had found out a lot about him in the times she'd taken refuge in his room. She often went there to escape when Sister Holmes was in one of her moods. She liked the darkness, the peace and quiet, and the unhurried sound of Flight Sergeant Chandler's breathing. Sometimes she would sit at his bedside and stare at him, wondering what he had once looked like.

She went to his bedside and picked up his wrist, feeling the steady beat of his pulse beneath her fingers. His right hand was surprisingly un-blemished, with a fine network of dark hairs on his strong forearm.

'Hello?'

Jennifer dropped his wrist and jumped back at the sound of a muffled voice coming from the bed. She'd wondered so often what his voice might sound like, she almost thought she'd imagined it.

But no, the figure in the bed was stirring, shifting against the pillows.

'Hello? Are you there? I know you're there, I can smell your perfume. Who are you?'

'I – I don't know. I mean – I'm not supposed to be here ... wait there, I'll fetch someone...'

She fled the room, straight into the arms of Miss Hanley, who was coming up the corridor with Sister Holmes.

'You again!' The Assistant Matron glared at her, but Jennifer was too flustered to care.

'He's awake!' she blurted out, interrupting Miss Hanley. 'Mr Chandler's woken up, and he – he's talking!'

Sister Holmes stared at her as if she were quite mad. 'Well, of course he's woken up,' she said. 'Mr Cooper has reduced his sedation. We're bringing him round. Although what you were doing in his room I have no idea,' she added sternly.

Jennifer lingered in the passageway outside Mr Chandler's room, listening as Sister Holmes spoke quietly to him, explaining where he was and what had happened to him. Their voices were so low she couldn't hear exactly what was being said, and she could only imagine how Philip Chandler was taking the news.

She ducked back into the sluice out of sight as Sister Holmes came out, half closing the door behind her. It was then that Jennifer remembered the duster she'd dropped as she fled Philip Chandler's room. She only hoped Sister hadn't spotted it, or she would be in real trouble.

She made sure the coast was clear, then opened the door as quietly as she could and tiptoed across the room to retrieve the duster. But as she was bending down to pick it up from under the bed, a voice suddenly said, 'It's you again.'

Jennifer straightened up slowly, the duster in her hand. She didn't speak.

'I know you're there. I can hear you breathing.'

Jennifer cleared her throat nervously. 'I – I just came to fetch this.' She held up the duster, then realised that he couldn't see it. 'Sorry for disturbing you.'

'That's all right. You've been in here quite often, haven't you?'

'How did you know?'

'I recognise your perfume. I thought I was dreaming it, but now I know it was real. You're real.'

There were footsteps coming up the passageway. 'I have to go,' Jennifer said. 'I'm not supposed to be in here.'

'Why not?'

Sister Holmes was calling her name now. 'I've got to go, or I really will be in trouble.'

She'd reached the door when he said, 'Wait.'

She paused, her hand on the doorknob. 'What?'

'What is that perfume?'

Jennifer smiled, in spite of herself. 'Evening in Paris.'

'Evening in Paris,' he repeated softly. 'I'll remember that.'

Chapter Nineteen

'Honestly, I've never seen her like this. She's usually the last person to lose her head over a man, but she's fallen for him hook, line and sinker. It's like he's cast a spell over her, or something...'

Eve and Cissy sat together in the small area off the Emergency Treatment Room, making up the dressings. It was the first job in Casualty, every morning.

'I'm not saying there's anything wrong with this Johnny, I'm just saying she should look before she leaps for a change. Although, of course, you can't tell Jen anything...' Cissy continued, snipping away at a large roll of gauze. 'But there's definitely something not quite right about him. I mean, where does he get all that money from? A businessman, Jen calls him. Funny business, if you ask me!'

Eve made what she hoped was a suitably sympathetic noise as she folded a piece of lint and packed it into the drum. She couldn't think of anything useful or interesting to say, but just listening seemed to be enough for Cissy when she was in one of her talkative moods.

'I'm sure she thinks I'm jealous,' she said. 'But what do I have to be jealous of, when I've got my Paul?'

'You're just worried about her, that's all,' Eve put in.

'Exactly!' Cissy nodded. 'I'm worried about her. You've hit the nail right on the head there, Evie.'

Evie. It was the first time anyone had called her that, and Eve savoured it. Anyone listening to them now might even think they were friends, she thought. Two friends gossiping together, the way Cissy and Jennifer gossiped.

'How is your Paul?' She chose her next topic carefully, not wanting to ruin the moment.

But she knew she was on safe ground with Cissy's boyfriend. He was all she ever wanted to talk about. 'I had another letter from him this morning,' she said. 'I brought it with me, look.' She pulled the blue envelope from inside the bib of her apron. 'I always keep his letters next to my heart,' she sighed. 'Would you like me to read it to you?'

Eve glanced nervously at the door. 'I'm not sure if we should...' she whispered. But Cissy was already pulling the letter out of the envelope and unfolding it.

Eve sat rolling bits of cotton wool into swabs on her knees as Cissy read out a long section of Paul's letter. It was difficult to make out what he was talking about half the time as there were so many names Eve didn't know, but that didn't matter. She felt as if she were being given a

176

glimpse into a new and fascinating world, full of love and romance and fun. She was sure Cissy's life must be every bit as exciting as any novel.

Halfway through her letter, Cissy stopped abruptly and said, 'Are you sure you don't mind me reading this?'

'Of course not? Why should I?'

'I dunno ... Jen always says I go on about him too much. I know I'm probably boring...'

'Not at all, I like hearing about it,' Eve assured her, and meant every word.

Cissy sent her a considering look. 'You know, you're a much better listener than Jen. I know she's my best mate, but between you and me, she only stops talking about herself long enough to draw breath!'

'I much prefer listening to talking,' Eve replied truthfully. 'Carry on, anyway – what else does Paul say?'

They spent the next ten minutes dissecting the contents of his letter, looking for hidden meanings behind his words. Eve was astonished at how much Cissy could read into a simple letter. She became quite giddy with it, and Eve was pleased to be taken into her confidence.

So pleased that she didn't hesitate later when Cissy asked her to treat a young boy whose scalp was crawling with lice.

'Be a mate?' Cissy had begged, and Eve was happy to oblige. As far as she was concerned, she really was Cissy's friend after their talk that morning.

But then, of course, when it was time for their break, Cissy immediately rushed off to join

Jennifer for another of their private conversations. All Cissy's resentment against her friend seemed to disappear into thin air as soon as they saw each other. Eve watched them walking together with their arms firmly linked, laughing over something, and tried not to mind. She wished Jennifer would be as friendly towards her as Cissy was, then perhaps she would be allowed to join in. She would like nothing more than to walk with them, her arms linked in theirs.

She returned to the Casualty Hall to find Oliver Stanton there, waiting with an empty wheelchair. She'd seen him a few times over the past two weeks, but only to nod to from a distance. Now he was blocking her way, and she would have no option but to speak to him. As Eve approached, she thought how very different he looked in his brown porter's overalls, his tousled fair hair shorn neatly over his ears.

He was staring out of the window across the courtyard, deep in thought. Eve was debating with herself whether she should speak to him when he suddenly looked up and saw her.

'Hello,' he greeted her. His faraway look was suddenly gone, replaced by a genuine smile.

'Hello.' Suddenly self-conscious, Eve searched for something to say. 'You've had your hair cut,' she blurted out finally.

He reached up to touch his bare ears. 'Mr Hopkins prefers all his new recruits to look smart,' he said.

'Are you – um – enjoying your job?' Eve asked.

'It's – interesting.' He chose his words carefully. 'I suppose it's not like being an art student in

178

Paris, though?'

His smile faded. 'No,' he said. 'No, it certainly isn't.'

'Stanton!' a voice roared out from the other side of the Casualty Hall. They both looked round to see another porter, George Geoffries, standing in the doorway. 'When you've finished your mothers' meeting, there's a patient waiting to go up to the ward,' he called out. 'If you can spare the time, that is,' he added with a nasty glance at Eve.

'I'm on my way.' Oliver took a step back and manoeuvred the wheelchair round. 'I'd best get on,' he muttered. 'Don't want to upset anyone, do I?'

Eve watched him follow George out of the Casualty Hall. Neither of them spoke.

She was still watching them when Cissy came up behind her. 'Were you talking to that porter?' she asked.

Eve started, blushing guiltily. Cissy sounded just like Aunt Freda. 'I wasn't doing any harm,' she said quickly. 'He spoke to me, so I answered him.'

'All the same, you shouldn't have anything to do with him. You know what he is, don't you?'

Eve frowned. 'What?'

Cissy leaned forward. 'A conchie.' She hissed the word, her lips curling as if she could hardly bear to say it.

Eve stared at her blankly. 'What's that?'

'Honestly, don't you know anything?' Cissy looked incredulous. 'He's a conscientious objector. That's why he's been sent to work here, because he's refused to join up and fight.'

179

'Why?'

'Because he's a coward!' Cissy spat. 'Honestly, I can't even stand to be near him. I think it's a disgrace that my Paul is out there, risking his life in the service of his country while *he's* swanning around here. He makes me sick. And I'm not the only one who thinks like that either,' she added. 'None of the porters can stand him. They wouldn't work with him if they didn't have to.' She tapped Eve on one shoulder with her fingertip. 'You take my advice. Don't have anything to do with him if you know what's good for you.'

Eve thought about the contemptuous way the porter had shouted at him, and the look on Oliver's face as he'd followed the other man outside. Poor Oliver, she thought. She understood all about being an outsider.

Chapter Twenty

'Not again!'

Dora put down her forceps as Jennifer Caldwell's laughter shrieked down the ward. She had been trying to remove fragments of shattered glass from a wounded soldier's face, and it wasn't helped by the VAD flirting on the other side of the screens.

She stood up and pulled aside the curtain. 'Caldwell?'

Jennifer jumped up from where she had been perched on the edge of a patient's bed. She

180

looked as if butter wouldn't melt. 'Yes, Staff?'

'Go about your work quietly, please. Just because it's Sister's day off, that's no reason to go wild.'

'Yes, Staff. Sorry, Staff.'

There it was again, that look of wide-eyed innocence. Dora knew very well she would be sitting on the patient's bed laughing again before she even had time to pull the screen closed.

'Leave her be, Nurse,' the soldier said, when she went back to her work. 'She's just having a bit of fun.'

'She's not here to have fun,' Dora muttered.

'She's a tonic.'

'She's a nuisance.' Only the previous night, Jennifer had managed to catch a blackout curtain on a gas boiler and nearly set fire to the ward.

The girl simply didn't think. Well, not about her duties anyway. She was too busy flirting, or admiring herself. Dora had even caught her gazing at her own reflection in the bathroom taps.

'The boys like her,' the soldier said.

'Only because she spends all her time flirting.'

'Exactly. That's what we need, especially the lads who've been badly injured. Having a pretty girl giving them the eye – well, it makes 'em feel more normal, if you see what I mean. She makes us feel like men, not circus freaks.'

'I suppose you're right.' Dora was thoughtful. At least that was a point in Jennifer's favour. Unlike Daisy Bushell, who wilted like a delicate flower at the first sight of an injury, Jennifer hardly seemed to notice. Probably because she was too preoccupied with her own appearance,

Dora thought sourly.

She tried to take the soldier's comments into account, but her temper snapped when she heard Jennifer's voice coming from Mr Chandler's room when she was supposed to be doing the beds and turning the patients with Daisy Bushell.

It was lucky Sister Holmes wasn't here, Dora thought. She'd already reprimanded Jennifer three times for straying into Mr Chandler's room. And those were only the times she'd caught her. Dora knew that in the month since Philip Chandler had regained consciousness, Jennifer had sneaked in to see him nearly every day.

She paused outside the door, listening. 'Go on,' she heard him say. 'Tell me.'

'Have a guess.'

'Blonde?'

'Wrong.'

'Brunette, then. I thought so. You sound like a brunette.'

She heard Jennifer's delighted laugh. 'And how do brunettes sound?'

'Like you. What colour are your eyes? No, don't tell me – blue?'

Dora flung open the door and Jennifer started to her feet, so quickly she upset a glass on Mr Chandler's locker.

'What have you been told about coming in here?' Dora demanded.

'I–' Jennifer started to say, but Philip Chandler spoke up for her.

'Don't be too hard on her, Nurse. I like a bit of company.'

Dora ignored him and turned to Jennifer. 'I'll

speak to you outside,' she said.

Jennifer followed her into the passageway and Dora closed the door behind them. 'You know only trained nurses are allowed in the private rooms,' she said.

'You heard what he said, Staff. He likes me being there.'

'And what's that got to do with anything?'

'I feel sorry for him. It must be lonely for him, lying there for all those weeks with no one to talk to. His parents hardly ever visit, and his fiancée's stationed in Scotland so she can't come to see him–'

'That really isn't your concern,' Dora said. 'You're here to follow orders. Besides, there's enough work to be done on the ward without you sneaking off, leaving it to everyone else.'

'I wouldn't have to sneak off if I was allowed to special him.'

Dora stared at her, and for a moment she wondered if she'd heard correctly. 'What did you say?'

'I was thinking – perhaps I should be allowed to help nurse him? He obviously likes me, and–'

'Only qualified nurses are allowed to special private patients,' Dora cut her off.

'Yes, but I could learn, couldn't I?'

There was no faulting the girl's confidence, Dora thought. 'You really think you could do the job of a trained nurse?'

Jennifer stared straight back at her. 'I'm sure I could if someone taught me,' she said.

If she hadn't looked so insolent Dora might not have done what she did next.

'Very well,' she said. 'Since you're so keen to learn, you can start by helping me to change Mr Chandler's dressings. Please prepare the trolley.'

That shook her. Jennifer's mouth fell open. 'Me, Staff?'

'Yes, you, Caldwell. You seem to think you're capable of doing some real nursing, so let's see, shall we?'

Dora saw the look of panic in Jennifer's eyes, and felt a brief moment of triumph. That would teach her, she thought.

But then Jennifer squared her shoulders and lifted her head up. 'Right away, Staff,' she said.

Now it was Dora's turn to be open-mouthed as she watched the girl walk off down the ward. What had she done? All she'd wanted was to shake her a little, take away some of her overconfidence. VADs weren't supposed to change dressings. Especially not for the likes of Philip Chandler. His injuries were so horrific, even some of the trained nurses quailed at the prospect.

But Dora couldn't back down now, and she suspected Jennifer wouldn't either. It was as if they were locked in a terrible game of dare, and neither of them wanted to be the first to admit defeat.

Jennifer was shaking as she pushed the trolley towards Philip Chandler's room.

You've done it now, my girl, she thought. You and your big mouth. Why had she had to answer Nurse Riley back like that? She was right, Jennifer had no business being in Philip Chandler's room. She had been defiant, and she should be punished.

184

She'd only gone in because she felt sorry for him. The other nurses all passed him by. They didn't think it hurt him, but Jennifer knew it did.

She couldn't imagine what gory horrors lay under those bandages, and she didn't want to know. But now, thanks to her own stupidity and cheek, she was going to find out.

Nurse Riley was waiting for her outside Philip Chandler's room. For a moment, Jennifer thought she was going to say it was all a trick and Jennifer didn't have to do it after all. But all Nurse Riley said was, 'You took your time.'

'Sorry, Sister.'

Jennifer met her eye. She could tell Nurse Riley was waiting for her to back down, to say she couldn't do it. All she had to do was say the words. But she was determined not to give Nurse Riley the satisfaction of seeing how terrified she was.

They entered the room together, Jennifer pushing the trolley. As she took her place beside Nurse Riley, Philip Chandler's head turned towards her.

'Evening in Paris,' he murmured.

'I beg your pardon?' Nurse Riley said.

'Jen– Miss Caldwell's perfume.'

'Is that right?' Nurse Riley's eyebrows rose. 'Miss Caldwell should know better than to wear scent on the ward,' she said sternly.

'Sorry, Staff,' Jennifer mumbled.

'I like it,' Mr Chandler defended her. 'It's how I know she's close by.'

Jennifer blushed, feeling the hardness of Nurse Riley's stare. It seemed to bore right into the side

185

of her head.

'We have come to change your dressings, Mr Chandler,' Nurse Riley told him.

'Both of you?'

'Miss Caldwell is going to assist me.'

Jennifer couldn't see the airman's face under the bandages, but she could sense his panic. 'I don't want her to see me,' he said.

'It'll be all right,' Jennifer reassured him, ignoring the stony look Nurse Riley sent her.

All the same, she had to steel herself as the staff nurse started to peel away the dressings. The last bandages came away, and Jennifer forced herself not to cry out at the sight of the hideous mass of swollen, burned flesh that had once been one side of Philip's face. Bile rose in her throat and she wanted to turn away, but she knew if she did she would never find the courage to look at him again. So she forced herself to stare unblinking as she passed the instruments to Nurse Riley.

'You've gone very quiet. Is it that bad?' He was trying to sound light-hearted, but she could sense the desperation behind his words.

'I've seen worse,' she said, hoping she sounded just as light-hearted. She knew his sight hadn't recovered enough for him to see her, but she also knew he was sensitive enough to read the slightest quaver in her voice. All the time her knees were pressed tight together to stop herself from swaying.

'That's a relief. I thought you'd fainted.' He addressed himself to Nurse Riley. 'She must have a strong stomach, eh, Nurse?'

'Yes,' Nurse Riley replied. 'Yes, I suppose she

must.' Then, just as Jennifer was feeling proud of herself, she snapped, 'The tulle-grass dressing, if you please, Caldwell.'

It took about twenty minutes to change Mr Chandler's dressings, although it seemed like a lifetime to Jennifer. But at last it was over, and Nurse Riley told her to clear up the trolley.

'And then make a cup of tea for both of us and bring it to the office,' she added. 'I think you've earned it, don't you?'

That was it. There was no praise, no thank you for the twenty minutes of gut-churning terror Jennifer had endured. But she still found herself smiling with pride as she headed for the kitchen.

If it was a test, she had a feeling she might have passed.

Chapter Twenty-One

It was a quiet Thursday morning in the Casualty Hall, and Eve and Cissy had been left in charge. Sister Dawson was in the Treatment Room, helping Dr McKay stitch up a man who'd fallen off his bicycle, while Nurse Kowalski was in Outpatients with Mr Cooper.

Thankfully, everyone seemed to be too busy enjoying the warm late July weather to come in with their various aches and pains. The rows of wooden benches were empty, except for a middle-aged man dozing in the corner. Eve sat at a table, checking a pile of surgical gloves for holes, while Cissy perched behind the booking-in desk, telling her all about a film she and Jennifer had been to see the previous night.

'It's about a woman who marries a mysterious widower and goes to live in his big house in the country,' she said. 'But there's a horrible old housekeeper who wants to get rid of her, because she's obsessed with his first wife.'

'What happens then?' Eve asked, blowing into a glove and holding it up.

'Oh, all sorts of things. The housekeeper – Mrs Danvers – makes the girl's life an utter misery, and the poor wretch just takes it. If it was me, I would have told the old witch to pack her bags and get out the minute I arrived – oh, look, here's the conchie,' Cissy groaned. 'What does he want, I wonder?'

Eve glanced up to see Oliver making his way towards them.

'I'm looking for Dr Jameson,' he said.

'Well, you won't find him here.'

'Do you know where he is? I have a message for him.'

'How should I know? I'm not his social secretary.'

Eve cleared her throat. 'I think he's doing his rounds,' she said quietly. 'He should be back in the next half an hour.'

'Thanks.' Oliver shot Cissy a dirty look then left, slamming the door behind him.

'You didn't have to be so rude to him,' Eve protested mildly.

Cissy shrugged. 'I've got no time for cowards.'

'You don't know he's a coward.'

'Then why isn't he fighting with the rest of our boys?'

Eve was silent. She'd been reading up about conscientious objectors in the library, and even though she knew now there was more to it than cowardice, she didn't want to start debating it with Cissy. Eve didn't want to antagonise her, especially when she probably wouldn't listen anyway.

'I hope you're not sticking up for him?' Cissy's eyes narrowed accusingly.

'Of course not,' Eve mumbled.

'I'm glad to hear it. Because I'm not sure I could be friends with someone who sticks up for his sort.'

Eve picked up the next glove. The truth was, she felt desperately sorry for Oliver. He always looked so forlorn, and she knew from listening to Cissy that he was having a hard time settling in at the hospital. Eve of all people knew how hard it was to be an outsider.

But at the same time, she couldn't risk her own position. Cissy might not be her friend, but she was the closest Eve had ever had to one, and she didn't want to risk that. Even if it did make her uneasy to see Oliver treated so badly.

'Anyway,' Cissy continued, 'as I was saying, about this film. It turns out the so-called perfect first wife was actually...'

Eve never found out, because at that moment a roar went up from the far side of the Casualty Hall. The man in the corner went suddenly rigid, shot to his feet, then promptly collapsed into a heap on the floor.

189

Cissy let out a scream. By the time Eve had got to him, he was jerking and twitching like a puppet tugged by invisible strings. His eyes were rolling in their sockets, and flecks of spittle were forming at the corners of his mouth.

'He's having a fit,' she said to Cissy, who hovered anxiously over her.

'What shall we do?'

Eve unfastened the collar stud at his throat, trying to remember what they'd learned at their First Aid class. 'Fetch a pencil or something,' she said. 'We need to stop him biting his tongue.'

Cissy handed her a pencil, and Eve jammed it between the man's teeth.

'Go and get help,' she ordered. Cissy didn't move. She stood over them, her hands clasped in front of her ashen face, rigid with anxiety. 'Now!' Eve shouted.

The sound of her voice was enough to shock Cissy out of her stupor. She jerked into life and rushed off.

By the time she had returned a few minutes later with Dr McKay, the man had stopped twitching and fallen into a deep sleep. It was so deep, Eve feared he might be dead. But when she slipped her hand against his chest she could feel the steady thud of his heart under his shirt.

Dr McKay kneeled down to examine him. As he worked, he asked Eve lots of questions about what had happened.

'How long did the fit last?'

'A couple of minutes.' But it had felt like a lot longer. Almost a lifetime.

'Did he go completely rigid, or twitch? Was it all

over his body?'

Eve tried to think clearly. 'It was mainly his legs,' she recalled slowly.

'And he cried out,' Cissy put in, still standing at a safe distance. 'Really frightened us, it did.'

'I'm sure it must have been a very nasty shock.' Dr McKay finished examining him and strung his stethoscope around his neck. 'We'll have him admitted and see what we can find. Can you sort out the paperwork?' he asked Cissy.

Eve stared down at the man and chewed her lip. Now the emergency had passed, delayed shock began to settle in as she realised what she'd done.

Dr McKay seemed to guess her thoughts. 'You did the right thing, Miss Ainsley,' he said. 'Your prompt action may have helped save his life.'

Sister Dawson said something similar to her when she found out about it later. Eve was still in a state of trembling nerves as she tried to go about her duties, but Sister Dawson called her into her office and made her a cup of tea. Eve was so overwhelmed she could barely manage to drink it.

'Dr McKay tells me your quick thinking saved the day,' she said. 'Tell me, how did you know what to do?'

'We learned it at the First Aid class,' Eve said. Although she had never imagined putting her knowledge to any use.

'You clearly have an aptitude for it. And I've noticed you're very good with the patients, too.' Sister Dawson put down her teacup. 'I wonder, have you ever considered training as a nurse?'

Eve blinked at her. 'I'm sorry, I don't understand–'

'I think you should consider studying for the State Examination,' Helen Dawson said. 'Matron has just announced that official training is going to start again at the hospital, and I would like to recommend you as a student. It would mean joining us full-time and training for three years, but I believe it would be worth it. You have the makings of an excellent nurse, just the kind of girl the Nightingale needs. I could talk to Matron about it, if you'd like?'

Eve stared at her, dazed. She had never dared to imagine that anyone would offer her such a chance. It was like a dream come true. 'I – I don't know what to say,' she murmured.

'You like working here, don't you?'

'Yes, of course.' More than she had ever thought possible. She looked forward to the three days a week she could escape from her aunt's shop and come to work at the hospital. She enjoyed the work and loved meeting the people there so much, it was even worth all the extra hours she had to put in slaving over her sewing in the workshop. The idea of being allowed to come every day, of actually training and passing exams, was almost too wonderful to contemplate. It was as if someone had suddenly taken all her dearest wishes, wrapped them up in a parcel and presented them to her with a big bow on top.

But even in her joy, Eve could picture her aunt, sour as a crab apple, grasping fingers reaching out to snatch her wonderful gift away from her.

'I'm sorry, Sister,' she said. 'I can't. My aunt needs me at the shop.'

Sister Dawson frowned. 'But surely she could

find someone else to help her? I can't imagine she would refuse you the chance to better yourself.'

There was no point even asking Aunt Freda if she could train. Freda Ainsley would never have been able to countenance the idea of her niece pursuing anything that gave her pleasure.

But even Aunt Freda couldn't spoil the fact that Sister Dawson had thought Eve worthy of anything.

Have you ever considered training as a nurse ... you're just the kind of girl the Nightingale needs.

The words reached deep inside her, warming a frozen part of Eve's heart. It was rare that anyone ever called her anything but hopeless, shameful or useless, and it was all she could do not to cry.

Chapter Twenty-Two

Every morning on the Male Acute ward was the same. Sister Holmes would come on duty at eight o'clock and carry out her inspection, with Nurse Riley at her side and Jennifer and Daisy Bushell bringing up the rear.

At the end of each bed, Sister would stop and greet each patient with the same words.

'Good morning. How are we feeling today?'

To which the patient would dutifully reply, 'Very well, thank you, Sister,' or, sometimes, 'Not too bad, thank you.' They all knew better than to complain.

Sometimes Sister would fire a question at Nurse

Riley about what kind of night a patient had spent, or what they'd eaten for breakfast, or something to do with their bowels. And Nurse Riley would always have an answer for her, without even consulting the patient's notes. Jennifer had no idea how she did it. She must have a magical memory, she decided.

By the time they had finished touring the ward, the porter would have brought up the morning post, and Sister Holmes would hand it out. The soldiers always received their letters gratefully, and there was much laughter and chatter around the ward, and a few sniffed back tears as they read their messages from home and opened their gifts.

This August morning there was one letter left in Sister's hand when she'd finished going round the ward.

'This is for Mr Chandler.' She handed it to Jennifer. 'Take it to him, if you please, Caldwell.'

'Yes, Sister.'

Delivering Mr Chandler's post and cleaning his room were tasks Jennifer had been given ever since that day she had watched Nurse Riley change the airman's dressings. It wasn't exactly the special nursing she'd hoped for, but it was a gesture at least. And it gave her the chance to pass the time of day with him.

Not that anyone else envied her the job.

'Rather you than me,' Daisy Bushell whispered as she made her way down to Philip Chandler's room. Daisy still couldn't bring herself to look at him, especially now his dressings had been removed.

194

As far as Jennifer was concerned, Mr Chandler was looking a great deal better. She had grown used to seeing his swollen, misshapen face, covered in shiny pink skin, and what was left of his blurred, blunt features. Only his eyes were swathed in dressings as his sight still hadn't returned.

But his other senses more than made up for it. As usual, his head turned towards Jennifer as she entered the room. 'Ah, Evening in Paris.' He breathed in and then let out a sigh of satisfaction.

'Shh, don't let on. I've already had a telling-off from Sister about wearing perfume. Besides,' she added, 'I do have a name, you know.'

'Would you rather I called you Caldwell?' He imitated Sister Holmes's stern tone.

'I suppose not.'

'So is this a social visit?' he asked.

'As a matter of fact, Sister sent me,' Jennifer said. 'You have a letter and I'm to read it to you.'

'A letter, eh? I suppose it's another one from my mother. Honestly, I'm sure she does nothing but write letters all day.'

Jennifer smiled. Eileen Chandler was certainly prolific with her pen. Scarcely a day went by without another letter arriving for her 'darling Phil'. After reading all their news aloud to him, Jennifer almost felt as if she knew the family. She had actually started to look forward to finding out about Mrs Chandler's latest spat with her fellow members of the WVS, and how Philip's younger sister had got on in her tennis tournament.

'Not this time.' Jennifer studied the rounded handwriting on the blue envelope. 'It looks like

195

Laura's handwriting.'

Laura Turnbull was Philip Chandler's girlfriend in the WAAF. She wrote less than his mother, once a week if he was lucky. Her letters were less chatty too, although Philip said it was because they had to be careful not to give away too much information.

'For all we know, you could be a fifth columnist, Miss Caldwell!' he'd said.

Jennifer pulled a chair to his bedside, sat down and opened the envelope. The notepaper inside was tissue-thin so more pages could be packed in. But in this case there was only a single sheet.

A chill of foreboding brushed over Jennifer's skin as she started to read.

'"Dearest Phil... This is a very difficult letter, and one I never imagined I should write..."' She stopped, realising what was to come.

'Go on,' Philip said.

Jennifer hesitated. 'Perhaps I should get Sister or one of the other nurses to read this?'

'Just read it, for God's sake!'

Jennifer cleared her throat and read on. It was a beautifully written letter, full of sorrow, begging for forgiveness and understanding. Laura had done her best to cope, she said, but finally she realised she couldn't. Things had changed so much, his accident had altered their lives for ever, and she wasn't strong enough, brave enough, to face what must be faced.

Jennifer glanced at Philip. He lay back against the pillows, as still as a statue.

'Go on,' he said gruffly.

'I can't,' she said, putting down the letter. 'It

doesn't seem right.' She felt like an eavesdropper, listening in on a lovers' conversation.

'Please,' he said. 'I want to hear what she has to say.'

He listened impassively, but Jennifer could feel her own anger rising with every word. She had never heard such self-pitying nonsense in her life. How dare the girl say *their* lives had altered for ever? It was poor Philip whose life had been destroyed, not Laura's. And just when he needed her most, she had deserted him. She hadn't even bothered to visit him, to find out for herself whether she could cope or not.

By the end of the letter, Jennifer was thoroughly disgusted by the coward who signed herself, 'Your friend for ever, Laura'.

Philip Chandler was quiet for a moment. Then he said, 'Well, that's that, then.'

He sounded so forlorn, Jennifer's heart went out to him. 'It doesn't have to be,' she urged. 'I could help you write back to her, if you like?'

'And say what?'

'I don't know...' She tried to think. 'Perhaps if she came to see you, you could talk to her?'

'I don't want her to come here. I don't want her to see me like this.'

'But if she loves you–'

'I don't want her to see me!' he repeated. 'Can't you understand that? It's better this way, for all of us. I'd rather she ditched me now than stayed with me out of pity.'

'Why do you think she'd only stay out of pity?'

'What other reason could there be? I'm not the man she fell in love with am I? Do you think I want to spend the rest of my life hearing the tremor in her voice, feeling her shrinking away every time I try to hold her hand?'

'The way you look shouldn't matter, not if she loves you.'

'You've been reading too many fairy stories! This isn't *Beauty and the Beast*. I won't be transformed by love into a handsome prince. Oh, perhaps in time a clever surgeon might be able to do something for me, but they'll never be able to turn me back into the man I was. Better that Laura remembers me that way, than as the deformed freak I am now.'

'Don't say that!' Jennifer cried. 'You're not a freak.'

'Aren't I?' He turned on her. 'You think I don't know the other nurses are repelled by me? Just because I can't see them, doesn't mean I don't hear what they say. They can't stand to look at me.'

'I'm not repelled by you,' Jennifer said quietly.

'But you wouldn't walk down the street with me, would you? You wouldn't hold my hand while everyone stared and pointed?'

Jennifer was silent. He was right, she realised with shame. And if she saw him in the street she probably would be repelled by him too.

'You see?' Philip said bitterly. 'You can't blame Laura for feeling the way she does, and neither can I.'

'You're not a freak,' Jennifer insisted quietly.

'Aren't I?' She heard the angry challenge in his voice. 'Then prove it.'

'How?'

'Kiss me.'

She stared at him in horrified silence. 'I – I can't–'

'Of course you can't.' His voice was bitter. 'For all your fine words, when it comes down to it, you're just the same–'

He didn't finish his sentence. Before she could change her mind, Jennifer lunged forward and planted her lips on his mouth. For a split second she felt him go rigid with shock, then his instincts seemed to take over and he responded, the tension leaving him.

'What on earth is going on?' Jennifer pulled away sharply at the sound of Sister Holmes's voice. She stood in the doorway, arms folded, bristling with outrage. 'Caldwell! Explain yourself!'

Jennifer opened her mouth to speak, but Philip got in before her. 'It wasn't her fault, Sister. It was mine. I asked her to kiss me.'

Sister ignored him, her furious gaze still fixed on Jennifer. 'My office,' she hissed. 'At once!'

'I don't believe it,' Cissy said.

'Nor can I,' Jennifer admitted with a grin. 'Honestly, Cis, I thought I was out on my ear for sure!'

Cissy shook her head. 'You must be the only girl in the Nightingale who could be caught kissing a patient and end up with a promotion!'

'I know!' Jennifer laughed. 'I'm still trying to take it in.'

She'd been convinced she was for the high jump when Sister Holmes marched her into her office. But instead of dismissing her, Sister had offered her the chance of taking responsibility for the ward on night duty.

It was the last thing Jennifer had been expecting.

'Perhaps she thinks you can't get into any trouble when everyone's asleep?' Cissy suggested.

'She doesn't know me then, does she?' Jennifer said. 'I'm going to have a party in the kitchen every night, and invite all the medical students.'

'I wish I could come,' Cissy sighed enviously. 'Honestly, Jen, talk about falling on your feet. But won't you miss your nights out?'

Jennifer shook her head. 'Not if it means I'll have my days free. And Johnny does a lot of his business in the evenings so it works out better...' She stopped talking, seeing her friend's sceptical look. Her boyfriend was still a sore point between them, and one they usually avoided. 'Anyway, working nights suits me fine,' said Jennifer. 'Especially if it means I don't have Sister breathing down my neck!'

'That's true,' Cissy agreed. 'And I suppose we can still go to matinees at the pictures on my days off, can't we?'

''Course we can.' Jennifer tucked her arm inside Cissy's. 'And you never know, you might be able to sneak into one of my late-night parties!'

Cissy laughed. 'Trust you to find a way to make mischief!'

'That's me!' Jennifer winked. 'Mischief's my middle name.'

But even though she didn't say so to Cissy, inside Jennifer was quietly proud that Sister Holmes had trusted her with so much extra responsibility.

Not that she'd ever admit it – she didn't want Cissy to think she was turning into a goody two shoes like Eve Ainsley!

'I still can't believe you actually kissed him, though,' Cissy marvelled, her nose wrinkling. 'What was it like? Was it really awful?'

Jennifer absently put her fingers to her lips, where she could still feel the imprint of Philip Chandler's mouth on hers. The kiss had taken both of them by surprise, in different ways.

'Funnily enough,' she said, 'it wasn't awful at all.'

Chapter Twenty-Three

Eve's hands were shaking so much she could barely hold the hypodermic syringe. As she pointed it upwards and plunged the piston to expel the air, the needle bobbed before her eyes, making it hard to read the figures on the barrel.

'That's it,' Sister Dawson's voice was quietly encouraging at her shoulder. 'Now you've got the right amount of fluid in the syringe, what do you do next?'

'Select a fleshy part of the arm or leg that is free from veins, purify it with a swab, then pinch a portion of it and introduce the needle into the lower part of the raised portion,' Eve recited from memory.

'Go on, then,' Sister Dawson said.

Eve pinched, aimed the needle, and taking a

deep breath, plunged it in. She quickly injected the dose, then pulled out the needle. But it wasn't until she was pressing a swab over the wound that she realised her mistake.

'I forgot to let go of the pinched portion before I injected,' she groaned.

She braced herself for a reprimand, but Sister Dawson just smiled kindly and said, 'At least you know what you did wrong. That means you'll remember it next time.'

'If there is a next time.' Eve gazed despairingly at her patient. She dreaded to think what would have happened if it had been a real person and not just a poor cushion.

'Of course there'll be a next time,' Sister Dawson said. 'You mustn't give up, Ainsley. Remember what I told you. You have the makings of an excellent nurse.'

Except I'm never going to be one, am I? Eve thought.

She still wasn't officially training, but Sister Dawson hadn't given up on her. Over the three weeks since their conversation, she had slowly been giving Eve more and more responsibility, as well as demonstrating different techniques and allowing her to practise in any spare moments she had.

Eve appreciated Sister Dawson's interest, but Cissy didn't.

'She's never offered to show *me* how to do anything,' she grumbled.

'Perhaps she would, if you asked her?' Eve suggested.

'No, thanks!' Cissy pulled a face. 'It's bad

202

enough doing everything we have to do, without taking on more work. And you needn't think you're getting out of the dirty jobs, just because Sister's got you giving injections and the like,' she warned. 'You're not a real nurse, you know!'

'I know that,' Eve said quietly.

'Just so long as you remember it,' Cissy said. 'And just so you don't start getting too much above yourself, you can take that rubbish down to the stoke hole.' She nodded towards the sack of soiled dressings leaning drunkenly against the back door.

'Why hasn't the porter been to collect it?' Eve asked.

'I don't know, do I? Perhaps that coward Stanton's dodging work as well as everything else these days.'

Eve felt a pang of guilt, but she stayed silent. It wasn't her business, she told herself. And it certainly wasn't her job to stick up for Oliver.

She went down to the basement. It was a warren of passageways, dark and low-ceilinged, opening out every now and then into a large storeroom lined with shelves. Eve's heart was racing as she hauled the sack down the steps and into the tunnel, reeking of damp and decay. It was worse than the cellar back at the shop.

In the heart of it lay the stoke hole, a vast furnace that looked like a portal to hell. Eve hurled the sack with all her might into its fiery mouth, then turned and blundered back into the darkness, anxious to find her way to the stairs as quickly as she could.

She was still groping her way along the dark

passageway when a deep-throated groan from somewhere in the shadows stopped her in her tracks.

It was her imagination, playing tricks on her again, she told herself, just as it had when she'd heard the ghost of her great-grandfather's apprentice shuffling in the dark of the shop cellar.

She hurried on, then she heard the groan again. 'Hello?' she called out in the darkness, her throat so parched with fear that barely any sound emerged. 'Who's there?'

'Over here.' She didn't know whether to be relieved or not when the voice called back.

'Hello?' She took a cautious step forward, craning her neck towards the sound. There was another groan, more human this time. The sound of someone in pain.

Forgetting her fear, Eve followed the twisting passageway and found Oliver Stanton sprawled on his back on the stone floor of one of the storerooms.

Eve threw herself down next to him. 'What happened?'

Oliver struggled to sit up, then collapsed back again with another groan of pain. In the dim light, his mouth glistened black with blood. 'My back ... it hurts to move.'

'Lean on me.' She draped his arm around her shoulders and slowly hauled him to his feet. 'I'd better get you to Casualty...'

'No!' Once upright he seemed to regain some of his strength. He pulled away from her, releasing himself from her arm. 'I'm all right. I was just – winded, that's all.'

'All the same, you need to let the doctor examine you.'

'I told you, I'm fine,' he snapped.

'You don't look it.' Eve peered at him. 'That's a nasty cut on your lip. You should get it cleaned up.'

'I'll have a wash in the Porters' Lodge.'

'It might need stitches. It could get infected if you leave it.'

He sighed. 'All right, if you insist. But I don't want any fuss,' he warned. 'And I'm not sitting in the waiting room.'

Fortunately, Dr McKay was alone in his consulting room. 'Good Lord, what happened to you?' he asked when he saw Oliver.

'I – smacked myself with a broom handle.' Oliver glanced at Eve, as if daring her to contradict him. She said nothing.

'Sounds rather painful.' Dr McKay tipped Oliver's head back to inspect the damage. 'Looks it, too. You'll need a couple of sutures in that lip, I'm afraid.' He turned to Eve. 'Can you clean him up for me?'

Dr McKay was summoned to give a second opinion on one of Dr Jameson's patients, leaving them alone. Oliver succumbed to Eve's ministrations in silence, only flinching the first time she touched the antiseptic swab to his cut lip.

'Why did you lie to Dr McKay?' she asked.

'I don't know what you mean,' he replied through clenched teeth.

'You didn't smack yourself with a broom. Someone hit you, didn't they?' He didn't reply. 'Who was it? One of the porters? I bet it was that

205

George Geoffries. I've seen the way he looks at you–'

'Does it matter?' Oliver cut her off.

She dipped another swab in the antiseptic and dabbed at his mouth. The blood had started to congeal, but his lips had swollen badly. 'You're lucky you didn't lose any teeth,' she commented.

Oliver made a small grunting sound from the back of his throat. It sounded like a pained laugh.

'He shouldn't be allowed to get away with it,' Eve said.

Oliver sent her a pitying look. 'Who's going to punish a man for hitting a conchie? Most people would give him a pat on the back. Like your friend Cissy, for instance.'

He was right, Eve thought. Cissy would think it was all a great joke.

'Anyway, I can't blame people for resenting me,' Oliver went on. 'They've all got loved ones fighting, and they're worried about them.'

'That doesn't make it right to go around hitting people!'

'Maybe not. But to understand all is to forgive all. *Tout comprendre c'est tout pardonner,* as the French would say.'

'So you're just going to turn the other cheek?'

'That's what my father would advise.'

That doesn't make it right either, Eve thought. 'So why aren't you fighting?' she asked.

'I don't believe in killing my fellow man,' he said simply.

'Don't you think it's right that we should stop Hitler?'

'Of course. I think he's a tyrant, but that doesn't

mean I want to take the lives of hundreds and thousands of innocent Germans. They're not my enemy.'

Eve frowned, considering his words.

'You've gone very quiet,' he said. 'I daresay you think I'm a poor sort, not going off to do my bit for my country?'

'It's none of my business.'

'That's not what your friend Cissy would say. She'd be furious if she could see you now, tending to my wounds.'

'You're a patient. It's my job.' Eve paused for a moment. 'You should stand up for yourself,' she said.

'You're a fine one to talk,' Oliver said quietly.

'What do you mean?'

'You let Cissy bully you.'

'I don't! Cissy and I get on well together.'

'So long as you're doing everything you're told.'

Colour scalded Eve's cheeks. She wanted to deny it, but she knew it was true.

The door swung open and Dr McKay came back in. 'Sorry about that,' he said breezily. 'Now, where were we?'

'I've just finished, Doctor.' Eve stepped back for Dr McKay to examine the wound.

'Jolly good. Let's see about getting you stitched up, shall we?'

Dr McKay was quick and skilful, and finished the job in a matter of minutes. 'There,' he said. 'With any luck you shouldn't have too much of a scar. Just be more careful about getting into a fight with brooms in future. Or anyone else, for that matter,' he added.

He knew, Eve thought, seeing the doctor's thoughtful look. Oliver's lie hadn't fooled him either.

Outside, in the passageway, Oliver said, 'We'd better leave separately. Don't want your friend seeing us together, do we? She might not approve.'

Eve was about to argue, then gave up. He was right, she thought. But how could she ever explain to him that she was used to doing as everyone wanted because it was safer for her that way? Oliver was so courageous, standing up for his beliefs, he would never have understood.

Chapter Twenty-Four

It was nearly midnight, but no one was sleeping.

Jennifer crept the length of the ward in her soft-soled shoes, surveying her charges by the dim light of her shaded torch. There were only half a dozen beds occupied now. Most of the men had been discharged, sent back into action. Those who remained were shifting restlessly in their beds, still waiting for the sleeping tablets the Night Sister had given them to take hold.

Not that anyone could sleep, with what was going on outside. There had been another air raid that evening, and outside the blacked-out windows the sky was alight with fire across the city. From far in the distance came the sound of bombs exploding and the muted roar of planes.

Jennifer was more excited than afraid. All week

208

the sirens had been sounding and on a couple of days bombs had gone off, lighting up the late-August night. But still it all seemed as if it was happening a thousand miles away.

Matron had ordered that mattresses be made up under the beds in case the men needed to take shelter there. But most of them preferred to lie in their beds and listen to what was going on outside. A couple kept up a running commentary, as calmly as if they were listening to a football match and not a dogfight in the sky.

'Did you hear that? That sounded close, didn't it? Oh, and there's another one. Now listen ... hear that? Those are our boys coming over, Spits if I'm not mistaken ... come on, lads, give 'em what for!'

Jennifer left them whispering excitedly and tip-toed up the passageway to Philip Chandler's room. He lay perfectly still in the darkness, his breathing low and even.

She started to turn away, but he said, 'Aren't you going to tuck me in?'

She smiled. 'I thought you were asleep.'

'With all that commotion going on? No chance.'

She crept into the room. 'It is rather lively out there, isn't it?'

'I wasn't sure if it was real or not. I thought I might be having another nightmare.'

'Is that what you dream about?'

He turned his ruined face towards her, his unseeing eyes meeting hers. 'What do you think?'

That was why he had had so many sleepless nights, she thought. The sound of the planes overhead must be like torture to him, reminding him of what had happened.

'Is there anything I can do?' she asked.

'You could hold my hand, if you like? I could do with the company.'

Jennifer shone her torch at the watch on her bib, checking the time. The medical students would be finishing their rounds soon. 'I can't,' she said.

'Of course not. I shouldn't have asked.'

'I would stay if I could. But I have things to do...'

'I understand. It's not as if I'm your only patient, is it?'

Guilt stabbed at her and she glanced at her watch again. 'I'm sure I could spare five minutes.'

'Really, it's all right. You get on with whatever it is you have to do.'

Jennifer hesitated at the door. 'Shall I fetch the Night Sister? She could give you something else to help you sleep.'

'I'd rather stay awake, if it's all the same to you. It's worse when I'm dreaming.'

His words stayed with Jennifer as she made her way back to the ward kitchen, where Mr Meredith and Mr Treacher were waiting for her. Jack Meredith already had the kettle on, and they were helping themselves to biscuits.

'We thought we'd make a start,' Jack said cheerfully. He and Tom Treacher made an odd pair, one tall, lanky and fair-haired, the other small and dark.

'Those biscuits are meant for the patients.' Jennifer slapped Tom's hand away from the tin and put the lid back.

Tom looked wounded. 'Have a heart, Jen,' he said through a mouthful of crumbs. 'We're starving students.'

'Give it up, Tom,' Jack said. 'You know Miss Caldwell doesn't have a heart. She's made of stone, eh, Jen?' He winked at her.

'You only say that because she's spurned your advances,' Tom said.

'And yours, my friend,' Jack reminded him.

'Yes, but in my case it's only a matter of time.'

'Shut up, both of you,' Jennifer snapped. Their midnight parties had become a ritual in the month or so she had been on nights. Every evening when the medical students had finished their rounds they would gather in the kitchen for tea. They would lark about and vie for her attention, and usually Jennifer loved every minute.

But not tonight. Her heart wasn't in it as she poured their tea.

'What's the matter?' Jack Meredith asked. 'You seem a bit on edge.'

'I expect she's nervous, aren't you? All those planes going over,' Tom replied for her.

Jack looked sympathetic. 'Do you want me to hold your hand?'

Jennifer thought of Philip Chandler. *You could hold my hand, if you like? I could do with the company.*

'No, thanks,' she said. 'And for your information, I'm not at all nervous,' she said to Tom.

'No, but I am. Aren't you, Jack?'

'Not in the slightest.' Jack Meredith cocked his head towards the distant sound of aircraft. 'It's about time this fight got going.'

'Some people have already had enough of fighting,' Jennifer said quietly.

'Come on, Jen, that's hardly the spirit!' Jack Meredith grinned. 'Remember what old Churchill said? "We shall go on to the end."'

'"We shall fight on the seas and oceans, we shall fight on the beaches,"' Tom joined in enthusiastically, mimicking the Prime Minister's voice.

'"We shall never surrender!"' Jack finished for him with a flourish, and they both laughed. 'I don't know about you, but I can't wait to join up,' he said.

'I imagine you'll get your wish soon enough,' Tom said. 'As soon as we're qualified, they'll pack us off to God knows where, to patch up God knows what.'

'I don't want to be a medic. I want to fight like everyone else.' Jack cocked his head, listening to the aircraft passing overhead. 'I quite fancy the idea of being a pilot, actually. If you ask me, they're the ones who are going to win the war for us. They're the ones who are out there now, protecting us...'

Jennifer thought again about Philip Chandler, lying in the darkness, paralysed with fear as the planes roared overhead. Too afraid to sleep.

'You have to go,' she said.

They stared at her in surprise. 'But we haven't finished our tea!' Tom protested.

'You can take it with you. But you have to go now. I have work to do.'

Jack spluttered with laughter. 'You, work?'

Jennifer glared at him, already shoving him

towards the door. 'Just leave,' she said.

'Come on, Jack,' Tom sighed. 'We'll come back tomorrow. She might be in a better mood by then.'

Philip was still lying awake when Jennifer returned to his room. 'Back again?' he greeted her. 'You can't keep away, can you?'

'It looks like it.' She smiled. 'I've finished what I had to do, if you still want some company?'

'Have your friends gone, then?'

She stared at him, nonplussed. 'How did you know?'

'I've heard you, every night. Don't worry, I won't tell.' She heard the smile in his voice. 'Why shouldn't you have a bit of fun? Life's grim enough, I reckon.'

Embarrassment froze her to the spot. He'd known she was lying all along.

'So are you staying, or are you just going to stand in the doorway all night?' Philip asked. 'It's all the same to me, but you might be more comfortable if you sat down.'

Jennifer stepped reluctantly into the room and pulled up a chair at his bedside. 'I've brought my sewing with me,' she said.

'What are you making?'

'Just some mending. Sister leaves me a load every evening, and expects me to have it done by the morning. And if I get through it all, I have to make–' She stopped herself before she could finish the sentence, but Philip's sharp ears picked up on it straight away.

'Make what?' he asked.

Jennifer hesitated. 'We have to sew shrouds,'

she said quietly.

'I see.' He paused, taking it in. 'Are you any good with a needle?'

'Not particularly. Sister's always pulling my work to bits. As if the people in the shrouds will notice a bit of poor stitching...' She stopped again, realising what she'd said. Silence fell for a moment, and then they both started laughing at the same time.

'So what do you want to do?' Jennifer asked, squinting to thread her needle by the dim light.

He pretended to think about it. 'Well, I don't think I'd be much use at playing cards,' he said. 'I couldn't see if you were cheating, could I?'

'We could talk,' Jennifer suggested.

'Let's do that.'

'What do you want to talk about?'

'You could tell me your life story.'

'It's not very interesting,' she warned.

'I'll bet it is. Tell you what, you tell me your life story and then I'll tell you mine. How about that?'

'If you like.'

And so that was what they did. As the bombs rained down outside, they talked. And they were still talking when the first pale fingers of dawn light appeared in the sky.

Chapter Twenty-Five

The church service had finished, and Eve was filing out of the doors behind her aunt when Reverend Stanton stopped her in the doorway.

'I've been meaning to thank you for helping my son after his accident.'

'Accident?' Eve echoed.

'He told me you helped get him to Casualty – after he fell off his bicycle?' Reverend Stanton smiled. 'Of course, his mother was absolutely frantic when she found out what had happened, but as I said to her, boys will be boys. I'm just grateful that you were there to pick him up and dust him off.'

He smiled at her and Eve smiled back. She wasn't sure if Reverend Stanton believed his son's story but his benign expression gave nothing away.

'So am I,' she murmured.

She went to walk away, but unfortunately for her Reverend Stanton was in a chatty mood.

'Oliver tells me you're doing very well at the hospital,' he said. 'They're talking about putting you forward for some proper nurse's training, he says.'

How did he know about that? she wondered. Eve glanced around in panic, but thankfully her aunt seemed to be out of earshot, talking to Mrs Peabody, another of the parishioners.

'They must think a lot of you,' Reverend Stanton commented. Then, in a lower voice, he added, 'Well done, my dear. You deserve it.'

'Eve!' Her aunt was calling her from further down the path. Eve gave Reverend Stanton a quick, embarrassed smile, then hurried off to join her.

It was too much to hope that Aunt Freda hadn't been listening. As they walked home through the park, she said, 'You didn't tell me you'd seen the Stanton boy?'

Eve was instantly wary. 'He works as a porter at the hospital.' She chose her words carefully, knowing that Aunt Freda would see through any lies in a moment.

'And what's all this about an accident?'

Eve looked up at the trees. It was barely a week into September, and the leaves were already turning golden. 'He – um – fell off his bicycle, and I found him and took him to Casualty.'

Aunt Freda's eyes narrowed. 'Are you sure you haven't been sneaking around again, meeting him in secret?'

'No, Aunt.'

'It wouldn't be the first time you've tried to pull the wool over my eyes, would it? Remember what happened to you last time you lied to me.'

How could she forget? 'I'm not lying to you, Aunt. I promise. I hardly know him.' She tried to keep the note of despair out of her voice, but her aunt still pounced on it.

'Don't you take that tone with me, young lady!'

'I'm sorry, Aunt.' Eve was immediately apologetic. If she allowed her aunt to work herself into

216

one of her black rages, she would have no peace for the rest of the day.

For once, mercifully, Aunt Freda seemed to let the matter drop. Or so Eve thought. But later, as they were sitting down to their meagre Sunday lunch, she suddenly announced, 'I've been considering the matter, and I don't think you should work at that hospital any more.'

Eve let her knife and fork fall on to the plate with a clatter. 'No!'

'We're far too busy in the shop. I simply can't spare you.'

Eve's throat went dry with panic. 'But I have to,' she said. 'It's war work...'

'Then you'll just have to find something else to do, won't you? Something that doesn't involve you spending half your time out of this house.'

Eve looked into her aunt's narrow, vindictive face and realised the truth. This had nothing to do with the shop. It was because she had heard Reverend Stanton saying how well Eve was doing. She could see her niece was enjoying her work, and couldn't bear to see her happy.

She would snatch it all away from her if Eve didn't fight to keep it.

She stared back down at her plate. 'I want to stay at the hospital. I like it there,' she said quietly.

Aunt Freda went white to her lips. 'What did you say?'

Eve heard the warning in her aunt's voice, but for once she recklessly ignored it. 'They've asked me if I'd like to train – you know, to become a proper nurse?' she said. 'It might be a good idea, don't you think? I'd be earning a proper wage, I could bring some extra money into the house. Perhaps you wouldn't have to work so hard,' she appealed to her aunt, but Freda was already shaking her head.

'I won't hear of it,' she said flatly. 'Now I've told you what's going to happen, and that's an end to it.' Her cold eyes fixed on Eve across the table. 'Really, I think it's high time you left that hospital, if it's filling your head with such silly ideas,' she said, her thin lips curling. 'You're getting above yourself, you really are.'

'Why shouldn't I get above myself?' Eve heard herself say. 'Why shouldn't I have a chance to make something of my life?'

She knew she'd gone too far. Aunt Freda rose slowly, drawing herself up to her full height. 'Make something of your life?' she echoed. 'You think you deserve more than I can give you, is that it?'

'No, Aunt,' Eve started to say. 'I'm very grateful, I really am.'

'And so you should be. Let me remind you, you'd be in the workhouse if it weren't for me.'

'I – I know, Aunt. I'm sorry.'

'You sound just like your mother.' Aunt Freda's fingers gripped the edge of the table until her knuckles turned white. 'She was never satisfied either. Always felt she deserved more. Selfish, selfish little whore. And now you're turning out just like her!'

Eve flinched from the sudden savagery in her aunt's face. 'I'm not,' she pleaded. 'I just wanted–'

The blow came out of nowhere, swiping across

her cheek and knocking her off balance. Out of the corner of her eye, Eve caught a blurred vision of her aunt's face, twisted with malice.

'I don't care what you want!' Aunt Freda hissed. 'You're not your mother. You don't do as you please. This is my house now, and I make the rules!' She rose up in front of Eve, her nostrils flaring. 'You will do as I say, and like it!'

Eve steeled herself for another beating, but thankfully her aunt stormed out of the room instead. Eve heard the door slam but she stayed where she was, crouched in her chair, too afraid to move. It wasn't until she heard the sound of her aunt's footsteps creaking on the floorboards overhead that she finally allowed herself to uncurl slowly and cautiously.

The first thing she saw when she looked up was Aunt Freda's wooden cross hanging over the mantelpiece. It had been there every day of her life, but it was the first time she really took in what it meant.

Without thinking, Eve locked her hands together in prayer. She couldn't remember a time when she'd truly prayed. She had spent hours saying prayers, watched over by Aunt Freda. But this was the first time she had really asked God for anything, or truly believed in what she was saying.

'Please God,' she whispered, 'grant me a miracle. Do something to change my life. And please God, do it soon!'

Chapter Twenty-Six

Kathleen Fox was in her office the following afternoon when the Germans launched their Blitzkrieg over London.

The first siren went off just before four o'clock, while she was having a meeting with the Clerk of Works about replacing the boiler in the nurses' home.

'Not again!' Mr Philips sighed. 'This is getting to be a blessed nuisance, isn't it?'

'It is indeed.' Over the past week or so, they had become used to the drone of the sirens as the evening approached, followed by the distant sound of aircraft and even a few explosions.

'I expect the south coast is due for another battering,' Mr Philips went on. 'Poor devils. Still, I daresay they're used to it by now.'

Outside in the courtyard Kathleen heard the sound of the nurses going through their evacuation procedure, spurred on by the booming tones of Miss Hanley. All the patients who were well enough took refuge on mattresses under their beds, while those who were very poorly were shifted, bed and all, into an underground passage beneath the office block. It was a tiresome business, especially when the All Clear usually sounded just moments after the last bed had been wheeled into place.

'I'd better go and inspect the wards, make sure

220

everything is all right.' She started to get up, but Mr Philips stopped her.

'We've got a bit of time, surely?' he said, helping himself to another biscuit. 'Might as well finish our meeting, since we're here.' He smiled benignly. 'My dear Matron, don't look so worried. We're as safe as houses here.'

No sooner had he said the words than there came the enormous roar of engines overhead.

'They're closer than usual, I think.' Kathleen got up and went to the window to look.

It was a fine September day, and there, high in the cloudless sky, were hundreds of glistening specks. As they drew closer, Kathleen realised they were planes, flying in formation, bombers hemmed in by fighters like bees around their queen.

Mr Philips came up behind her. He let out a low whistle. 'Bless my soul,' he murmured.

There was a tremendous crash, and the next thing Kathleen knew she was prostrate on the floor, Mr Philips lying over her, crushing her beneath his considerable weight.

'Perhaps we should put our meeting off until later,' he said, clambering to his feet and brushing himself down while he tried to cling to his last shred of dignity. 'Bit close for comfort, if you ask me.'

He was right. It was as if the bombers were aiming straight for them. Crash after crash shook the building around her as Kathleen toured the wards to make sure everyone was safe. The nurses and VADs were doing their best to keep up the patients' spirits, smoothing down beds and serving tea, wearing their tin hats over their caps.

Even Sister Holmes seemed slightly rattled as she went between the beds, checking everything was in place.

'All present and correct, Matron,' she reported briskly.

'Very good, Sister.' Kathleen checked her watch. 'And no ill effects on the patients?'

'Not at all, Matron. Between you and me, I think some of them are quite enjoying the excitement.' Sister Holmes flinched slightly as a crash overhead showered her immaculate uniform with plaster dust.

Mr Cooper caught up with Kathleen as she made her way down to Casualty.

'Grim, isn't it?' he said.

'Very,' she agreed. 'Let's hope we get the All Clear soon.'

'I'm not sure we will, Matron.' He looked apprehensive. 'Have you seen what's happening out there?'

'I haven't had the chance to take a good look yet. Is it as bad as it sounds?'

'It's horrendous. There are fires burning all over the East End. They must have been aiming for the docks, but they've destroyed everything in their path. It's like hell out there.'

Kathleen shuddered. 'I'm on my way to Casualty now to see what needs to be done.'

'I'll walk over with you. By the way, I've asked for volunteers, and a dozen students are coming in to help. They're prepared to stay all night, if need be. They might as well. I shouldn't think anyone will sleep through this,' he added grimly.

In Casualty some of the medical students had already arrived, most of them in a state of high excitement, as if they were in the middle of a great adventure.

'I've heard they've had to send for pumps from the rest of London, to try and put out the East End fires,' one said.

'Did you notice that awful smell? I thought it was a gas attack until I realised it was a paint store burning at the docks,' another put in.

'They've got it worse in Silvertown, so I hear. It's gone up like a rocket.'

Mr Meredith had come from a cricket match, still in his whites. 'It's too bad,' he complained. 'Just as I was coming in to bat, too.'

Ambulances were already lining up in the yard, having battled their way through the blazing streets. In Casualty Sister Dawson looked dazed but calm among the chaos as she and her nurses worked their way through the patients, assessing their injuries and sending them off to be treated. The benches were filled with shocked, blackened faces; people sat huddled in blankets, with bandaged heads and crudely splinted limbs.

Dr McKay emerged from his consulting room and went over to speak to Helen Dawson. Kathleen saw the look that passed between them, and the way his hand brushed hers in a quick, tender gesture of reassurance.

She didn't begrudge them their little secret. She only wished she'd someone to hold her hand, too. Looking around her, she felt the terrible weight of responsibility weighing down her shoulders.

After she'd talked to Helen and satisfied herself that all was well, she headed up to the roof.

Mr Cooper was right, it was quite a sight. The river seemed to be on fire, turned to a crimson ribbon by the reflection of the countless fires that blazed along its banks. To the east, the jagged remnants of buildings were illuminated horribly against the red glow of the sky, and the air was filled with thick smoke and the endless jangling of fire bells. It was like a vision of hell.

She spotted a familiar figure on the other side of the roof, her tall, solid build silhouetted against the fierce, bright sky. Miss Hanley stood to attention, her tin hat planted squarely on her head, armed with her stirrup pump as she scanned the horizon.

She had been on fire-watching duties every night for the past week. Even on the nights when there was no sign of a bomber in the sky, Miss Hanley had insisted on coming up to the roof to watch out for incendiaries.

'It's my duty, Matron,' she'd said stolidly when Kathleen tried to persuade her to come down. 'I can't desert my post.'

She had plenty to keep her busy tonight, Kathleen thought. It seemed as if the whole world was on fire.

She left without speaking to Miss Hanley, and went back downstairs to the operating theatre, where Mr Cooper and Dr Jameson were already busy. Matron caught Sister Theatre as she skimmed past with a tray of dressings.

'How are you getting on?' she asked.

Poor Sister Theatre looked as if she might

collapse. 'It would go a great deal faster if we had some help,' she admitted frankly. 'We could use the third operating theatre if we had another scrub nurse. But the ones I've been sent don't have the experience.'

'I'll do it,' Kathleen offered promptly.

'Oh, Matron, would you? It would be such a help.' Sister Theatre looked anxious. 'But won't you be needed elsewhere?'

'Not at the moment. Everyone seems to be coping very well.' In truth, she was beginning to feel rather useless, wandering from place to place when everyone else was so busy. 'It's been a while since I worked in Theatre, but if I can be of any use to you...'

'I'll get one of the VADS to sort you out with a cap and gown,' Sister Theatre said promptly.

For the next few hours, Kathleen assisted Mr Cooper as he treated crushed limbs, set bones and stitched up gaping wounds. They worked quickly and steadily until sometime after midnight, when there was a sudden crump sound over their heads and everything went black.

Everyone froze. In the darkness, Kathleen heard Mr Cooper's voice, muffled behind his mask. 'What the devil is going on?'

'I think we must have been hit, sir,' Mr Jessop the anaesthetist replied. 'It's taken out the electricity cable.'

'Well, I hope they sort it out soon, before I stitch this abdomen up the wrong way,' Mr Cooper replied calmly.

A moment later, a VAD arrived bearing two hurricane lamps. Across the operating table,

225

Kathleen caught Mr Cooper's blue eyes twinkling over his mask.

'Candlelight, eh?' he remarked dryly. 'How romantic.'

By half past four the following morning, thankfully the bombing had abated and the final All Clear sounded.

Kathleen was shaking and exhausted as she made her way back to her office to be greeted by Miss Hanley, looking entirely unruffled and none the worse for spending the whole night on the roof in the middle of an inferno.

'Good morning, Matron,' she greeted her. 'Would you like a cup of tea?'

'Yes, please.' Kathleen sank down behind her desk. The inkwell lay on its side and papers were scattered all over the floor. Was it really only a few hours ago she and Mr Philips had been calmly discussing the new boilers? It felt as if the whole world had changed since then.

'It sounds as though Jerry's decided to go home,' Miss Hanley remarked, as she poured them each a cup.

'And not a moment too soon,' Kathleen agreed.

'Fortunately we don't seem to have sustained a great deal of damage apart from the loss of electricity,' Miss Hanley said. 'And at least the emergency generator is working now.'

Another explosion crashed in the distance and it was all Kathleen could do not to fling herself under her desk. But Miss Hanley didn't spill a drop of tea.

The woman has nerves of steel, Kathleen thought.

'I shall have a meeting with Mr Philips today, and see what can be done,' Kathleen said. 'Let's hope we can get everything back in order soon.'

'Until the next time,' Miss Hanley said darkly.

Kathleen frowned. 'Don't you think we've seen the last of it?' she asked.

Miss Hanley sent her a wise, weary look over the rim of her cup.

'Oh, Matron, I don't think it's even begun,' she said.

Chapter Twenty-Seven

As dawn broke and the bombing subsided, Dora was waking up with her family in the public shelter in Victoria Park.

Not that she had been allowed a wink of sleep. The shelter was crammed with people, so many there wasn't room for everyone to lie down or even sit. Dora had been lucky enough to find a small space for her and the twins to settle in, but other poor souls had been forced to stand all night, crushed up against each other as the bombs came down around them. As if that wasn't bad enough, the brick walls oozed damp, and some places were ankle deep in dank, cold water. Added to that the overpowering stench of unwashed bodies, and the overflowing buckets behind a thin curtain that served as the only toilet, and it was a miracle any of them had survived the night.

Dora had tried not to show her own fear for

Danny's sake, hiding her nerves and trying not to flinch as the planes came lower and louder, and each crump of bombs seemed to come nearer and nearer. But the twins had picked up on her underlying terror. They clung to her, whimpering and fractious, and nothing she could do would settle them. Danny, meanwhile, sat hunched, his arms wrapped around his knees, face buried, quivering like a nervous racehorse and humming the same song, 'You Are My Sunshine', over and over again to comfort himself.

'Bloody hell, don't you know any other songs?' exclaimed an irritable man beside them.

'You leave him alone!' Dora snapped back. 'Can't you see he's frightened?'

'We're all bloody frightened,' the man grumbled, but he didn't say any more. It was just as well. The mood Dora was in, she would have gone for him. Fear and sleeplessness had made her nerves as taut as piano wire.

And she wasn't the only one either. Around her, all she could hear was ill-tempered bickering.

It was a huge relief when the All Clear sounded, and they tumbled out of the shelter into the pale dawn light.

'Right, that's it,' Nanna declared, wincing as she stretched her cramped limbs. 'I ain't spending another night in that place. If my time's up, I want to go in the comfort of my own bed.'

'That's if you've got a bed any more,' someone said. 'From the sound of what was coming down all night, I reckon we'll be lucky if there's anything left.'

Danny whimpered, and Dora put her arm around him. 'Come on, Dan, it ain't going to be that bad,' she said, even though her heart was in her mouth at the thought of what they might find waiting for them.

Little Alfie was indignant. 'What about Octavius? What if he's been blown up?'

'Let's go and see what's what before we start getting ourselves in a state, shall we?' Rose Doyle said.

Dora hardly recognised the landscape around her as they trudged back to Griffin Street. The dawn light barely penetrated the thick, choking fog of smoke, ash and dust from the fallen houses. It was as if she'd found herself tipped into a strange, ruined land, full of shattered buildings. People walked in disbelief among the piles of rubble that had once been homes. Even the firemen and the ARP wardens looked stunned and exhausted. On the corner of Brigg Street, two First Aid workers were searching the ruins of a collapsed house, grimly dragging oil-cloth bags.

'Wh-what are they looking for?' Danny asked.

'They're rescuing people, I expect,' Little Alfie said wisely.

'That's right, ducks. They're rescuing people,' Dora said. No need to upset anyone with the truth, she decided.

They turned the corner on to Griffin Street and Dora let out the breath she'd been holding all the way from Victoria Park.

'There, what did I tell you?' she said to Danny. 'All safe and sound.'

'Not all,' Nanna said grimly. 'Looks like the Prossers have caught it.'

The Prossers' house had taken the force of a blast. It was as if one wall had been ripped away by a giant claw, leaving the patterned wallpaper on the remaining wall exposed and vulnerable.

'Oh, those poor people!' Dora's mother was instantly sympathetic. 'As if they haven't already suffered enough, losing their son.'

'It's cruel,' Nanna agreed, shaking her head.

For a moment they were all silent in their sympathy for their neighbours. But they were interrupted when Little Alfie, who had been rummaging in their backyard, gave a joyful cry.

'Octavius is safe! Look, the tin bath landed over him.'

'Oh, well, that's something to be thankful for, ain't it?' Nanna muttered under her breath. 'Poor Mr and Mrs Prosser ain't got a home to go to, but at least the bleeding rabbit is all right!'

On the other side of the street, Mr and Mrs Prosser were in the middle of an argument with an ARP warden.

'I'm telling you, you can't go near it. It ain't safe,' he was telling them.

'But all my belongings are in there!' Mrs Prosser was trying to be brave, but tears were etching tracks down her grimy face. 'Everything I have, all my memories...'

'There's nothing I can do about that,' the warden insisted. 'You've got to clear off.'

'Clear off where?' Mr Prosser said. 'This is our home.'

'You'll have to call into the relief office,' the

ARP warden said. He reminded Dora of Mr Hopkins the Nightingale's Head Porter with his stern, officious manner. 'They'll tell you where the nearest rest centre is.'

'I ain't interested in any rest centre!' Mrs Prosser plonked herself down on an upturned dustbin, her arms folded. 'I've told you, I ain't leaving here.'

'We'll have to do as he says, love.' Mr Prosser spoke gently to his wife. 'Don't look like we've got much choice.'

'But all my memories are in that house.' Mrs Prosser looked up at her husband, tears shimmering in her eyes. 'All the photos of our boy...'

'Come in and have a cup of tea,' Rose Doyle offered. 'You look like you could do with one. Then we can sort out what you're going to do next.'

Mr Prosser nodded. 'Thanks, Rose.'

As they traipsed into the house, Nanna turned to Dora and said, 'I suppose this means we'll have to make room for two more waifs and strays.'

'I reckon you're right,' Dora agreed. Her mum could never turn her back on anyone in trouble, whoever they were.

But looking at Mrs Prosser's tearful face, it seemed it would take more than tea and sympathy, or even a bed for the night, to make up for everything she'd lost.

After they'd had their tea and she'd made sure Danny and the twins were settled, Dora prepared to go to work.

Nanna was outraged. 'You mean to tell me you're going out after what's happened?'

'They'll be expecting me.'

'But half the East End's in ruins!'

'All the more reason why I should go, ain't it?' Dora said. 'There are bound to be some casualties, after last night.'

'She's right,' her mother put in. 'I reckon they'll need her at that hospital.'

'And we need her here!' Nanna insisted. 'What if they start dropping bombs again? What are we going to do then?'

'They won't,' Dora said. 'I reckon they've done all the damage they're going to do.'

'Well, I don't think much to it.' Nanna folded her arms across her chest, a sure sign of her disapproval. 'A family should be together at a time like this. Blood's thicker than water, so they say. I don't know what you'd do if anything happened to us and you weren't here,' she said darkly.

'Nothing's going to happen to us, Mum,' Rose Doyle said. 'You get yourself off to work, love, and take no notice of your nan.'

'Oh, no, don't take any notice of me,' Nanna grumbled. 'I've only been on the earth seventy years. What do I know?'

All the beds in the Male Acute ward were occupied again, but Dora was met at the doors by Sister Holmes, who told her to report to Casualty.

'I'm not saying we couldn't do with you, but their need is greater than ours at the moment,' she said.

She was right, too. As Dora crossed the yard, there was a line of ambulances waiting outside

232

the Casualty Hall. Inside, the rows of wooden benches were filled with people nursing various wounds, or huddled under blankets. Women from the WVS moved around them, handing out cups of tea and sandwiches.

Dora found Helen propped against the door to one of the consulting rooms. She looked as shell-shocked and weary as the patients in the waiting room, her brown eyes circled by purple rings of exhaustion. The lacy strings of her bonnet drooped loosely under her chin.

She managed a smile when she saw Dora. 'Goodness, you're a sight for sore eyes! How was your night?'

'Better than yours, by the look of it.' Dora's gaze fell to her friend's blood-spattered apron. 'Have you slept at all?'

'I think I dropped off for half an hour just after dawn, but I can't remember.' She rubbed her face. 'Oh, Dora, you wouldn't believe it. It's been utter chaos here. They've had three theatres on the go, and they've all been working flat out all night.'

'I'm not surprised,' Dora said. 'Hitler's taken a right old chunk out of the East End. Whole streets have just gone.'

Helen shuddered. 'Those poor people.'

They were interrupted by one of the VADs, a pert-looking blonde. In contrast to everyone else's bedraggled appearance she looked as if she'd enjoyed a good night of beauty sleep with her fresh face and platinum curls tucked under her cap.

'Excuse me, Sister, but Ainsley hasn't reported

for duty,' she said.

Helen frowned. 'Hasn't she? That isn't like her.' She looked at Dora. 'Oh, God, I do hope nothing's happened to her.'

'Where does she live?'

'Down by the docks, I think.'

Dora's heart sank. 'In that case, I'm afraid something might well have happened,' she said.

Chapter Twenty-Eight

'I don't understand. What was she doing in the cellar?'

'I don't know, my dear,' Reverend Stanton replied. 'Perhaps she was taking shelter there?'

'But why wasn't she in the Anderson shelter with her aunt?'

Eve could hear them talking as she sat shivering under a blanket, but she didn't know what to make of it. She didn't know what to make of anything any more. One minute she was in the workshop, mending a pair of trousers, and the next she was being lifted out of the wreckage by strangers in uniform.

The last thing Eve remembered as they took her away was the sight of her aunt's cash register, lying amid a heap of splintered wood that had once been the shop counter.

Now she was here, in the church hall with all the other dispossessed people. But there was no sign of Aunt Freda.

Reverend Stanton's daughter Muriel approached her with a tea tray. 'Here you are. I've put extra sugar in it.' She held out a cup but Eve didn't take it.

'Have you seen my aunt?' she asked.

Muriel's smile wobbled. 'Drink your tea, dear. It will make you feel better.' She put the cup down on the floor beside her.

Eve stared at it. She didn't deserve to feel better. 'This is all my fault,' she whispered.

She hadn't realised she'd said the words aloud until she caught sight of Muriel's quizzical look. 'What on earth do you mean?' she asked.

Eve shook her head. How could she answer that? Muriel was too good-hearted. She would never understand how someone could be as wicked as Eve.

Muriel hurried off with her tea tray, and Eve looked around her. Reverend Stanton had turned the church hall into a temporary rest centre for the homeless. The empty space where her aunt and the other ladies of the church had once held bazaars was now lined with mattresses. Families had set up camp there, surrounded by a hotch-potch of whatever belongings they had managed to retrieve.

Eve recognised the young mother who rented a room two doors down from Aunt Freda's house. She sat on the floor, baby in her arms, her four other grubby-looking children crammed on the mattress around her. She claimed she was a widow, but Aunt Freda reckoned she knew better.

'I daresay none of those children has the same father,' she always said. 'I'd be surprised if she knew who half of them were.'

Aunt Freda would certainly not approve of this woman being offered shelter in the church hall. 'God's house is no place for the ungodly,' she would have declared.

The young woman looked up, caught Eve's eye and sent her a wobbly smile of sympathy. Eve automatically slid her gaze away. Her aunt's training was so drilled into her, she responded without thinking.

Besides, she didn't deserve the woman's sympathy. Not after what she'd done.

This was all her fault. She had prayed for a miracle to change her life, and God had punished her for it. He had sent down destruction, and all these poor people had paid the price for her blasphemy. A great weight of guilt and shame sank over her shoulders like a cloak.

And what about Aunt Freda ... had she paid the price too, Eve wondered. No one had said what had happened to her.

Oliver Stanton came into the hall with an armful of blankets. He spotted Eve and handed the bedding to one of the volunteers, then came over to her, threading his way between people, side-stepping mattresses.

'Eve! Thank God you're all right. I heard about your shop–'

'Where's my aunt?' she cut him off.

Oliver frowned. 'Isn't she here?'

'I haven't seen her, and no one will tell me where she is. Please, I need to find her. I need to know if she's safe...'

Her desperation must have shown in her face.

'Wait here,' Oliver said, then turned and pushed his way back through the crowd.

Eve watched him conferring with his father, saw the frown Reverend Stanton cast in her direction, and her heart sank. By the time Oliver had made his way back to her, she had prepared herself for the worst. So it caught her off guard when he said, 'They've taken her to the Nightingale.'

Hope flared inside Eve. 'You mean she's not dead?'

He shook his head. 'So far as Father knows, her injuries aren't too bad – wait!' he said, as Eve shrugged off her blanket and got to her feet. 'Where are you going?'

'To see my aunt.'

'But you can't go out there. The sirens have just sounded again.'

'I've got to see her.'

Oliver thought for a moment. 'In that case, I'm coming with you,' he said.

Aunt Freda sat upright in the hospital bed, no less fearsome for her borrowed nightgown and the plaster cast on her arm.

'This is utterly ridiculous,' she snapped. 'I don't even know why they're keeping me here... I want to go home.'

'Now Mrs Ainsley, you know what Sister said. You need to rest.' The nurse smoothed the bedclothes down around her. Eve caught the girl's tight smile and guessed her aunt had not been making herself popular.

'Rest!' Aunt Freda rolled her eyes. 'How can I

237

rest when there's so much to be done?' She turned to Eve. 'How is the shop? Is it badly damaged?'

Eve took her time, pouring her aunt a glass of water from the jug on her bedside locker. 'Why don't you have a drink?' she offered.

'I don't want a drink!' Her aunt knocked the glass from Eve's hand, sending it skittering across the floor. 'Do you think I'm a fool, child? I know there's something you're not telling me. What's happened to my shop?'

Eve picked up the glass. At least it hadn't broken, she thought, otherwise Sister would have something to say about it.

But finally she couldn't avoid her aunt's stern gaze any longer. 'I'm afraid it's gone,' she said.

'Gone? What do you mean, gone?' Aunt Freda was scornful.

'It was destroyed, Aunt.'

'You mean – there's nothing left?'

Eve shook her head. 'I'm sorry.'

She saw her aunt's expression falter. That little tailor's shop had been Aunt Freda's life. It had been left to her by her father, entrusted into her safekeeping. And now it was no more.

Seeing her aunt looking so vulnerable touched Eve's heart.

But it didn't last for long. A moment later Aunt Freda had rallied, her invincible armour back in place.

'Then we mustn't waste another moment,' she declared, throwing back the bedclothes with her free hand. 'You must go straight to the shop, salvage everything you can. Take a wheelbarrow...'

'Aunt Freda–'

But her aunt wasn't listening. 'I must telephone the insurance agent,' she muttered. 'It's about time they did something to earn their money, after all those premiums I've paid. Then we must find suitable new premises...'

'Mrs Ainsley, what do you think you're doing?'

Sister Edgar's voice rang out down the ward, stopping even Aunt Freda in her tracks.

Eve watched with trepidation as the ward sister approached. Sister Edgar was a large woman, as broad as Aunt Freda was whip-thin. They made a formidable pair as they faced each other.

'Get back into bed at once,' the sister ordered.

Eve was sure no one had ever spoken to her aunt like that before. Aunt Freda must have been taken by surprise by it too, because she did as she was told.

'That's better.' Sister Edgar tweaked the bed-clothes back into place. 'You remember what the doctor told you? You mustn't overexcite yourself in your condition.'

'The doctor is talking nonsense!' Aunt Freda said. 'I've never had a day's illness in my life.'

'Then you've been very fortunate indeed, given what he said,' Sister Edgar replied.

'Why? What did the doctor say?' Eve looked from one to the other of the two women.

'Nothing worth repeating,' Aunt Freda dismissed, tight-lipped.

'Dr McKay has discovered your aunt has a weak heart,' Sister Edgar explained. 'It's not too serious at the moment, but she needs complete rest.' Aunt Freda rolled her eyes. 'He's having her transferred to a convalescent home later on today.'

239

'He might think that, but I'm not going,' Aunt Freda declared.

'You don't have any choice,' Sister Edgar said. 'It's either that, or suffer the consequences.'

'But I have a business to run...' She faltered again, and Eve saw another flash of vulnerability in her flinty eyes. 'At any rate, I can't go,' Aunt Freda said shortly.

'The arrangements have been made'

'Then you can cancel them, can't you?'

Eve looked from one to the other. It felt as if she was witnessing an epic battle between two titans.

'Perhaps you should go, Aunt?' she put in quietly. 'If the doctor thinks it would be for the best.'

'Oh, you'd like that, wouldn't you?' Aunt Freda turned on her savagely. 'I daresay you'd like nothing better than to be left to your own devices. You could get up to all kinds of wickedness then, couldn't you?'

Eve caught Sister Edgar's eye. 'I didn't mean that, Aunt.'

'I'm sure you didn't.' Aunt Freda's mouth curled. 'Well, if I have to go then you're coming with me,' she said. 'You'll have to find somewhere to live since the shop–' She stopped talking, braced herself and moved on swiftly. 'You might as well move down to the country too.'

'But where will I stay?' Eve asked helplessly.

'I don't know, do I? I expect Reverend Stanton will be able to help. I'm sure he knows of some God-fearing people who will take you in.' She nodded to herself, satisfied with her solution. 'Tell him to come and see me, and we'll sort something out.'

The All Clear had sounded by the time Eve left the hospital. She was surprised to find Oliver still waiting for her outside, leaning against the gates. Had he been standing there all through the raid? she wondered. He straightened up when he saw her.

'How is she?' he asked.

'They're sending her away to a convalescent home. The doctor says she has a weak heart.' Even as she said it, Eve couldn't believe there was anything weak about Aunt Freda.

'What about you? What will you do?'

'She wants me to go with her.'

'What about your work?'

Eve suddenly remembered their argument the previous night, and the prayer that had started it all. She had prayed for her life to change, and it certainly had.

'I'll give it up,' she said. 'It's what Aunt Freda wants anyway.'

'And what about what you want?'

Eve stared at Oliver. She couldn't remember anyone ever asking her that question before. She was so shocked she couldn't think of anything to say.

'I thought you liked working here?' he prompted.

'I do.'

'Then why can't you stay? You don't have to follow your aunt down to the country if you don't want to.'

'It's what Aunt Freda wants,' she repeated.

'But–'

'Look, you don't understand,' Eve cut him off abruptly. She was already feeling bitterly disappointed enough, without him making it worse.

On their way back to the church hall, Eve decided to stop at what was left of the shop to collect some of her aunt's belongings.

'It might make her feel better if she has some of her things around her,' she told Oliver.

'Do you want me to come with you? I could help you to carry something?'

She shook her head. 'I'd rather go on my own, if you don't mind?'

Eve wasn't sure how she would react when she turned the corner and saw the pile of rubble, splintered glass and fallen masonry that had once been her home. All around her, people were weeping as they picked over the ruins of their houses. But Eve was shocked by how little she felt. It was the only home she had ever known, and yet she couldn't feel sad at its loss. Instead all she felt was a strange sense of – release. It was as if the walls of a prison had come down around her.

She didn't even bother to look for any of her own belongings. She had nothing of any value to her, Aunt Freda saw to that. Instead she carefully climbed the pile, shifting pieces of debris here and there to try to find something of her aunt's.

A well as a photograph of her grandparents, she found a wedding picture in a splintered wooden frame. Aunt Freda and Uncle Roland were smiling grimly side by side, her arm locked through his, as if to stop him escaping from her. The glass was cracked jaggedly from top to bottom, separating them.

Eve also found Aunt Freda's jewellery box, lying on its side. It was empty.

'Looters,' a policeman watching over the site told her wearily. 'They go through the bombed-out houses, looking for stuff to nick.' He shook his head. 'They want stringing up, I reckon.'

Then why don't you stop them? Eve wanted to ask. She wondered if the policeman filled his pockets too, when no one was looking. Perhaps he was hiding Aunt Freda's rose-gold bracelet, or the locket Uncle Roland had given her. It was horrible, not knowing who to trust.

She looked further, and managed to find her aunt's chest of drawers buried under some shattered roof tiles. At least Aunt Freda would have the comfort of some of her own clothes, Eve thought.

When she returned to the hospital the following morning, Reverend Stanton was with her aunt, deep in conversation. Eve's heart sank. They were probably discussing who would take on the burden of having her to stay, she thought.

Reverend Stanton turned to her with a smile as she approached.

'Ah, Eve. We were just talking about you.' He beamed. 'Your aunt was telling me you need somewhere to stay near her while she's convalescing?'

'That's right.' Eve glanced at her aunt's stony expression, and instantly felt wary.

'Unfortunately, I don't know anyone down in

that particular part of the country,' Reverend Stanton said regretfully. 'But I do have another suggestion. How would you like to come and live with us at the vicarage?'

Eve stared at him. 'Do you mean it?'

'It seems like the perfect solution,' he said. 'And it means you could continue your work here. You'd like that, wouldn't you?'

It was more than she could have ever imagined. Hope bubbled up inside her, but Eve kept her gaze fixed on her shoes. If Aunt Freda saw any hint of joy on her face she would never agree.

'What do you think, Aunt?' she asked cautiously.

Aunt Freda's mouth was so tense her lips had almost disappeared. 'I think she would be far too much trouble for you, Reverend,' she said.

'Nonsense, we'd love to have her. And I'm sure she can't be any more trouble than our two!' he said.

'You don't know her,' Aunt Freda said darkly. 'She has sin in her soul.'

Eve's cheeks burned with shame, but Reverend Stanton didn't seem troubled by her aunt's comment. 'Then what better place to live than with a man of God?' he said blandly.

Even Aunt Freda couldn't argue with that. Although from the look on her face, she would have dearly loved to try.

Chapter Twenty-Nine

After nearly a week of bombing day and night, Jennifer was simply too tired to be afraid any longer. Nights spent on the ward and days spent in the nurses' basement shelter, listening to the explosions and the rapid, noisy retort of the ack-ack guns had taken their toll on her, leaving her exhausted and bad-tempered.

But most of all, it was the state of her hair that troubled her. She refused to be seen in public in her curlers, which meant that every time the air-raid siren sounded, she had to remove them all before she could go to the shelter. Then, when the All Clear came, she had to put them in again before she could get some much-needed sleep. Sometimes it happened two or three times during a daylight raid, which meant she was awake more often than she was asleep. And even then the results of her efforts were disappointing. For once she was glad of the ugly starched cap she had to wear, because at least it covered her limp and lacklustre waves.

Luckily they didn't have too many patients to look after. The morning after the first big raid, a fleet of Green Line buses had arrived to ferry the bomb casualties down to the safety of the sector hospital in Kent. The patients who were left behind were moved down to the basement. The low-ceilinged warren of cellar wards might have been cramped and dark, but it was a lot easier staying down here than transporting the patients and their beds in the lift every time the siren sounded.

She was giving Philip Chandler his cocoa last thing at night when he broke the news that he, too, had been given his marching orders for the following day.

'They've found me a place down in Sussex that specialises in plastic surgery,' he said. 'Apparently they can do wonders.'

'They'll turn you into a film star,' Jennifer said.

He grimaced. 'Boris Karloff, perhaps.'

'You're not that bad.'

'Aren't I? I'll have to take your word for it.'

Jennifer carefully held the spout of the feeding cup to his damaged mouth. 'Have the doctors said when you might get your sight back?' she asked.

He shook his head. 'No one seems to know. I suppose it's a blessing in disguise. If I could see myself in a mirror the shock would probably kill me!' He paused. 'I'm sorry I never got to see you, though. I would have liked to know if you look like I imagine you.'

Jennifer smiled, intrigued. 'And how do you imagine me?'

He thought for a moment. 'Medium height,' he said at last. 'Slim. Blue eyes. Dark curly hair, not too long. Small turned-up nose, pointed chin.'

Jennifer laughed. 'Goodness, you've built up quite a picture, haven't you?'

'And am I right?'

'More or less,' she admitted. 'Except my eyes

are green.'

'I like green eyes.'

She took the cup away and dabbed his mouth with the linen napkin. She was glad he couldn't see her blushing.

'I'll miss you,' he said.

'Go on, you'll forget all about me when you've got all those new nurses to flirt with!'

'I mean it. I'll miss our chats every night.'

'Me too.' It had become a habit over the past couple of weeks. Once she'd made sure all the other patients were resting comfortably, Jennifer would sit at Philip's bedside and they would talk until morning. She had started to look forward to it all day, gathering little titbits and stories to tell him. She had never had a man listen to her the way Philip Chandler listened. Most of the men she knew were too interested in showing off.

Even Johnny, she thought. She loved being with him, and she loved being seen in all the fancy nightclubs and restaurants he took her to, but she couldn't imagine ever talking to him the way she talked to Philip Chandler.

Perhaps it was because she didn't really think of Philip as a man, she thought. She didn't feel the need to impress him the way she did other men. Especially Johnny.

'Anyway,' she said briskly, folding the napkin in her lap, 'I'm being moved back to days soon, so we wouldn't be able to talk for much longer in any case.'

'Will you write to me?' Philip asked.

'I'm not really one for writing letters.'

'If I write to you, will you read it? Or aren't you

one for reading either?'

She smiled. 'We'll see.' She stood up.

'Where are you going? Don't you want to stay and talk?'

'I thought you might want to get some sleep, if you're leaving in the morning?'

'I'll have plenty of time to sleep when I get there.' He put out his hand. 'Stay,' he said. 'We've only got one more night, and I hardly know anything about you.'

Jennifer laughed. 'You know everything about me!'

It was true, she realised. She had told him more about herself than she had ever told anyone.

'Then tell me again,' he said. 'Please?'

The following morning the porters brought down a big urn of tea from the dining room, and Jennifer served the breakfasts. There was no kitchen down in the basement, so the men had to make do with bread and jam.

She was in the makeshift preparation area, a small section of brick-lined corridor curtained off from the rest of the ward, when Daisy Bushell came in to start her morning duty. She looked as tired as Jennifer felt, her tin hat perched incongruously on top of her linen cap.

'What a night,' she said, stifling a yawn with the back of her hand. 'I didn't get a wink of sleep with those blessed ack-ack guns firing all night. Honestly, they make more racket than the German bombers!' She watched Jennifer eking out the margarine, trying to make it stretch to the last slice of bread. 'Anything I can do to help?'

'You can spread the jam for me.' She pushed the plate towards her.

Daisy picked up the knife. 'Did we get any more patients in during the night?' she asked.

'Only three. A chest wound, an amputated leg and an old boy collapsed with chest pains on his way to the air-raid shelter.'

'That's not bad.'

'I know. And they're all leaving for Kent first thing this morning.'

Daisy dipped her knife in the jam pot and spread it thinly over the bread. 'They're not the only ones. What's this I hear about your airman being transferred?'

Jennifer frowned. 'He's not my airman,' she muttered.

'That's not what I heard.'

'What's that supposed to mean?'

Daisy smiled archly at her. 'Oh, come on! We all know he's got a soft spot for you.'

'So what if he has? I can't help it, can I?'

'Rumour has it you have a soft spot for him, too.'

Jennifer put down her knife and turned to face Daisy. 'It isn't like that,' she said quietly.

'Isn't it? I've heard you spend half the night sitting at his bedside, having cosy chats.'

'We're only talking.'

'I'm sure you are.' Daisy shrugged. 'I'm just telling you what I've heard, that's all. Tongues are wagging all over the hospital.'

Jennifer turned cold. 'What are they saying?'

'As I said, that you and Mr Chandler are very – fond of each other. Although personally I can't

249

see the attraction.' She shuddered delicately. 'He gives me the creeps.'

'I'm not attracted to him!' Jennifer raised her voice in frustration. 'I just feel sorry for him, that's all.'

'If you say so,' Daisy replied, with an infuriating look on her face. It was all Jennifer could do not to grab her by the tin hat and stick her head in the jam.

Just before she went off duty, Jennifer went to say a final goodbye to Philip Chandler. She took a moment to pinch her cheeks and tease her curls into some kind of shape, even though she knew he couldn't see her.

He was still in bed, his blue uniform neatly pressed and hanging up beside him. It gave her a pang to see it.

'I've come to say goodbye,' she said.

'You needn't have troubled yourself.'

His tone was icy, like nothing she'd heard from him before. Jennifer frowned. 'Are you all right?' she asked.

'Not particularly, since you ask. I heard every word you said to your friend earlier on.'

She froze. 'You know I didn't mean–'

'Didn't you? You sounded as if you meant every word. Unlike when you were talking to me.' His mouth twisted contemptuously. 'And all the while I thought we were getting on, you were passing time with me out of pity. Just goes to show what a fool I was, doesn't it?'

'I wasn't–'

'You know how I feel about being pitied. You know how much I hate it.'

'But it wasn't like that... I didn't mean...'

'It's all right, you don't have to pretend with me any more. I think we both know where we stand now, don't we?'

'At least let me explain,' she begged.

'I'd rather you didn't. In fact, I'd rather we didn't speak to each other again.' He shifted against the pillows. 'I'd like you to leave now, please,' he said quietly.

Jennifer stood her ground, reluctant to go until she'd said her piece. Except she had no idea what to say.

'Will you still write to me?' she asked quietly.

He turned to her, and Jennifer could see the scorn written all over his ruined features.

'What do you think?' he said.

Chapter Thirty

The air-raid siren sounded at half past eight in the evening, just as Dora was starting her night duty in Casualty.

It had become a weary routine over the past month. Each bombing raid would bring dozens of casualties, sometimes forty a day, and another fifty during the night. Most of them would be treated and sent home, but the most serious cases would be transferred up to the ward. Dora never knew what was going to greet her when she reported for duty, but it was always a heartbreaking sight.

In spite of all the horrendous injuries she witnessed every day, the bombing had ceased to trouble her. She knew her family would be safe in the shelter, and after four weeks of day and night bombing, she had got used to the sound of the explosions and the sight of baskets of incendiaries falling from the sky, lighting up London. She had even got used to the casualties, although it was their desperate courage, rather than their horrific wounds, that really affected her.

Everyone had a horror story to tell, of friends, neighbours or loved ones lost, of homes and belongings destroyed. But Dora never heard a word of complaint from anyone.

'We can take it,' they would say with grim satisfaction. 'If old Hitler reckons he can beat us with a few bombs, he's got another think coming!'

As Dora changed into her uniform in the cloakroom, Cissy Baxter the blonde VAD was changing out of hers, ready to go home.

'I'm supposed to be going to the pictures,' she said as she shrugged on her coat. 'I hope they don't stop the film halfway through and turf us all out like they did last time. It's not fair when you've paid good money for your ticket.'

Dora smiled to herself. Typical, she thought. There were people in Casualty whose homes had been reduced to rubble, and Cissy Baxter was moaning about missing the end of a film!

Once she'd changed into her uniform, Dora and Dev Kowalski filled the stone hot water bottles and put them in the beds in the recovery ward to air the sheets. They had just finished when one of the medical students, Mr Meredith, arrived.

'What are you doing here?' Dora asked.

Jack Meredith puffed up his chest. 'I'm filling in for Dr McKay.'

God help us, she thought. Jack Meredith did his best, but he was very young and didn't possess an ounce of David McKay's experience or skill. Dora only hoped they didn't get too many serious cases in that night, with Mr Meredith holding the fort.

She might not have been looking forward to the night ahead, but Jack obviously was. He paced the Casualty Hall, checking his watch.

'When do you think it's all going to get going?' he asked. 'They've usually started the night strafe by now.'

'Perhaps they're going to give us a night off?' Dora suggested.

'Do you think so?' Jack Meredith's disappointment was almost comical.

'Tell you what, I'll make us a cup of tea while we wait for the next bomb to drop,' Dora offered.

'And biscuits,' Jack Meredith called after her. 'See if they've got any biscuits.'

'I'll see what I can do.' Dora smiled and pushed open the kitchen door.

In the kitchen, Helen was still in her uniform, making up an urn of tea.

Dora looked at the watch on her apron bib, then back at her friend. 'Aren't you supposed to be off duty by now?' she asked.

'I thought I might as well put the kettle on before I go, to save you a job. You're bound to be needing tea, once the ambulances start to arrive.'

'I daresay we will, but I'm perfectly capable of making it.' Dora took her friend's arm and guided

253

her towards the kitchen door. Helen's arm felt painfully slender under the thick fabric of her dress. 'Go on with you. It's supposed to be your night off.'

'I know, but I feel so guilty.' Helen chewed her lip. 'We've been run off our feet for the past week. I should be here to help...'

'You should be resting,' Dora said firmly. Helen and David McKay had been working night and day for almost a month.

'But the beds in the recovery area need to be aired...'

'Kowalski and I did it half an hour ago.'

'And you'll need to make sure we have enough dressings,' Helen said. 'I checked the drums this morning, but I know we got through quite a lot this afternoon...'

'I'll see to it,' Dora sighed. 'For gawd's sake, anyone would think you didn't want a night off!'

Helen smiled wearily. 'David has bought tickets for the theatre,' she said. 'But I should think we'll probably sleep all the way through the performance–'

Before she could finish her sentence, a tremendous crash of what sounded like a thousand windows exploding shook the walls around them and plunged them into darkness.

'What was that?' Helen whispered. 'Have we been hit?'

'It sounds like it.'

Dora went to open the kitchen door and was immediately lost in a dense, choking cloud of smoke and dust, and the sickening stench of explosive.

It was a night of hell.

By the time the sun came up the following morning, six people had been found dead, buried under the rubble of what had once been the Casualty department.

At ten o'clock, Kathleen Fox had to present her official report to an emergency meeting of the hospital Trustees, and Mr Philips the Clerk of Works.

'Four of the dead were casualties, brought in following the bombing raids.' Kathleen recited the words dully as she stood clutching the edge of the table for support. Beneath her calm surface, she fought the desperate urge to curl up in a ball and sob her heart out. 'There were also two members of staff – a second-year student nurse, Devora Kowalski, and a junior houseman, Mr Jack Meredith.'

A murmur went around the table. Kathleen glanced at James Cooper, sitting opposite her. He looked as shattered as she felt. They had both worked tirelessly all night, helping to pull people from the wreckage. He'd changed into a clean shirt, but his surgeon's fingers were still rimed with dirt and his jaw was shadowed with stubble.

'And what about the damage to the building?' Constance Tremayne, Chairwoman of the Trustees, turned to the Clerk of Works.

Mr Philips consulted his notes. 'The wreckage from the explosion has buried the transformer room,' he said. 'We hope to have enough of the debris moved by this afternoon to repair the DC cable, but in the meantime the building is without

255

any electricity. And of course, there is the problem of the main Casualty Hall being damaged beyond repair.'

'Quite,' Mrs Tremayne said. 'I suppose under the circumstances it would be appropriate to contact the Area Medical Officer and ask him to send any future casualties elsewhere, at least until we can have a new department running. Wouldn't you agree, Matron?'

Kathleen blinked at Constance Tremayne. She could hear the other woman speaking but somehow the words didn't make any sense.

'I'm sorry–' she started to say, but James Cooper answered for her.

'I've already spoken to him and made the necessary arrangements.'

'Excellent. Now, I suppose we'll have to discuss where to situate the temporary Casualty department...'

Kathleen allowed the conversation to wash over her, numb with disbelief. Six people had lost their lives, among them a young nurse and a doctor, and Mrs Tremayne was more concerned about when the electricity could be reconnected.

She thought about her meeting with Mr and Mrs Kowalski, first thing that morning. They had come to the hospital because they had wanted to see where their daughter died.

It had been a heartbreaking visit. Mr Kowalski and his wife had sat in her office, glowing with pride as they talked about their daughter.

Kathleen had expected anger and blame. But instead they had thanked her for taking such care of their child. 'Miss Fox, you gave Devora the chance to do a job she loved, and we will always be grateful for that,' Mr Kowalski had said, wringing her hand in his.

Afterwards she wished he had raged at her. Rage would have been easier for her to deal with than his humbling gratitude.

The meeting dragged on. Kathleen barely listened to the debate about irregular gas supplies, and the inspection of the chimney above the office block. All she wanted was for it all to be over, so she could creep away and be alone.

Finally, everyone grew tired of listening to themselves speak, and the meeting ended.

As Kathleen moved towards the door, James Cooper appeared at her side.

'Would you care to have some coffee with me in my office, Matron? I think we have some matters to discuss,' he said quietly. At the same time, his strong hand closed around her elbow, guiding her gently but firmly towards the door.

She followed him to his office, still numb with shock. Outside the tape-crossed windows, she could hear the sound of the workers shouting to each other as they began clearing away the debris in the yard. Risking a glance out, she glimpsed the horrifying scree heap of blocks of masonry, steel girders and wreckage that had once been the Casualty department. Immediately she thought of poor Nurse Kowalski.

In his office, James ignored the coffee pot and poured her a large brandy.

'You look as if you need it,' he said.

Kathleen took a gulp, letting her head relax against the back of the leather wing chair as the fiery warmth spread through her limbs.

'Thank you,' she said.

He took the armchair opposite hers and re-garded her thoughtfully over the rim of his glass. 'I have to drive down to Guildford to meet Jack Meredith's parents this afternoon,' he said.

'I've already met the Kowalskis. They came to the hospital this morning.' She took another steadying gulp of brandy.

'How was it?'

'As awful as you might expect.'

'I'm sorry.'

'Don't be. I'm not the one with a daughter lying dead in the hospital mortuary.' She hadn't meant to sound so short, but the Trustees meeting had worn away at her reserves of civility.

'We should be grateful there aren't more in there, after what happened,' James Cooper said.

Kathleen stared at him. He was right, she thought. But that was small comfort to her, or the Kowalskis.

She stared down at her hands, her nails broken by her efforts to claw away the fallen rubble.

'I was so naïve,' she murmured. 'I truly didn't think any harm would come to the hospital. I thought we would be safe.'

'You weren't to know. None of us were.'

'That's just it. I should have known.' She put down her glass. 'I was the one who wanted the Nightingale to stay open,' she said. 'Don't you remember? The Trustees wanted to evacuate when the war started, but I argued that we needed to stay in London.'

'And it was the right decision.'

258

'Is it? Two young people are dead now because of it.'

'And a lot more might be dead if we'd closed our doors,' James Cooper said. 'This hospital has saved hundreds of lives in the past month. Lives that might well have been lost if we hadn't been open to receive the wounded. And besides, you weren't the one who dropped that bomb, were you?' He leaned forward, his eyes holding hers. 'Don't blame yourself, Kathleen. You weren't the only one who decided to keep this hospital open. We all wanted to stay, including Nurse Kowalski and Mr Meredith. Don't take that burden of guilt on your shoulders, for God's sake or it'll drive you mad.'

Kathleen stared into his steady blue gaze and immediately understood why he was such a good doctor. His deep, soft voice had the power to calm and comfort the most frayed nerves. She sat for a moment, grateful for his quiet strength.

'Thank you,' she said finally. She stood up, smoothing down her uniform. 'I'm sorry, you must think me very foolish.'

'We are all allowed to be a little foolish, under the circumstances.'

Are we? A mental picture came into her mind from the previous night, of David McKay in evening dress, running towards the wreckage while everyone else was running away, crying out Helen's name. And then, when she'd appeared, stumbling out of the ruins of the building, the way they'd fallen into each other's arms, clinging together, so frantic and desperate they no longer cared who saw them.

Kathleen badly wanted to fall into someone's arms now, to cry for Nurse Kowalski and Jack Meredith and all those other poor souls who had sought refuge in Casualty that night and paid with their lives. She wanted someone to stroke her hair, and hold her, and tell her everything would be all right...

'Everything will be all right,' James Cooper said.

She stared at him, wondering for a moment if somehow he'd seen into her mind. Or perhaps he was just wishing the same thing, she thought.

Chapter Thirty-One

Johnny was waiting for Jennifer in his usual place on the corner, lounging under a lamp-post, smoking a cigarette. But this time he wasn't alone.

He was deep in conversation with a woman, a hard-looking blonde a few years older than Jennifer. She felt a strange, panicky stirring in the pit of her stomach as she watched them, their heads close together, laughing.

Jennifer hurried towards them. As she drew closer, Johnny glanced at her out of the corner of his eye. He leaned forward, whispered something to the woman and put something in her hand. She hurried off before Jennifer could reach them.

Johnny turned to her, tossing away the end of his cigarette. 'Hello darling,' he greeted her. 'You're looking beautiful today.'

Usually she would have enjoyed the thrill of his admiring gaze travelling down from her head to her toes and back again, but not today.

'Who was that?' she demanded.

'Who?'

'That girl you were talking to.'

'Oh, her.' He shrugged. 'A friend.'

'What did she want?'

'Just passing the time of day, that's all.'

There was an impatient edge to his voice, and Jennifer knew she should let it go, but she couldn't. 'You gave her something,' she accused. 'What was it?'

'Blimey, you're asking a lot of questions today, ain't you?' He was smiling, but his eyes were chilly.

'Tell me.'

He shifted from one foot to the other, hands thrust into his pockets. 'If you must know, I was doing her a favour. She asked me to get something for her, and I was just handing it over. It was a bit of business, that's all.'

'What kind of business?'

'My business.' There was no mistaking the edge to his voice now. Even Jennifer knew better than to push it. She had learned quickly that Johnny's mood could change like the wind, especially when it came to discussing his business affairs. Not that Jennifer was really interested, anyway. As long as he had the money to take her out, that was all she cared about.

But as they walked towards his car, she couldn't stop herself from asking, 'Is she a good friend of yours?'

Johnny smiled lazily. 'What's up? You're not

261

jealous, are you?'

'Of course not!' But as soon as she heard the words, Jennifer realised that was exactly what she was feeling.

The shock almost stopped her in her tracks. She had never, ever been jealous in her life. She had never known that horrible, uncertain feeling uncurling in the pit of her stomach, every nerve ending suddenly on alert, sensing threat.

She knew she had made plenty of other people jealous in her time. She rather enjoyed seeing the fear on other girls' faces when she flirted with their boyfriends in front of them. And it gave her a thrill when young men fought with each other like dogs over a bone because of her.

But she had never cared for anyone enough to experience true jealousy, until now. It was a horrible, vulnerable sensation, she realised, entrusting your heart to another person. Especially when that other person was as slippery as Johnny Fayers.

'I'm glad to hear it,' he said. 'I can't stand jealous girls.'

Jennifer was wise enough to take the hint. 'Lucky I ain't then, eh?' she replied. 'Besides,' she added, with a touch of contempt, 'why should I be jealous of someone like her? That blonde hair came straight out of a bottle, I'll bet.'

Johnny laughed. 'Too right!' he agreed. 'She isn't a patch on you, love.' To Jennifer's relief he put his arm around her and everything was all right again. 'Come on, let's go and have some fun.'

He took her up to Lyons Corner House in the Strand for afternoon tea. Usually, Jennifer would have felt very grand as she sat in the window seat, nibbling on dainty sandwiches and wishing someone she knew would walk past and see her. But this time she felt the weight of the world on her shoulders.

'Come on, out with it.' Johnny smiled across the table at her.

'I dunno what you mean.'

'You've had a face as long as a fiddle ever since we got here.' He leaned back in his seat. 'What's up? Potted meat sandwiches not to your taste?'

'No – no, they're lovely.' Jennifer took another half-hearted bite to prove it.

'What is it then?' Johnny sighed irritably. 'Don't tell me you're still thinking about that girl? I told you, she's just a friend.'

'It's not her.' Jen bit her lip. 'It's my dad,' she said finally.

Johnny frowned. 'What about him?'

'He wants to meet you.'

There, she'd said it. 'He's been on and on about it,' her words tumbled out in a rush. 'My mum told him about you, and he wants to make sure you're a respectable young man!'

She mimicked his voice, desperately trying to make light of it. Don't hate me, she pleaded silently, watching Johnny's face across the table.

She had hoped her mum might forget that Jennifer had a boyfriend. But as usual, Elsie Caldwell never forgot anything. And she'd stayed true to her promise to tell Jennifer's father, too. All hell had broken loose, and the only way Jennifer could calm him down was to promise to introduce her new boyfriend.

Johnny lit up a cigarette, his movements

agonisingly slow. 'I don't know about that,' he said.

'Please? It won't be too bad, I promise. Just come for tea, that's all. It'll be worth it for my mum's cooking!' She laughed, trying to lift the sudden tension that had descended over the table. 'I'm sorry,' she said. 'I wouldn't ask you, but my dad's very protective of me.'

'He ain't going to think much of me then, is he?'

'You don't know that. Please, Johnny?'

He shook his head. 'I dunno, Jen.'

'He'll like you, I promise.'

'And what if he doesn't?'

'He will. I'll make him like you,' Jennifer said firmly.

'Got him twisted round your little finger, have you?' Johnny exhaled a thin stream of smoke out of the corner of his mouth. 'I bet you're good at doing that.'

Perhaps she was, once. But Johnny was the only one she couldn't control, which was why he fascinated her so much. Fascinated – and terrified.

She licked her lips nervously. 'So will you come?' she asked.

He paused for a long time. Too long. 'Sorry, Jen, I can't,' he said.

'Why not?'

'Because it's all a bit serious, ain't it? Meeting your mum and dad sort of makes everything official. Next thing, he'll be asking me what my intentions are, and before I know it I'll be down on one knee with a ring in my hand!'

He roared with laughter. Jennifer stared at him

264

blankly. Why was it so funny? she wondered. It was what she'd planned, after all. They'd been courting for three months, longer than she'd ever been out with any other man. Besides, Cissy and Paul were beginning to talk about settling down together, and Jennifer was determined to beat her friend to the altar. She'd even daydreamed about the kind of wedding dress she would have.

She screwed up her fists tightly and fought the urge to punch him. If any other man had laughed at her, she might have done just that.

'Isn't it serious, then?' she heard herself ask in a small voice.

'Not serious enough for me to face your dad!' Johnny roared with laughter again, then stopped when he saw her stony face. 'What's the matter? You didn't think I was going to pop the question, did you?'

'Don't be daft.'

Johnny must have read the disappointment on her face because he reached across the table for her hand. 'Sorry, Jen, I didn't mean to upset you,' he said. 'I thought you understood we were only having a bit of fun?'

A bit of fun?

There was nothing fun about her feelings for Johnny Fayers. Jennifer knew she should get up and walk away, but she couldn't bring herself to do it. She was afraid he might not follow her, and that would be it for them.

'If you don't mind, I think I'd like to go home now.'

'But you haven't finished your tea.'

'I've lost my appetite.'

Johnny narrowed his eyes. 'I hope you're not sulking?' he said.

'Of course not.' She folded her napkin and laid it down on the table. 'I'd just like to go home, that's all.'

She wanted him to apologise. But all he did was lift his hand to summon the nippy. 'If that's what you want,' he snapped.

They drove home in silence, with Jennifer feeling utterly wretched. She'd ruined everything. Johnny wouldn't want to see her again, she was sure of it. He would drop her, and take up with that hard-faced blonde instead.

She had never been dropped by anyone before.

He parked a couple of streets away from her house as usual, and Jennifer struggled to get out of the car before he could say anything to her. She had just managed to get the door open when he suddenly said, 'Wait. Before you go...'

This is it, she thought, steeling herself. She had made up her mind she wouldn't cry, but she could already feel tears pricking the back of her eyes.

'What?'

'I've got something for you.' He reached into the inside top pocket of his jacket and pulled out a long red leather box.

Jennifer fixed her gaze on it. 'What is it?'

'Open it and find out.'

Inside the box was the most beautiful rose-gold bracelet, fine links with a dainty little diamond clasp.

Jennifer's anger disappeared. 'It – it's beautiful.'

'Do you like it?'

'I love it.' She draped it across her wrist. The pinkish gold glowed against her skin.

'Here, let me.' He fastened the bracelet for her, his strong fingers brushing hers. 'You see?' he said, holding on to her hand. 'Now would I give you a present like that if I wasn't serious about you?'

She smiled reluctantly. 'I suppose not.'

'You're a lovely girl, and if I ever settle down it will be with someone like you. But I'm just not ready at the moment. You understand that, don't you?'

She nodded, sniffing back her tears. 'Yes, Johnny.'

'Now let's not have any more sulking, shall we?' He dropped a kiss on top of her head.

Jennifer skipped home, utterly elated, stopping every couple of minutes to admire the bracelet. It was the nicest thing anyone had ever given her, and she couldn't wait to show it off.

Wait until Cissy saw it! Paul had never bought her such an extravagant gift, not even for her birthday.

This was proof, Jennifer decided. Proof that Johnny truly cared about her. Perhaps he wasn't ready to get engaged, but he was still serious about her in his own way.

Her mother poked her head out of the kitchen when Jennifer let herself in. 'You're early,' she said.

'Hmm.' Jennifer picked up the post from the hall table and flicked through it. 'Anything for me?' she asked.

'No, why? Are you expecting something?'

Jennifer had written to Philip Chandler nearly two weeks ago, apologising for what had happened the last time she'd seen him. She'd felt sure he would write straight back, but so far she'd heard nothing.

It took her by surprise that he hadn't replied. Surely he couldn't stay angry with her? It wasn't fair. She hadn't even meant what she'd said.

She missed him. The ward seemed a lonely place without their daily chats for her to look forward to.

'No,' she said. 'I'm not expecting anything.'

Perhaps Philip had found another nurse to flirt with? No sooner had the thought occurred to her than Jennifer felt jealousy uncurling in the pit of her stomach, for the second time that day.

Chapter Thirty-Two

During the first two weeks of October, London suffered an almost constant barrage from the Luftwaffe. Day and night, German bombers screamed overhead, raining down incendiaries and explosives and spreading terror throughout the city.

And the Nightingale suffered more than its fair share.

One night a high-explosive bomb destroyed half the administration block. Kathleen had to move to a temporary office in one of the basement equipment stores, setting up her desk among stacks of old X-ray tubes and boxes. No sooner had she got herself settled than the following night a basket of incendiaries hit the dispensary, sending it and the staff dining room up in flames.

Then, while they were still struggling to recover, two days later another bomb hit a chimney, sending it crashing down through three floors of what had once been the main ward block. It broke Kathleen's heart to stand in the remains of Holmes ward, looking down to the ground far below, where Sister's desk lay crushed under a heap of fallen masonry. Just a few months ago, she had been so proud when they'd managed to get the ward redecorated and finished in time to treat the casualties from Dunkirk. Now all their hard work was reduced to rubble, along with everything else.

The one blessing was that no one had been seriously hurt in the blast. By the time the bomb struck, all the wards had been moved down to the basement, along with the operating theatres, the temporary Casualty department and the nurses' accommodation. Old parts of the cellar Kathleen had never even known existed were now pressed into service as makeshift wards, sleeping quarters and dining rooms. Closer to the stoke hole, the Red Cross had taken up almost permanent residence, dispensing tea and sandwiches as the dining room was no more.

The Nightingale's staff lived underground like moles, working, eating and sleeping in the dimly lit warren of corridors and only emerging into the outside world to survey the damage around them. By the middle of October, everyone had dragged their beds down to the basement, where they were packed together as tightly as in a public shelter, with only curtains to separate them. Every night, Kathleen had to pick her way over the sleeping bodies of doctors, students and ward sisters to find herself a spare mattress. It wasn't uncommon to see a medical student propped up against a wall, his head lolling on the shoulder of a sleeping consultant.

The nurses and VADs behaved as if they were at Girl Guides camp, laughing and singing songs and setting each other's hair. Meanwhile, the medical students discussed the bombs dropping around them as if they were commentating on a cricket match.

'There goes another basket of incendiaries, lighting up the way... Now wait a minute, here comes his mate ... there! I bet that's got the docks again. I'm surprised there's anything left.'

But when Kathleen toured the wards during the night, she was surprised to find the patients all sleeping like babies, in spite of the deafening noise of the ack-acks in Victoria Park.

'They're exhausted, poor things,' one of the night nurses commented. 'I expect they feel a lot safer here than they do in their own homes.'

Kathleen couldn't imagine why they had so much faith in the hospital, when the building was falling down around their ears.

At least the debris in the courtyard was gone now, thanks to the hard work of Mr Philips and his men. But Kathleen still averted her gaze every time she had to pass the spot where the Casualty department had come down. She couldn't walk past the broken ruins of the building without thinking of poor Nurse Kowalski and Jack Meredith.

As far as Kathleen was concerned, she would have razed the whole lot to the ground. But the Trustees had other ideas.

'We must consider reopening Casualty,' Mrs Tremayne announced at their last meeting. 'I have spoken to Dr McKay, and he says the present arrangement in the old laundry is simply not practical for the volume of casualties they have to deal with.'

'Is that possible?' Another trustee, Gerald Munroe, turned to Mr Philips.

'Well...' The Clerk of Works sucked his teeth. 'I've had a word with the Borough Engineer, and he reckons most of the treatment rooms and consulting rooms are still intact. It's only really the Casualty Hall itself that has been destroyed.'

'Could it be rebuilt?'

'Not without considerable time and cost.'

'Perhaps we could make do without a waiting area for the time being? I know it isn't ideal, but at least it would mean the treatment rooms could be used...'

Kathleen looked from one to the other of the Trustees in disbelief. 'But it isn't safe!' she burst out finally. 'You saw what happened last time the Casualty Hall was hit by a bomb. Are you seriously proposing we make doctors and nurses go back to work somewhere they might be killed at any time? The patients and doctors and staff would be like sitting ducks, waiting for the next

271

bomb to hit.'

'They are in any case,' Gerald Munroe pointed out quietly.

'We all are,' Mr Philips put in.

'And we need to do something,' Mrs Tremayne said. 'As Dr McKay said, we can't go on treating dozens of patients in a cramped, unlit basement.'

'Then perhaps it would be better to inform the Area Medical Officer that we're not in a position to take any more patients?' Kathleen snapped back.

There was a murmur of dissent around the table. As usual, Mrs Tremayne's view held sway, and the meeting ended with the Clerk of Works being sent off to patch up what was left of the Casualty Hall. Kathleen came out of the meeting feeling very agitated, to hear the drone of yet another air-raid siren.

A tide of weary, resigned-looking nurses, tin helmets perched on top of their caps, started to trudge down to the basement. Kathleen should have followed them, but she couldn't face another moment crammed into the narrow, overheated space. Instead she turned and went in the opposite direction, up the emergency staircase that led to the roof.

It was just past six and the sky was growing dark. Silhouetted against the moon on the far side of the roof stood the lone figure of Miss Hanley in her tin hat, watching for fires. The last person she wanted to see. Kathleen was about to slink away when Miss Hanley called out to her.

'Bomber's moon tonight, Matron.'

Kathleen turned around. 'I beg your pardon?'

'It's a clear night.' She pointed skywards towards the moon, bright in the cloudless sky. 'That means they'll be over soon. Hundreds of them, I expect.' She gazed around her. 'There'll be some blazes tonight.'

Kathleen stared at her. The Assistant Matron's eyes were gleaming in the darkness, almost as if she relished the prospect.

'But our boys will be more than a match for them,' Miss Hanley went on. 'Did you hear the news? They say we've managed to shoot down a record number of Germans on the south coast. That's something, isn't it?'

'I honestly can't bring myself to listen to the news any more,' Kathleen admitted.

Miss Hanley couldn't have looked more scandalised if Kathleen had produced a swastika armband from her pocket. 'Not listen to the news, Matron? But – how do you know what's going on?'

'I don't think I want to know.' Kathleen stared out over the broken landscape below them, bracing itself for another onslaught. London can take it, everyone kept saying. But it didn't seem that way to her.

Miss Hanley looked at her questioningly. 'Is everything all right, Matron?'

Kathleen laughed. What a question, with half of London smouldering around them!

'Why do you stay up here night after night, Miss Hanley?' she asked.

The Assistant Matron puffed out her cheeks. 'It's my duty, Matron.'

'Yes, but what's the point? The hospital is still

collapsing around our ears, in spite of your best efforts. Frankly, there's very little left of the building to be destroyed.'

Miss Hanley looked confused for a moment. Then she frowned. 'That sounds rather defeatist, Matron.'

'Of course I'm defeatist!' Kathleen's last shred of patience, the fragment she had been holding on to throughout the Trustees' meeting, now slipped away from her. 'Look around you, Miss Hanley. We've been defeated, or hadn't you noticed? We have nothing left. No gas, no electricity, no water half the time. Our buildings have either been blown up, or they're falling down around our ears. Our nurses are exhausted, trying to cope in desperate conditions. But even then we can't even look after more than a handful of patients because we don't have the equipment or the resources or even the beds to cope.'

'Mr Philips will sort it out,' Miss Hanley insisted stoically. 'And once the Casualty department is up and running again–'

'For how long?' Kathleen cut her off. 'How long before there's another bomb? How long before something else falls down, or someone else gets killed?'

A muscle in Miss Hanley's square jaw twitched with tension.

'Then what do you suggest we do?' she said.

Kathleen's shoulders slumped. 'I don't know,' she sighed. 'I don't know anything any more. Everyone keeps coming to me for answers, and I have no more to give.'

She started to walk away, and had almost

reached the steps when Miss Hanley called after her, 'If you'll pardon me for saying so, Matron, I think you're looking at this in the wrong way.'

Kathleen hesitated. 'I don't know what you mean.'

'You look around and see ruined buildings and no electricity. I see Mr Philips and his men working round the clock to clear away rubble and get everything running smoothly again. You see exhausted nurses struggling to cope. I see resourceful girls sterilising instruments over Primus stoves, and doctors operating under umbrellas while plaster dust showers down on them. You see despair, Matron. I see people who are dedicated to keeping this hospital running.' Miss Hanley came closer, her broad, masculine shape outlined against the moonlight. 'Do you remember a few months ago, you told me that there was more to a hospital than bricks and mortar? It was the people who made a hospital, you said. I didn't understand what you meant at the time, but now I think I do.'

She jabbed her finger in the direction of the courtyard below. 'You're right, this hospital has been badly damaged. But it stays open because of the spirit of the people in it. I thought you had that spirit too, Matron.' She sounded disappointed. 'What happened to the woman who rallied her troops to decorate a ward when no one else thought it could be done?'

'I'm afraid she's gone, Miss Hanley.' She disappeared a long time ago, Kathleen thought. She was wiped out of existence by the constant bombing raids, leaving a cynical shell in her place.

'Then you must find her again,' Miss Hanley said briskly.

'Why?'

'Because it's your duty!' The Assistant Matron's eyes glittered with fervour under the shadow of her tin hat. 'The staff of this hospital rely on you for inspiration, guidance. If you give up...'

Kathleen shook her head. 'I'm sorry, but I'm too tired,' she said. 'Why don't you do it, as you're so determined to see this thing through? You've always wanted to take charge, now's your chance.'

Miss Hanley shook her head. 'I know where my strengths lie, Matron, and where they don't. I realise I could never understand people the way you do. I lack your – compassion.'

Kathleen smiled in spite of herself. Only Miss Hanley could pay someone a compliment and make it sound like a criticism.'

'We all have our part to play, Matron. Mine is to watch out for fires. Yours is to lead us through this war with our heads held high.'

Kathleen looked back at her assistant. Miss Hanley hadn't made a move, but Kathleen still felt as if she had been given a good hard kick in the backside.

Chapter Thirty-Three

A large sign hung from what was left of the Casualty Hall, greeting Eve as she came on duty two days later.

'The Nightingale Hospital – open for business as usual.'

'A bit more open than usual, if you ask me!' Oliver nodded towards the makeshift tarpaulin wall billowing like a sail in the early-morning breeze. 'Someone's got a sense of humour.'

'I don't care, so long as it means we can move out of that horrible basement,' Eve replied. The novelty of trying to dress wounds by the light of a hurricane lamp had worn off a long time ago. 'That sign is funny though, isn't it? I wonder who put it up?'

As if in answer to her question, an opening in the tarpaulin flapped aside and Matron emerged, her arms full of linen, and marched purposefully across the courtyard.

As she passed Eve, she beamed and said, 'Good morning, Miss Ainsley. Lovely day, isn't it?'

Eve glanced around her at the chilly grey autumn morning. Icy spots of rain were beginning to dampen her shoulders, and cordite-scented smoke lingered on the air from the previous night's raids. But Matron's smile was so bright and convincing, Eve couldn't help but smile back and say, 'Yes, Matron.'

'Do you like the sign? Rather fun, isn't it? I thought we might as well let people know we're still going strong.'

'Someone's in a good mood,' Oliver remarked as they watched her walking away, humming to herself.

'She is, isn't she?' Eve was glad to see Miss Fox smiling again. The last few days had depressed them all, especially when all the wards came down. But the sign showed they were fighting back. It was a message of hope, of defiance.

'Don't look now, but your friend's coming.' Oliver glanced over his shoulder towards Cissy, who was sauntering up the drive behind them. 'Better make myself scarce. Wouldn't do for her to see us talking to each other, would it?'

'Oliver, wait...' Eve started to say, but he was already gone, making his way across the yard to the Porters' Lodge.

Eve watched him go, his shoulders hunched against the October chill. Poor Oliver. He didn't talk about his work, but she knew that the other porters still treated him like an outcast. It filled her with shame that she didn't defend him, especially in front of Cissy when she owed him and his family so much. The Stantons had been kind to her, giving her much more than a roof over her head for the past six weeks. They had taken her into their hearts, shown her for the first time what it was like to be part of a proper, loving family. For the first time in her life Eve didn't have to creep around in fear, wondering where the next punishment, the next harsh word was coming from.

It had taken a while to get used to not having to

278

be afraid all the time. But every day Eve felt herself slowly blooming, like a flower opening in the sun.

In that time she'd also got to know Oliver better, and she understood why he had chosen not to go and fight. She appreciated that his decision hadn't been an easy one, that he'd searched his soul and his conscience for a long time before he decided what had to be done. It certainly wasn't that he was a coward, as everyone believed. If anything, Eve thought he'd shown a great deal of courage in standing up for what he believed was right. She dearly wished everyone could see him for the kind-hearted young man he truly was.

Especially Cissy. Sometimes Eve felt as if she was the bigger coward for not standing up to Cissy when she criticised Oliver.

One of these days, Eve told herself. But her fledgling friendship was too new, too much of a novelty, for her to want to spoil it just yet.

Cissy came up behind her, looking disgruntled.

'What's all this?' she said, nodding towards the Casualty Hall. 'Does this mean we won't be working in the basement any more?'

Eve nodded. 'I think so.'

Cissy pulled a face. 'Well, that's just typical, isn't it? I liked the basement. I won't be able to sneak off to the stoke hole for a cigarette any more.'

Inside the tent, a weary-looking Nurse Riley greeted them and told them to get on with preparing the dressings.

'We had a busy night, and our supplies are running low,' she said.

'Bossy!' Cissy stuck her tongue out at the nurse's retreating figure. 'Jen warned me she was a slave-driver, and she was right. Well, Riley needn't think I'm hurrying!'

Ten minutes later they sat in the treatment room, rolling the cotton wool into swabs.

Cissy watched Eve rolling them on her knees for a moment, then said, 'You know, I've heard that if you roll them under your bosom it makes you more shapely.'

Eve looked doubtfully down at her chest, flat as a pancake under the bib of her starched apron. 'I'm not sure it would work on me,' she said.

'You never know,' Cissy said kindly. 'Can't hurt to have a go, can it? After all, we girls need all the help we can get to improve our looks, with everything so short these days.'

'I don't think anything would improve mine!'

'Don't be silly. You could look all right, you know, if you wore a bit of make-up and did your hair nicely.' Cissy squinted at her, sizing her up. 'You're not exactly Lana Turner,' she declared finally, 'but you could definitely improve on what you've got. And not all film stars are that pretty,' she added. 'They just know how to make the best of themselves, that's all. I could show you, if you like?'

Eve concentrated on the cotton wool ball she was rolling. 'I don't know about that,' she murmured.

'Why not? You want to look nice, don't you?'

'Yes, but I don't think my aunt would like it.'

'But your aunt isn't here, is she?' Cissy pointed out.

Eve didn't reply. Aunt Freda might be tucked away down in the country, but fear of her still lingered in Eve's mind. She could still hear her aunt's harsh voice jangling in her mind.

Just like your mother... Selfish, selfish little whore...

Perhaps she was right, Eve thought. Perhaps, without her aunt's guiding influence, Eve's wantonness was finally emerging. She would never have even thought about doing anything to her hair if Aunt Freda had been there.

Her panic must have shown on her face because Cissy said scornfully, 'For goodness' sake, I'm only going to put a few curlers in your hair!'

'All the same, I'll have to ask Mrs Stanton.' She would know, Eve thought. Mrs Stanton was a vicar's wife, after all. She would be able to guide her.

'Why do you need anyone's permission?' Cissy asked. 'It's your hair, you can do as you like with it.'

Eve stared at her. Until that moment, the idea had never occurred to her. She had been so used to pleasing other people, the idea of pleasing herself was all too much for her.

'But I suppose you're right.' Cissy's next comment took the wind out of her sails again. 'I mean, you don't want to embarrass the vicar, do you?' Her voice was heavy with sarcasm. 'Poor you,' she sympathised. 'It can't be much fun, having to lodge at a vicarage. I expect they're as dull as ditchwater, aren't they?'

Eve cleared her throat nervously. 'Actually, I'm having a nice time,' she said. 'The Stantons have been very kind to me.'

Every day was a revelation to her. Muriel had lent her novels and magazines to read, the likes of which Eve had never seen before. Mrs Stanton had started to teach her the piano and Oliver had promised to show her how to sketch, even though she was sure she would never have half his talent.

She was allowed to listen to the radio, not just to the news broadcasts but to all kinds of other programmes like *It's That Man Again* and *Scrapbook*. They discussed the news over breakfast and tea. At first Eve had sat mutely listening to the others giving their opinions. She had panicked the first time Reverend Stanton asked her what she thought. Even more surprising, they had actually listened to her. No one had mocked her, or criticised her, and she didn't have to worry about getting the strap if she said the wrong thing.

All the same, she was nervous of broaching the subject of Cissy doing her hair. Mrs Stanton seemed very kind and easy-going, but what if Eve offended her in some way? What if Aunt Freda was right and she betrayed her true nature by suggesting it? Perhaps the only reason they were so kind to her was because they didn't yet know how wicked she really was. If she said the wrong thing she could easily give herself away, and then where would she be?

It wasn't until they were clearing the table after tea that Eve finally plucked up the courage to ask.

'I wondered...' She kept her eyes fixed on the sink as she filled it, not daring to look over her shoulder. 'Would it be all right if one of the girls

wearing her thoughtful look, as if trying to work out what to say and how to say it. The last time Jennifer had seen that expression on her friend's face was when she had thought about bleaching her hair two years ago. She'd been so set on the idea, it had taken all Cissy's courage to persuade her not to do it.

Finally Cissy said, 'You do know what Johnny's up to, don't you? I mean, you know what business he's really in?'

'What do you mean?'

'He's a black marketeer, Jen. All this stuff he gets hold of for people ... it's stolen.'

Jennifer felt the hot blush rise in her cheeks. 'Of course I know what he does!' she snapped. 'Do you think I'm stupid or something?' Johnny had never told her and she had long since stopped asking. But she had worked it out for herself.

Cissy stared at her. 'And you don't mind?'

'Why should I?' She shrugged. 'It's nothing to do with me.'

'But it's stealing!'

'Oh, come off it, Cis! It's not like he really robs anyone, is it? It's only stuff that falls off the back of lorries. Everyone does it,' Jennifer added carelessly.

That was what she told herself anyway.

But it took a lot for her to swallow her shame. Especially when her father came home and told them about the latest theft from the bombed-out dock warehouses. And the last thing she needed was Cissy to get all holier-than-thou about it and make her feel worse than she already did.

'Anyway,' Jennifer added, 'I don't see you com-

plaining when he brings you stockings and lipstick!'

That got her. Cissy retreated into guilty silence.
Jennifer was silent too, but out of hurt and anger.
She was really disappointed in her friend. First
Cissy hadn't been nearly impressed enough when
Jennifer showed off the bracelet Johnny had given
her. Then she'd refused to come out dancing, and
now she was being very hurtful about him.

If she was a real mate she would be pleased for
her, instead of trying to make her feel bad. God
knew, Jennifer had listened to Cissy going on
about Paul often enough!

Or at least, she used to. It shocked her to realise
how far apart she and Cissy had drifted since
they'd started working in the hospital. They didn't
even have lunch together any more, since the
dining room had been destroyed.

But Cissy was her only real friend and Jennifer
didn't want to lose her. And if that meant swallowing her pride and making the first move, then
so be it.

'I don't want to fall out, Cis,' she wheedled.
'Can't we just be friends?'

'I suppose so.' Cissy sent her a sidelong smile.

'I'd really like us to go out tonight.' Jennifer
nudged her. 'Go on, it'll be like old times, you and
me down the Palais.'

'I told you, I can't.'

'What are you doing that's so important?'

Cissy paused. 'I promised Eve she could come
round so I could do her hair,' she said quietly.

She was blushing when she said it, and with
good reason. Jennifer stared at her.

286

'You what? Why?'

Cissy lifted her shoulders. 'I feel sorry for her.'

'You feel sorry for her?' Jennifer echoed. She could hardly believe what she was hearing. 'We are talking about the same girl, aren't we? The one we used to make fun of at those First Aid classes?'

'She's all right once you get to know her,' Cissy defended. 'You should come round, too. Then you could...'

'No, thanks!' Jennifer grimaced. 'Spending the evening with that drip isn't my idea of fun, thank you very much!'

'I told you, she's not that bad once you get to know her.'

'I'll take your word for it,' Jennifer said. 'Honestly, Cissy, I would have thought the last thing you'd do is waste your time on someone like her!' She stared at her friend in frustration. 'Are you sure you can't just tell her you've had a better offer?'

Usually she could have twisted her friend around her little finger. But for once Cissy was being surprisingly stubborn. 'I told you, I promised.'

There was something about the way she said it, and the shifty way she couldn't meet Jennifer's eye, that made her feel there was more to it than Cissy was letting on.

'I thought I'd just give you a few pin curls, because they're easy and won't take as long to set,' Cissy said.

She fluttered around Eve, winding strands of

hair around her fingers and fastening each curl in place with a hairpin. Eve watched her admiringly.

'You're so quick,' she said. 'I don't think I could ever manage it the way you can.'

'It's not that difficult once you get the knack. Jen and I used to do each other's all the time...'

Cissy's voice tailed off and Eve saw her face fall, reflected in the mirror she held in her hands. Eve knew Jennifer and Cissy had fallen out because Jennifer had made a point of grabbing her at the WVS van and telling her all about it earlier that day.

'I s'pose you know you've ruined Cissy's evening?' she'd said. 'She wanted to come out dancing with me but she can't because she doesn't want to let you down.'

Of course Eve had tried to put it right straight away by telling Cissy she didn't have to come. 'We can easily make it another evening,' she'd said. But Cissy just firmed her mouth and said, 'Jen said that to you, did she? She had no right to interfere.'

'She wasn't interfering,' Eve assured her hastily. 'And besides, I don't mind.'

'No, but I do,' Cissy said. 'You're coming round to my house tonight, just like we planned,' she told Eve firmly.

'But Jennifer...'

'Believe me, Jennifer's the last person I want to see at the moment. And she'll stay out of my way if she knows what's good for her!'

But Eve still felt guilty as she sat in the kitchen of the Baxters' home. She shouldn't be there, she thought. This was Jennifer's place, not hers. It was Jennifer who should be here, gossiping with Cissy before going off on their night out.

Even Cissy's mother seemed surprised to see Eve, although once Cissy had introduced them she had smiled and welcomed their visitor and offered her tea and a piece of cake.

'Not sure what it tastes like, though,' she'd said cheerfully. 'You just can't get the ingredients, can you?'

Now she fussed around them in the kitchen, complaining about Cissy's combs and clips and pins being scattered over the table.

'Look at all this mess! Why do you have to spread yourself about and take over everything?' she sighed.

Eve was mortified and rushed to tidy them up, but Cissy said, 'Take no notice, she doesn't mean it.'

Eve glanced warily at Mrs Baxter, waiting for her to react. But the woman simply smiled and shook her head at her daughter's antics. 'I dunno why I waste my breath,' she said.

Eve eyed them both uncertainly in the mirror, still not sure what was happening. Aunt Freda would have expected her to do as she was told straight away, or be given a smack round the face. Seeing Cissy and her mother, and Mrs Stanton and Muriel, Eve realised she still had a lot to learn about how mothers and daughters treated each other.

Cissy put in the last curl. 'There,' she said. 'That's done. Now while we're waiting for it to set, I'll give you a bit of make-up.'

Eve shrank back in her seat. 'Oh, no,' she said.

'Really, I couldn't.' Having curls was one thing, but going back to the vicarage with her face painted was another.

Cissy laughed. 'Don't look so frightened, it's just a bit of powder and lipstick. You won't look like someone who hangs round the docks, I promise.'

Eve stared at her, mystified. The only people who hung around the docks were stevedores and sailors and the like. She couldn't think why any of them would wear lipstick. 'I – I don't understand,' she ventured.

Cissy and her mother exchanged disbelieving glances. Then Cissy laughed and said, 'It doesn't matter. You wait there, I'll go and get my make-up bag.'

Eve submitted patiently as Cissy went about her work, dabbing on powder and rouge, and shaping Eve's lips with a stub of pink lipstick. 'I haven't got a lot of this left, but Jen reckons her Johnny might be able to get me some...'

Once again, she stopped herself, and her face took on a taut, angry look that Eve didn't understand. She wanted to ask about it, but Cissy looked too cross as she took out her mascara, spat on it then worked the brush into the dense black block.

Her mood had recovered by the time she'd finished. 'There,' she said, gazing into Eve's face like an artist studying their latest canvas. 'No, don't look at yourself yet. Let me take your curls out first so you get the full effect.'

It was much quicker to unpin the curls than it had been to put them in. Cissy released each one in turn, and carefully combed it out. Eve felt a curl tickle her cheek.

'Trust me, it looks lovely,' Cissy said. 'You'll have all the boys running after you by the time I've finished.'

Eve glanced up at her in dismay from under lashes weighed down by sooty mascara.

'But I don't want anyone running after me!'

Cissy slanted a smile at her. 'Oh, come on! You must have someone you like, surely?'

For some reason, a picture of Oliver Stanton came into Eve's mind.

'I knew it!' Cissy laughed with triumph. 'You're blushing, which means there is someone. And I bet I know who it is, too.' She slowly combed out another curl and fluffed it up with her fingers. 'I don't blame you,' she said. 'He is rather handsome, I must say.'

Eve frowned at her, until Cissy went on, 'I mean, I don't go much for fair-haired men myself, but Dr Jameson is very good-looking.'

'Dr Jameson?' Eve repeated blankly.

'That's who you've got your eye on, isn't it? I'm right, aren't I?' Cissy said. Then, without waiting for an answer, she went on, 'If you ask me, he definitely likes you, too.'

'Me?' The idea was so ridiculous Eve almost laughed. 'I don't think he's even noticed me.'

'Of course he has. I've seen him giving you the eye, don't you worry.' Cissy nodded knowingly.

Eve stared down at her fingers, lacing them together nervously in her lap. This was all a revelation to her, and she sincerely hoped it wasn't true. She had no wish for a boyfriend, and if she

291

thought Dr Jameson had any interest in her she would be so embarrassed she would probably never be able to face him again. But Cissy understood far more about all this sort of thing than Eve did, so maybe she was right.

'There, that's it.' Cissy adjusted the last curl and stood back to survey her handiwork, tweaking a curl here and there until finally she was satisfied. 'You can look in the mirror now,' she said.

Eve held up the mirror and stared at her reflection. She barely recognised the girl gazing back at her. The bouncy curls framed a small, heart-shaped face, softening the narrow angles and making her look almost pretty. Cissy's subtle make-up enhanced her wide eyes and the cupid's bow of her mouth.

Cissy's mother came bustling back in. She stopped in her tracks in the doorway when she saw Eve.

'Oh, love, that does suit you,' she said. 'You look a treat, you really do.'

Cissy smiled, obviously pleased with her creation. She turned to Eve. 'Well? What do you reckon?'

'It looks – lovely,' Eve whispered.

'I told you, didn't I?' Cissy grinned triumphantly. 'I said all you needed was a bit of help.'

'It's like magic. I never imagined I could look like this.'

Cissy blushed at the praise, but Eve could tell she was pleased with herself. 'It's nothing, really,' she shrugged. 'Just a few curlers and a bit of make-up. I could show you how to do it yourself, if you like? Then you could look like this every day.'

Eve shook her head. 'Oh, no, I couldn't do that.'

'Why not? What harm would it do to brighten yourself up a bit?' Cissy grinned. 'You never know, you might catch Dr Jameson's eye!'

Now it was Eve's turn to blush. Her thoughts flew to her aunt. Freda Ainsley would have had a fit if she'd thought Eve was flaunting herself in front of a man.

Bad blood will out. That's what she would have said.

'I'd better not,' said Eve. 'But I'd like to keep it on for tonight, if that's all right? I'd like to show Mrs Stanton and Muriel.'

And Oliver, a small voice inside her head added. Eve pushed the thought away.

Mrs Stanton was playing whist with Muriel and Oliver when Eve walked in.

'There are you, dear. Did you have a nice–' Mrs Stanton looked up and stopped dead when she saw Eve. 'Oh, my goodness! What have you done to yourself?'

All Eve's fragile self-confidence instantly crumbled. 'Is it too much?' she asked anxiously.

'No, it's beautiful. Truly beautiful. You just look so – different, that's all.'

Mrs Stanton and Muriel got up from the table and came over to study Eve. The next thing, they were stroking her curls and admiring her make-up and asking all kinds of questions about what Cissy had done and how she'd managed to achieve such a miraculous transformation.

For once, Eve didn't feel embarrassed at being the centre of attention. Instead she felt absurdly pleased and almost like a real girl as she chatted to them about lipstick and mascara. But all the time she was looking at Oliver, waiting for his reaction. He hadn't even glanced up from his cards since the first look he'd given her when she walked into the room.

Mrs Stanton finally turned to him. 'What do you think, Oliver? Doesn't she look lovely?'

Eve turned nervously to him and waited as he raised his gaze from his cards. 'I think you look exactly like your friend Cissy Baxter. But I suppose that's the point, isn't it?' he replied, his voice full of disgust.

With that, he put down his cards and walked out of the room.

'Oliver!' Mrs Stanton called after him. She turned back to Eve, instantly apologetic. 'I'm sorry, my dear,' she said. 'I really don't know what's got into him. He isn't usually so offhand.'

'It's all right,' Eve mumbled. It shouldn't matter, she told herself. She thought she looked pretty, and so did Cissy and Mrs Stanton, and Muriel, and everyone else. So why should she care what Oliver thought?

But she did care. More than she liked to admit.

Chapter Thirty-Five

Nick was coming home.

The letter Dora had longed for was waiting for her when she came in from duty one evening. She read it aloud to Danny while they were feeding the twins.

Danny frowned. 'What does em– embar–'

'Embarkation leave,' Dora finished for him. 'It means Nick's allowed home for a few days before the army sends him away again.'

Danny's face fell. 'Y-you mean he's got to g-go and fight again?'

Dora wished she could have lied to her brother-in-law, to make him feel better. But he had to know the truth.

'Yes,' she said heavily.

'But I d-don't want him to go. Wh-what if he gets h-hurt?'

'He won't.'

'He got hurt l-last time.'

Dora looked at Danny's earnest face. He was spooning food into Walter's mouth, concentrating on getting every spoonful past the baby's pursed lips without spilling any. Danny was right, she thought. He might not understand everything he was told, but she couldn't argue with his simple logic.

'I know,' she sighed. 'But what can we do? Nick has to go.'

'You c-could talk to him?' Danny looked up at her, his pale eyes shining with hope. 'Nick l-listens to you. He w-wouldn't go if you t-told him not to.'

'It's not your brother I'd have to talk to, love. It's the army.'

'Then you c-could talk to them?'

His faith was almost heartbreaking. In Danny's world, she and Nick could move mountains.

'I wish I could, ducks. But even I couldn't take on the British army.' Dora smiled bracingly. 'Anyway, listen to us. Here we are, being all gloomy when we should be happy he's coming home. We've got to keep smiling, Danny, for Nick's sake. We don't want him going off to war feeling all worried because we're fed up, do we?'

Danny shook his head. 'I – I suppose not.'

'That's the spirit. Let's just think about making this leave really special for him, shall we? So he can go off wherever he's going with some nice memories, and he won't have to worry about us.'

The idea seemed to cheer Danny up. 'I can sh-show him how I've b-been looking after the b-babies,' he said.

'That's right. He'll be proud of you.'

Danny smiled shyly. 'I w-want him to be proud of me.'

Danny insisted on sleeping with Nick's letter under his pillow. When Dora crept downstairs to the outhouse in the middle of the night, he was lying awake, trying to read it in the dark, struggling to recognise all the words from memory.

Dora smiled to herself. The poor lad hadn't seen his brother for seven months, the longest they'd ever been apart. She knew they missed each other dreadfully, and she only hoped Nick would be cheered up when he saw how Danny was flourishing.

The following morning, Little Alfie arrived back from one of his early-morning scavenging trips with some pieces of shrapnel and the news that the hospital had been hit yet again.

Dora sighed. 'What is it this time?'

'I dunno. But I saw a couple of fire engines going in there earlier on, and there was lots of smoke.'

'I hope it ain't Casualty again! We've only just started to put ourselves together after the last time.'

'I'm surprised there's anything left of the place,' Nanna commented.

'Ain't you worried one of them bombs will get you, Dor?' Little Alfie asked.

Dora glanced at Danny. He was playing with Winnie, but she could tell from his stiff posture that he was listening to every word.

'Don't be daft,' she shrugged it off. 'They haven't managed to hit me so far, have they?'

'Yes, but I thought you said one of the nurses had been killed...'

'Anyway, I'd best be off.' Dora hurriedly shoved the last of her belongings into her bag and headed for the door.

'I'll w-walk up the alley with you,' Danny said, scrambling to his feet.

Dora knew why. They'd barely got through the back gate before he said, 'I d-don't want you to g-go, Dora.'

She stifled a sigh. 'Look, Dan, you don't want to worry about what Little Alfie says.'

'It ain't j-just that.' He chewed his lip. 'I don't like it when y-you're away. The t-twins don't like it either.'

'That's why I need you to look after them for me,' Dora said. She laid her hand on his sleeve. The bones of his forearm jutted through his shirt. No matter how much her mum tried to feed him up, Danny always stayed as skinny as a rake. 'Don't you worry about me, I'll be home tonight, same as usual.'

He gazed at her with pale, trusting eyes. 'You p-promise?'

'I promise, love. And in the meantime, you just make sure you look after the kids for me, all right? They won't get scared if you don't.'

He nodded, his expression serious. 'I'll s-sing to them,' he said. 'They like that. *You are my sunshine...*' His quavering voice rose into the morning air.

'That's the spirit, Dan. You just sing to them and cheer them up till I come home, eh?'

There was no sign of the fire engines, although a pall of smoke still hung in the air. Dora made her way to the Casualty Hall and pushed aside the canvas flap that served as a doorway.

For once, mercifully, they weren't busy. Less than a dozen patients occupied the pair of wooden benches, the only remnants of the old Casualty Hall. The VADs Cissy Baxter and Eve Ainsley were handing out blankets and hot water bottles to keep out the October chill that blew

298

through the thin canvas walls. But there was no sign of any fire damage, Dora was pleased to see.

She hurried to the cloakroom to get changed. Helen came in as Dora was fastening her apron.

'Good morning,' she greeted her friend, trying to stop her teeth from chattering. 'Cold, isn't it?'

'Good thing, too,' Dora said. 'I heard the place was on fire.'

'Oh, that.' Helen rolled her eyes. 'It was just a stray incendiary that landed on the roof. Miss Hanley managed to put it out with her stirrup pump long before the fire engines arrived.'

'Good for her,' Dora said.

Helen smiled. 'Isn't it odd? A few months ago the very idea of a fire would have kept us talking for weeks, but now we hardly think about it unless the building falls down around our ears.'

'I know what you mean,' Dora agreed. 'Nothing seems very shocking any more, does it? Not since poor Dev Kowalski...'

They were both silent for a moment, lost in their thoughts. Nurse Kowalski's name might not be mentioned so much any more, but her death still hung like a shadow over them all. Dora remembered the young nurse's kindness on her first day, when she'd been so nervous.

Dora had just finished getting changed when she found the doll in her bag. She pulled it out with a groan.

'What's that?' Helen asked.

'Raggy Aggy. Winnie's doll. She won't go to sleep without it.'

'Do you want to take it home?' Helen asked.

Dora paused, torn. Going home would mean

changing out of her uniform again. On the other hand, she could be there and back in fifteen minutes...

While she was still trying to make up her mind, the familiar drone of the air raid siren filled the air.

Helen smiled ruefully. 'Looks as if Winnie might have to wait to be reunited with Raggy Aggy.'

Dora gazed down at the scruffy doll in her hands. 'I'm sure she can. She won't need it until she has her nap this afternoon. I can take it back when I have my break...'

As it was, Dora was kept so busy for the rest of the morning that she forgot about the doll. The next few hours brought a steady stream of minor injuries: wounds from falling shrapnel and shattered glass, cuts and bruises, and a couple of elderly people who had collapsed from shock and exhaustion.

It was strange, she thought, how everyone seemed to have grown used to having bombs dropping around them. After nearly two months of air raids day and night, life went on much as usual these days. Most people scarcely bothered to rush for the shelters any more, preferring to stay in their own homes instead. They were tired from all the disturbed nights, but otherwise undaunted.

Everyone who came in dropped a couple of coins in the collecting tin Matron had set up on the booking-in desk. As well as the casualties, there was also a steady stream of people bringing in gifts, including food from their own rations.

'Just a little gift, Nurse,' they would say. 'It ain't

300

much, but every little helps, eh?'

And then, just before teatime, Dora was getting changed to go home when the siren sounded again.

'You're not going now, surely?' Helen asked her.

'I've got to, even if I have to make a run for it.' Dora unfastened the stud on her collar. 'Danny will be worried if I'm not back on time, and Winnie will be frantic for—'

She was cut off by a loud crash, which threw them both to the floor and plunged the room into darkness.

'Not again!' Helen picked herself up, straightening her bonnet. 'Really, this is too bad.'

'Did they get us?' Dora eyed the cloakroom door nervously. The last time she had opened it after an explosion, she'd been greeted by a huge, smoking pile of rubble. The shock still haunted her.

Helen seemed to guess what was going through her mind. She headed purposefully to the cloakroom door and threw it open.

Outside, much to Dora's immense relief, everything was much as it had been, although the VADs and the patients seemed to be in an ungainly heap behind the booking-in desk where they had taken shelter.

'Thank God!' Helen breathed, echoing Dora's thoughts.

'But it must have been close, for us to feel it like that,' Dora said.

'We'll soon find out, won't we?' Helen said grimly.

It wasn't long before the ambulances started to arrive. By now, Dora was familiar with the drill. She and Helen went out into the yard to meet them, climbing into the back of each vehicle to assess the wounded. The seriously injured were sent straight down to Theatre or to the Emergency Treatment Rooms, while those with minor injuries were sent to the Casualty Hall to wait for their wounds to be dressed.

And then there were those for whom it was too late. They were dispatched straight down to the mortuary.

Dora hated sifting through the bodies, discarding the dead and deciding what to do with the living. It felt all wrong.

In between these duties she listened to the First Aiders and the ambulance drivers talking among themselves, sharing their scraps of news.

'It was a really nasty one, on the railway line,' the ambulance driver told her, lighting up a cigarette with shaking hands. 'Very messy business. I'm surprised you didn't get it here.'

'We caught the tail end.' Dora climbed into the back of the ambulance. Another burns victim. She could smell the scorched flesh before she pulled back the blanket. 'Where did it hit, exactly?'

'Griffin Street. Flattened the whole place.'

Dora froze, her hand halfway to the blanket. Suddenly she didn't want to see who was underneath.

Chapter Thirty-Six

'You mustn't blame yourself. There was nothing you could do,' her mother said again.

Dora couldn't trust herself to reply. She clutched her twins tighter to her and buried her face in Winnie's neck, desperate for reassurance. She hadn't been able to bring herself to let them go since she'd found them in the church hall rest centre. Her mother, brother and sister sat in a row, blankets around their shoulders, white-faced and silent with shock.

By contrast, Winnie and Walter hadn't stopped crying. They looked at her, mouths gaping, cheeks wet, inconsolable with misery.

Dora knew exactly how they felt.

'But I don't understand,' she said. 'Danny was so frightened of the explosions, he'd never go out by himself.'

'It was Winnie's doll.' Little Alfie broke his silence, his gaze fixed on the empty space in front of him.

Dora's heart quickened. 'Aggy?'

Her mother nodded. 'We were on our way to the shelter, but Danny kept saying we'd left it behind. He'd been looking for it all afternoon, said she wouldn't settle without it. I tried to tell him it didn't matter, that we'd manage. But he must have gone back for it anyway.' Rose's eyes were huge and dark in her white face. 'By the

303

time I realised he was gone, it was too late. The whole street went down like dominoes.'

'We've lost everything!' Bea started to cry, and Rose comforted her. Dora watched them and wanted to smack her sister. Danny was dead, and all Bea could think about were her lost belongings.

Danny was dead.

No matter how many times she said it, it still didn't seem real. Only a few hours ago he'd been playing with the twins, babbling to them in that daft baby talk, so excited because his brother was coming home...

'Nick!' She hadn't realised she'd cried his name aloud until she saw the three faces staring blankly at her. 'He'll have to be told,' Dora said, recovering herself quickly. 'He's coming home in a few days. He needs to know before he–'

Dora stopped talking, grief and pain choking her. She closed her eyes, but she couldn't shut out the painful thoughts that filled her head, of Nick turning up on their doorstep, all smiles, looking forward to seeing his family again. And then having to break the news to him that his beloved brother was dead.

No. Dora's mind rejected the thought. She would rather never see her husband again than have to put either of them through that.

'We'll tell him, don't worry,' her mother soothed.

'I don't know what he'll say...' It would break his heart, Dora knew it. And it would be all her fault. She had let him down. She'd promised that she would take care of his family, and she had

304

failed. Nick would never forgive her, she was certain of it.

'It wasn't your fault.' Rose's voice changed, hardening. 'You've got to stop blaming yourself, love.'

Dora stared at her. What was her mother talking about? Of course it was her fault.

She had the doll, Raggy Aggy, still stuffed in her bag. Dora couldn't bear to touch it, or even to look at it. If only she'd taken it home when she'd first realised she had it, Danny would never have tried to go back to the house and look for it.

Better still, if she hadn't left her family in the first place...

Danny hadn't wanted her to go to work. It was so unlike him to make a fuss, and yet that morning he'd all but begged her not to leave them. It was almost as if he knew...

But she'd let him down. She'd put her own selfish desires before her family, and look what had happened. Now Danny was dead, and Nanna was in hospital, and her babies had no home.

'What are we going to do?' Little Alfie's plaintive voice cut into her thoughts.

Dora glanced up and realised they were all looking at her – her mother, her brother, her sister, even her babies were staring up at her with wide, trusting eyes. They all expected her to be the strong one, to come up with the answer, to look after everyone. How could they possibly still rely on her when she'd let everyone down so badly? she wondered.

Fortunately, her mother stepped in. 'I've been talking to one of the ARP wardens,' she said. 'He says we've got to go to the Administrative Centre, down at the public library. They'll sort us out with our cards and our ration books, and all the other bits and pieces we've lost. Then we'll have to go to the Assistance Board, and the Housing Department ... and I suppose we should see about getting some of our things salvaged...' Her voice sounded bright, but Dora could see the weary despair in her eyes.

'What about Nanna? Will she be all right?' Little Alfie piped up.

'She'll be fine. They'll be looking after her lovely in that hospital. Ain't that right, Dora?'

She caught her mother's desperate look, and this time managed to rouse herself to say, 'Mum's right, Alfie. They'll take good care of her.'

'She ain't going to die, is she?'

'No, ducks, Nanna will be fine. She's just had a funny turn with her heart, that's all. You'll see, she'll be right as rain in a day or two.'

But Nanna had looked anything but right as rain when Dora went to see her in the hospital earlier. It had broken her apart all over again to see her strong grandmother laid so low. When had her indomitable Nanna Winnie become so old and frail? Why hadn't Dora been caring for her instead of nursing strangers?

Worse still was breaking the news to Nanna Winnie that Danny was dead, and that her own beloved home, the house where she'd first lived as a young bride, was reduced to nothing more than rubble and dust.

Seeing her grandmother's trembling fingers plucking at the bedcovers while she fought so hard to stay strong had been almost more than Dora could stand.

And now it was her mother who was doing her best to stay strong as she explained to Little Alfie that by the time Nanna was well enough to come out of hospital, they would have a nice new home for her to live in.

'But it won't be like Griffin Street, will it?' he said.

'No, love,' Rose admitted sadly. 'It won't be like Griffin Street.'

'I don't want a new home,' Little Alfie said. 'I want to go back to Griffin Street. I want our old house back, and everything to be the same as it was.'

Dora met her mother's gaze over his dark head. If only they could go back, she thought. How differently she would do everything next time.

But the whole world had changed in the space of an hour. Her life had completely turned upside down, and Dora wasn't sure she could cope with it any more.

'Dora?' She looked down to see Little Alfie at her shoulder, looking up at her.

'What, love?'

'Do you think Octavius managed to escape? Only I asked the ARP blokes, and they couldn't find him. I expect he ran away, don't you think?'

Dora couldn't meet her brother's trusting gaze. He was looking to her for reassurance, just like everyone else. But for once she was too exhausted to give it.

Kathleen Fox looked across the desk at Dora

Riley and wondered when the poor girl had last had a wink of sleep.

'I heard about what happened,' she said quietly. 'It's a terrible tragedy. You have my condolences, Nurse Riley.'

Dora nodded, but she didn't speak. As usual, she looked as if she was fighting to stay in control of her emotions.

'Have your family found somewhere else to live?' Kathleen asked.

'Not yet, Matron,' Dora's voice was tight. 'They're staying in a rest centre. But they might be able to go and stay with my aunt in Haggerston.'

'I see.' Kathleen paused. 'And you've decided to resign from the hospital?'

'I think it's for the best.'

Best for who? Kathleen wondered. Not Dora, judging by her wretched expression. 'And may I ask why?'

Dora winced. 'I've realised my place is with my family, Matron.'

'Well, I'll be very sorry to lose you,' she said. 'You're an excellent nurse.'

'Thank you, Matron.'

'When would you like to leave?'

'Straight away, if possible. My grandmother is in hospital, and my mother and family need me. They're not coping too well in the rest centre...'

'Very well. As I said, I shall be sorry to lose you. But I certainly wouldn't want to keep you here if your heart is no longer in it.'

'Thank you, Matron.'

As Dora reached the door, Kathleen said, 'But

don't forget, if you ever change your mind and want to come back, I would be very happy to have you.'

For the slightest fraction of a second, Kathleen thought she saw a flicker of regret in Dora Riley's muddy green eyes.

'Thank you, Matron,' she said stiffly. 'But I can't see myself ever changing my mind.'

Chapter Thirty-Seven

'You're late.'

Aunt Freda's greeting was typically chilly. Eve gritted her teeth and tried to smile.

'I'm sorry, Aunt,' she said, as pleasantly as she could manage. 'The trains are very difficult at the moment. It took me a long time to get here.'

'Perhaps you should have left earlier, in that case.'

Eve ignored the comment. She shrugged off her coat and hung it over the back of the chair at her aunt's bedside, then sat down. 'How are you feeling, Aunt?'

'How do you think I'm feeling?' Freda snapped back. 'I'm stuck here in the middle of nowhere, the staff couldn't care less, and I'm in great pain. And they never give us anything to eat.'

'I've brought you some sweets,' Eve said, delving into her bag. 'Barley sugars, your favourite. And look.' She rummaged around and produced an orange from the depths of her bag. 'Mrs Stanton managed to get some from the greengrocer's. Wasn't it kind of her to think of you?'

No need to tell her aunt that Mrs Stanton had actually bought the orange for Eve, and that she'd decided to save it.

She was proud to be able to offer her aunt such a treat, but Aunt Freda accepted the fruit and put it in the bowl on her bedside locker without thanks or comment.

Eve tried again. 'You're looking well,' she said. 'The country air must agree with you.'

'I very much doubt it. We're driven mad by planes going over day and night. And if it's not that, it's the wretched troop lorries trundling back and forth, shaking us out of our beds. I never get a wink of sleep. I might as well be at home...' she started to say then stopped, pressing her thin lips together.

Poor Aunt Freda. Eve knew it couldn't be easy for her, being uprooted and moved to the middle of the country. And she'd lost her home and livelihood, too. No wonder she looked every one of her fifty years.

As usual, it was the shop that Aunt Freda wanted to talk about. 'Have you spoken to the Borough Engineer?' she demanded. 'Has he said when they're going to start rebuilding?'

Eve was silent for a moment. The Borough Engineer's office had actually told her they had no immediate plans to rebuild her aunt's shop, or any of the other buildings on their street. But how could she possibly explain that to her aunt? Especially when the poor woman was pinning all her hopes on coming back to London.

'I have spoken to them,' she began carefully. 'But they say they're rather busy at the moment...'

'Busy, my foot!' Aunt Freda retorted. 'You have to be firm with these people, don't allow yourself to be fobbed off. Those wretched civil servants will try and get away with anything if you let them.' She gave a frustrated sigh. 'I can see I shall have to write to them myself if I want to get anywhere. I knew I shouldn't have left it to you. I might have known you'd make a mess of it.'

'But Aunt–'

'Don't argue with me, child.'

'No, Aunt,' Eve said meekly.

Aunt Freda stared at her. 'There's something different about you,' she declared.

Eve put up her hand to her blushing face. She hadn't worn make-up or curled her hair since the day Cissy showed her how a couple of weeks earlier. But she still braced herself, afraid that somehow her aunt would know what she'd done. As Aunt Freda always told her, she could sniff out sin.

Finally, her aunt sat back and said, 'You've put on weight. That's what it is.'

Eve didn't know whether to be relieved or dismayed. 'I – I don't think I have, Aunt.'

'I thought I told you not to argue with me?' Aunt Freda stared down her long nose at Eve. 'It doesn't suit you,' she said flatly. Then she added, 'I hope you're not gorging yourself at the Stantons' expense?'

'No, Aunt!'

'And you're helping out and making yourself useful, as I told you?'

311

'Yes, Aunt.' No point in telling her that Mrs Stanton refused all offers to cook and clean around the house. Aunt Freda would only say Eve hadn't tried hard enough. Desperate to impress her aunt, she said, 'I'm learning the piano. Mrs Stanton has been giving me lessons.'

Her aunt frowned at her. 'And whose idea was that?'

'Mrs Stanton's. She says I'm quite good.'

'I daresay she was just being kind,' Aunt Freda dismissed. 'Really, Eve, you shouldn't take advantage of their good nature. Piano lessons, indeed! I'm sure Mrs Stanton has better things to do!'

'But she offered,' Eve said lamely, then flinched as her aunt turned on her.

'You mustn't make a nuisance of yourself,' she hissed. 'Remember, you're not a house guest. You're only there thanks to their Christian charity, and you should do your best to stay out of their way as much as possible and not impose on their good nature. They don't want you acting as if you're part of the family.'

'But they seem to quite like me...'

Aunt Freda sent her a withering look. 'Of course they don't like you!' she snapped. 'They've taken you in as a favour to me. Do you really think they'd want to know you otherwise?'

The journey home was just as long and difficult as the way down had been, except now it was dark, and the wind was lashing the rain against the windows, and the train finally gave up and pulled into a siding three miles from London. Eve didn't have the money for a taxi so she walked the rest of the way. At least she didn't have to fear the dark for once, as the sky glowed orange with the light from distant incendiaries, and the ground shook with the crump of bombs from the planes swooping overhead. By the time she reached the vicarage, her heart was in her mouth and her legs were shaking so much they could barely hold her up.

The house was in darkness as she crept in. But as she passed the door to the library, she was surprised to see a welcoming fire blazing in the hearth.

She put her head round the door. Oliver sat in one of the leather wing armchairs beside the fire, a sketch pad balanced on his knees. The firelight gave his fair hair a burnished glow as he bent over his work.

He looked up at her and smiled. 'There you are! Mother was wondering if you'd got lost. It was all I could do to stop her sending out a search party.'

They don't like you, she heard her aunt's voice saying in her ear. *They've taken you in as a favour to me...*

'I'm sorry,' Eve murmured, taking off her coat. 'I didn't realise anyone would be waiting up for me.'

'I had to promise Mother I would, otherwise I think she would have had half the constabulary out looking for you.' Oliver peered at her. 'You're soaking wet,' he said. 'Is it raining that badly?'

'My train terminated in Essex. I had to walk the rest of the way.'

'You've walked all that way in this rain? You'll catch your death.' He put down his sketchbook and stood up. 'Here, let me help you.'

He helped her off with her coat and hat. 'Go and sit by the fire, for heaven's sake. Would you like some cocoa? Mother left you some supper in the kitchen too, if you'd like it?'

Eve's stomach growled at the mention of food. She hadn't eaten since breakfast. 'That's very kind,' she murmured. 'I'll go down and get it.'

She moved to the door but Oliver stopped her. 'Keep warm,' he said sternly, pointing to the armchair he'd just vacated. 'I'll bring it up to you on a tray.'

'Really, you don't have to go to so much trouble.'

'It's no trouble. Mother would be furious if I allowed you to get pneumonia.'

His sketchbook was lying or the armchair where he'd abandoned it. As she approached, Eve could just about make out the rough pencil outline of a figure. But before she could see any more, Oliver grabbed the book and flipped it closed.

'Just trying something out,' he muttered. 'Not sure if it works or not. Now, about that cocoa...'

Eve perched uneasily on the armchair, gazing into the flames. All the time her aunt's words kept swimming through her mind. *You're only there from their Christian charity, and you should do your best to stay out of their way as much as possible... They don't want you acting as if you're part of the family...*

Was she imposing on the Stantons' good nature by sitting here, warming herself by their fire? Eve wondered. They were so kind, it was hard to tell.

Oliver returned with her supper on a tray and set it down in front of her. Eve looked up at him. 'Aren't you eating?'

He shook his head. 'I had something earlier, with the rest of the family.'

She felt a little self-conscious at first, with him sitting opposite her, watching her eat. But she was so tired and famished, she soon forgot he was there as she tucked into her cold ham and pickles.

'You don't have to stay up with me,' she ventured. 'I don't want to keep you, if you'd rather go to bed?'

'I'd rather stay and chat to you, if you don't mind? I could work while we talk.'

Eve paused, her fork halfway to her mouth. She couldn't remember anyone ever asking if she minded anything.

'How was your aunt?' Oliver asked, flipping open his sketchbook and picking up his stubby pencil. 'I daresay she was pleased to see you, wasn't she?'

Eve thought about Aunt Freda sourly picking over the gifts she'd been given, rejecting the book Eve had chosen and turning her nose up at the barley sugars, even though a week earlier she'd insisted they were her favourites. 'Oh, yes,' she said. 'We had a lovely time.'

'Then why do you look so sad?'

Eve looked up at him sharply. 'I don't know what you mean?'

'It's in your eyes,' he said. 'You're always smiling, but your eyes are always so full of sadness.'

Eve lowered her gaze, suddenly self-conscious again. 'It's all right,' Oliver said. 'I don't think anyone else notices. Only me. It's one of the perils of being an artist,' he said wryly. 'I'm used to seeing behind people's faces.'

Can you see behind mine? Eve wanted to ask. But she didn't really want to know the answer.

'You haven't answered my question,' Oliver reminded her after a moment. 'Why are you so sad? Has your aunt said something to upset you?'

Eve gazed down at her plate, picking over her food. Then she asked, 'Do you think your parents mind having me here?'

Oliver looked genuinely surprised. 'What makes you ask that?' Then his eyes narrowed. 'Did your aunt put that idea in your head?'

'I just wondered.' Eve still didn't look at him, although she could feel him watching her intently, his pencil still moving restlessly over the page. 'I am very grateful to you for having me here,' she said. 'But I don't want to impose on your charity for too long...'

'Charity?' Oliver echoed. 'What makes you think we're offering you charity?'

'Aren't you?' At last she lifted her eyes to meet his, and was surprised by the look of tenderness she saw there.

'Not at all,' he said. 'My parents love having you here. We all do,' he added, so softly Eve wondered if she'd imagined him saying it. 'Anyway,' he went on briskly, 'my mother would never hear of you leaving. You're like a second daughter to her. And Muriel loves having a sister. Between you and me, I think she's always wanted one. I've been a lifelong disappointment to her,' he said, pulling a face.

Eve smiled. 'Everyone has been very kind to me.'

'Kinder than your own flesh and blood, from what I gather.'

Oliver muttered the comment under his breath, and once again Eve wondered if she'd heard him properly. 'What do you mean by that?' she asked.

His face flushed in the firelight. 'Nothing,' he said. 'It's just something I've noticed, that's all…'

'For your information, my aunt has been nothing but kind to me,' Eve told him sharply. 'She took me in when I was just a baby, gave me a name and a roof over my head. If it hadn't been for her, I would have ended up in an orphanage, or the workhouse. And she taught me a trade, so I could earn my own living.'

'And never paid you a penny,' Oliver murmured.

'Why should she? I should have been repaying her for everything she did for me!' Eve parroted back the words she'd heard so often while she was growing up.

'You're right,' Oliver said quietly. 'I shouldn't have criticised her. She's your family, after all.'

'Yes, she is.' Ridiculous as it was, Eve felt a sudden pang of longing for her aunt's chilly kitchen. Difficult as Aunt Freda might be, at least Eve had felt she belonged there.

She picked up her tray and stood up. Oliver closed his sketchbook again and looked up at her in dismay. 'Where are you going?'

'I'm taking this back to the kitchen,' Eve said stonily.

He sighed. 'I've upset you, haven't I? Look, I'm sorry. I shouldn't have said anything – Eve, come back!'

But she was already out of the door and heading for the kitchen. It wasn't that she was angry with Oliver, but he was far too observant for her liking. And Eve didn't want him seeing behind her face. Not for anything.

Chapter Thirty-Eight

Jennifer dropped the letter in the postbox and immediately regretted it.

What was she thinking? It was the fourth time she'd written to Philip Chandler in the two months since he'd left the hospital, and he hadn't replied once. She had long since given up looking out for the postman.

If she'd had any sense, she would have given up writing to him by now. Why couldn't she take the hint? If Philip Chandler had ever been interested in her, he certainly wasn't now. She didn't even know if her letters were getting through to him. For all she knew, he could have been transferred to another hospital, or even sent home.

But still she wrote. Even though she told herself every letter would be the last, as the days went by the urge to write would grow stronger and stronger, until she couldn't stop herself from picking up her pen again.

Her letters to Philip had become like a diary for her. She told him all the news about the hospital, about where she'd been and what she'd been up to. But she also talked about her feelings, just as she had when they used to talk every evening. She shared all her fears and frustrations, about her work, Cissy, even Johnny... It felt strange in a way, writing down her innermost thoughts to someone she barely knew. Perhaps knowing that Philip may never read them made it easier to tell him how she really felt.

This letter had been all about her friendship with Cissy, and how it had turned sour because of Eve Ainsley. Although once she'd written it down, Jennifer began to realise that perhaps Eve wasn't the real cause of her problems. She had neglected Cissy, and so Cissy had taken up with Eve to teach her old friend a lesson.

And it had worked. Jennifer was determined not to drift apart from her any more, which was why she had arranged for them to go to the pictures that night. She wanted to make a special effort with her friend, to show her how sorry she was that she'd taken her for granted.

So she was very put out when she saw Cissy coming up the street arm in arm with Eve Ainsley.

'What's she doing here?' The words were out of Jennifer's mouth before she could stop herself.

Eve looked as if she might take flight, but Cissy tightened her grip on her arm. 'It was my idea,' she said. 'Eve's never been to the pictures before, so I said she could come with us. I said you wouldn't mind?' Her gaze was fixed on Jennifer, hard and meaningful.

Jennifer looked at Eve. Trust her to poke that pointed little nose in where it wasn't wanted! 'It's a free country, I suppose,' she shrugged.

They made an awkward group, walking to the

picture house. Jennifer had been looking forward to a good gossip with Cissy, but it was difficult with Eve there, hanging on to every word. She looked such a sight, too, shrouded in a drab, shapeless coat that must have been at least three sizes too big for her. Didn't the girl own any nice clothes? Jennifer wondered.

She did her best to ignore Eve and leave her out of the conversation, but Cissy kept drawing her back into it. In the end it was Jennifer who felt like a gooseberry, listening to them gossiping about Casualty, and one of the doctors who had apparently taken a shine to Eve.

'It's true,' Cissy said. 'I definitely saw him smile at you this morning.'

'Dr Jameson smiles at everyone,' Eve murmured, a tide of colour sweeping up her face.

'Yes, but it was the way he smiled. You must have noticed it, surely?' Eve shook her head. 'Trust me, a man doesn't smile at a woman in that way unless he's interested in her. Isn't that right, Jen?'

'I wouldn't know, I wasn't there,' Jennifer reminded her.

But Cissy didn't take the hint and soon they were off again, discussing Dr Jameson and his supposed interest in Eve. Privately, Jennifer couldn't imagine why anyone as good-looking and lively as Simon Jameson would ever look twice at a drip like Eve, but she didn't voice her thoughts. Cissy was fussing over Eve like a mother hen, and Jennifer had a feeling her friend would turn on her if she said a word out of place.

It was even worse when they got to the cinema.

Eve was irritatingly wide-eyed as the usherette showed them to their seats, gazing around at their grand surroundings like a child in a toy shop. Jennifer would have made a sharp comment but Cissy sat protectively between them, sharing her sweets with her new friend. She seemed utterly charmed by Eve's excitement.

'Look at her,' she whispered to Jennifer. 'I'm glad we invited her, aren't you?'

Luckily the first Pathé News film lit up the screen, saving Jennifer the trouble of replying. She stared up unseeingly at the flickering images of the Duke of Kent inspecting a brand-new type of aircraft, her mind elsewhere.

This was all wrong, she thought. It was supposed to be her and Cissy, not Cissy and Eve. Six months ago she would have laughed at the notion that her best friend would go off with anyone else, let alone a timid little mouse like Eve Ainsley. Yet here they were, whispering together as if Jennifer didn't exist.

Mindlessly, she found herself fiddling with the gold bracelet on her wrist for reassurance. Perhaps she shouldn't have come. She could have gone out with Johnny instead. At least she knew he cared about her...

The Pathé film ended, and the lights went up again before the main feature. Cissy was still talking to Eve, but she didn't seem to be listening any more. Her attention was fixed on Jennifer's bracelet.

'Where did you get that?' she asked in a small, flat voice.

'My Johnny gave it to me.' Jennifer held up her

wrist so they could admire the bracelet, pleased that the attention was on her for once. 'Do you like it?'

Eve didn't reply. But the way she was staring at the bracelet sent an uneasy feeling creeping up the back of Jennifer's neck. She tweaked the sleeve of her jumper down over her wrist, concealing the bracelet from sight.

Cissy stepped in. 'What's wrong?' she asked Eve. 'Are you all right? Do you need some air?'

Eve stared at Jennifer's wrist. 'I know that bracelet,' she said. 'It belongs to my aunt. It was stolen after our house was bombed.'

There was a short, awkward silence. Jennifer could feel Cissy looking at her, her gaze reproachful. *You see,* she seemed to say. *What did I tell you?*

Jennifer turned on Eve, wild with outrage. 'Are you implying my Johnny is a thief? You don't even know him...'

'No, but I know that bracelet,' Eve insisted quietly.

'You must be mistaken. It probably just looks like your aunt's bracelet, that's all...'

'My aunt's bracelet has a diamond missing from the clasp.'

Cissy turned to Jennifer. 'Let's have a look,' she said.

Jennifer tucked her arms around herself. 'No.'

'Go on, Jen. Then we'll know it isn't the stolen bracelet, won't we?'

Jennifer glared at her. She didn't like the way Cissy was looking at her, as if she already knew the truth. She was supposed to be Jennifer's friend.

Why wasn't she sticking up for her, instead of taking Eve's side?

'Show us,' Cissy said.

She made a grab for Jennifer's wrist but she jerked her arm away. 'Leave me alone! I don't have to show you anything.'

'Because you know we're right,' Cissy said.

So it was 'we' now, was it? Two against one. Except, for the first time, Jennifer was the one being left out.

'I don't have to prove anything to you. If you were a real friend you'd believe me,' she said.

'I am your friend. That's why I'm trying to make you see sense. It's about time you found out what that Johnny Fayers is really like, Jennifer Caldwell!'

They glared at each other. The lights lowered again, and the heavy red velvet curtains drew back slowly. Jennifer stumbled to her feet and started to move along the row, fighting to get out.

She half expected Cissy to get up and follow her, but it was Eve who called out to her.

'Wait!' she cried. 'I'm sorry...'

'Leave her,' Cissy muttered. 'Let her go, if that's what she wants.'

Her mother and father were in the kitchen when Jennifer let herself in.

'You're early,' Elsie Caldwell said.

'The projector broke down, so they cancelled the film.'

It was a stupid lie, but all Jennifer wanted to do was escape. She didn't need a barrage of questions from her mother.

323

'That's a shame. I've heard it's a good one, too.' She looked past her daughter's shoulder towards the hall. 'Did Cissy not come home with you?'

'No,' Jennifer said. 'No, she didn't.'

Her mother and father looked at each other, but said nothing. They probably thought she and Cissy had had another of their fallings out. But this time it was more than just a spat. Jennifer didn't think she would ever forgive her friend for humiliating her like that.

She went upstairs to the sanctuary of her own room. She sat down heavily on the bed and steeled herself to take off the bracelet. Until a few hours ago, she couldn't stop admiring it. Now she could hardly bear to touch it.

As she went to undo the clasp, as usual her thumb found the tiny hollow where the diamond was missing. She hadn't liked to point out the flaw to Johnny when he first gave her the bracelet. And as time passed, she had stopped noticing it.

Until now. She wrenched off the bracelet and flung it across the room.

Eve had ruined everything. Again.

It was the first film Eve had ever seen and she had been looking forward to coming to the cinema. But she couldn't concentrate on the black-and-white images flickering across the vast screen in front of her. Even when the picture magically burst into colour and Dorothy and her friends began their magical journey to the Emerald City, Eve was too preoccupied to notice.

She should never have said anything, she

thought. But she couldn't help it. The words were out the minute she'd seen Jennifer flaunting her aunt's bracelet, showing it off so proudly on her wrist.

She hadn't meant to humiliate her, and she certainly hadn't meant to drive her away.

'I should apologise,' she said to Cissy as they walked home afterwards.

'Why? It wasn't your fault. If anyone apologises it should be Jen.'

'But she was so upset...'

'Good,' Cissy said firmly. 'Perhaps it will make her wake up at last and realise what kind of man that Johnny Fayers really is.' She turned to Eve. 'I've a good mind to tell my dad.'

'You can't do that!' Eve was shocked. 'What if Jennifer got into trouble?'

'It would serve her right,' Cissy muttered. 'It might even drum some sense into her.'

'Please don't,' Eve begged. 'She's upset enough, without us making it worse.'

'I suppose you're right,' Cissy agreed heavily. 'But all the same, he can't be allowed to get away with it. We should do something, surely?'

'I think if anyone does anything, it should be Jennifer.'

Cissy laughed harshly. 'She won't! She's far too besotted with him. If he told her black was white, she'd believe him.'

I'm not so sure, Eve thought. She'd seen the distraught look on Jennifer's face as she rushed out of the cinema. Cissy might not believe it, but Eve had a feeling Jennifer Caldwell had finally woken up to the truth.

Chapter Thirty-Nine

Nick came home on the day of his brother's funeral.

Dora could feel the tension in his body as she stood beside him at the graveside. Like her, he was fighting hard to contain his emotions. But Dora could sense the torrent of pain behind his blank-eyed stare.

They had barely spoken since he'd come home. Nick was quiet, lost in his thoughts. The only time Dora had seen him smile was when the twins crawled into his lap, stroking his hair and planting sloppy kisses on his face.

Dora wished she could go to him, too. She longed to wind her arms around his neck and bury her face against his broad chest, just to be close to him so they could comfort each other. But there was something so chilly and forbidding about him, she didn't dare.

She had longed to see him, but dreaded it at the same time. She knew their reunion would be difficult, but she had never imagined he would be so cold towards her She was desperate for re-assurance, but he could barely bring himself to look at her.

And Dora knew why, too. Nick blamed her for his brother's death almost as much as she blamed herself.

She sneaked a glimpse at his profile now, standing beside him at the grave. His face was expressionless, as if it had been carved from stone. His flattened boxer's nose and strong jawline were as familiar to her as her own, and yet Dora hardly recognised them any more.

But then, she barely recognised much about her life after the past week. Her days had become an endless round of trudging around Bethnal Green, going from one office to the other, queuing up at one place for identity cards, another for ration books, emergency relief, clothes, and everything else they needed. Other people had grumbled, but Dora was thankful for the excuse to keep herself busy.

There was a time when she might have sought refuge in her work, losing herself in the comforting hospital routine. But not any more. As far as Dora was concerned, it was her work that had caused Danny's death. He was dead because she'd put her own selfish needs first, instead of staying at home and looking after her family. If only she had been there to comfort her baby daughter instead of putting all the responsibility on to Danny's young shoulders. He had been doing what she was supposed to do, taking care of her children.

The funeral ended, and the mourners started to walk away from the grave. Dora reached for Nick's hand. It hurt to see him flinch from her touch. When his fingers finally closed around hers, his grip was cold and lifeless.

They were supposed to go to Auntie Brenda's house in Haggerston for the funeral tea. Dora and her family were staying there until they could find somewhere else to live. But on the way Nick suddenly announced that he wanted to go for a walk to clear his head.

'I'll come with you,' Dora offered straight away, but Nick shook his head.

'I'd rather be on my own, if you don't mind?'

She watched him go, hands thrust in his pockets, shoulders hunched against the cold.

'Just leave him be, love.' Her mother came up behind her. 'He's got a lot on his mind, that's all. He'll come round in the end.'

But Nick didn't come round. He didn't return to the house until later that evening, and then he insisted on sleeping in an armchair in the kitchen, even though Dora's mother and sister had moved into the front parlour to give them some privacy while Nick was on leave.

Dora lay awake, staring at the ceiling, feeling utterly rejected and miserable. She knew that Nick was grieving, but surely this was the time when they should have been together, comforting each other. What did it say about her marriage that her husband couldn't even bear to sleep in the same bed as her any more?

On her mother's advice, she put up with it for two long days. Two days of silence, and two nights of sleepless misery. Dora tried to keep her distance, understanding only too well that it was Nick's way to retreat into himself when he was angry or upset. But all the while she could feel their precious time slipping away. Tomorrow he would be gone, off to God knows where. She had no idea when or if she would ever see him again.

It was that thought that finally made her creep downstairs in the middle of the night to see him.

He wasn't asleep. He was in the armchair, a blanket pulled up to his chin, staring into the dying embers of the fire. Dora hesitated for a moment in the doorway, watching him. The firelight's glow softened the hard planes of his face. With his grim mask down, he looked so lost it touched her heart.

He looked up sharply when she walked in. 'Dora?'

She smiled. 'Can't you sleep either?'

He shook his head and turned his gaze back to the fire. Dora crossed the room, her legs suddenly trembling, and sat down on the rug at his feet. As she leaned against him, she felt his body stiffen. It hurt, but she forced herself to ignore it.

'You're leaving tomorrow.' Her voice sounded loud in the shadowy silence of the kitchen. 'Do you know where they might send you?' He shook his head. 'When will you be back?'

'Can't say. Might not be for a while.'

'How long?'

'A couple of years, maybe.'

She twisted round to look up into his expressionless face. 'Two years?'

He lifted his broad shoulders. 'That's what everyone reckons.'

The flat tone of his voice filled her with anger. 'You don't seem very upset about it?' she said.

'What am I meant to do, then?'

You're meant to love me, she thought. You're meant to put your arms around me and tell me it's not my fault, that everything will be all right.

But it was too late for that, she realised bleakly. It wasn't just Danny who had died. Their marriage had died with him.

And it was all her fault.

Dora gazed into the dying firelight and silently prayed for the strength to get through what had to be done next. 'I'm sorry,' she said flatly.

'So am I.'

'I know I let you down, and I know you'll never forgive me for it, but I want you to know how sorry I am. Believe me, if I could go back and change what happened I would. I would rather I'd died that day than poor Danny.'

'Don't say that.'

'It's true. I know how much he meant to you, and it's my fault he's dead. Believe me, you can't hate me any more than I hate myself. But I can't live the rest of my life like this, with you blaming me. I'd rather we just walked away from each other now than see that hatred in your face.'

Nick was silent for a long time. When Dora risked a glance at him, she saw a single tear running down his face.

'Is that what you think?' he said hoarsely. 'That I hate you?'

'That's why you've been avoiding me, isn't it? That's why you won't talk to me, or hold my hand, or share a bed with me—'

'It's not because I hate you. It's because I hate myself.'

Dora frowned. 'I don't understand?'

'I promised to look after you, and Danny, and the babies. It was my job to protect you.'

'But how could you?' Dora said. 'You weren't here.'

'Exactly. I should have been here, looking after

you all. I shouldn't have left you to cope without me.' His jaw clenched with tension. 'I let you down,' he said.

Dora stared at him, and suddenly it dawned on her why her husband couldn't meet her eye, couldn't touch her. He was ashamed because he felt he'd failed her. Just as she felt she'd failed him. They were locked together in a world of guilt, each blaming themselves for what had happened.

And in reality, neither of them was really to blame.

'I thought you didn't love me any more,' she whispered.

'Oh, Dora, I love you more than anything in the world.' Nick reached for her, finally, and when his strong arms went around her it was as if a dam had broken, engulfing them both in the warmth and light and love they'd been denying themselves for so long.

'When I heard about Danny, it broke my heart.' Nick's voice was gruff with emotion. 'But at the same time I was relieved because you and the kids were safe. All I could think about was getting back to you. But then when I saw you, I felt so ashamed that I'd put you in danger.'

'You didn't put us in danger,' Dora said. 'You didn't drop that bomb, Nick. Any more than I did.'

'All the same, I knew I couldn't protect you. And I need to protect you, Dora. I need to know you and the kids are safe.' He pulled away from her, holding her at arms' length. 'I want you to go away,' he said. 'I want you to take the twins and leave London.'

'But where will we go?'

'I don't know. I don't care where you go, so long as you're safe.' He stared down at her, his eyes wretched. 'I don't know what I'd do if I lost you, Dor. I just don't know...'

'Just as well you ain't going to lose me, then.'

At last she could put her arms around him, feel the reassuring strength of his body against hers.

'I don't want to leave you,' he whispered into her hair.

'You don't have to. Not until tomorrow.' She smiled up at him, her hands cupping his face, feeling the rough stubble of his chin against her fingers. 'We've already wasted enough time, don't you think?' she whispered.

Chapter Forty

'I've got something for you,' Johnny said.

Jennifer's heart sank, and she was instantly reminded of Cissy's words.

It's about time you found out what that Johnny Fayers is really like.

She'd tried to ignore her friend's comment, told herself Cissy was just jealous, that she didn't know Johnny the way Jennifer did. But then she had to admit she didn't really know him herself at all. They were just two strangers, pretending to have a good time together.

From somewhere outside came the distant wail

of the air-raid siren, but nobody moved. No bomb would ever dare penetrate the tiny subterranean club where they sat drinking champagne in the middle of the day.

Jennifer looked around her. The private club had always seemed so like Johnny, glamorous and lively. But now she realised it reminded her of him because it was dark and full of secrets.

All those shady corners, filled with characters just like Johnny. Hunched over tables, doing deals. How had she never noticed what lay beneath the showy façade?

'Go on,' Johnny said, pushing the package towards her.

Jennifer stared down at it, filled with dread. Please, she begged silently. Please don't prove Cissy right.

'Aren't you going to open it?' Johnny's smile hardened. 'Don't look so worried, it ain't an unexploded bomb!'

Jennifer unwrapped it with trembling hands, and tried to smile when she saw the bottle of perfume.

'Evening in Paris – that's the one you like, ain't it?' Johnny's grin was back in place, so sure of himself. 'You said you'd nearly run out, so...'

She tried again to smile as she unscrewed the stopper and took a long sniff. Evening in Paris. An image of Philip Chandler came into her mind, and the sharp suddenness of the pain took her breath away.

He'd probably forgotten all about her and her perfume by now, she thought.

From far above came the muted whine of aircraft, followed a moment later by the retort of the ack-ack guns.

'Do you like it?' Johnny was watching her keenly from across the table.

Jennifer replaced the stopper and put the bottle back on the table. 'Where did you get it?' she asked.

He tapped the side of his nose. 'What have I told you about asking questions?'

Usually she would have giggled, but this time uncertainty welled up inside her. 'Where did you get it, Johnny?' she repeated.

His smile faded. 'One of my business connections,' he replied. 'Someone owed me a favour.'

'Are you sure you didn't steal it?'

His expression darkened, and Jennifer felt instantly wary, knowing she had crossed a line.

'What are you saying, Jen?' The lightness of his voice belied the storm clouds gathering in his eyes.

Jennifer opened her mouth, then closed it again. It would have been much easier just to say nothing, to step away from the brink of an argument. But she couldn't go on turning her back on the truth for ever.

'I just want to know, Johnny,' she said quietly. 'Did you steal it?'

He stared at her for a long time. She kept her fingers crossed under the table. If he denied it, she would believe him and everything would be all right.

'No,' he said finally. 'I didn't steal it.'

There. He'd said it. Now everything could go back to normal and she could be happy again.

Except there was something in his guarded reply...

'But someone did?' she said.

'What if they did? How do you think I get hold of all these presents for you? They don't just fall out of the sky with the bombs, y'know.'

Jennifer stared at him, dazed. Even now, she wanted him to deny it, to tell her she was being silly. But they were past lying, she realised.

'You don't need to look so shocked,' Johnny mocked her. 'You ain't that naïve.'

'Perhaps I am,' Jennifer said sadly. She'd thought she was so sophisticated, sipping champagne and hobnobbing with rich people. And if she was honest, she had known about Johnny's shady business dealings, and even found them a little thrilling.

But now she realised that all this time she had been swimming hopelessly out of her depth. And she was starting to drown.

'I thought it was just black-market stuff,' she said.

'Shh! Keep your voice down!' Johnny hissed, glancing around. 'I told you, I'm a businessman. I see an opportunity, and I grab it.'

'Even if it means robbing people who've lost their homes, their families?'

'I dunno what you're talking about,' he muttered.

'I'm talking about this.' Jennifer slid the bracelet off her wrist and put it on the table between them. 'A girl at work recognised it, Johnny. It belonged to her aunt. It was stolen when their house was blown up. This, and a few other bits and pieces,

335

which I'm sure you know about.'

She went to move but his hand flashed out, encircling her wrist painfully where the bracelet had been, pinning it to the table. 'Have you told anyone else about this?' he snapped.

'No, of course not.'

'Are you sure?'

'I told you, didn't I?' Jennifer tried to twist free from his grasp, wincing at the pain. 'Let go, Johnny. You're hurting me.'

He released her, then snatched up the bracelet and slid it smoothly into his pocket. 'You'd better not say anything either,' he warned.

'Why would I go round telling people my boyfriend is a thief?' She rubbed the tender skin where his fingers had dug into her flesh.

She must have pricked his conscience because he looked away. 'Everyone's doing it,' he muttered. 'The police and the ARP wardens, they're the worst. They're the real villains, making out they're helping people, when all the time they're just helping themselves.'

'And that makes you better than them, does it?' Jennifer said. 'Because you're an honest thief?'

He glared at her, his eyes hostile 'I dunno what you're looking so high and mighty about. You were happy enough to drink my champagne and take my presents. Showed off to your friends about them, too, I shouldn't wonder.'

'Only because I didn't know where they came from.'

'Do me a favour! You're worse than my customers, pretending they haven't got the faintest idea that they're buying ill-gotten gains. At least I

336

admit what I do.'

He was right, Jennifer thought. Supply and demand, he'd called it. She'd demanded, and he'd supplied. She was as guilty as he was, in her way.

But not any more. Jennifer squared her shoulders and looked at him. 'I want you to stop,' she said.

He stared at her for a moment, then laughed. 'You're joking, ain't you?'

'You could find another job,' she urged him. 'Something legal.'

'You're right,' he said. 'I could give up my business, everything I've worked for, and become – I don't know – a bus conductor. Or maybe I could get myself a nice job at that hospital of yours, shifting bodies about?'

Jennifer flushed. 'I'm not saying you have to do anything like that. You could make money some other way. You're clever,' she urged him. 'And you know lots of people. I'm sure you could find something.'

He set his jaw. 'I'm happy as I am, thanks.'

'But those people you steal from – they've lost everything.'

'They won't miss a bit more then, will they?'

She stared at him across the table, gazing intently into that rugged face and trying to remember what it was that had ever attracted her to him. How had she ever felt a thrill, looking into those stone-cold eyes?

'If you don't give it up I'm leaving you,' she said.

A slow, insulting smile spread over his face. 'You really do think a lot of yourself, don't you?

Do you seriously imagine I'd give up the chance to make good money, just for a little tart like you?' He took out his cigarettes and lit one with deliberate slowness. 'If you want to leave, you know where the door is.'

For a moment, she sat rooted to the spot with humiliation. People were starting to look at them, glancing up from their own business.

She rose to her feet with as much dignity as she could muster. 'Right, I'm going,' she said. 'But I think you should know I'm going to tell my dad about you.'

She'd lashed out to upset him, but the minute she saw his smile disappear Jennifer knew it was a foolish move to threaten him.

'You what?' he said.

'You heard.' She lifted her chin and forced herself to meet his gaze, even though her heart was fluttering against her ribs.

She'd backed away from him and was nearly at the door by the time he reached her. Before Jennifer knew what had happened, he'd pinned her to the wall. 'Now you listen to me,' he said. 'You ain't going to say a word to anyone. Not if you know what's good for you.'

'And what are you going to do about it?'

'You'll find out. I don't like people crossing me.'

All around, the walls seemed to be closing in on her. She could hear the rumble of bombs overhead, like the rumble of thunder.

'Oh, Johnny...' She gave him the sweetest smile she could muster. Then, in the swift movement her father had taught her, she brought her knee

338

up sharply between his legs.

For a second his hard eyes registered shock and pain. Then he doubled over, giving her enough time to reach the door.

'Jen! Come back here!' His voice seemed a long way behind her as she ran up the flight of steep stone steps back to the street.

'Catch me!' she called over her shoulder, pushing open the wooden door. The cold, bright November day seemed to hurt her eyes and she paused for a second to catch her breath.

And then, suddenly, she heard someone cry out. Jennifer turned to look in their direction – and she knew no more.

Chapter Forty-One

Jennifer had a dream. She was floating on a cloud with a bright light all around her, and far below her she could hear her parents' voices. Her mother was crying and her father was trying to comfort her. Except he didn't sound like her father. His voice was low and shaking, as if he was trying to stop himself crying, too. Jennifer wanted to call out to them, but she was too far away, and she couldn't make them hear her.

She felt something tugging at her, pulling her out of her dream. But she resisted. She didn't want to leave the floating warmth of her cloud behind and drift back to the cold, hard earth.

And then she opened her eyes and she was still

dreaming, still floating. Only this time they weren't just voices – she could see her mother sitting beside her, and her father. Just as in her dream, he had his arm around her mum's shoulders, comforting her.

Jennifer tried to speak, but her face was stiff and painful, as if she was wearing a tight mask. The pain made her cry out, and her mother looked up.

'She's awake! Alec, she's awake! Oh, thank God!' Elsie was smiling, but tears streamed down her face.

'I'll fetch someone,' her father said.

Fetch someone? Who? Jennifer tried to look around, but everything seemed blurred, shrouded in a strange mist. She could just make out dim pools of lamplight, white-painted brickwork, and a smell that seemed very familiar to her. Disinfectant, mingled with the slightest tang of damp...

Her father returned with a tall figure in a grey dress. As the woman drew closer, Jennifer recognised Sister Dawson.

But it made no sense. If she was in hospital, why was she lying down and not tending to the patients?

Suddenly it all came back to her, a torrent of memories flowing into her head at the same time, overwhelming her. The club, Johnny, their argument ... the images came too thick and fast for her to see them properly.

Sister Dawson was checking Jennifer's pulse and breathing, calm and professional as ever. All the while Jennifer's mind was racing, trying to piece together what had happened. But everything was like a jigsaw puzzle, fragments of a picture that didn't seem to fit together.

She remembered running up the steps, into the street. Then someone had called out to her, a warning...

And then nothing.

'Johnny?' She tried to say his name, but her tongue refused to move in her mouth.

'Jen?' Her mother's face loomed anxiously in front of her. Poor Elsie Caldwell looked as if she'd aged ten years. 'What did you say, love?'

'Johnny...' Tears of frustration pricked her eyes, stinging her face as she struggled to speak.

Sister Dawson laid a calming hand on her shoulder. 'Don't try to move, my dear,' she said. 'Dr McKay has given you some morphia for the pain. It'll wear off in a while.' Sister Dawson lifted one of Jennifer's eyelids to check her pupils. 'But I'm afraid you'll be rather sore when it does.'

'She's lucky to be alive,' her father said. 'When I first saw her in that ambulance...' He shuddered. 'I've got used to seeing casualties, I can tell you. I've seen a lot worse than our Jen, too. But when you turn up to something like that and find your own daughter covered in blood–' His shoulders heaved, and it took a moment for Jennifer to realise that he was crying. She tried to reach out for him, but her limbs didn't seem to belong to her.

'She's luckier than most,' her mother said. 'It would have been a different story if she'd been in that club with those other poor souls. Buried alive, they were. Doesn't bear thinking about, does it?'

Johnny...

'What happened – to Johnny?' she managed to

341

ask. She saw the quick look that flashed between her mother and father and immediately knew the answer. 'Is – is he dead?'

Elsie Caldwell leaned over and patted her hand. Jennifer felt the weight of her fingers, but no warmth. It was as if her skin was dead. 'I'm so sorry, love.'

Johnny was dead. Before Jennifer could take in the information she felt herself being pulled backwards into the numbing fog of sleep, until she was flying, floating, drifting again on her cloud, with her mother and father and Sister Dawson and the troubles of the world far below her.

But this time her dream was more vivid. She was on the street outside the club, and someone was calling to her, trying to warn her. Everyone was running, and she tried to run too. But then came the sound of shattering glass, and suddenly she was being thrown through the air.

She woke up, flailing and gasping for breath. It felt as if a thousand wasps were crawling over her skin, stinging her all at once with white-hot shards of pain.

'Jen?' There was no sign of her parents, but Cissy was at her bedside, in her uniform. She was smiling, but her white, worried face and red-rimmed eyes gave her away. 'You're awake at last.'

'My – face...' Jennifer could make a sound, but still struggled to shape her swollen lips around the words. She could feel the skin splitting as she tried to speak, blood oozing from painful wounds. Her head felt as if it had been filled with hot, molten metal.

Oh, God, what was happening to her?

She tried to touch her face, but Cissy took hold of her hand.

'Not yet,' she said. 'Wait until I've finished.'

It was then Jennifer saw the forceps in her friend's hand. In her lap, tiny fragments of bloodied glass glittered like ghastly rubies in a receiver dish.

A wave of sickness welled up inside her. 'Bad?' she asked.

'Not too bad.' But Cissy's hand was trembling as she leaned in to remove another piece of glass. She was a terrible liar, Jennifer thought.

She pulled out the glass, and Jennifer flinched in pain. 'Does it hurt?' Cissy asked, immediately anxious. 'Shall I fetch the doctor, see if he can give you any more morphia?'

Jennifer shook her head. 'Not morphia ... mirror.'

'I don't think that's a good idea,' Cissy started to say, but Jennifer grabbed her hand.

'Mirror,' she repeated, forcing her painful mouth to say the word clearly. She stared at Cissy, trying to signal with her eyes what she couldn't manage with her voice, imploring her friend to help her.

Cissy's round blue eyes filled with tears. 'Honestly, Jen, I think it's for the best if you don't see,' she said.

'Want – to.' She tightened her grasp on her friend's hand. 'Please?'

Cissy glanced around, then set down the dish and forceps and hurried off.

She returned a moment later with a small hand mirror. 'I really shouldn't be doing this, you

343

know,' she said, looking around. 'I expect Sister will have a fit.' She went to show Jennifer her reflection, then hesitated. 'Are you sure about this? Perhaps I should fetch the doctor first, see what he says?'

'Please, Cis.'

Cissy sighed, and angled the mirror above Jen's head for her to see her reflection. 'It's not as bad as it looks, really,' she said lamely.

But one glance told Jennifer that it was worse. Much worse.

Chapter Forty-Two

'Cup of tea, love?'

Dora pressed a cup of strong brew into the cold hands of the woman in front of her. She and her family had arrived before dawn, the latest to be bombed out of their home.

There had scarcely been any raids in the month since early November. But the previous night Hitler had sent a handful of bombers over to remind them all they still weren't safe in their beds.

And Mrs Gibbons and her family had caught the worst of it. Dora recognised the shock on the poor woman's face as she struggled to come to terms with what had happened to her.

'Cheers, ducks.' Mrs Gibbons gave her a tired smile and took a slurp of tea. 'Ah, that's better.' She smacked her lips appreciatively. 'Although I must say, it'll take more than a cuppa to sort out my problems,' she sighed.

'I know it's hard at the moment,' Dora sympathised. 'But I'm sure you'll find somewhere else to live soon.'

'I hope so, love. This place is nice enough, but I wouldn't want to spend Christmas here.'

Dora and the other WVS volunteers had tried hard to make the rest centre look a bit more festive as Christmas approached. Someone had unearthed a box of old decorations, and now the school hall was strung with tinsel and paper garlands. It was an incongruous sight next to the exhausted faces of families who had lost everything.

At least Dora and her family had started to get back on their feet. The Corporation had found them a couple of nice rooms at the top of a tenement house in Roman Road. It wasn't the same as Griffin Street – her mum missed her backyard and Nanna didn't like all the stairs – but they had a place to call their own.

Dora had tried to do as Nick said and persuade them to leave London, but Nanna wouldn't budge.

'I don't care how many bombs he drops, Hitler ain't chasing me out of the East End,' she declared defiantly. 'You lot can go if you like, but I'm staying put.'

After that, there was no question of Dora leaving her family. She couldn't imagine being separated from her mum, and knew she would only worry herself to death if she and the twins left them behind in London.

But at the same time she worried that she hadn't taken Nick's advice. What if something happened to the babies because they'd stayed in the city? It was that fear that haunted her, robbing her of sleep. Sometimes she would sit at the window all night, staring out at the dark sky, watching for danger.

And when she did sleep, she always dreamed about Danny.

Even though she tried to smile and make the best of things for the sake of her family, Danny's death still hung over her like a dark shadow. Sometimes she would wake in the early hours after a vivid dream, convinced he was in the room with her. Or she would be sitting up in bed, keeping watch, and she would hear him singing.

'You are my sunshine, my only sunshine...'

She missed him desperately, but the twins missed him even more. They would call out for him, holding out their arms, waiting to be picked up. Then they would cry when Dora appeared instead.

'He ain't here, sweetheart,' she would say, tears pricking her eyes. 'I only wish he was.'

She couldn't blame Danny for haunting her. She had let him down so badly, no wonder he hadn't forgiven her. She wasn't sure she would ever forgive herself.

Her mother came to join her as she washed up. Rose Doyle worked alongside her at the rest centre for a couple of hours a day. Dora insisted on bringing the twins with her. She had scarcely let them out of her sight since the night of the bombing.

'I'm worried about the Trewell boy,' said Rose. 'He's got an awful cough. Been up all night, so his mum says.'

'She needs to take him to a doctor, in that case.'

'She doesn't want to send for one. Between you and me, I think she's a bit frightened of doctors since her husband died.' Her mother paused, and Dora knew what was coming next. 'Couldn't you take a look at him?'

Dora shook her head. 'I can't, Mum.'

'But why not?'

'Because I don't do that any more. I look after my own family, I don't care for other people's.'

'You don't mean that. I've never known you turn your back on anyone in need.'

Dora looked into her mother's face, and knew she was right. Try as she might, she couldn't ignore a plea for help.

'Where is he?' she sighed.

Paddy Trewell was seven years old, and usually a lively boy. Dora often saw him running around the rest centre, playing with his toy train. But now he lay listless on a mattress, racked with a cough that shook his skinny little body.

Dora put her hand to his forehead. 'There doesn't seem to be any fever, which is a good sign,' she told his worried mother, who sat anxiously beside him. 'Just keep him warm, and make sure he gets plenty of rest.'

'Easier said than done in this place!' Mrs Trewell said grimly.

Paddy Trewell coughed again. His little chest went into spasm, his ribs jutting painfully through his skin with every cough.

347

'He also needs something for that chest,' Dora said. 'An inhalation of turpentine or Friar's Balsam would be best.'

'I've got some liniment, would that help?' her mother offered.

Dora nodded. 'It might relieve the pain, at any rate,' she said. 'Bring it here, and I'll show you how to rub it into his chest. Bear in mind, you'll need to do it every couple of hours...'

'You know, you're wasted here,' her mother said later, after Dora had shown Mrs Trewell how to treat her son's cough. 'You should be back at that hospital, not here making cups of tea.'

Dora held up her hand. 'I don't want to hear it,' she said flatly.

'But–'

'I'm never going back to nursing, and that's an end to it.'

She went to finish the washing up, but her mother followed her. 'I don't understand why not,' said Rose. 'I thought you enjoyed it?'

'I did.'

'Well, then.'

'I enjoyed it too much, Mum. That was the trouble.'

Matron had tried to warn her on that day back in the spring when she went to ask for her job back. She'd told Dora that nursing would consume her entire life and test her priorities, and she was right. Except Dora had got her priorities wrong. She'd put her work above her family, and Danny had paid the price for it.

Rose Doyle sighed. 'How long are you going to go on punishing yourself, Dor? You know it wasn't your fault Danny died. And stopping nursing ain't going to bring him back, is it?'

'I know that,' Dora said quietly.

She scrubbed at a pan, until she felt her mother's hand on her arm. 'He wouldn't have wanted you to go on punishing yourself, love,' she said quietly. 'He would have wanted you to help people.'

'I am helping people, Mum.'

'Not like this,' Rose said. 'I mean really helping. Why don't you go back to nursing, love? I'm sure they could do with you at the hospital–'

'Don't, Mum,' Dora cut her off. 'I can't go back, all right? Don't ask me again.'

The truth was she couldn't even walk past the hospital without averting her gaze. Just the thought of going back through those gates made her feel sick.

But she had to. By the following day, Paddy Trewell had got much worse. Dora could feel the burning heat coming off his face before she'd even put her hand near his sweat-glistened cheek.

'You need to get him to hospital,' she told his mother.

'Can't you do anything?' Mrs Trewell begged. 'Maybe some more of that liniment–'

Dora shook her head. 'Liniment won't help now the infection's taken a hold. Hospital's the best place for him, honestly.'

Mrs Trewell's lip trembled. 'But I'm scared,' she said. 'They took my Albert into hospital and he never came out...'

'Paddy will be all right, I promise,' Dora assured her. 'But he needs proper treatment.'

'Will you come with us?' Mrs Trewell asked.

'I can't.'

'Please, Dora? I'd feel a lot better about it if you were there.'

'I've got to stay here and look after the twins.'

'They'll be fine with me,' Rose Doyle stepped in. 'You go, Dora. Do what you can for little Paddy.'

Dora sighed. As her mother said, she could never turn her back on anyone in need. More's the pity, she thought.

It took all her courage to walk through the hospital gates. By the time they reached the courtyard, Dora was trembling so much she couldn't face going into the Casualty Hall.

'You go in,' she urged Mrs Trewell. 'I'll sit out here and wait for you. It's all right, I'll be here if you need me,' she said, when the other woman looked reluctant.

'Promise?' Mrs Trewell said. 'Promise you'll stay here?'

'I promise.'

She sat down on the bench under the plane trees in the middle of the courtyard, huddled in her coat against the December chill. How strange that the trees and the bench had stayed standing when so many of the hospital buildings had come down around them, she thought.

There was building work going on around the Casualty Hall. The tented structure remained around what was left of the building, its sign still resolutely in place.

The Nightingale Hospital – open for business as usual.

They'd laughed about it when Matron had it put up, but it had made them feel proud, too. As if it was somehow one in the eye for Hitler. They were standing up to him, defying him.

And now they were rebuilding the walls of the Casualty Hall, making it bigger and better than ever by the look of it.

'Dora?' She swung round. Helen stood behind her, navy blue cloak wrapped around her shoulders. 'I thought it was you.' She smiled. 'What are you doing here? You haven't come to ask for your old job back, have you?' Her face brightened hopefully.

Dora shook her head. 'One of the kids at the rest centre was taken poorly. I see you're rebuilding?' she changed the subject, nodding towards the Casualty Hall.

'At last!' Helen said. 'I must say, I'll be glad to work in a real building again. That tent gets a bit chilly at this time of year, and we practically have to wrestle the blankets off the nurses to give to the patients!' she laughed.

'I can imagine.'

Helen nodded towards the building and beamed with pride. 'Can you believe we raised most of the money to rebuild it from that collecting jar Matron left on the booking-in desk?'

'Never!'

'It's true. You'd be amazed what people put into it. One man walked in and stuck a five-pound note in, just because he was so proud of us for staying open through the Blitz! And those workmen are mostly volunteers,' she added. 'Just ordinary people, giving their time and their labour for nothing, because they want to put the Nightingale back together again.' She turned to Dora, smiling. 'It's wonderful when you think about it, isn't it?'

A lump rose in Dora's throat, and she could only nod in agreement.

It was wonderful indeed. And it made her proud that she had once been a part of it. Seeing it again made her realise why she had been so reluctant to come back to the hospital. It was because she knew how much she still missed it.

As if she could read her thoughts, Helen suddenly said, 'Are you sure you wouldn't like to come back? I'd love it if you did. A few more of our nurses have gone off to serve abroad, and we're desperately short. And now David's leaving, too—' she stopped short, biting her lip.

Dora stared at her. 'Dr McKay's been called up?'

Helen nodded. 'He's joining the medical corps. He's been wanting to go for a while, but he didn't want to leave while London was being bombed. But now the Germans seem to be laying off us for a while, there isn't as much to keep him here.'

'Except you,' Dora said.

Helen lifted her shoulders in a graceful shrug. 'We all have to do our bit. I understand that.'

'Doesn't make it any easier, does it?'

'I suppose not.' She managed a brave smile. 'But really, I'm no worse off than hundreds of other women, am I? We see them in here every day, wives and mothers who have had to send their men off to war. I'm lucky that I've been able to keep him with me for so long. But I always knew this day would come...'

Her voice tailed off, but Dora could read only too clearly the thoughts behind her unhappy dark eyes. Poor Helen. She had already had her heart broken once in her young life. She dearly hoped her friend never had to endure that pain again.

'Anyway, I think I'd find it easier to bear if I had a friend here,' Helen went on, pulling herself together. 'Are you sure you wouldn't consider coming back?'

'I can't,' Dora said. 'I'm sorry.'

Helen paused. 'I understand, you know,' she said. 'You can't help blaming yourself when someone close to you dies. You constantly ask yourself if there was anything you could have done differently. When Charlie died, I blamed myself too.'

'That was different,' Dora said. 'You couldn't have stopped him getting scarlet fever.'

'And you couldn't have stopped that bomb dropping.'

'No, but I could have been there.'

'And then you might have died too, and the twins would have been without a mother.' Helen sent her a considering look. 'Are you sure you're not just punishing yourself by turning your back on something you love? Because I'm sure Danny wouldn't have wanted you to do that–'

'Stop,' Dora begged her. 'I've heard it enough from my mum. I don't want to talk about it, please?'

Helen nodded. 'Then I won't try to force you,' she said. 'But please, promise me you'll think about it at least?'

Dora nodded, but she already knew what her

353

answer would be.

Perhaps Helen was right, she thought. Perhaps she was punishing herself. But if so, it was the right thing to do. Danny had lost his life, and the least she could do was to lose something that she treasured, too.

I am doing the right thing, aren't I, Danny? She sent the thought up into the empty air.

Just then Dora spotted Mrs Trewell across the yard, and went over to meet her.

'What's happened? How's Paddy?'

'They've taken him in,' she said in a choked voice. 'But it's all right, the doctor said they'll be able to treat him. He reckons he'll be as right as rain in a day or two. He's already brightened up no end, especially once he got a look at all the toys on the Children's ward!' Mrs Trewell gave Dora a shaky smile. 'Thanks for talking some sense into me.'

'That's all right. We all need someone to talk sense into us sometimes.'

As they walked back across the courtyard, Dora heard a sound that stopped her in her tracks.

'What is it?' Mrs Trewell frowned. 'What's wrong?'

Dora held up her hand to silence her. She turned her head, listening for the sound. At first she thought she'd imagined it. But then she realised it was one of the workmen, up a ladder, singing. His voice drifted down to her, carried on the chill wind.

'You are my sunshine, my double Woodbine, my box of matches, my Craven A...'

Mrs Trewell smiled. 'It's a daft song, isn't it?

354

I've heard some of the men singing it in the shelter. Those ain't the real words, though.'

'I know,' Dora said quietly. But she wasn't listening to the words. She was listening to the oh-so-familiar tune, drifting down from the top of the ladder, as if it was coming down from heaven.

Chapter Forty-Three

The day after she'd arrived home from hospital in Kent, Jennifer was helping her mother to put up Christmas decorations when Cissy called round.

'Tell her I'm not in,' Jennifer said immediately, peering through the net curtains.

'Don't be daft.' Her mother smiled at her encouragingly. 'Cissy's been dying to see you. She asks after you all the time.'

'I mean it, Mum,' Jennifer pleaded. 'Tell her I'm not well enough for visitors. Tell her I'm not ready...'

'It'll do you good,' Elsie Caldwell said. 'Besides, you can't hide away for ever, you know. You've got to get used to seeing people again.'

She went to answer the door and Jennifer automatically put her hand up to her face, feeling the roughness of her skin under her fingers. Everyone said the scars were healing well, but Jennifer hadn't looked in a mirror since that day she'd woken up in hospital after her accident.

She had spent the past month in the Nightingale's sector hospital, recovering from a fractured skull. She'd been glad to be able to hide herself away. She knew she looked a terrible sight, her shorn head hidden under a hospital cap, her face a sickening mess of tiny cuts. Her hair had started to grow back, but she could still feel the rough line of the scar that crawled across her scalp underneath.

She heard her mother talking to Cissy in the hallway and concealed herself behind the Christmas tree, pretending to be draping tinsel from its branches.

But even then, she noticed Cissy flinch when she walked in and saw her friend. It was the first time they'd seen each other since that day in the hospital. Any faint hope Jennifer might have had that she was looking better vanished the moment she saw the appalled expression in her best friend's eyes.

A second later Cissy's bright smile was back in place. 'Hello, stranger,' she greeted Jennifer.

'Hello yourself.' Jennifer kept her eyes fixed on the piece of tinsel she was draping, as if it was the most important thing in the world.

'How are you?'

'All right, I s'pose.'

'I'm glad to see you,' Cissy said. 'I would have come down to visit you, but I couldn't get any time off from the hospital.'

'It's all right. I didn't really want visitors anyway.' Jennifer nodded towards the small bag in her friend's hand. 'What have you got there?'

Cissy blushed. 'It's a Christmas present for

356

you,' she murmured. 'Only–' She stopped talking abruptly.

'Only what?'

'Nothing.' Cissy's blush deepened. 'You might as well have it anyway.' She thrust it into Jennifer's hands as if she couldn't wait to be rid of it. 'I was so pleased when I found it ... you can hardly get them anywhere these days.' Her words tumbled out in a rush. 'I didn't stop to think... I'm sorry...'

Jennifer opened the bag and stared down at the powder compact in her hands. Once upon a time she might have been delighted to receive such a gift, but now it seemed more like an insult.

'Reckon it'll take more than a bit of powder to make me look better.' She tried to sound light-hearted, but she couldn't keep the bitterness out of her voice.

'As I said, I didn't stop to think that you–'

'That I might look like a monster?' Jennifer finished for her.

Cissy blushed. 'I didn't mean that,' she mumbled.

'You might as well have it back, anyway.' Jennifer went to hand it over, but just at that moment her mother came in.

'What's that you've got? Oh, is it a present? Isn't that kind of Cissy, Jen? I'll put it somewhere safe for you, shall I?' She took the compact and put it in her apron pocket. 'I'll go and put the kettle on, shall I?' she went on briskly. 'You'll stay for a cuppa, won't you, Cissy?'

Jennifer willed her to say no, but Cissy smiled politely and said, 'Yes, thank you, Mrs Caldwell.'

Elsie Caldwell bustled off, leaving the two girls

alone. The silence stretched between them, awkward and unfamiliar.

'You didn't have to stay, you know,' Jennifer said.

'I wanted to. I've been looking forward to a good old gossip.'

Jennifer sent her a sceptical look. 'How come you've hardly said a word, then?'

Cissy looked uncomfortable. 'Your tree's looking nice,' she commented at last.

'It will be, when it's finished.'

'Can I help you?' Cissy offered.

'You can unravel that tinsel, if you like.'

They worked together in silence. Usually they would have been chatting away nineteen to the dozen, but now they struggled to find something to talk about.

As Jennifer hung the baubles from the tree, she was aware that her friend was staring at the ornaments on the mantelpiece, the pictures on the walls, her own shoes ... anything but at Jennifer's face.

'I look a fright, don't I?' she said finally.

'No, no, of course not,' Cissy said quickly.

'Then why can't you look at me?'

Cissy slowly lifted her gaze to Jennifer's face, then glanced quickly away. 'The scars are healing up nicely,' she mumbled.

'So they tell me.'

'And your hair's growing back. It suits you short.'

'No, it doesn't.' Jennifer smoothed her hand over her dark cap of wispy curls. Losing her crowning glory was nearly as heartbreaking as having her face ruined.

The silence stretched between them. Jennifer cleared her throat. 'So,' she said. 'What have you been up to?'

'This and that. It's not been so busy at the hospital since all the bombing stopped, and they've started to admit patients again instead of sending them down to the sector hospital. There's even talk of opening up a couple of the main wards again, once they've finished repairing the buildings.'

'That'll be nice,' Jennifer replied without enthusiasm. The last thing she wanted to talk about was hospitals, as she'd spent the last month in one. But she couldn't think of anything else, so she let Cissy carry on as she finished decorating the tree.

'Actually, I'm going to start training properly,' Cissy said. 'I've talked to Matron about it, and she says I can start in January.'

Jennifer frowned. 'You, a nurse?'

'Why not? I know I didn't like it much when we first started, but I've actually started to enjoy the work, especially now they've moved me up to the Female Acute ward.'

'Wonders will never cease,' Jennifer muttered.

'Eve's signed up too. You should join us, it'll be fun.'

'No, thanks,' Jennifer said. 'I've seen enough of hospitals to last me a lifetime, thank you very much.'

'But you always enjoyed nursing,' Cissy said. 'And you were a lot better at it than I was. You'd be a natural–'

'I don't want to!' Jennifer cut her off abruptly.

'Besides, you've got your friend Eve now. And you know what they say – three's a crowd.'

Cissy lowered her gaze. 'Don't be like that,' she said quietly.

How do you expect me to be? Jennifer wanted to shout at her. In the space of a few minutes everything had been ruined for her. That shattered window had scarred her inside and out, taking away her looks, her confidence, her whole life.

And to cap it all, her best friend could hardly bear to look at her.

'Anyway, what else has been going on?' she changed the subject briskly. 'Any gossip?'

Cissy thought for a moment. 'They're holding a dance at the hospital, just after Christmas,' she said. 'Matron's organised it to try and cheer us all up after the awful year we've had.' She flicked Jennifer a quick look. 'You should come.'

'How can I?' Jennifer replied bitterly.

'I don't see why not. You worked at the Nightingale right the way through the Blitz. You should be there. Everyone else is going, all the doctors and nurses. Go on, it'll be a laugh!'

'I don't feel like it.'

'But you love dancing!'

'Not any more.'

Cissy looked as if she might argue, but decided against it.

They were saved from more awkwardness as Jennifer's mother popped in with the tea. Cissy drank hers quickly, then announced she had to go.

'Off somewhere special, are you?'

Cissy looked at the floor. 'I promised Eve I'd

help her find something to wear for the Christmas dance,' she replied quietly.

'Eve, eh?' Jennifer felt another flash of jealousy. 'That sounds like fun.'

'Why don't you come and help, too?' Cissy offered. 'You know you're much better at picking clothes than I am.'

'No, thanks.'

'I'll come round and see you again tomorrow, shall I?' Cissy said.

Jennifer shrugged. 'If you're not too busy with Eve,' she couldn't stop herself sniping.

Cissy's face crumpled with sadness. 'Don't, Jen,' she begged.

Jennifer turned away. 'Just go,' she muttered.

Her mother came back in when Cissy had left. 'She didn't stay long,' she commented.

'She had other plans.'

'So I heard.' Her mother picked up the tea tray. 'You should have gone with them.'

'And listen to those two gossiping together all the time?' Jennifer shook her head. 'Besides, she only invited me because she felt sorry for me.'

'How can you say that? Cissy's your best friend.'

'Not any more.' Jennifer turned her face to stare out of the window at the wintry December street outside. The sky was a dirty yellowish-grey and snow had started to drift out of the sky. 'I'm better off on my own,' she said.

'Is that why you don't want to go to that dance?'

Jennifer glared at her. 'You were listening all the time?'

'I couldn't help overhearing, could I? Anyway, why don't you want to go? It would have done you good.'

'To have all those people staring at me ... pitying me? I doubt it.'

'No one would do that.'

'Look at me, Mum! I'm a freak.'

'Only in your own mind.' Elsie Caldwell set down the tray and stared at her for a long time. 'You might have a few scars but you're still a pretty girl. If you looked in the mirror, you'd see that.'

Jennifer shuddered. 'I don't want to.' Seeing herself for the first time in hospital had shocked her so much, she didn't want to do it again.

'But the scars aren't nearly so bad now...'

'They're still there. I can feel them.'

Her mother planted her hands on her hips. 'So what are you going to do? Hide yourself away for ever?'

Jennifer was silent. The truth was, hiding herself was exactly what she wanted to do. She didn't want to have to face anyone. She couldn't bear the idea of everyone looking at her, pitying her. She hadn't even wanted to come home to London. She preferred to be buried down in the country, among strangers, people who didn't know her and who didn't matter.

'Cissy's right,' Elsie Caldwell said. 'You should ask for your job back at the hospital, maybe start training properly like her.'

'No!'

'But you used to enjoy it.'

'They wouldn't want someone like me working

on the ward.'

Her mother sighed, the fight going out of her. 'Have it your own way,' she said. 'But you're going to that dance, Jennifer Caldwell.'

'I am not!'

'Oh, yes, you are. I know you're worried, but you're not going to get over anything by hiding yourself away. You're going, even if I have to drag you out of this house myself!'

'What do you think of this one?' Eve frowned critically at her reflection in the mirror. 'I know it's not much at the moment, but if I took up the hem a few inches, and shortened the sleeves, and put in a couple of darts here...' She turned to look at Cissy, who was staring blankly into space. 'Cissy?'

'Hmm?' Cissy looked at her, smiling vaguely.

'The dress?' Eve reminded her. 'What do you think of it?'

'It looks ... very nice.'

Eve gazed back at her reflection. The rose-pink taffeta dress was far from nice. It was big and fussy and old-fashioned, which was probably why it had lain unclaimed and unloved at the bottom of Mrs Stanton's jumble pile for so long. But with her trained tailor's eye, Eve knew she could transform it into something special.

All she needed was Cissy's approval. She might have the skill, but she had no confidence when it came to deciding what suited her. She desperately needed Cissy's flair to make her believe she could pull it off.

But Cissy was miles away, and had been ever

since she'd arrived at the vicarage.

Eve put down the dress. 'What is it?' she asked.

'Oh, nothing,' Cissy sighed. But she bit her lip when she said it, a sure sign she was anxious.

'You can tell me.' Eve paused, then said, 'It's Jennifer, isn't it?'

She knew Jennifer had come home from hospital earlier that day, and she also knew Cissy had been to visit her. Eve had been wondering all afternoon whether Cissy would even remember she was supposed to be helping her to choose a dress. She was convinced that once the pair were reunited Cissy would forget all about her.

But Cissy had turned up just when she'd said she would, with a face as long as a fiddle. Something had gone wrong, Eve knew.

Sure enough, at the mention of Jennifer's name, Cissy's blue eyes filled with tears.

'Oh, Eve, it was awful!' she cried. 'She's changed so much. I don't mean her scars or anything. It's like she's a different person in here.' She put her hand to her heart. 'I couldn't even talk to her, and you know how Jen and I always liked to talk. But she was so cold – almost like she's lost interest in life. She didn't even want to come to the Christmas dance. Reckons she doesn't like dancing any more.' She rummaged in her sleeve and pulled out her handkerchief to dab her eyes. 'I never thought I'd see the day Jen Caldwell turned down a night out dancing!'

'Perhaps she needs time?' Eve suggested. 'She's just come home from hospital, after all. Everything's bound to feel a bit strange until she finds her feet.'

'Do you think so?' Cissy sniffed. 'I suppose you could be right. It was such a shock, seeing her like that. It was almost like she didn't want to know me any more.'

'I'm sure she'll be all right once she's got used to being home,' Eve said.

'I hope so.' Cissy smiled gratefully at her. 'Thanks for talking some sense into me, Evie. You're a good friend, you know that?'

A good friend. Never in her life could Eve have imagined having a friend like Cissy Baxter.

But at the same time, a small unworthy part of her hoped that Cissy wouldn't renew her friendship with Jennifer. Because then there might no longer be any room for Eve in her life.

Chapter Forty-Four

As soon as Jennifer walked into the dance, she realised she had made a terrible mistake.

It was all too much for her. The bright lights, the loud music, the laughter – after so many weeks hiding away, it was like a horrible dream. The kind of dream where she found herself lost in an unfamiliar place with no clothes on, and everyone was staring at her.

They were staring at her now. Jennifer could feel several pairs of eyes boring into her back as she slunk around the edge of the dance floor to join the row of wallflowers.

She burned with shame. Once upon a time she

would have felt nothing but pity for them, sitting there so hopefully, clutching their glasses of punch and waiting for someone to ask them to dance. But now she was the one to be pitied. Even though she kept her gaze fixed on the dance floor, pretending to be absorbed in watching the dancers spinning around in front of her, she could hear the other girls whispering together, glancing her way, then whispering again.

Jennifer put her hand up to her face, an automatic gesture of self-protection. She wished she'd swallowed her pride and asked Cissy to come with her. At least she would have had a friend, someone to talk to. But Jennifer had only made up her mind to come at the last minute, because her mother nagged her into it.

'You'll enjoy it,' she'd kept saying. 'Go on, you need an excuse to get yourself dressed up.'

So now here she was, in an old dress, wishing she had never listened to her mother. No amount of make-up could cover her scars, and her hair hadn't grown enough to curl into anything like a nice style.

She heard one of the girls giggling, and something inside Jennifer snapped. She turned on them. 'Had a good look? Perhaps you'd like to take a picture, so you can show all your friends?'

The girl turned red. 'We weren't talking about you.'

'No, of course you weren't!' Jennifer sneered back. 'You think I can't hear you, whispering and laughing behind your hands? You're not exactly an oil painting yourself, you know!'

She looked away in disgust, in time to see Cissy

coming into the hall, arm in arm with a pretty girl in a pink dress. Cissy saw her, waved and came over, dragging her friend behind her.

'Jen! Why didn't you tell us you were coming? We would have waited for you.'

'I – I didn't make my mind up until the last minute.' It was only when the girl in the pink dress drew nearer that Jennifer realised with a shock that it was Eve Ainsley.

But it wasn't the Eve she remembered. Make-up transformed her ordinary features, widening her grey eyes and giving a glossy pink softness to her mouth, while her light brown curls perfectly framed her face.

And that dress – well, it could have come straight off the catwalk of Elsa Schiaparelli herself, nipping in at her tiny waist then flaring out over her hips, giving the illusion of curves to her skinny shape.

But it wasn't just the clothes and make-up that were different. Eve seemed to glow, as if lit from within. Jennifer couldn't stop gawping at her.

Cissy smiled, guessing her thoughts. 'What do you think?' she said proudly. 'She looks all right, doesn't she?'

Jennifer caught Eve's shy smile, and felt a painful stab of jealousy. She instantly put her hand up to her own face, feeling the roughness of her scarred skin under her fingers.

'You look nice, too,' Eve complimented Jennifer. 'That dress really suits you.'

She was trying to be kind, Jennifer realised. But the last thing she needed was to be patronised by the likes of Eve Ainsley. Just because she'd had her hair done and was wearing a dress that fitted her for a change, that was no reason for her to get all high and mighty. Underneath those bouncy curls, she was still the same insipid little creature she had always been.

Not that Cissy could see that. She looked completely besotted with her creation.

'We're just going to get some punch,' she said, taking Eve's arm again. 'Why don't you come with us?'

Before Jennifer could reply, Dr Jameson and her old medical student friend Tom Treacher came over to them.

'Good evening, ladies,' Simon Jameson greeted them smoothly. 'My friend and I were wondering if you might dance with us?'

His gaze skimmed over Jennifer, and she was already smiling before she realised he was holding his hand out to Eve and not her.

Jennifer glanced at Tom, but he was looking away as if he didn't know her. She quickly tried to hide her embarrassment, but Cissy's sharp eyes must have caught it, because she said, 'Sorry, we can't.'

Jennifer interrupted her. 'You can go and dance, if you like,' she said. 'Don't mind me. I'll go and get some of that punch.'

Cissy chewed her lip, reluctance written all over her face. 'You will wait for me, won't you?' she said.

'Of course.' Jennifer shrugged.

'Promise?' Cissy was still watching her friend over her shoulder as Tom Treacher led her on to the dance floor. 'Promise you'll wait there till I come back?'

'I promise,' Jennifer mouthed back. She kept the smile pinned to her face until they had disappeared among the dancers. Then she hurried away.

Her mother would be furious with her, but Jennifer didn't care. She had had all the humiliation she could bear for one evening.

Fortunately her mother was out visiting a friend when Jennifer arrived home, but her father was in the kitchen, listening to the nine o'clock news on the wireless. She tried to tiptoe down the hall, but as she reached the foot of the stairs he called out, 'Is that you, Jen?'

Her heart sank. 'Yes, Dad.'

She heard the creak of his old armchair as he stood up and came into the hall to greet her. 'You're home early, love. Didn't you enjoy the dance?'

'Not really.' She shrugged. 'To be honest, I'm a bit tired.'

'That doesn't sound like you. What happened to the girl who used to come home at dawn on the back of a milk float?'

Jennifer glanced at him in shock. 'How did you know that?'

'There's a lot of things I know, love.' Alec Caldwell's eyes twinkled. 'Like I know it ain't tiredness that's brought you home early. Am I right?'

Jennifer caught her father's kindly gaze and suddenly all the fight flooded out of her. 'Oh, Dad!'

The next thing she was in his arms and he was comforting her, just like he used to do when she was a little girl and had fallen over and hurt her knee.

'Come on,' he said, his arm around her shoulders. 'Let's have a cuppa and you can tell me all about it.'

As they sat together in the kitchen, Jennifer told him about the dance, and about how everyone had looked at her. Her father listened sympathetically.

'Are you sure you ain't just seeing and hearing what you want to?' he asked.

'I don't want people staring at me, or talking behind my back.'

'No, but it's what you expect, so that's what you think is happening.' Alec Caldwell regarded her over the rim of his teacup. 'Either way, the question is what are you going to do about it?'

'I dunno what you mean.'

'I mean, are you going to hide away, or are you going to go out there with your head held high?'

'I know what I'd like to do,' Jennifer murmured into her cup. 'I just want to lock myself in my room and stay there.'

'That doesn't sound like my Jen.'

'Yes, well, I'm not your Jen any more, am I?' she snapped back. 'The explosion – what happened – it changed me, Dad. You only have to look at me to see that.'

'I look at you every day,' her father reminded her. 'And all I see is my beautiful little girl.'

Jennifer turned her gaze towards the dying fire. Of course, he would say that, wouldn't he? He was her father, and she would always be beautiful to him.

'Other people see something different,' she muttered. 'They see a monster.'

Her father sighed. 'That ain't true, girl, and you

370

know it.'

'I don't care anyway. I'm never going to face anyone again.'

'Oh, yes? And how are you going to manage that, then? You can't lock yourself away, no matter how much you might feel like it.'

'Want to bet?'

Her father shook his head. 'Look, I can't take away what happened to you, no matter how much I wish I could.' His face filled with sadness. 'But I won't allow you to ruin your life over it.'

'My life's already ruined.'

'No, it ain't. Not if you don't let it be.'

'So what am I supposed to do?' Jennifer asked.

'You've got to get out there and face the world.'

'I tried that, remember?'

'I don't mean going out tonight,' her father dismissed. 'I mean getting yourself back in the land of the living. Going back to work would be a start–'

'Oh, no.' Jennifer was shaking her head before he'd reached the end of his sentence. 'You've been talking to Mum, ain't you? I bet she's put you up to this. But I ain't going back to the Nightingale, Dad. I can't do that.'

'You've got to do something, love.'

'Then I'll find a job somewhere else. In a factory, or an office or something. There's plenty of other war work I could do. Just don't ask me to go back to that hospital, please!'

But for once her father stood firm. 'Until you're twenty-one, you'll do as you're told, my girl,' he said. 'And I'm telling you, the best thing you can do now is put that uniform on and get back to that hospital!'

'I'm sorry,' Eve said for what seemed like the hundredth time.

Dr Jameson smiled down at her. 'Stop apologising,' he said. But Eve could see the pained look that flashed across his face every time she trod on his feet. He was such a good dancer, he must despair of her, tripping over her own feet and stamping on his toes. He was probably wishing he'd asked Jennifer to dance instead of her, she thought.

She tried to remember to do what Cissy had told her, and smile up into his eyes while they were dancing, but embarrassment stopped her from lifting her gaze past his bow tie. She only hoped he couldn't feel how clammy her hands were.

The tune ended and another began. Eve started to move away, grateful to escape, but to her astonishment Dr Jameson held on to her hand.

'Can't we have another dance?' he pleaded.

'Are you sure?' She eyed him uncertainly, not sure if he was making fun of her. 'I'm not a very good dancer,' she pointed out, as if he hadn't noticed that by now.

'You know what they say. Practice makes perfect.'

Eve glanced at Cissy, already making her way off the dance floor.

'I can't,' she said. 'I need to see my friend.'

'The next dance, then?'

'If you like.' He probably would have found himself another partner by then, she decided.

Eve caught up with Cissy by the punch bowl. 'I can't see Jen anywhere, can you?' Cissy said, looking around. 'I hope she hasn't gone home.'

A thin thread of jealousy snaked its way into Eve's heart. She wanted to tell Cissy all about her dance with Dr Jameson, to share the exciting details with her and hear her opinion. But Cissy seemed more preoccupied with Jennifer.

'I shouldn't have abandoned her like that,' she said. 'She was bound to be a bit nervous about coming here on her own.'

'Probably better for her to go home, in that case.'

Eve knew she'd said the wrong thing when she saw Cissy's frown. But then she sighed, and said, 'I suppose you're right. I'll go and see her tomorrow, make sure she's all right.'

The music changed, and suddenly Dr Jameson reappeared at Eve's side, claiming her for another dance. She was going to refuse him again, but Cissy nodded her encouragement.

'Go on,' she whispered. 'This is your big chance.'

Eve tried to smile as she followed him on to the dance floor. Cissy was right, she told herself. This was her big chance.

This was the night the ugly duckling turned into a swan, and she had to make the most of every minute.

Chapter Forty-Five

It had taken some effort to organise the dance, but it was worth it.

Kathleen gazed around the room with satisfaction. With the threat of air raids still present, the disused ward on the top floor was considered unsafe for patients, but it made a splendid place for a dance, transformed with tinsel and garlands. Mr Hopkins had even performed a Christmas miracle and found a small tree, which they'd decorated with a star on top.

Everyone was there, from student nurses to sisters, housemen to consultants. They had all made an effort and dressed up for the occasion, as if determined to forget the hardships and troubles of the past year and simply enjoy themselves.

Even Miss Hanley was there, looking stately in dark green brocade, keeping vigil by the punch bowl to make sure none of the medical students got any ideas about adding their own ingredients.

'I suppose this means we won't be getting a cascara cocktail this year?'

Kathleen turned round to see Mr Cooper standing behind her, looking smart in his evening suit.

'Not if Miss Hanley has anything to do with it,' she said.

'She's no fun.' His mouth quirked.

374

'Fun? Have you forgotten the year someone laced it with antimony and half the ward sisters ended up in the sick bay?'

He pulled a face. 'That was fairly ghastly, wasn't it?'

'Ghastly isn't the word.'

'So what do you say?' he asked. 'Shall we live dangerously, and risk a glass?'

'Why not?' She smiled back. 'Although I feel quite confident with Miss Hanley as guardian,' she added.

'Oh, me too.'

She watched him as he made his way to the punch bowl. James Cooper was a handsome man, but his evening suit gave him the look of a matinee idol. Some of the young nurses were sending him longing looks as they sat in a row around the dance floor, she noticed.

He returned and handed her a glass of dubious pink liquid. 'Cheers,' he said. 'And may I say how beautiful you're looking this evening?'

Kathleen looked down at her dress. The dark blue velvet was more serviceable than glamorous. 'Thank you,' she said. 'One has so few opportunities to dress up these days.'

'Unless one's idea of dressing up is a siren suit and tin hat.' He raised his brows at her over the rim of his glass.

'True.' Kathleen looked around the crowd. 'Is your wife not with you this evening?'

His smile slipped a fraction. 'No,' he said shortly. 'I'm afraid Simone dislikes hospital parties.'

'I suppose they must be rather dull if you don't know anyone?'

'Quite.' He downed some of the punch, then winced.

Kathleen looked at him apprehensively. 'Oh, dear, don't tell me they've managed to put alcohol in it, after all?'

'No,' he said, 'just the opposite, in fact. It might be improved if they had.' He leaned in towards her and said, 'Fortunately I've taken the liberty of bringing a flask of medicinal brandy with me, if you're interested?'

Kathleen laughed, shocked. 'Mr Cooper! I'm surprised at you.'

'Do you want some, or don't you?'

Kathleen sipped the sugary pink punch. It was rather unpalatable. 'I'm supposed to be setting a good example to the nurses,' she said.

'Then we'll have to be discreet, won't we?' He laid his hand on her arm and guided her to the back of the room, as far from Miss Hanley as they could manage.

'I bet you were a holy terror when you were a student!' Kathleen said, as he topped up her glass from the small leather hip flask.

He smiled roguishly. 'I had my moments.' He raised his glass to her. 'Cheers.'

'Cheers.' Their eyes met and held for a moment. In the background, the band struck up a lively tune.

'Do you remember that day we redecorated the ward?' he asked suddenly.

Kathleen nodded. 'How could I forget? It was a very rash decision of mine.'

'It was a very brave decision,' he corrected her. 'It was also one of the happiest days of my life.'

He looked so wistful when he said it, Kathleen wondered if she'd heard him correctly.

'This tune was playing then as I recall.' He paused for a moment, his head cocked, listening.

'"The Lambeth Walk",' Kathleen nodded. 'Everyone was dancing to it.'

'Do you want to dance now?'

His question took her by surprise. She glanced around at the couples who had already taken to the floor. 'I'm not sure if that's appropriate.'

'Why not?'

Without knowing why, she looked towards Miss Hanley, still keeping her fearsome watch over the punch bowl.

'May I remind you, Miss Fox, that you are Matron of this hospital, not Miss Hanley?' James Cooper said softly.

'All the more reason why I shouldn't make a fool of myself in front of the junior staff.' She looked longingly towards the dance floor, terribly tempted. She had always loved dancing when she was young. 'Besides, it's such a long time since I danced, I'm not sure I'd even remember how,' she said ruefully.

'Then allow me to show you.' He took the glass out of her hand and guided her towards the dance floor. 'It's like riding a bicycle,' he promised. 'You never forget how to do it.'

Fortunately, by the time they'd taken to the floor, the music had changed to a sedate foxtrot. Kathleen was grateful for the change of pace. She wasn't sure she would be able to keep up with the lively to and fro of 'The Lambeth Walk', let alone master all the steps.

'This is much more to my taste,' she said.

'Mine too.' He pulled her gently into his arms.

He seemed to hold her closer than he should, so close she could breathe in the scent of his expensive cologne. Kathleen hardly dared tilt her head, knowing that if she did she would be gazing straight into his eyes, her face only inches from his. But at the same time, she felt the pull of his gaze until she couldn't look away any longer...

And then the siren sounded, drowning out the music, and every muscle in Kathleen's body tensed.

Not again, she thought. Please God, not tonight. Let us have one night of joy, at least...

The double doors flew open and two of the medical students burst in, their faces alight with excitement.

'They've got St Paul's!' one of them exclaimed. 'The whole city's alight!'

Everyone ran to see what was going on, donning their tin hats and climbing the metal staircase to the roof for a better view. Only Kathleen and James stayed behind, holding back as the tide of people rushed past them.

'Aren't you going up to look?' he asked.

She shook her head. 'I don't think I could bear it. I've seen enough destruction over the past few months to last me a lifetime.'

'I know what you mean.' He took out his hip flask and passed it to her again. 'I hope to God they haven't really got St Paul's,' he muttered. 'I don't know why, but it would just feel like the end.'

Kathleen nodded in mute understanding. As

378

the Blitz had raged around them, wreaking destruction day and night for weeks, the cathedral had remained untouched, a proud and defiant symbol of the city's enduring heart. If that heart were destroyed, then perhaps the heart would go out of the people, too.

'I thought it had stopped,' she whispered. 'I really thought they'd leave us alone now.' For the first time in months she had allowed herself the faintest hope. The Luftwaffe had turned its attention to other cities, and much as Kathleen pitied them, at the same time she couldn't help feeling a kind of relief. They had started to emerge from their basements, to feel the cold December air on their faces.

'Perhaps it's just for tonight?' James suggested.

'It won't be. This is the beginning of another assault. We didn't cave in last time, so he's trying again. And this time it will be even worse.' Her voice hitched, betraying her despair.

'It'll be all right,' James soothed. 'We'll get through it.'

'I don't think I can bear it, not again. I'm not brave enough...'

'You're braver than you think.' He reached out and took her hand, a brief squeeze of reassurance which imperceptibly took on a new meaning when his fingers slowly curled around hers, his thumb tracing her knuckles with a delicate touch that made her catch her breath. Kathleen froze, not daring to breathe. She knew she should pull away, but after standing alone for so long, it felt too good to have someone to hold on to. If she didn't move, didn't acknowledge what was happening, perhaps the moment would never end.

And then, suddenly, it did.

They sprang apart like guilty children as the ward doors flew open and Miss Hanley appeared.

'I'm sorry to interrupt you, Matron ... Mr Cooper ... but I'm afraid we have an emergency.'

Chapter Forty-Six

A young woman had gone into labour in Stepney. The ambulances had all been diverted to the city to deal with bomb casualties, and there was no one to help her.

'Isn't there someone else who can assist? A mother or a neighbour?' James Cooper asked.

Miss Hanley shook her head. 'It was a neighbour who made the call. The poor girl has been in labour for some hours, and it sounds like a complicated delivery. The neighbour said the mother is exhausted and showing signs of distress.'

James frowned. 'I suppose I shall have to go and see her.'

'But you can't!' The words were out before Kathleen could stop them. 'It's far too dangerous out there.'

'What choice do I have?'

They looked at each other for a moment. 'Then I'm coming with you,' she said.

He shook his head. 'I couldn't allow you to do that. As you said, it's far too dangerous.'

'But you're going to need a nurse with you.

380

And I'm not prepared to risk another girl's life out there.'

An explosion crashed overhead, shaking the ground and making them both flinch. They stared at each other for a moment, then he said shortly, 'Very well. I'd appreciate your help.'

Outside the air was filled with smoke and the smell of cordite. There were no ambulances to be had, so James said they would take his car.

'In that case, we'll need mattresses,' Kathleen said.

James stared at her. 'I beg your pardon?'

'I've seen it done on a delivery van a couple of months ago. We'll strap a couple to the roof of your car. It might not stop a direct hit, but at least it will offer us some kind of protection. That's the idea, anyway.'

They made an odd sight, driving through the streets of the East End with a pair of old hospital mattresses strapped to the roof of their car. Meanwhile, a fierce firework display exploded over the city, lighting up the night sky with a spectacular fiery glow of red and amber, every building seemingly ablaze.

It was difficult to find the house. They kept being directed away by the ARP wardens and the firemen. On practically every corner they were told, 'You can't come through here, half the street's come down.'

'It's like hell,' James commented, as he swung the car round yet again. 'I'm half expecting to get there and find the poor girl giving birth on the pavement.'

'Don't.' Kathleen shuddered. 'Look, they've shut

that road off, too. Perhaps we're better off abandoning the car and trying on foot?'

He sent her a quick look. 'Are you sure? It seems rather hectic out there.'

As if to prove it, an incendiary exploded on the roof above them, showering them with sparks.

Kathleen covered her head with her hands. 'We've survived this far,' she said grimly.

They ran for it. James grabbed her hand in the darkness, pulling her through the debris-strewn streets.

When they found the house, the door was already open, and, once inside, they could hear the sound of screaming.

'It's coming from round the back,' James said. 'She must be in the shelter.'

In the backyard, they were met by an anxious-looking woman.

'Oh, thank God you've come!' she cried. 'I've put her in the Anderson shelter, just in case. She's in a terrible way, poor kid.'

James went straight to the shelter while Kathleen took charge in the kitchen. She instructed the woman to boil some water and find as many clean towels as she could.

'I tried to help her,' the woman said. 'I've had five myself, so I thought I knew what was what. But when I saw how much she was struggling...'

'Is it her first?' Kathleen asked, as she washed her hands with a slab of hard green soap.

The woman nodded. 'And she's just found out her husband's been killed. He was in the RAF, shot down in a dogfight, he was. This baby's all she's got left, bless her heart.'

James Cooper had already examined the girl by the time Kathleen got to the shelter.

'The baby's breech,' he said. 'She's fully dilated, but I can't feel the feet.'

'So the legs are extended? No wonder it's taking so long.' Kathleen looked at the poor girl, sprawled on the earth floor of the shelter. She looked exhausted, but Kathleen knew her labour pains would not be enough for her to push the baby out by herself. 'Should we try to get her to hospital, do you think?'

'There's no time.' James's face was rigid, but Kathleen could read the calculations going on behind his eyes. A breech presentation, legs extended, usually required a caesarean in a first-time mother. 'Give her a sedative, and let's see if we can help her.'

The next half an hour felt like the longest of Kathleen's life. She stayed determinedly at James's side, checking the baby's heartbeat as he struggled to deliver the child. He was utterly silent, all his concentration focused on getting the legs out, then carefully rotating the baby's body to bring the shoulders and arms down before he could deliver the head.

Kathleen held her breath as he performed the last part of the manoeuvre. She saw the child's lifeless-looking body emerge, its bluish-grey skin mottled with blood and greasy white vernix, and her hopes sank. But then, miraculously, a hiccup shook the tiny body and the baby let out a thin, reedy cry that filled the tin shelter, just as the All Clear was sounding.

'It's a boy.' James's voice was choked. As he

383

turned to Kathleen she saw the emotion written all over his face.

And she found herself crying too, later, when she placed the baby in his mother's arms for the first time. She and the neighbour stood at the foot of the bed, tears running down their faces as they watched the young woman's face light up at the sight of her baby son.

'Poor love,' the older woman said. 'She hasn't had much to smile about up till now. Perhaps this next year will bring us all something good, eh?'

'Let's hope so.' Kathleen smiled through her tears.

They drove back to the hospital, through the now-quiet streets. The bombs had stopped falling, but the firemen and the ARP wardens were still out, dampening down the fires among the smouldering wreckage.

'It's been quite an evening, hasn't it?' James broke the silence.

'This is one Christmas dance I certainly won't forget in a hurry.' Then Kathleen remembered something and glanced down at herself. 'You do realise we're still wearing evening dress?'

'Good Lord, so we are!' James laughed. 'What on earth must that poor woman have made of us, turning up like this? We look as if we've just come from the opera!'

After an evening of such high drama, the last thing Kathleen wanted to do was sleep. So when James suggested they should have a nightcap to celebrate the baby's safe arrival, she accepted without hesitation.

They went down to his office in the basement. It was a tiny space, made even more cramped by the heavy wooden desk, leather chairs and examination couch crammed into it. Behind the desk was a mattress, strewn with bedclothes.

Kathleen sat in one of the armchairs, her knees almost touching James's as they toasted each other with a glass of sherry.

'To a good night's work,' he said. 'Thank you for coming with me. I couldn't have managed it without you.'

'I'm glad I was there. After all the death we've seen recently, it makes a nice change to bring a life into the world.'

'Even so, it took a lot of courage to head out in the middle of an air raid.' He regarded her over the edge of his glass. 'Didn't I say you were brave?'

Kathleen blushed, remembering how she'd crumbled in front of him. She could still feel the imprint of his hand on hers.

She turned away, changing the subject. 'I see you're still sleeping down here,' she commented, nodding towards the mattress on the floor. 'I suppose you've had a few late nights in Theatre recently?'

'Actually, I've left my wife.'

Kathleen whipped round to face him. 'Oh, God, I had no idea. Why didn't you say something when I asked about her earlier?'

'I didn't feel it was the right moment.'

'I'm so sorry.'

'Don't be. It's something I should have done a long time ago, if only I'd had the courage.' He took a steadying gulp of his drink.

'So why now?' Kathleen asked.

He paused for a while, considering. 'I suppose the war made me realise that life is too short to spend it with the wrong person,' he said at last.

His eyes met hers, a look so sudden and unexpected it caught her unawares. Kathleen tightened her hands around her glass to stop them trembling.

'What will you do now?' she asked.

'I don't know,' he admitted heavily. 'As far as I'm concerned, Simone can have everything. It's all she's ever been concerned about anyway. We'll live apart until she can sue me for desertion. Unless she gets bored and decides to commit adultery, of course.' Something about the way he said it made Kathleen think that it wouldn't be for the first time.

'I'm sorry,' she said again. 'No matter what the circumstances, it can't be easy to end a marriage. After all, there must have been some happy times?'

'Must there?' he said bleakly. 'I don't think either of us has been happy for a very long time. In fact, it dawned on me that the happiest moments I'd had recently were the ones I'd spent with you.'

The air was suddenly sucked from the room, making it difficult for her to breathe.

He must have noticed Kathleen's stunned expression because he said wryly, 'I think we had better call it a night, before I tell you how I feel about you and frighten you off for ever. If I haven't terrified you enough already.'

There it was. The moment when Kathleen

knew she should put down her drink, bid him a polite goodnight and then close the door on what might have been. But instead she stayed rooted to the spot.

'Do I look terrified?' she said.

Hope sparked in his eyes, nearly breaking her heart. 'Do you mean it?' he whispered.

Once again, she knew she should go, do the sensible thing. But the pull of attraction was too strong for her to resist.

She thought about the woman's words, back at the house where they'd delivered the baby.

Perhaps this next year will bring us all something good.

It was about time, Kathleen thought. She had spent too long alone, doing her duty. She was tired, and she was lonely, and she yearned for someone to spend her life with.

James Cooper was watching her, his gaze melting into hers.

'So what are we going to do about it?' he asked softly.

Chapter Forty-Seven

It came as a surprise to Dora's family when she announced she was going back to work at the Nightingale at the beginning of January.

'What made you change your mind?' her mother asked.

'I just think it's about time I made myself useful

again,' Dora replied. She didn't try to explain that it was a random snatch of song she'd heard from a workman that had convinced her it was the right thing to do. Her mother would think she'd gone potty, and even Dora wasn't so sure when she stopped to think about it.

But in spite of the sign she had been given, it was still a wrench for her to leave the twins. She'd already come close to losing them once. Was it tempting fate too much to leave them again? she wondered.

It was only the fact that she'd given her word to Matron to return to the Nightingale that made her leave the house on that cold, dark January morning. The twins were already awake in bed, laughing and waving their arms at nothing, and chattering in their own funny language.

'I'll be back soon, I promise,' Dora whispered, planting kisses on their fat cheeks. As she pulled away, she noticed Raggy Aggy's woolly head poking out from under the covers. Where had she come from? Dora wondered. She hadn't been able to find her anywhere when she'd put the twins to bed the previous night.

She must have been lost in the bedclothes all the time, Dora decided, tucking the doll under Winnie's arm.

Matron had assigned her back to the Male Acute ward, which had thankfully emerged from the basement and was now in one of the newly restored ground-floor wards. Sister Holmes was in high spirits as she inspected her new home, filling the linen stores and cupboards and directing the porters around as they wheeled in the beds.

'Although goodness knows how long we'll be allowed to stay here this time,' she said to Dora. 'I daresay we'll be back in the basement before the month is out. Honestly, I can't keep up with it all. One minute we're upstairs, then we're down. Another minute we have so many patients we're having to put extra beds in the corridor, the next we're packing them all off on a bus to the country while we sit twiddling our thumbs! Still, we're here for the time being,' she said. 'I suppose we must be grateful for small mercies. And at least now I have a properly trained staff nurse to assist me again, which is something,' she added.

Dora glanced at Daisy Bushell, who was busy polishing the bed frames. Her face was red with effort, loose locks of fair hair falling into her eyes. 'Has Bushell not been very helpful, Sister?' she asked.

Sister Holmes sent her a withering look. 'Bushell,' she said, 'is as much help as a leaky bedpan. But what she lacks in skill she makes up for in enthusiasm, I suppose. Which is more than can be said for Jennifer Caldwell.' She counted another pile of towels and ticked them off on her list. 'You do know Caldwell is also joining us today?' she said.

'No, I didn't, Sister.'

'Indeed. Matron has seen fit to bless us with Miss Caldwell's presence again.' Sister Holmes finished counting the pile of pillowcases, then frowned and started again. 'She seems to think the girl would benefit from being in familiar sur-roundings, given everything that has happened to

389

her.' She finished her counting for the second time and put another tick on her list.

'Why? What happened to her, Sister?'

'Oh, of course. You won't have heard, will you? The poor girl was injured in a bomb blast. Ended up with a fractured skull and some very nasty scarring from the falling glass. Quite honestly, I'm surprised she wants to see another hospital, after spending so long as a patient. But I suppose we all have to do our bit, don't we? Now, are these the only drawsheets we have? I thought I'd ordered more.'

If Sister Holmes hadn't warned her Jennifer Caldwell was coming, Dora would never have recognised her. She barely knew the withdrawn young girl who reported for duty. Unlike the Jennifer Caldwell who used to burst into the ward at least ten minutes late every morning, wearing an incorrigible grin and last night's make-up, this version seemed to shrink before Dora's eyes, standing quietly with one hand pressed to her cheek as Sister handed out the work lists.

But it was her eyes that Dora noticed, far more than the pinkish scars that peppered her thin cheeks. The pretty green eyes that had once sparkled with laughter and defiance were now filled with sadness and defeat.

'Welcome back, Caldwell,' Dora greeted her.

'Thank you, Staff.'

'I heard about what happened to you. I'm sorry.'

'And I'm sorry for you, too, Staff. About your husband's brother, I mean.'

Dora tensed against the swift dart of pain. 'So what made you decide to come back?' she asked.

390

Jennifer's expression was stony. 'My dad,' she said shortly. 'He told me I had to come. I tried to find other work, but there was none available.'

Dora saw the way her head hung down, as if she couldn't bring herself to face anyone, and understood.

'I'm sure we can find something useful for you to do here,' she said.

But as the day wore on, Dora found she missed Jennifer's merry laughter that used to ring out down the ward, bringing Sister Holmes scuttling angrily from her office more often than not. There was no laughter now, and no flirting as Jennifer silently set about her work. Even Daisy Bushell kept out of her way after her first attempts at conversation were met with snappish replies.

Dora watched Jennifer thoughtfully. She kept her head down as she worked, never making eye contact with anyone, her jaw set, as if grim determination alone could get her through the day.

'And to think I was worried she might be too lively!' Sister Holmes said. 'Now it seems we have the opposite problem. Oh, well, as long as she gets on with her duties and doesn't upset the patients, I suppose we'll just have to tolerate it.'

But the patients had other ideas.

'Cheer up, love, it might never happen!' one of the young men called out to Jennifer as she helped serve the midday meal.

She stared at him blankly. 'I beg your pardon?'

It was the first time Dora had heard her utter more than a word since she'd come on duty, and she looked up from doling potatoes on to plates to listen.

'I said cheer up,' the young man said, less sure of himself now. 'You're far too pretty to be miserable–'

He didn't have the chance to finish his sentence. Jennifer slammed his plate down hard on his bed table, splashing soup all over his covers. Then she turned on her heel and stalked off down the ward.

Dora thrust the plate and serving spoon into Daisy Bushell's hands and hurried over to where the young man sat, looking bewildered.

'I didn't mean to upset her,' he said. 'I was only trying to make her smile.'

'I know,' Dora reassured him. 'You didn't do anything wrong, she's just in a funny mood, that's all. Let me go and fetch a cloth to clean you up.'

She found Jennifer in the kitchen. She was leaning against the sink with her back to the door, her slim shoulders heaving.

'What was that about?' Dora asked. 'You're lucky Sister didn't see you, she would have torn you off a strip.'

'He was making fun of me.'

'No, he wasn't. Why would you think that?'

'You heard him. He called me pretty.' Jennifer's voice was dull, flat.

'That's hardly making fun of you.'

'Isn't it? Look at me!' She swung round, her face wet with tears.

Dora regarded her steadily. 'I am looking at you,' she said.

'I'm hardly pretty, am I?' Jennifer's voice was hard with self-mockery.

Dora suddenly understood. 'You know, you can

hardly see the scars.'

'Of course you can see them!' Jennifer snapped back. 'I look like a freak!'

'No, you don't. Have you seen yourself lately?'

Jennifer turned away, her back to Dora. 'I never look at myself. Not any more.'

'Then it's about time you did.' Dora snatched up the small mirror propped on the window sill and thrust it at her. 'Go on, take a look.'

Jennifer hung her head so her chin was pressed against her chest. 'I don't want to.'

'Go on!' Dora grabbed the girl roughly by the shoulders and tried to turn her, but Jennifer averted her gaze from the glass. Her face was so twisted with pain and emotion that Dora gave up. The girl had already been through enough.

She laid the mirror face down on the draining board. 'You should take a look,' she said quietly. 'Perhaps if you did, you might see what the rest of us are seeing.'

Chapter Forty-Eight

'He's asked you out? Oh, that's wonderful. Of course, I knew he would. I told you he liked you, didn't I?'

Cissy was as pleased as Eve had known she would be. All morning she had waited to tell her friend the good news, hugging the secret to herself until they were sitting in the students' kitchen, watching Sister Parker the Sister Tutor demonstrating how to make various invalid drinks.

'When?' Cissy wanted to know. 'Where is he taking you? Do you know what you're going to wear?'

Eve laughed, fending off the questions. 'I don't know,' she confessed. 'I think we're going out to dinner.'

'Dinner, eh? I bet it'll be somewhere posh.'

'Do you think so?' Eve chewed her lip anxiously.

'Don't look so worried about it.' Cissy grinned at her. 'I bet there are a lot of girls who'd love the chance of a romantic dinner with Dr Jameson!'

'But I've never been out with anyone before. How will I know what to do, what to say? What if I make a fool of myself?'

'You won't.' Cissy patted her hand kindly. 'You've got me to help you, haven't you? We'll meet up one night after work and talk about it. We can decide what you're going to wear. I expect I've got something you can borrow...'

Eve went back to her notes, feeling pleased with herself. Truth be told, she had been more excited about the prospect of telling Cissy that Simon Jameson had asked her out than actually going on the date. The idea of going out with the handsome houseman filled her with dread.

But Cissy was pleased, which was the main thing. Eve basked in the glow of her friend's approval.

Once Sister Parker had taught them the intricacies of beef tea, peptonised milk and Imperial drink, it was time to return to the Casualty department. As they stepped out into the crisp January day, Cissy whispered, 'Actually, I've got some news myself. Can you keep a secret?'

Eve looked at her, intrigued. 'You know I can. What is it?'

'I'm engaged.'

Eve stopped dead. 'What? When?'

'Paul telephoned me last night. I know it's not exactly a romantic proposal, but he wants us to get married on his next leave.'

'When's that?'

'I don't know, that's the trouble. He won't know either, until the last minute. But it probably won't be until the spring at least.' Laughter burst out of her. 'Can you imagine? I'm getting married!'

'I'm so pleased for you, I really am. But why do you want to keep it a secret?' Cissy had waited so long for Paul to pop the question, Eve imagined she would want to shout the news to the world.

Cissy's pretty face creased in a frown. 'It's Jennifer,' she said. 'I'm not sure how she'll take the news. She's been in such a funny mood lately.'

'You haven't told her?' Cissy shook her head. 'But I thought she'd be the first to know.'

'She would have been – once. But you know what she's like. I can't even talk to her these days.'

Jennifer Caldwell had come back to work a fortnight ago, but in all that time they'd hardly seen or spoken to her. She kept herself to herself. They didn't even see her at mealtimes, as she only came to the dining room when most of the nurses had gone.

Cissy had tried to be friendly, chatting to her and inviting her out with them when they went to the pictures. But Jennifer always refused, and in the end Cissy had given up asking.

'But surely she'll be pleased for you, if she's your friend?' Eve said.

'I'd like to think so, but I'm just not sure.' Cissy looked wistful. 'We'd always talked about getting married, you see, and how we'd have our weddings at the same time. Although between you and me, I reckon Jen always thought she'd be the first. She was always the first to do everything, you see.' She smiled sadly. 'But now, after what's happened to her – I'm just worried she'll be hurt, that's all.'

'She's bound to find out sooner or later.'

'I know, but I want to wait until I can find the right way to break the news to her. You promise you won't say anything?'

'Cross my heart.'

Cissy grinned. 'At least I can talk to you,' she said. 'I've been dying to have a good natter to someone about it. You know me, I'm not one to keep things to myself!'

The next minute they were deep in discussion about dresses, and flowers, and what kind of wedding Cissy wanted. But excited as she was, all the time Eve was painfully conscious that Cissy would rather have been discussing all the details with Jennifer.

She liked to think she had finally won Cissy's friendship, but Jennifer's larger-than-life presence still loomed like a shadow over them. If they were at the pictures or visiting the fair, Cissy would say, 'Oh, Jen would love this,' or, 'That was always Jen's favourite.' Or, if they were having a heart-to-heart, she would chime in with, 'Jen always used to say...' as if Jennifer's opinion was the only one that counted. Eve tried not to mind, but at the same time she couldn't help feeling resentful that Cissy missed Jennifer so much. It made her feel as if she wasn't quite good enough to fill the other girl's shoes.

After they'd finished for the day, Eve returned to the vicarage. The Stantons were out visiting family in Essex, except for Oliver, who was at work. But as usual Mrs Stanton had left Eve a cold supper in the kitchen.

She smiled at the sight of the snowdrops sticking out of the tiny bud vase that Mrs Stanton had set on the tray for her. She had grown so fond of the Stantons in the four months she had been living with them. Her aunt still regularly reminded her that she wasn't part of their family and had no right to be there, but Eve still couldn't help feeling as if she belonged. Given from Christian charity or not, it was the closest to a loving home she had ever known.

Now she was a fully fledged student nurse at the Nightingale, and the training school had returned to London from the country, Matron had offered Eve the option of moving in to the students' home. Usually it would have been compulsory for all students to live in, but the war had changed that as well as everything else. The hospital was short of accommodation, thanks to all the bomb damage, so nurses living locally could have the choice of staying at home if it suited them.

Eve had decided to stay at the Stantons'. She had been nervous about asking them, convinced

397

they would want to be rid of her. But to her surprise Mrs Stanton had said, 'Well, of course you must stay, my dear. We'd be sorry if you left us.'

And then there was Aunt Freda to think about. She had entrusted her niece to the Stantons' care, and would be furious if Eve left without her permission.

Eve put down her fork and pushed her plate away. The thought of her aunt was enough to rob her of her appetite.

After four months in the convalescent home, Aunt Freda had recovered her strength enough for the doctors to consider discharging her. She was already making plans, writing to various London estate agents to enquire about finding a place for them to live.

Eve knew her aunt couldn't stay an invalid for ever, but the thought of returning to her old life made her feel ill.

She had already half planned that if that day came, she would take the chance of moving into the students' home. She knew Aunt Freda wouldn't be pleased about it, and would do her best to stop her. But the past few months had taught Eve that she was strong enough to resist her aunt's bullying.

At least, she hoped she was.

After she'd finished her supper and washed up her dishes, Eve set about the mending Mrs Stanton had left for her. The vicar's wife had been insistent that she didn't expect Eve to work for her keep – 'We're just pleased to have you here, my dear' – but Eve liked to feel she was contributing something. And using her sewing skills was something she could do very easily.

But it wasn't just the family's mending she did. After seeing how she'd transformed that old jumble dress for the Christmas dance, Muriel and Mrs Stanton had asked her to perform the same magic on their old clothes. She'd reshaped dresses, added sleeves and hemlines, and had even turned an old tablecloth into a work blouse for Muriel. She was currently refashioning a worn-out pair of Reverend Stanton's trousers into a skirt, unpicking the seams and adding contrasting panels of fabric from a remnant Mrs Stanton had picked up at the market.

Eve had set up her machine in the attic room, so her work wouldn't disturb the rest of the family. Oliver also sometimes used it as a studio. He'd obviously been working there before he left for work because his easel was set up in a corner, with a canvas propped on it. It was a picture he'd been working on for weeks, and even though Eve knew he didn't like anyone looking at his work before it was finished, she couldn't resist creeping across the room to take a peek.

She expected to see one of his landscapes. Oliver had produced some hauntingly beautiful sketches of the bombed-out buildings of London, perfectly capturing the pathos and dignity of the ruined city. But this time it was a portrait.

A portrait of her.

Or rather, a portrait of the girl she used to be, before Cissy taught her to curl her hair and she'd spent her wages on the last lipstick in Woolworth's. Before she had become the girl she wanted to be.

She was sitting at her sewing machine, working. Her head was bent, and her hair hung limply on either side of her pale face. Even her posture seemed apologetic, her shoulders hunched as if she had no right to occupy too much space.

Eve stared at the picture, repelled and enraptured at the same time. No one had ever painted a portrait of her before. She couldn't imagine anyone taking that much interest in her yet Oliver had captured her in every line.

But what he had captured, what he had exposed on the canvas, made her feel angry and vulnerable. It reminded her too much of the person she was trying to forget. She wished he could have painted her as she was now, pretty and confident, with a smile on her face. Not the old, scared Eve she had once been.

There was a paint-stained cloth lying on the table. She picked it up and threw it over the picture. But as she worked at her machine, she could feel the old Eve taunting her from behind her veil.

Oliver came home from duty at the hospital an hour later. Eve heard him coming up the stairs to the attic, but kept her eyes fixed on the seam she was sewing.

He stopped in the doorway. 'Oh! I didn't realise you'd be here.'

'I had some sewing to finish.'

Out of the corner of her eye, she saw him move towards the easel.

'You've seen the picture, then?' he said.

'Yes.'

'I was going to show it to you, but I wanted to

wait until it was finished.' He was silent for a long time, and Eve could feel the question burning inside him, wanting to be spoken. Finally, he said, 'What did you think?'

Eve considered it for a moment. 'It's very good,' she replied. There was no denying the skill that had gone into creating it. 'But it isn't very flattering, is it?'

'What do you mean?'

She looked up at him. He was standing at the easel, frowning at the picture as if he were seeing it for the first time.

'I look so ugly and unhappy.'

'Not to me. I think you look beautiful.'

She looked at him sharply, wondering if he was making fun of her. But his face was sincere.

'It's a picture of how I used to be before...'

'Before you started trying to be someone else?' he finished for her.

'Before I changed,' Eve corrected him firmly. 'Anyway, why shouldn't I try to be someone else, if it makes me happy?'

'Does it make you happy?'

How could he even ask that question? She was the happiest she had ever been in her life, surely he could see that?

'I'm not saying there's anything wrong with changing who you are,' Oliver went on. 'As long as you're not doing it to please anyone else.'

'I'm not.'

'Aren't you? It seems to me you've turned into Cissy Baxter's pet.'

Eve gasped, outraged. 'Cissy's my friend!'

'Only because you do everything you're told.

Everything you do, the way you act, even the way you dress – it's all approved by her, isn't it?'

Eve wanted to deny it, but she knew it was true. 'So what if it is? She's only giving me her advice.'

'Is that what you call it?' Oliver's mouth curled. 'What kind of friendship is it when you're only allowed to do what's acceptable? A true friend should care about you whatever you're like.'

Eve suddenly thought about Cissy, so worried about Jennifer's feelings even though she'd done nothing to deserve her friendship.

As if he knew what she was thinking, Oliver said, 'Cissy doesn't care about you, anyway. She's just using you because she's fallen out with Jennifer and she needs to have a new stooge.'

His comment was like a blow to the stomach, hurting Eve so much that she couldn't speak for a moment. Oliver must have realised he'd gone too far, because he said, 'I'm sorry, I shouldn't have said that. It was hurtful.'

Eve didn't speak. She carefully finished the seam she was sewing, then broke off the thread and folded her work away.

All the time she could feel him watching her. 'I'm sorry,' he said again. 'I didn't mean to upset you, truly. I just wanted to make you understand, Cissy doesn't have your best interests at heart.'

'And you do?' she snapped at him. 'You know what's best for me, do you?'

'I want you to be happy–'

'I am happy.'

'Only because you're pretending to be someone you're not. Can't you see, Eve? There's nothing wrong with who you are.'

His words haunted her as she lay in bed that night, staring into the darkness, unable to sleep.

There's nothing wrong with who you are.

What did he know about it? Perhaps she was trying to be someone else, but what was wrong with that, if it made her happier and more confident?

She thought about the unhappy wretch in the picture, all defeated eyes and hunched shoulders.

There's nothing wrong with who you are.

He was wrong, she thought. There must have been something terribly wrong with who she was, if her own flesh and blood couldn't find it in their heart to love her.

Chapter Forty-Nine

Kathleen was having tea in Fortnum's with James Cooper when Constance Tremayne walked in.

'Oh, no!' Panic surged through Kathleen at the sight of the neatly suited figure, hair done up in a tight bun, making her way across the Fountain Restaurant towards them. 'We should leave–' She glanced around for a means of escape.

James, by contrast, was very relaxed as he sipped his tea. 'Calm down,' he said. 'We're only having tea together. What's wrong with that?'

Kathleen stared at him in disbelief. 'But she's the head of the Trustees! Oh, no, she's seen us. She's coming over. Now what do we do?'

'Smile, darling.' James turned in his seat as Mrs

403

Tremayne bustled over. 'Mrs Tremayne!' he greeted her warmly. 'How lovely to see you.'

'Mr Cooper... Matron.' Constance Tremayne fixed her beady eyes on Kathleen. 'I'm surprised to see you here, I must say.'

'Dedicated as we are, even we need some time off from the Nightingale,' James said smoothly.

'Indeed.' Mrs Tremayne's mouth pursed. 'I'm just surprised you choose to spend your free time together, that's all.'

Kathleen felt the blush sweeping up her body, starting from her toes. It had reached her knees by the time James said, 'Actually, we were discussing Nightingale business. The new drainage system, in fact. Won't you join us?' Much to Kathleen's horror, he waved to the waiter for a spare chair.

'Thank you, but I'm already meeting someone.' Mrs Tremayne looked at Kathleen again. Her piercing gaze seemed to go right through her. 'Have a nice time, won't you?'

'And you, Mrs Tremayne,' James said.

As Mrs Tremayne walked away, Kathleen leaned towards him and hissed, 'What were you thinking? Why did you invite her to join us?'

'Because I knew she'd say no.' He lifted the lid on the teapot and peered inside.

'She might have said yes.'

'And spend all afternoon discussing drains? I very much doubt it. I think we need some more hot water. Or shall we order a fresh pot?'

Kathleen stared at him, lost between exasperation and admiration. 'You have nerves of steel,' she said.

'Of course I do. I'm a surgeon. Besides, it's far less suspicious than jumping about like a cat on hot bricks,' he added, sending her a meaningful look.

'I suppose you're right. But I can't help it.' Mrs Tremayne made Kathleen nervous at the best of times, but now...

She was still watching from across the restaurant. Kathleen looked away, convinced guilt was written all over her face. She and James Cooper might be innocently taking tea together now, but a few hours ago she'd been in his bed.

'If only it hadn't been Mrs Tremayne,' she said. 'You know how deeply moral she is, and how much she detests me. She would have a field day if she thought I was having an affair with a married man.'

'You make it sound so tawdry. My wife and I are living apart, remember?'

'I know, but you're still a married man in the eyes of the law.' And, more importantly, in the eyes of Mrs Tremayne. 'We could both lose our jobs.'

'In that case, perhaps we should run away together?'

Kathleen smiled reluctantly. 'That sounds like a wonderful idea.'

'I mean it. I want to be with you, more than anything in the world.'

'And I want to be with you.'

'Then what are we waiting for? Why don't we just pack our bags and go?'

She caught the gleam in his eyes and realised he was deadly serious. 'Where would we go?'

'I don't care. Anywhere, as long as it's with you. I'm sick of sneaking about, hiding away. I want to be able to tell the world how much I love you.'

'You can tell the world, as long as you don't tell Mrs Tremayne!' Kathleen joked, flicking her gaze over to the other woman, sitting in a corner of the restaurant.

'I'm serious, Kathleen. I can't wait two years for this divorce to come through. I want to be with you now, and to hell with Mrs Tremayne and everyone else.'

'And what about your career?'

'I'm sure I'll find work at another hospital. Or if not, I'll give it up and become a sheep farmer, or a shoemaker, or anything at all. Just as long as you're there with me.'

He started to reach across the table but Kathleen drew away from his hand. James sighed with frustration.

'Isn't that what you want?' he pleaded. 'For us to be together?'

'You know it is.'

In spite of having to keep their romance a secret, the last few weeks had been the happiest of Kathleen's life. She hadn't loved anyone the way she loved James Cooper, or been loved so completely either. Her only regret was that she had missed out on so many years of feeling this way.

And yet...

'Running away isn't the answer,' she said. 'It won't solve our problems, it will only create more.'

'Then we'll deal with them. Together.'

Together. Just hearing the word warmed her.

'It's still a big step,' she said.

'Promise me you'll think about it, at least?'

'Of course I will.'

'I love you, Kathleen.'

'I love you too, James.'

His hand snaked across the table again, his fingertips brushing hers. And this time she didn't pull away.

When Kathleen returned to the Nightingale, the first person she met was Veronica Hanley.

'I've just had a meeting with the cook,' she announced, dropping a pile of papers on to Kathleen's desk. 'She tells me you haven't agreed next week's menus with her yet.'

'Oh, dear, I completely forgot. I'll go and talk to her–'

'It's quite all right, Matron, I've already attended to the matter.' Miss Hanley pursed her mouth. 'Although in future it would be preferable if you could try to remember these things. We all have to pull together if this hospital is to run properly, you know.'

'Of course, Miss Hanley. I do apologise.'

Kathleen smiled through gritted teeth. The idea of running away with James Cooper had never seemed more tempting.

Chapter Fifty

'Now don't forget, try to look interested in what he's saying, even if you don't understand it. If you don't, just smile and nod. And whatever you do, don't look bored!'

'But what if he *is* boring?' Eve asked Cissy's reflection in the mirror.

'That doesn't matter. You've still got to make him feel as if he's the most fascinating man on earth. And *you've* got to be fascinating, too,' Cissy warned, pulling a pin out of Eve's hair so that a curl tumbled down to her shoulder.

'How do I do that? You know how tongue-tied I get, I'll never think of anything clever to say.'

'Oh, you don't have to be clever. Men don't like women who are too clever.' Cissy combed the curl around her fingers. 'In fact, try not to say anything at all. Just sit there and look mysterious, as if you've got a secret. You know, like Bette Davis?' She sighed at Eve's blank look. 'Like this.'

Eve studied Cissy's mysterious face. She looked more like she had a stomach ache than a secret.

It was all very nerve-racking. She was relieved Cissy had the morning off and could help her prepare for her lunch date.

'I didn't realise there was so much to remember.' If she'd known going on a date with Simon Jameson was going to be this complicated, Eve would never have agreed to it in the first place.

'Why do I have to remember all these rules, anyway?'

Cissy sent her an almost pitying look. 'Because you have to captivate him,' she said patiently. 'You have to be the woman of his dreams.'

'Yes, but surely if I really were the woman of his dreams I wouldn't have to pretend to be – ow!' Eve yelped as Cissy pulled out another curl and yanked her scalp with it.

'And you have to suffer to be beautiful, too,' Cissy said primly.

Eve suddenly thought of Oliver, and what he'd make of it all. He would probably laugh at her, she decided. Or say that it proved his point: she was pretending to be someone she wasn't.

Which was true, she thought. A lot of what Oliver had said made sense to her now, no matter how much she might have denied it at the time. She had modelled herself on Cissy and Jennifer because she wanted so badly for them to like her, and didn't believe anyone could ever accept her as she was.

But Oliver had. It was there, in the portrait he'd painted of her. He'd seen the real Eve, and he still liked her. Not only that, he preferred her the way she used to be.

She wished she still had the portrait so she could look at it again and try to see what he'd seen in her. But the day after their argument, she'd found it discarded in a corner of the attic. Seeing it abandoned had hurt Eve deeply. Oliver had taken so much trouble over it, and in rejecting it she felt he'd also rejected her.

'There, all done.' Cissy stood back to admire her

handiwork. 'You look lovely, Evie. Simon Jameson won't know what's hit him.' She paused to tweak a loose curl into place. 'Y'know, I've got a funny feeling about you two. I think you might really hit it off. You might even end up getting married.'

'Stop it! I'm only going out for lunch with him. I might decide I don't like him.' But even though she was smiling, Eve felt a prickle of unease. This was all going too far, too fast. She felt as if she was hurtling along the track of someone else's life.

'Oh, you will,' Cissy predicted confidently. 'Jen and I have always had a soft spot for him, so I expect you will, too.'

Eve left Cissy's house, promising to report back with all the details at work the following morning, then returned home to the vicarage to get changed.

It was nearly midday and Mrs Stanton was putting on her hat ready to go and play the organ for choir practice when Eve let herself in.

As usual, Mrs Stanton was full of admiration for Eve's appearance. 'Your hair looks so lovely like that,' she said. 'I hope your young man's worth all this effort!'

'He's not my young man,' Eve said. 'To be honest, I hardly know him.'

Mrs Stanton sent her a shrewd look. 'You're not getting cold feet, are you?'

Eve was so grateful she could have hugged her. At last, someone was allowing her to say how she really felt, instead of telling her what she was supposed to feel.

'I'm not sure,' she admitted. 'I think I like him,

but I don't know if I like him – in that way. But I won't be able to tell unless I go out with him, will I? And Cissy keeps telling me we're made for each other, so I suppose she must be right...'

Mrs Stanton turned away from the mirror to face her. 'Do you want to go out with this young man or don't you?' she asked.

'I don't want to let anyone down,' Eve said lamely. 'Everyone's expecting me to go.'

'If I were you, I'd worry less about other people's expectations and more about what you want.'

Eve blinked at her. The idea of ever trusting her own judgement was such a revelation to her, she didn't know what to think.

'Go upstairs and get changed,' Mrs Stanton said kindly. 'He's not due for another half an hour, is he? That'll give you a while to make up your mind what you want to do.'

Eve's pink dress was laid out on the bed where she'd left it that morning. And next to it there was a piece of paper that she hadn't seen before.

She picked it up. It was another sketch, this time in pastels. A portrait of her looking pretty in her rose-pink dress, her hair curling softly around her flushed cheeks.

Once again, Oliver had captured her perfectly. But what caught her eye were the words he'd written underneath.

Hope you like this better. It was a labour of love. Oliver.

In a sudden rush of emotion, it came to her. She was doing this all wrong. Mrs Stanton was right, she was trying to live up to everyone else's expectations, trying to be the person they wanted her to be, instead of doing the things that would make her truly happy.

She thought she had been liberated when she escaped Aunt Freda. But really all she was doing was swapping one person's set of rules for another. Whether it was Aunt Freda or Cissy, they both insisted on telling her how she should look, how she should behave, who she should speak to.

And she'd listened to them, because she had grown up needing to please everyone.

But not any more.

Eve heard the knock on the front door and apprehension surged through her. If she was going to start living her own life, now was the time to do it.

She would explain to him, she decided as she went downstairs. If Simon Jameson was as nice a man as he seemed, he would surely understand that she'd had second thoughts. All she had to do was tell him she'd changed her mind...

'Eve?' Mrs Stanton appeared in the doorway to the sitting room as she reached the bottom step. 'You have a visitor.'

Eve followed her into the room. 'You're early–' she started to say, then realised it wasn't Dr Jameson.

There, standing by the fireplace, was Aunt Freda.

'Really?' she said. 'Looking at the state of you, I'd say I'm already too late.'

Chapter Fifty-One

Mrs Stanton came up behind Eve. 'Well, this is a nice surprise, isn't it?' she said tightly. 'But you really should have warned us you were coming, Mrs Ainsley. As you can see, both Eve and I are going out this afternoon. Isn't that right, Eve?'

Eve couldn't speak, couldn't even open her mouth to make a sound. Aunt Freda had her pinned helplessly with her basilisk stare. She suddenly felt exposed and vulnerable in her pretty dress and make-up.

This couldn't be happening. Any moment she would wake up and find it was all a horrible dream.

'Her young man is picking her up soon,' Mrs Stanton went on.

'Is he now?' She had forgotten how sharp Aunt Freda's voice was, rapping out the words as if she was aiming stones. 'Well, you can tell him he's not welcome.'

'Now, just a minute—' Mrs Stanton started to argue, but Aunt Freda whipped round to face her.

'I've discharged myself from hospital and come all this way to see my niece because the Lord came to me in a vision and told me she needed saving. And it looks as if I was right to come, doesn't it?' Eve felt herself shrivelling under her aunt's piercing gaze, what little confidence she

413

had turning to dust.

'I beg your pardon?' Mrs Stanton's voice rose indignantly. 'Are you saying we haven't looked after Eve?'

'I entrusted her to your care believing she would be kept on the righteous path,' Aunt Freda said. 'But instead I find that you've allowed her to turn into some kind of – harlot!'

'A harlot?' Mrs Stanton gasped in disbelief. 'Just because the child is allowed to take a bit of pride in herself doesn't make her wicked, Mrs Ainsley.'

'That's all you know, isn't it?' Still Aunt Freda's gaze was fixed on Eve. 'Perhaps I didn't make it clear, Mrs Stanton, but my niece has bad blood in her veins. She is sinful to her very bones. I'd hoped you and her husband would give her the discipline she badly needs.'

'I think Eve has had all the discipline she needs, growing up with you! What she badly wants now is a bit of kindness. When I think what a terrible state she was in when she first came to us. The poor girl was a bag of nerves–'

'You can save your well-meaning nonsense for your friends in the WVS,' Aunt Freda cut her off. 'I know my own niece, thank you very much. Now I'll thank you to leave us alone.'

She turned away from Mrs Stanton, dismissing her. Mrs Stanton looked as if she would have argued, but Eve stepped in.

'It's all right,' she said quietly. 'Aunt Freda's come all this way to see me, it's only right that I should speak to her.'

Mrs Stanton looked doubtful. 'Are you sure,

my dear? I'm certain they can manage without me at choir practice for one day if you'd like me to stay.'

'You heard her,' Aunt Freda snapped.

'I'll be all right, honestly,' Eve said. Mrs Stanton's kindness had overwhelmed her, but she knew she owed it to her aunt to listen to her.

'Well, you know where I am if you need me.' Mrs Stanton laid her hand on Eve's arm. 'Don't forget, my dear, you're safe here,' she whispered. 'You have no reason to fear. Remember that.'

Eve nodded in mute acknowledgement, too choked to speak.

Mrs Stanton looked past her to where Aunt Freda stood by the fire, stiff as a poker. 'But let me just say this to you, Mrs Ainsley. From what I can see, the only bad blood in your family is running through your veins, not Eve's!'

And then she was gone, leaving them alone.

'Well?' Aunt Freda demanded. 'What have you got to say for yourself?'

As the shock of seeing her aunt again subsided, Eve began to feel calmer. All the old fears were still there, lighting up her nerve endings. But this time they were overlaid with a sense that, for the first time, she didn't need to run and hide. In the eight months she had been working at the hospital, Eve had seen and dealt with situations that previously she could never have imagined. She had been tested to the limit, and she had emerged stronger. She had developed a proper spirit, and Aunt Freda was never going to break it again.

Besides, she wasn't in Aunt Freda's house any

more. There was no leather strap, no dark and haunted cellar, no punishment her aunt could give her.

You have no reason to fear. Remember that.

She faced her aunt. 'What do you want me to say, Aunt Freda?'

Her air of calm only seemed to enrage her aunt further. Cords of rage stood out on her thin neck.

'Answering me back now, are you? You've grown bold, haven't you? And what's all that paint on your face?'

Eve put her hand up to her cheek. 'It's make-up, Aunt.'

'You look like a Jezebel.'

'All the girls wear it. Even Muriel Stanton.'

'Muriel Stanton isn't the daughter of a whore!' Aunt Freda's mouth curled. 'Although I daresay her mother lets her get away with anything. I really expected better of Reverend Stanton, but I can see now this is a home of loose morals, just like all the rest.'

'You can't say that. The Stantons have been very kind to me.'

'Too kind!' Aunt Freda snapped. 'You've been allowed to get above yourself. Look at you, bold as brass. The sooner I get you out of here, the better.' She nodded towards the door. 'Go and pack your bags,' she said. 'We're leaving.'

Panic surged through Eve. 'Leaving?'

'I've rented us some rooms in Battersea. I've decided I need to get you away from this area, make a new start. Once I've got the money from the insurance, I'll buy a new shop and we'll start the business up again...'

416

But Eve had stopped listening. All she could see was everything she had achieved, everything she had learned to treasure, being taken away from her. 'I don't want to go,' she said.

Aunt Freda's head reared back in disbelief. 'What do you mean, you don't want to go? You'll do as you're told, my girl. Do I have to remind you, you're in my care until you're twenty-one?'

'I don't care,' Eve said. 'I won't go. If you won't let me stay here, I'll move to the nurses' home at the hospital–'

The ringing slap came out of nowhere, catching her unawares. 'How dare you answer me back!' Aunt Freda's face was twisted with rage. 'You're just like–'

'My mother? So you're always telling me.' Usually Eve would have known better than to mention her mother. But the blow must have dislodged something in her brain, because she suddenly felt strangely unafraid. 'But I've only got your word for that, haven't I, Aunt? Because you've never told me anything about her. I'm not even allowed to see a photograph of her.'

She saw her aunt flinch, and realised with a shock that Freda Ainsley was nervous. It was all very well for her to wield her sister's name like a weapon, but she didn't like it used against her.

'What was she like, Aunt?' Eve asked. 'Why did you hate her so much?'

'I'll tell you what she was like, shall I?' Aunt Freda recovered herself. 'She was an evil, conniving little whore. Only no one else could see it but me because she had the face of an angel and could twist anyone she liked around her little

417

finger.' Freda's face was bitter. 'I did everything,' she said. 'I stayed at home, ran the business, looked after our parents while she ran around doing exactly as she pleased. But did I get any thanks for it? Of course I didn't. My father adored her all the same, even left her half the business when he died. The business that I'd worked to build up, that should have been all mine!'

'Is that why you hated her so much? Because you were jealous of her?'

'Jealous of her? Oh, no, you've got that wrong.' Aunt Freda laughed. 'Lizzie was the one who was jealous. She couldn't let me have anything to call my own. She had everything, but that was never enough for her. Whatever I had, whatever I cared for, she had to take it away from me. The business, our parents – even the man I loved!'

Realisation suddenly dawned, like a light coming on. 'Uncle Roland was my father, wasn't he?'

Aunt Freda went utterly still and silent, as if she'd been turned to stone. When she finally spoke, her voice barely rose above a murmur.

'I wanted her to go away and have it, to give it up quietly. But of course she couldn't even spare me that, could she? She wanted to flaunt it in front of me. And she knew how much I wanted a child of my own...' She swallowed hard, her throat moving convulsively. 'She never said anything, and neither did he, but I knew. I could see it in the way they looked at each other, all those secret little smiles when they thought I wasn't watching... But at least the Lord was on my side.' Freda smiled maliciously. 'I prayed to Him for deliverance and He answered my prayers. He punished her for her sin. But then they made me look after you, her bastard child.' She raised her gaze to fix on Eve. Her eyes were full of hatred. 'My mother insisted on it. She said I could finally have the child I'd always wanted. I had to watch you grow up, knowing where you came from, and no one cared that I was dying inside.'

Eve thought about Uncle Roland, patiently teaching her his trade.

'It's in your blood,' he used to say. Eve had always thought he meant her mother's blood. But now she understood the truth.

No wonder it had always enraged Aunt Freda to see them together.

She looked at her aunt as if seeing her for the first time. Suddenly she realised the pain Freda must have endured, being forced to bring up a child she couldn't love. Had her mother loved Uncle Roland? Eve wondered. Or was she conceived out of spite, as Aunt Freda seemed to believe?

Not that it really mattered. When she looked at her aunt now, all Eve could feel was compassion.

'Oh, Aunt, I'm so sorry.'

Aunt Freda turned on her, her face twisted with anger. 'How dare you feel sorry for me!' she bit out. 'I don't want your pity! I don't want anything from you!'

She moved to hit her again, but Eve sidestepped the blow.

'Don't, Aunt, please,' she begged. 'It doesn't have to be like this. I know you're angry, but it's not my fault. You don't have to hate me.'

'Hate you? *Hate* you? I should have done away with you when you were first born! You don't know how many times I longed to put a pillow over your face while you were sleeping. But he was always watching over you... He loved you, you see. More than he ever loved me. She took him away from me once, and then you did it all over again!'

Aunt Freda flew at her, knocking Eve backwards. The next thing she knew, her aunt was on top of her, pinning her down, hands like sharp claws around Eve's throat, digging into the delicate skin of her neck.

'Aunt ... please...' Eve stared up into the contorted face, the bloodshot eyes full of rage, and realised with a shock what she had always suspected: that Aunt Freda was capable of killing her.

Then, as if a switch had been flicked off, the life suddenly seemed to go out of her aunt and she slumped against Eve, pinning her down with her dead weight.

Eve pushed her off and struggled to her feet. Aunt Freda lay lifeless, face down on the rug.

'Aunt Freda!' Eve scrambled to feel for her pulse. At first there was nothing, then she felt a faint flickering under her fingers. 'Aunt Freda, wake up!' She sat back on her heels. 'Oh, God, please help her!'

The knock at the door made her jump. Eve shot to her feet, torn between staying with her aunt and finding help. In a split second she made up her mind and rushed to the front door.

There, standing on the doorstep, was the answer to her desperate prayer.

'Sorry,' said Dr Jameson. 'Am I late?'

Chapter Fifty-Two

Jennifer crouched beside the big tub in the ward bathroom, cloth in hand, and steeled herself.

It was only a quick look, she told herself. Just a quick glimpse of her distorted reflection in the shining chrome of the bath taps. All she had to do was open her eyes, for a second, then close them again. Where was the harm in that?

But her throat was dry and her heart was drumming against her ribs as she moved closer, counting inside her head. One ... two ... three...

'What are you doing?'

Jennifer shot to her feet as the door opened and Daisy Bushell stood there.

'Nothing,' she mumbled. 'Just polishing the taps, that's all.'

'They look shiny enough to me.' Daisy shrugged. 'Have you finished in here? Only Nurse Riley says I have to run a bath for the new gastric patient before I can go off for lunch.'

'All done.' Jennifer folded the cloth, pleating it between her fingers. She would try again later, she decided. No point in rushing these things.

You've been saying that since Christmas, a small voice inside her head replied.

'Good news about your friend, isn't it?'

Jennifer looked round. 'What?'

'Your friend Cissy. Any idea when the wedding might be? I hope it's soon. I think spring weddings are smashing, don't you?'

'Cissy's getting married?'

'That's the general idea, when someone gets engaged!' Daisy grinned at her through a rising cloud of steam. 'I expect you'll be a bridesmaid, won't you?'

But Jennifer wasn't listening. 'Who told you she was engaged?'

'Oops!' Daisy put her hand to her mouth. 'Sorry, it was supposed to be a secret, wasn't it? But I haven't told anyone else, honestly. I heard her discussing it with Eve Ainsley yesterday. I thought I could talk to you about it, as you're her best friend. I mean, it's not as if she'd keep it a secret from *you*, is it?'

Jennifer looked down at the cloth, bunched between her fingers.

'You'd be surprised,' she muttered.

As soon as lunchtime came, Jennifer rushed down to the basement dining room to find Cissy. To her relief, for once she didn't have her little lap dog Eve with her.

'Jen!' Cissy looked up as she approached. She looked so touchingly pleased to see her friend, for a moment Jennifer almost forgot to be angry.

But then she remembered. 'When were you going to tell me you were engaged?' she demanded.

Cissy didn't even bother to deny it. She stared down at her empty plate. 'Who told you?'

'Never mind who told me! What I want to know is, why didn't *you* tell me?'

'I wanted to, honestly. I just didn't know how.'

Jennifer dropped down into the chair opposite

her. 'What do you mean, you didn't know how? I'm supposed to be your friend, aren't I?'

'I know.' Cissy looked thoroughly miserable. But Jennifer knew she was just feeling sorry for herself.

'It's all right,' she said bitterly. 'I know the real reason why you didn't want to tell me. And you don't have to worry, I won't embarrass you on your wedding day!'

Cissy stared at her blankly. 'What are you talking about?'

'You don't want me to be a bridesmaid, do you? You're worried I'm going to ruin your wedding pictures with my ugly face.'

To her fury, Cissy laughed. 'You're joking!' Then, seeing Jennifer's expression, she sobered and said, 'That's not what you really think, is it? Honest to God, Jen, the thought never crossed my mind.'

'Why else would you keep it such a secret?'

'If you must know, I didn't tell you because I was worried you'd be upset. You know how we've always talked about getting married at the same time? I didn't want you to feel left out.'

'Left out?' Jennifer gave a hollow laugh. 'That's a good one! You sneak around, getting engaged in secret and then telling everyone but me, and then you say it's because you don't want me to be left out? I might be ugly, Cis, but I'm not a fool!'

'You are if you think I'd leave you out because of the way you look!' Cissy shot back. 'Of course I want you to be a bridesmaid.'

'Don't sound too excited about it, will you?' Jennifer said sarcastically. 'It's all right, you don't have to ask me just because you feel sorry for me. I'm sure your new friend Eve would be happy to take my place. Heaven knows, she has done in every other way!'

'And why do you think that is?' Cissy jumped to her feet. Her cheeks turned mottled pink, the way they always did when she was angry. 'Why do you think I go around with Eve all the time, and not you?'

'Because she's prettier than me, I suppose.'

'It's because you're never there! All you've done since you got back from hospital is hide yourself away. Whenever I've asked you to go out dancing or to the pictures, you always make an excuse not to come.'

'Do you blame me? Would you want to go out if you looked like this? Would you like to go out, knowing everyone is pointing at you, whispering behind your back?'

'Oh, for heaven's sake! Why do you have to keep on about your wretched scars? Nobody even notices them except you!'

'That's easy for you to say,' Jennifer mumbled.

'You know what? You're right, I don't want you to be my bridesmaid. But it's got nothing to do with you being ugly, or me being ashamed of you. It's because I'm worried you'll ruin my big day by being miserable and going on about yourself all the time! Because that's what you are these days, Jennifer Caldwell. Miserable and selfish–'

Cissy shut up when the jug of water hit her full in the face. Jennifer didn't know which of them was more shocked: Cissy, dripping from head to foot, or herself standing there with the empty jug in her hand.

'Caldwell and Baxter!' Miss Hanley's booming voice rang out across the dining room. 'Matron's office at once, if you please!'

It had taken Kathleen hours to write her resignation letter.

She had been trying ever since that morning, but every time she made a start, Miss Hanley seemed to interrupt her with some trifling matter or other. The laundry order had arrived with several pillowcases missing, a nurse had broken a thermometer, one of the porters thought he smelled gas near the stoke hole... Every hour seemed to bring a new problem, and each time Kathleen had to put her letter aside to deal with it.

It was difficult enough to write in the first place. But she had thought long and hard about what James had said and had finally realised that he was right. She loved him, so why shouldn't they be together?

Of course it would be a big step to leave the Nightingale. It had been her first Matron's post, and she liked to think that in the seven years she'd been there she'd made an impression on the place.

First – and last, she corrected herself. She would never run another hospital, not once the news about her and James became public knowledge. There would be a scandal for sure, especially as he was still married.

But none of that mattered, she reminded herself, as long as they were together and happy. And she deserved to be happy. She had never been loved by a man, and she dearly wanted to enjoy it while she could. She had already given enough years to nursing. Now she deserved some time for herself.

She was still trying to put her thoughts down on paper when Miss Hanley interrupted her yet again.

Kathleen laid down her pen. 'What can I do for you this time, Miss Hanley?' she said with forced patience.

'Two VADs, Matron, fighting in the dining room.'

'Fighting?'

'Like cats,' Miss Hanley confirmed. 'One threw a jug of water over the other.'

'How extraordinary.'

'Indeed, Matron.' Miss Hanley glanced at the letter on the desk in front of Kathleen. 'Excuse me for asking, Matron, but I couldn't help noticing you've been dealing with that piece of paperwork for some time. Is it something I could do for you?'

'No, Miss Hanley. It's a personal matter.'

'But if you're busy, I could always–'

'As I said, Miss Hanley, it's personal.' Kathleen slid a paperweight over the letter so her Assistant Matron couldn't read it. 'Now, I suppose we'd better see what those VADs have to say for themselves.'

Chapter Fifty-Three

Dora checked her watch again and stared in frustration at the double doors. It had been nearly an hour since she'd sent Jennifer Caldwell off for her lunch break. Until she returned, Dora couldn't go for her own lunch, which meant she wouldn't get all her work finished before her duty ended, which meant she would have to stay later...

If my kids are asleep by the time I get home, I'll strangle her, she thought. Putting Walter and Winnie to bed, and being able to snuggle up with them while they covered her face with warm, wet goodnight kisses, was the highlight of Dora's day.

It was Daisy Bushell who put an end to the mystery. She galloped back on to the ward, ignoring the rule about not running except in case of fire or haemorrhage.

'You'll never guess what, Staff?' she cried, eyes shining with excitement. 'Caldwell's been hauled up in front of Matron – for fighting, would you believe?'

Dora sighed. She could believe it, only too well. She had learned not to put anything past Jennifer Caldwell.

What was the wretched girl fighting about anyway? she wondered. Although given her permanently low mood, it wouldn't take much to provoke Jennifer. These days she seemed to go through life with her head down and shoulders hunched, looking for trouble.

'I don't care if she's gone ten rounds with Max Baer, she should be back here,' she said crossly.

'I could hold the fort, Staff, if you want to go for your lunch?' Daisy offered.

Dora thought about it for a moment. She knew Sister Holmes didn't put a lot of faith in Daisy Bushell's abilities. But she was willing enough, and she'd more or less stopped fainting at the sight of blood.

'I suppose it wouldn't hurt,' she agreed reluctantly. 'As long as you promise not to try and do anything? If anyone needs a nurse, go next door and find Nurse Padgett.'

'Yes, Staff,' Daisy agreed cheerfully. 'Don't worry, I won't kill anyone while you're gone!'

I hope not, Dora thought as she headed across the courtyard.

She met Helen Dawson coming out of the basement dining room.

'You'd better hurry up, lunch is nearly finished,' her friend greeted her. 'The dining room was nearly empty when I left.'

'Just my luck!' Dora sighed. 'Lucky I'm not that hungry.' She smiled at Helen. 'How are you, anyway? Long time, no see.'

'I know. We've been sorting everything out for the grand reopening of the Casualty department.'

'How is it coming along?'

'Oh, it's grand. Almost restored to its former glory.' Her smile faltered. 'It's a pity David isn't here to see it. He would have been so proud.'

'Have you heard from him?' Dora asked.

Helen nodded. 'I had another letter from him

this morning. He's almost finished his basic training, so he reckons they'll be shipping him out soon. He doesn't know where they're sending him yet, though.'

'If he's anything like Nick I don't suppose he'll know until he gets there!' Dora said ruefully. She noticed her friend's wistful face and said, 'He'll be all right, you know. I'm sure he can take care of himself.'

'I know,' Helen sighed. 'It's just going to be so hard to say goodbye. It was upsetting enough when he went off to the army camp for his training, so I don't know what I'll be like when he finally gets his embarkation date.'

'It ain't easy, but you have to put a brave face on it for his sake,' Dora advised. 'What else can you do? I mean, it ain't like you can stow away on the ship with him, is it?'

She laughed, but Helen didn't. Her friend looked thoughtful, her dark brows drawing together over her brown eyes.

'It might not come to that,' she said quietly.

Now it was Dora's time to frown. 'What do you mean?'

'Oh, nothing.' A moment later, Helen's smile was back in place. 'Just something I've been thinking about lately, that's all.'

'And what's that?'

'I'll explain later. I need to discuss it with Matron first. Anyway, I mustn't keep you,' Helen went on. 'You'd best get down to the dining room before they close. You know what they're like about pulling those shutters down...'

'You're right. I'll be seeing you. And don't get

429

any ideas about stowing away!' Dora called after her.

'I told you, it might not come to that.'

Dora couldn't shake off her friend's comment as she headed for the basement. It wasn't like Helen to be so mysterious. What was she planning? Dora wondered.

She went to push the door open to go down to the basement, but it was stuck. She pressed her shoulder against it, but she still couldn't shift it.

Then, as she was leaning her weight against it, she suddenly heard a voice as clear as day whispering in her ear, 'G-go home, Dora. Go home n-now.'

She stopped, still leaning against the door, and looked around. There was no one in sight. She knew there wouldn't be, because there was only one person that voice belonged to.

'Danny?' she whispered.

'G-go home, Dora. Th-the twins...'

Without thinking, she turned and ran across the courtyard, through the archway and down the drive. Mr Hopkins and his hospital Home Guard unit, who were practising their drill outside the Porters' Lodge, scattered like ninepins as she sprinted past them.

'Oi, you!' Mr Hopkins called after her. 'You know nurses aren't allowed out of hospital in their uniform. I'll report you, so I will!'

By the time she got home, her lungs were nearly bursting. Her mother looked up in surprise as Dora fell through the door.

'What on earth–'

'Where are the children?' she demanded.

430

'Having a nap. Why…?'

Dora didn't wait to hear the end of her mother's sentence. She pushed past her into the bedroom, her heart pounding painfully.

Winnie and Walter were fast asleep, their thumbs lodged in their mouths. Raggy Aggy slept between them, under Winnie's arm.

Dora stared at them, watching their chests rise and fall, her own heartbeat slowing down with each breath.

Her mother came in behind her. 'What's happened? Are they all right?'

'Yes, they're fine.'

'What on earth is it, love? You looked like you'd seen a ghost when you came in.'

Dora looked rueful. 'I dunno about that, Mum. But I reckon I've just heard one.'

Her mother listened, mystified, as Dora told her what she'd experienced. 'I know it sounds daft, but I heard him, Mum. Just as clear as I'm talking to you,' she said.

'I believe you, love. And Danny loved those kiddies so much, it wouldn't surprise me at all if he was watching over them. But why should he tell you to go home, when they're as right as rain?'

That was when they heard it. The unmistakable sound of a distant explosion.

Eve and Dr Jameson were silent as they followed the ambulance in his car.

'Well,' Simon Jameson said finally, 'as first dates go this is certainly unusual.'

'I'm sorry,' Eve apologised again. It was all she

had said since the ambulance arrived.

'Don't be. It's not your fault your aunt was taken ill.'

Eve closed her eyes briefly against the memory. 'Will she be all right?' she asked.

Simon's face grew sombre. 'I hope so,' he said. 'But she should never have discharged herself from that convalescent home.' He glanced sideways at Eve. 'You did everything you could,' he said.

'No, I didn't. I panicked when she collapsed. I just didn't know what to do...'

'Anyone would be the same. It's one thing when it's a stranger, but it's another when it's a loved one, isn't it? Anyway, you mustn't blame yourself.'

It was such an ironic comment, Eve almost smiled. Blaming herself was exactly what she'd been doing for years. She had gone through her whole life thinking that it was her fault her aunt didn't love her, that she must be a truly terrible person.

But now she realised that it was the circumstances that were at fault, not her. Her aunt couldn't love her, no matter how hard she might have tried.

'I don't,' she said. Not any more, she added silently.

The ambulance pulled up so suddenly, Simon had to swerve to avoid running straight into the back of it.

'What the–' He stopped the car and got out. Eve followed him. 'What's going on?' he called out to the ambulance driver.

'We've just been told we're being diverted to the London,' the driver told him.

'The London? Why?'

'Been a big explosion at the Nightingale, apparently. Rumour is an unexploded bomb's just gone off. They're not allowing anyone near it.'

'Oh, my God,' Simon muttered.

'Oliver!' Eve hadn't realised she'd said his name out loud until Simon turned to frown at her. 'I've got to go,' she said.

'But your aunt...'

'Will you go with her, make sure she's all right?'

'Well–'

'Please?' Eve begged. 'I have to go to the Nightingale. There's someone I need to see.'

'You heard what the driver said. They're not letting anyone through.'

'I have to try. Please?'

Dr Jameson pulled a wry face. 'So now you're abandoning me for another man,' he said. 'This really is turning into a very strange first date indeed.'

Chapter Fifty-Four

'Matron? Matron, can you hear me?'

Kathleen heard someone calling her name and opened her eyes to dense blackness. She tried to breathe, but the thick, gritty air filled her throat like sand, making her cough and retch.

'Oh, Matron! Thank God you're alive!' Miss

433

Hanley's voice came out of the darkness from somewhere to her left. Close, or far away? Kathleen couldn't tell.

'Miss Hanley?' She tried to move towards the sound, but something was pinning her down. She put out her hands, touching splintered wood and torn leather. Her armchair, lying on top of her. How had that happened?

'I'm over here, Matron.' Veronica Hanley's voice was a hushed whisper. 'I think I must be against a wall, but it's difficult to tell ... no, don't try to move. You might upset something and bring more down on top of us.'

Kathleen gingerly flexed her limbs. Apart from the weight of the armchair pinning her, there was no pain, and apparently no bones broken.

'How are you, Miss Hanley?'

'I'm alive, Matron. As to anything else, I really couldn't say. What happened, do you think? Not an air raid, surely? I didn't hear the siren, did you?'

Kathleen reached out in the blackness, exploring. Her hand grazed rough stone, great boulders of it heaped up like walls around her.

Like a tomb.

'Whatever it was, we're well and truly trapped,' she said. She lifted her head and called out, 'Hello? Is there anyone down here with us?'

A faint whimper came from further away, to her right this time, beyond a wall of fallen masonry.

'Hello?' Kathleen called out again. 'Who's there?'

'C-Caldwell, Matron,' the voice came back, reedy with terror.

Of course, Kathleen thought. The VAD she had just reprimanded.

'Is Baxter with you?'

'Yes, Miss. But I don't know if she's–' On the other side of the rubble barricade, the girl started to cry.

Kathleen struggled to ease herself free from the chair that was pinning her down, and crawled through the darkness towards the sound of weeping. Groping ahead of her, her fingers grazed against a wall of rubble and she started to try to pull pieces of it free, before she remembered Miss Hanley's warning. She had no idea how precarious the barrier was on the other side, and she didn't want to bring an avalanche down on the girls.

But further down the rubble heap, where it met the wall, she found a chink. She flattened herself on to her belly and felt a rush of air on her face. Somehow the fallen masonry had wedged itself in such a way as to leave a narrow gap between the wall and the floor.

Kathleen tested it with her hand, trying to gauge its size. It was barely wide enough for her to get her shoulders through.

'Matron?' Miss Hanley's voice came from behind her. 'Where are you?'

'I'm just here, Miss Hanley. I thought there might be a way through ... but it's too small.'

Exhausted and frustrated by her efforts, Kathleen stared helplessly into the darkness of the hole. 'Try to stay calm, Caldwell,' she called out. 'We'll be rescued soon, I'm sure. But in the meantime, you need to be brave and do what you can for your friend. Do you understand?'

'Y-yes, Matron.'

'It will be all right, Caldwell. Just sit tight and wait.'

Her reassurance seemed to work, because the girl gradually stopped crying. A moment later Kathleen heard her murmuring voice, talking to her friend.

'It's all right, Cis,' she heard her say. 'Matron says we're going to be rescued soon. This is a right pickle, isn't it? But we'll be safe soon, you'll see.'

Hearing her broke Kathleen's heart. She remembered that these were the two girls who only a few minutes before had been standing truculently before her, refusing to look at each other.

'Do you think we will be rescued, Matron?' Miss Hanley said.

'Of course. They're probably looking for us now.' Kathleen stared up at the ceiling. Her mouth and throat were gritty with dust and dry with fear.

At least I hope so, she thought.

Think, Jennifer told herself.

It wasn't something she did very often, she realised now. She preferred to drift along, pleasing herself and making up her mind on a whim, while everyone else danced around her. But suddenly, in the space of a few seconds, life had become very serious. Now she was certain that her life and Cissy's depended on her coming up with a plan, doing something right for once.

She had been in a situation like this before, but

then she had known nothing about it until she woke up in a hospital bed. Was this better or worse? she wondered. It was more frightening, but at least she was conscious. And she wasn't in any pain either. Although she was aware of rubble all around her, miraculously she was untouched.

Unlike Cissy, who lay as motionless as a doll beside her.

'Cissy? Cis, wake up.' Jennifer couldn't see in the darkness, was only aware of her friend's body lying beside her. She was like the dummy they'd used in the First Aid classes, lifeless and heavy-limbed.

Think.

Jennifer cast her mind back desperately to those classes, trying to remember something of what she'd been told. Why on earth hadn't she listened when she had the chance, instead of playing the fool all the time?

And as for that pathetic row she'd had with Cissy – it all seemed so ridiculous now. Unimportant, like her scars. She would willingly suffer any kind of disfigurement if it meant she and Cissy would be safe.

Think.

Light. That was what they needed. Nothing would seem so bad if she could see what she was facing, good or bad.

There was a torch in Cissy's shelter bag. They were supposed to carry them all the time, but typically Jennifer had given up once the air raids lessened. But Cissy hadn't. Jennifer was sure her friend had had her bag with her when they were summoned to Matron.

She groped around in the darkness, her hands scraping over broken bricks and fractured shards of wood and metal. How none of it had injured her was a miracle. And then another miracle happened, and somehow there was Cissy's shelter bag under her hand.

As she was groping inside for the torch, Cissy suddenly stirred beside her. Jennifer's heart leaped. 'Cis?'

Cissy groaned, as if waking up from a long sleep. She must have opened her eyes, because the next moment she was panicking and struggling in the darkness. 'W-what happened? Where are – ow, my leg!' She screamed in pain.

From somewhere on the other side of the rubble wall came Matron's calm, strong voice.

'Is everything all right, Caldwell?'

'Yes, Matron. Cissy's just woken up.'

'That's good news, my dear. Try to keep her calm, won't you?'

'Yes, Matron.' Jennifer rummaged in the shelter bag. 'You heard her, Cis. Keep calm and don't try to move. I'm just trying to find – ah, here it is.' She produced the torch and switched it on, then immediately wished she hadn't as the pool of light illuminated a terrifying landscape of jagged walls, shattered furniture and a mountain of fallen debris, all seen through a thick veil of grey dust.

'We're trapped, aren't we?' Cissy's voice came out of the gloom, trembling and fearful.

'Don't be so melodramatic, Cis. Now, let's take a look at you.' Jennifer turned the beam on to her friend. Cissy's face came into view, hazy through the dust, but unharmed. 'Well, you look all right,' said Jennifer. 'Did you say your leg was hurting?'

Cissy nodded. She tried to move it and winced with pain. 'I think it might be broken,' she whispered.

Jennifer ran her hand carefully along the length of Cissy's leg. She had no idea what she was looking for, but Cissy hissed with pain when she reached a spot in the middle of her shin.

'It doesn't seem broken,' she said. 'I'd better put a splint on it, just in case.'

'You, put on a splint?' Cissy managed a short laugh.

'Why not? I think I can remember how to do it.' Jennifer searched around, and found the broken leg of a chair. 'This should do nicely.'

'You do know it's supposed to be padded, don't you?'

'Of course I do! You don't have to order me about, Cissy Baxter, just because you're training to be a nurse now!' Jennifer circled around in the darkness with her torch, but she couldn't see anything. 'I know, I'll use my apron.'

As she reached over to help unfasten the strings, Cissy said, 'You needn't think that I'll forgive you, just because you're doing this. This is all your fault, Jen Caldwell!'

'What? How do you work that out? I didn't ask the roof to fall in on us, did I?'

'No, but if you hadn't thrown that jug at me, we wouldn't be here!'

'And if you'd told me you were getting married, we wouldn't be here either!'

Jennifer stopped talking then, suddenly realising how pathetic it sounded.

Cissy seemed to be thinking the same thing. 'What are we doing, Jen?' she sighed. 'We could die at any minute and we're arguing about jugs of water and weddings!'

'I know,' Jennifer said. 'I'm sorry.'

'Me, too. You're right, I should have told you I was getting married. I don't blame you for being upset. I know I'd have been, the other way around.'

Jennifer kept her head down, padding the splint. 'It doesn't matter.'

'Yes, it does. But it wasn't because I didn't want you as a bridesmaid, honestly. You do believe me, don't you?'

Jennifer nodded. 'I don't blame you for being angry with me. I know I've been unbearable lately. I've driven everyone mad, haven't I?'

'Just a bit!' Cissy winced as Jennifer tied the splint in place. 'But I could have been a bit more understanding, all the same. I just wanted the old Jen back.'

'I thought you'd replaced me,' Jennifer said in a low voice.

'No chance! I like Eve, but you'll always be my best friend. It's always been you and me, hasn't it?'

'True.' Jennifer smiled at her. 'And when we get out of here, I promise I won't be nearly so miserable.'

Cissy cast her gaze gloomily towards what was left of the roof. 'If we get out of here,' she said.

Chapter Fifty-Five

'They've gone very quiet. I hope they're all right.'

Kathleen listened, trying to hear the voices of Cissy and Jennifer from beyond the rubble. 'How long has it been now, do you think?'

'An hour. Perhaps two.'

Kathleen gazed up at the roof. 'They're taking a long time to reach us, aren't they?'

'I suppose it's a delicate process,' Miss Hanley replied. 'And we don't know how much debris there is lying above us. If it's anything like when the Casualty Hall came down...' Her voice trailed off.

Kathleen shuddered. Why did she have to mention the Casualty Hall? That was the day six people had died, some crushed by falling masonry, others buried alive. It had been the worst day of her life. So far.

'I'm sorry, Matron, that wasn't very comforting, was it?' Miss Hanley sighed in the darkness. 'I'm not terribly good at offering words of solace, I'm afraid. But I have every confidence that help will be here soon.'

Kathleen looked across at her. Now the thick dust had settled and her eyes were growing used to the dark, she could just about make out the Assistant Matron's shape in the gloom, slumped against a wall.

Her voice sounded weak and tired. 'Are you all

right, Miss Hanley?'

'Yes, thank you,' she replied stoically. 'Just a little cold, that's all.'

'I wish I had a blanket or something I could offer you.' Kathleen scanned around in the darkness. 'I keep looking for my cloak. I know it must be here somewhere...' Not that she knew where to look. It was as if someone had put all the contents of her office in a cup, shaken them up and rolled them out like dice.

'It doesn't matter, Matron, really. I'm just making a fuss over nothing.'

Kathleen crawled over to her, clambering over the remains of what had once been her bookcase. 'We'll have a nice hot cup of tea when all this is over. What do you say to that, Miss Hanley?'

'That would be very acceptable, Matron.' There was a smile in Miss Hanley's voice. 'I could do with something to get this dust out of my throat.'

Kathleen leaned against the wall beside her. 'I wonder what caused the explosion? It can't have been an air raid.'

'Perhaps it was gas? I did mention one of the porters thought he'd smelled something this morning...'

'So you did.'

There was a long silence. Then Miss Hanley said, 'Did you ever finish your paperwork, Matron?'

'What paperwork?'

'The letter you've been trying to write all morning.'

'Oh, that.' Was that only today? It seemed like

such a long time ago now. 'No, I never did finish it.'

'Perhaps you were never supposed to resign?' Miss Hanley spoke in a hushed tone.

Kathleen whipped round to stare at her, glad the darkness hid her own shocked expression. 'How did you know?' she hissed back.

'We've been working together for some time, Matron. I understand you better than you might imagine.' Miss Hanley glanced over at the shattered wall, as if to make sure the girls on the other side couldn't hear her. 'I know about you and Mr Cooper, too. Don't worry, you haven't given yourself away,' she assured Kathleen. 'Not to anyone else, at any rate. But I guessed something might be going on, after I saw you together at the Christmas dance. That was when it all started, I suppose?'

'Yes.' There was no point in denying it. After today, it wouldn't matter anyway.

'And I imagine you're planning to leave the hospital, start a new life together?'

There was something slightly mocking about the way she said it that made Kathleen's hackles rise. 'You make me sound like a lovesick schoolgirl,' she accused.

'I beg your pardon, Matron, I hadn't meant it to sound like that. As I said, I don't always choose my words carefully.'

Kathleen felt the weight of the silence that followed. She might not choose her words carefully, but Miss Hanley could make a silence say everything she couldn't.

'We do want to be together,' Kathleen said finally. 'And yes, we are planning to leave London.

443

I deserve to be happy,' she blurted out, wondering why she even felt the need to justify herself to Miss Hanley. The Assistant Matron would never understand anyway.

'Indeed, Matron,' Miss Hanley replied. 'But I wonder if you ever could be happy, knowing it was at the expense of another?'

Kathleen turned to face her. She couldn't make out her face, just the denser shadow of her profile in the darkness. 'Mr Cooper and his wife are living apart. His marital problems were nothing to do with me,' she said.

'I'm sure they weren't. I've met Mrs Cooper and she seemed a thoroughly disagreeable woman. But she is also a very troubled one.'

Kathleen knew all about Simone Cooper and her troubles. James had told her about his wife's wild mood swings, her violent passions. There was a time when he'd even considered sending her away to Austria for psychiatric treatment, but he couldn't bring himself to do it.

'She will find it hard to cope alone, I daresay,' Miss Hanley said. 'And if I know you, Matron, you will find it very difficult to live with that.'

'And what about me?' Kathleen knew she sounded peevish, but she couldn't help it. 'Should I sacrifice my own happiness just so Simone Cooper can live the life she wants? Perhaps I find it difficult to cope alone, too. Have you thought about that?'

'Oh, Matron.' Miss Hanley sounded almost pitying. 'You have coped alone all this time, haven't you?'

'Yes,' said Kathleen, 'and I'm sick and tired of

444

it. I want someone I can lean on for a change.'

'But women like us don't need a man to lean on.'

'Women like us?'

'Strong women. Women of a deeply moral character.'

Kathleen laughed in spite of herself. 'You've never described me as having a deeply moral character before! If anything, I thought you had the opposite impression of me.'

'Then I'm genuinely sorry. Because I truly think you are one of the strongest, most moral people I know.'

Kathleen suddenly found it hard to swallow, and not just because of the dust clogging her throat. She could feel Miss Hanley's eyes on her in the darkness.

'Oh, I don't blame you for wanting to walk away. Why shouldn't you fall in love and be happy, if that's what you really want? But I would be very disappointed if you left now. The Nightingale needs you.'

'And I need to be loved,' Kathleen said. 'Although you probably wouldn't understand that.'

'I do understand, Matron, better than you might think.' Miss Hanley's voice was tired. 'I know you may not believe it, but I have known great loneliness too. But unlike you, I've found solace in my work, and in my friends here. The Nightingale is my home, my family. It's all I need. But you're different. I certainly can't blame you for wanting to find your happiness elsewhere.'

Kathleen stared at her. She was so used to her Assistant Matron being judgemental, it came as a shock to find out she had a softer side.

'It's not for me to choose your path for you,' Miss Hanley went on. 'You must do that for yourself. But you know I trust your judgement, Matron.'

How many times had she heard Miss Hanley say that? But this time Kathleen felt as if her Assistant Matron truly meant it.

'Thank you,' she said.

'Hello? Is anyone there? Can you hear us?'

A shaft of light pierced the gloom above their heads.

'Hello!' Kathleen left Miss Hanley's side and crawled to the centre of the room towards the light.

'Matron?' a man's voice called out. 'Are you all right down there?'

'We are quite well, thank you.' It was all she could do to stop herself from bursting into tears.

'How many of you are there?'

'Four, I believe, Miss Hanley and myself, and two VADs, Jennifer Caldwell and Cicely Baxter.'

There was a pause as the information was relayed down the line. Then the voice called out, 'We'll come down to you. Stay where you are.'

Even then, it seemed to take an agonisingly long time before the first of the rescuers was lowered down to them. Two porters and a fireman came down first, followed by James Cooper, his medical bag in his hand. It was all Kathleen could do not to rush into his arms, and she could tell from his face that he was fighting not to do the same.

She flinched as the fireman shone his lamp

around the room. 'Where are the others?' he asked.

'Trapped through there.'

As the fireman went off to examine the rubble wall, Kathleen let her hand brush against James's in the darkness. The contact was electric.

The fireman returned, looking grim. 'If we start to clear it, it could bring the whole lot down,' he said, confirming Kathleen's worst suspicions. 'I don't know how we can get them out without injuring them, or worse...'

'There's a gap down there,' Kathleen pointed it out. 'But I don't think it's big enough to get through.'

'Couldn't the girls crawl through it to us?' James suggested.

'One of them might be able to, but I think Miss Baxter has an injured leg. She won't be able to get through without help, and Miss Caldwell won't be strong enough.' Kathleen shook her head. 'Someone would have to crawl through and help them.'

'I'll do it,' one of the porters, a skinny, fair-haired young man, offered straight away.

'Are you sure?' the fireman said. 'What if you dislodge something and it all comes down on you?'

'We've got to do something, haven't we? Besides, I'm a conchie, not a coward.'

He was staring at the other porter when he said it. Kathleen had no idea what was going on, but the older man looked away, clearly ashamed.

'You're right, it is the only way,' the fireman said. He handed the young man a torch. 'Take this with you,' he said. 'And be careful, lad.'

As the young man started to inch his way through the narrow gap, James turned to Kathleen. 'Are you all right? No bones broken?'

'Not as far as I know.'

'Then you should get out. The porter will help you...'

Kathleen shook her head. 'Miss Hanley should go first.'

'I'm sorry, Matron, but I'm not going anywhere.' Miss Hanley's weary voice came out of the darkness.

James Cooper swung his lamp in a wide arc, illuminating the Assistant Matron, and Kathleen nearly screamed. Sweat glistened on the ghastly mask of Miss Hanley's white, bloodless face. Another sweep revealed her lower half was hidden from view, crushed under a towering heap of masonry.

'Miss Hanley?' James got to her first when Kathleen's own legs failed her.

'I'm afraid I've lost a great deal of blood, Doctor. And I can't feel my legs. I – I believe my back may be broken.' The Assistant Matron's voice faltered slightly. Why hadn't Kathleen realised there was a reason she'd sounded faint and weak in the darkness? 'I don't think I would survive the rescue.'

'No!' Kathleen's cry of anguish filled the darkened cavern.

'Take her,' Miss Hanley said to James. 'Keep her safe. Please.'

James took a step towards her, but Kathleen shrugged him off. 'I'm not going,' she told him. 'I'm staying here.'

'Please, Matron, you need to go,' Miss Hanley's voice sounded more like a sigh now. 'It's your duty.'

Kathleen squared her shoulders, even though tears were running down her face. 'May I remind you, Miss Hanley, that I am Matron of this hospital? I don't need you to tell me my duty!'

Miss Hanley's mouth curved in a weary smile of recognition. How many times had Kathleen flung those words at her in the seven years they had worked side by side?

Not that she had ever taken any notice.

'I'll stay with her,' James promised, his hand on Kathleen's arm. 'I'll give her something – for the pain,' he said quietly.

Kathleen's gaze flew to his, understanding. A merciful morphia shot that would shorten her suffering.

Miss Hanley understood too. It was written all over her tired, wise face. 'I'm sure Mr Cooper will look after me,' she said.

'And so will I,' Kathleen said, settling herself down beside her.

'Matron—'

'I mean it, Miss Hanley.' She reached for her assistant's hand. It felt as big and solid as a man's.

James started to intervene, but Veronica Hanley shook her head.

'Leave her be, Mr Cooper,' she said, fingers tightening around Kathleen's. 'I'm afraid Miss Fox will never be told.'

'Neither will you,' Kathleen said.

Miss Hanley smiled, the fight going out of her. 'Then we make a good pair, don't we?'

Chapter Fifty-Six

As it turned out, Cissy's wedding wasn't quite the grand affair she'd hoped for.

Three days after they had been rescued, Paul telephoned out of the blue to say he'd been given twenty-four hours' leave the following week, and could they possibly organise the wedding by then?

The next few days were a flurry of activity, but everyone pitched in. While Cissy queued at the register office for a special licence, Mrs Stanton and her WVS volunteers pooled their rations to come up with the ingredients for a cake, and Eve set about making a dress from a length of parachute silk. It wasn't exactly Norman Hartnell, but everyone agreed it was close enough.

Unfortunately, they could only get hold of enough fabric for one bridesmaid's dress.

'You should have it,' Jennifer said to Eve. 'You're the one who's stayed up day and night sewing, after all.'

But Eve refused. 'It wouldn't feel right,' she said. 'You're Cissy's best friend. You should be her bridesmaid.'

Eve was still stitching the hem as they got ready on the morning of the wedding.

'She hasn't stopped, has she?' Cissy remarked as Jennifer put curlers in her hair for her. 'But I suppose it takes her mind off what's happened,

450

doesn't it? It must have been terrible for poor Eve, don't you think, her aunt dying so suddenly? Her heart, wasn't it?'

Jennifer watched Eve, her head bent over her sewing, humming to herself as she worked. She wasn't sure it had been so terrible. Although her face was full of sorrow, she also looked as if she'd had a huge weight lifted from her shoulders.

But then, that might have been her new boyfriend's influence, Jennifer thought.

Cissy still hadn't got over seeing Eve throw her arms around Oliver and plant a huge kiss on his lips after their rescue. Everyone was in shock, especially Cissy.

'You know, I could have sworn she had a soft spot for Dr Jameson,' she'd marvelled. 'Just goes to show, doesn't it? Appearances can be deceptive. Not sure I like the idea of a conchie at my wedding, though,' she'd added in a low voice. 'Dunno how my Paul will feel about it either.'

'I'm sure he'll be fine when you tell him that conchie helped to save your life,' Jennifer reminded her.

'I suppose you're right,' Cissy agreed. 'Who'd have thought he'd turn out to be such a hero?'

'As you say, appearances can be deceptive.'

Jennifer finished putting in Cissy's curlers and fastened a scarf around her head to keep them in place.

'Right, your turn,' Cissy said, getting up from the chair to let Jennifer sit down.

'Oh, I'll be all right,' Jennifer dismissed this, her gaze cast down. 'I'll just put a comb through my hair...'

451

'Jennifer Caldwell! This is my wedding and you'll do as you're told!' Cissy planted her hands on her hips. 'Besides, you want to look your best if–' She stopped abruptly.

'If what?' Jennifer asked.

'Nothing,' Cissy said. But her enigmatic smile told a different story. She really was a terrible liar, Jennifer thought. 'Anyway, sit down and let me put some curlers in, and I don't want to hear another word about it!'

Jennifer slid into the chair reluctantly. She stared down at her hands folded in her lap as Cissy set to work.

Cissy sighed. 'I do wish you'd learn to look past those scars, Jen. Everyone else has.'

I wish I could too, Jennifer thought. But they went too deep.

At Cissy and Paul's wedding reception at the local pub, Jennifer lingered on the edge of the dance floor, watching the other couples whirling around in each other's arms, and trying not to feel too jealous that she was the only girl in the room without a partner.

'Not dancing, then?' a man's voice asked behind her.

Jennifer's heart sank. She didn't want to have to turn round and see that flash of revulsion in his eyes before he had time to hide it behind a smile. She didn't think she could bear it, not again.

Her hand went up automatically to cover her cheek. 'I'm not really one for dancing,' she muttered.

'That's not what you used to tell me. You said

you used to love the Palais on a Friday night.'

Without thinking, Jennifer swung round – and found herself staring into the steady gaze of Philip Chandler.

She had never seen his eyes unclouded before. They were sharp and brown, the colour of chestnuts. She'd never seen him on his feet either. It surprised her to see how tall and well-built he was in his smart RAF uniform. His features, though still damaged, were starting to take on a better appearance, thanks to the surgeons' skill. As had his smile, which lit up on seeing her.

'Philip?'

'You recognise me then?' He sounded disappointed. 'And there was me, thinking I'd been transformed into a handsome prince.'

But Jennifer was too shocked to laugh at his joke. 'What are you doing here?'

'I'm a guest at your friend's wedding, same as you are. She wrote and invited me, told me you'd be here.'

Jennifer frowned. 'Didn't you get my letters?'

Philip's smile dimmed ever so slightly. 'Yes, I did,' he said quietly.

'So why didn't you write back?'

'I didn't know what to say,' he admitted. 'I was angry when I first left the Nightingale. I didn't really care what you said. I thought you still pitied me.'

Jennifer winced, remembering what he'd overheard. 'I didn't,' she said.

'I know that now. But by the time I realised your letters were sincere, I thought I'd left it too late. I thought you might have forgotten about me, until

453

your friend wrote and told me how much you were missing me.'

Jennifer whipped round to look at Cissy, whirling over the dance floor in the arms of her new husband. 'She told you that?'

'Well, not in so many words,' Philip admitted. 'But she did suggest that you might like it if I could come and see you. Was she right?' He eyed her cautiously.

'Yes,' Jennifer said. 'Yes, she was.'

'I'm glad to hear it.' He smiled with relief. 'Because it took me a long time to wangle a twenty-four hour pass from the hospital, and I wouldn't want to think I'd wasted my time!'

'You're still at the hospital?' Jennifer asked.

'Of course. There's a long way to go before I recover my matinee idol good looks, you know.'

He grinned at her, completely untroubled by the interested stares he was attracting from around the dance floor. And much to her suprise, Jennifer found she was untroubled by them too.

'How did you know it was me?' she asked him, as they moved around the dance floor in a stately foxtrot. 'You've never seen me before.'

Philip sniffed the air appreciatively. 'Evening in Paris,' he said. 'I'd know it anywhere. And besides, you're just as beautiful as I imagined you,' he added.

She frowned for a moment, thinking he was making fun of her, then realised he meant every word.

He could see past her scars. Perhaps it was time she started to do the same.

Chapter Fifty-Seven

On a damp Friday morning in February, Dora joined the ranks of other nurses and ward sisters to pay her respects at the funeral of Veronica Hanley.

They made a solemn group, standing in their uniformed rows around the grave. But all the time, Dora couldn't shake off the thought:

It could have been me.

Her family had indulged her when she told them about hearing Danny's voice warning her, but Dora knew deep down they didn't really believe her. Danny was dead, and any idea that he might have been looking out for her from beyond the grave was just wishful thinking.

But Dora knew. She had heard his voice as clear as if he'd been standing at her shoulder. And then there was the basement door – when she'd leaned against it, she could swear it felt as if someone was pressing their weight against it from the other side, trying to keep her out.

Danny was looking out for her, she was certain of it. And the idea warmed and comforted her. It was his way of letting her know that he didn't blame her for what had happened to him. That he wanted her to go on living, for Nick and for the twins.

And that was just what she was going to do. However long this wretched war lasted, she was going to stick it out and see it through to the bitter end, for Danny's sake.

The funeral ended and they began to drift away from the graveside, back to the hospital. As she followed the other nurses, Dora heard a familiar voice calling her name. She turned round and started at the sight of the tall, slender figure standing under the trees.

She walked over to meet her. 'You did it, then,' she said.

'Yes,' Helen replied. 'I did it.'

Dora looked her friend up and down. She looked so different in her grey military uniform, her peaked cap perched on her sleek dark head. 'You look more like a soldier than a nurse,' she commented, her throat suddenly dry.

'I'll be back in my ward dress and apron once I start work. And there'll be another cap to learn to fold properly!' Helen tried to smile, but there were tears sparkling in her brown eyes.

'I hope it's easier than the one they gave us here on our first day!' Dora joked back, her throat clogged with emotion. Don't cry, she told herself. Whatever you do, don't cry.

They were silent for a moment. 'Do you know where they're sending you?' Dora managed to ask.

Helen shook her head. 'Not yet. But David thinks we'll be stationed together.'

'That's good.' Dora stared at the ground, not trusting herself to meet Helen's eye.

'It's what I want,' Helen said firmly.

'I know.'

Dora still couldn't believe her friend's bravery, following the man she loved into an uncertain future. But at the same time she knew that if she had the chance to be with Nick, she would have taken it in a moment, war or no war.

She wasn't upset for Helen, because she knew it was what she wanted. She was upset for herself, because it was someone else being taken away from her, another strand of her life that was unravelling. She wasn't sure how much more of it she could stand.

'I'll miss you,' Helen said.

Dora prided herself on being tough and keeping herself together, but those three words almost undid her. It was a moment before she could allow herself to say, 'I'll miss you, too. The old place won't seem the same without you.'

'I'll be back before you know it.'

'You just make sure you are.'

The silence stretched between them. Then Helen said, 'Well, I'd best be going.' She reached out and squeezed Dora's hand. 'I mean it, you know. I will be back. And I'll bring David and both our brothers and your Nick with me, I promise.'

Dora's fingers tightened impulsively around Helen's. 'I'll keep you to that,' she said.

After the other nurses had gone, Kathleen stood for a moment, her head bowed, saying her own private goodbye to the courageous woman whose judgement she had come to trust more than she'd ever imagined she would.

'It's hard to believe she's really gone, isn't it?'

Kathleen looked round. James Cooper stood behind her, sombre in his black suit.

'Yes, it is,' she said. 'I keep expecting to see her

coming down the passageway to find me, with yet another complaint or question.'

'I don't suppose you miss that?'

'Actually, I already do,' Kathleen replied with a sad smile.

Once she had thought Veronica Hanley was a tyrant whose sole purpose was to frustrate her. But over the past months she had come to realise that her deputy was a deeply caring person, a woman who believed in doing her duty, and did it unflinchingly.

An image of her in her tin hat, fearlessly fire-watching on the roof while bombs exploded around her, came into Kathleen's mind. That was what she would always remember about Veronica Hanley. Her indomitable spirit.

James Cooper fell into step beside her as they approached the main hospital block. Kathleen knew what was coming, and she was dreading it, almost as much as she had been dreading the funeral.

'I haven't seen you for a while,' he said.

'I've been very busy, trying to sort out the repairs.'

'I thought you were just avoiding me?'

Mr Philips and his men were out in force again, patiently trying to move the rubble. A team of volunteers had joined them, forming a human chain as they shifted the weighty lumps of rock away from the bomb site. Kathleen could hardly bear to look at it.

James, on the other hand, couldn't take his eyes off it. 'I nearly went mad when I realised you were buried under that,' he said quietly. 'I thought I'd lost you.' Then he paused and said, 'But I did lose you, didn't I?'

Kathleen allowed herself to look at him at last. He was so handsome, it almost broke her heart.

'You're not coming away with me, are you?' he said.

'I can't,' she said. 'It wouldn't be right. Not while the Nightingale needs me.'

'I need you!' He smiled sadly. 'But I suppose some things are never meant to be, are they?'

'No,' she said. But it had been wonderful while it lasted. A romantic fantasy she would never forget for as long as she lived.

'Did you ever think you would do it?'

'I was writing my resignation letter when the explosion happened.'

His mouth twisted. 'So just a few hours more and you might have been mine.'

Kathleen didn't reply. She knew Miss Hanley was right. She would never have been happy, knowing it was at someone else's expense.

They walked a little further, towards the main ward block. For the time being Kathleen's office had been moved to one of the rooms adjoining a disused ward.

'What will you do?' she asked. 'Will you stay?'

'Would you like me to?'

There was no answer to that. Seeing him every day, knowing she would never be able to hold him or even touch him again, would be torture to Kathleen.

But then, so was the thought of never seeing him again.

'I've arranged to transfer out to the sector hospital,' he answered her question. 'I think that might be best under the circumstances, don't you?'

She nodded. 'And will your wife be joining you?'

He sent her a haunted look. 'I don't think so.'

'It might be a good idea,' she said. 'You never know, perhaps it would be good for you to make a new start?'

James Cooper sent her a long, sad look. 'That's what I'd hoped for,' he said. 'A new start.'

Kathleen deliberately turned away so she wouldn't see the pain in his face. It was the same pain as she was feeling.

She turned her attention back to the men working on the site. The bomb had exploded right in the centre of the hospital, tearing out its heart.

She knew how it felt.

'It's an ugly scar, isn't it?' James commented, following her gaze.

'Scars heal. You of all people should know that.'

'And do you think the Nightingale will ever heal?'

Kathleen lifted her chin. 'I'll make sure it does,' she said.

The publishers hope that this book has given you enjoyable reading. Large Print Books are especially designed to be as easy to see and hold as possible. If you wish a complete list of our books please ask at your local library or write directly to:

Magna Large Print Books
Magna House, Long Preston,
Skipton, North Yorkshire.
BD23 4ND

This Large Print Book for the partially sighted, who cannot read normal print, is published under the auspices of

THE ULVERSCROFT FOUNDATION